# THE UNITED FEDERATION MARINE CORPS' LYSANDER TWINS

## BOOK 2
# ESTHER'S STORY: RECON MARINE

Colonel Jonathan P. Brazee
USMCR (Ret)

Semper Fi Press

Author Website: http://jonathanbrazee.com
Email List Sign-up: http://eepurl.com/bnFSHH

Acknowledgements:
I want to thank all those who took the time to pre-read this book,
catching my mistakes in both content and typing. Thanks to
Jymsym for his editing. And once again, a special shout out goes to
my cover artist, the award-winning Jessica Tung Chi Lee. You can
see more of her work at: http://www.jessicatcl.com/news.html.


Original cover art by Jessica TC Lee

Cover graphics by Steven Novak

Dedicated to

Signalman First Class Douglas A. Munro, United States Coast Guard

Awarded the Congressional Medal of Honor
for actions on Guadalcanal as set forth in the following citation:

*For extraordinary heroism and conspicuous gallantry in action above and beyond the call of duty as Officer-in-Charge of a group of Higgins boats, engaged in the evacuation of a Battalion of Marines trapped by enemy Japanese forces at Point Cruz, Guadalcanal, on September 27, 1942. After making preliminary plans for the evacuation of nearly 500 beleaguered Marines, Munro, under constant risk of his life, daringly led five of his small craft toward the shore. As he closed the beach, he signaled the others to land, and then in order to draw the enemy's fire and protect the heavily loaded boats, he valiantly placed his craft with its two small guns as a shield between the beachhead and the Japanese. When the perilous task of evacuation was nearly completed, Munro was killed by enemy fire, but his crew, two of whom were wounded, carried on until the last boat had loaded and cleared the beach. By his outstanding leadership, expert planning, and dauntless devotion to duty, he and his courageous comrades undoubtedly saved the lives of many who otherwise would have perished. He gallantly gave up his life in defense of his country.*

# Jordy Enclave, Nouvelle Bretagne

"Sergeant Hammerschott, where are you? You need to bring up your squad now!" Lieutenant Esther Lysander shouted into her mic.

She could see her Third Squad leader's avatar on her display, so she knew that the sergeant was still 200 meters from the small raised edge of the roadbed where Esther had ordered him, but her frustration was mounting over his progress, or rather, lack thereof.

"Sorry, Lieutenant, but we're under heavy fire. We can't move," the sergeant passed back, the stress in his voice evident despite the comms filters flattening out his words.

"We're all under heavy fire, Hammerschott, and I need you to move now. If you won't, I'll put someone in charge who will!"

"Aye-aye, ma'am. I'll try."

"No, you won't 'try.' You'll do it and do it now! And get some return fire going. If they can see you, you can fire at them, too!"

Esther blinked her outgoing comms back to the platoon command net and studied her display.

*How in the hell has it gone to shit so fast?* she wondered.

Esther had known that there was a possibility of action, and part of her had hoped she would see it. She was a proven combat veteran, after all, and a fight with the Legion would give her a chance to flex her command muscles under fire. Never in a million years, however, would she have guessed that it would all fall apart so quickly.

The mission had seemed so routine. While out on their initial orientation patrol, she'd received orders to check out a distress call from a farmhouse. She'd diverted the platoon off the highway and up the long dirt road leading to it, stopping on the near side of the open bottomlands. A dragonfly overflew the house, spotting nothing, and satellite scanning picked up no emissions.

1

Esther placed Second Squad in the treeline to the south of the open area, Third to the east, and sent First to investigate. Once Sergeant Ngcobo entered the house, all hell erupted.

"Staff Sergeant Fortuna, I need you to stay on Hammerschott's ass. I need him to provide the covering fire so First can disengage," she passed to her platoon sergeant on the P2P.

"Roger that."

*I hope he can handle that, at least,* she thought as she pulled up the known Legion firing points.

So far, her platoon sergeant had been less-than-impressive despite his sterling combat record. She'd address that though after the fight.

*Think, Esther, think!* she implored herself as if some magic solution would suddenly appear on her display.

It didn't.

Facing her 33 remaining Marines were at least two platoons of legionnaires, one dug in along the high ground to the north, another maneuvering through the swamp to the west. Both units had been well-cloaked from surveillance, but as one platoon opened fire and the other started moving, their positions were revealed to the Federation scanners. The only saving grace was that the legionnaires were not in the Rigaudeau-4 combat suits, and the platoon approaching through the swamp was moving slowly through the tangled morass.

Sergeant Ngcobo was pinned down at the farmhouse at the base of the hill. He'd lost three Marines KIA and two WIA, and his only egress was right under the legionnaire platoon on the high ground. The singing of not one but two "chat-chats" was evidence enough that if he made a break for it, his squad would be cut down in the open. The Chauchat 46's might be old tech, but the 7.8 mm rounds packed a big punch, strong enough to defeat the Marines' STF[1] body armor, the "bones" inserts that went into their combat utilities (their "skins").

---

[1] STF: Shear-Thickening Fluid, a liquid-based armor that thickened to a solid when subjected to a shock.

Esther had taken her platoon into a trap, pure and simple. The call for assistance from the farmhouse had been staged at worst, monitored by the Legion at best. It was probably the former as Sergeant Ngcobo hadn't found anyone in the house. Either way, First Platoon, Kilo 3/14 was in deep shit.

And the legionnaires had selected the terrain well. The farmhouse was 500 meters away from her across a wide, grassy bottomland, a decent-size creek meandering back and forth towards and past the house and the small vineyard. The creek drained into the swampy marsh to the west, widening and disappearing into the trees. To the north, on the far side of the house, was the high-ground, the 100 meter-high last gasp of the more gradually rising foothills to the east that eventually led to the Jaune Range, a series of 4,500-meter high peaks. A single road was cut through the bottom land on the east side, crossing the creek on a sturdy-looking bridge in front of the house. The only access in and out of the area was to the south. While it technically wasn't one, it might as well have been a box canyon.

"Ter, I really need fire on that high ground," Esther passed to the XO. "We're getting chewed up."

"I'm working on it. We've got a time-on-target of 27 minutes for air, and arty is still down."

"Twenty-seven minutes isn't going to cut it. We need it now!"

"I know, I know. But the Storks aren't going in without cover."

"Fuck those cowards," Esther said, cutting the connection.

She knew she was being unfair. The Legion was well-armed, and their *Cerf* man-packed missiles were a huge threat for the lumbering Storks. They needed either Wasp support to neutralize the threat or Boomer drones to jam the Cerf's acquisition systems.

But those were her Marines pinned down, Marines she barely knew yet, but hers none-the-less.

She knew she was running out of options. In another 25 minutes or so, the Legion platoon maneuvering from the west would emerge within 100 meters or thereabouts from the farmhouse. She could pull back Second and Third Squads and break contact to the southeast, but that would mean abandoning First Squad. That obviously was not going to happen.

She could engage the platoon from the swamp as the legionnaires emerged, but only two of her squads, along with her attached M449 HMG team would have fields of fire, and her chances of success with the other Legion platoon on the high ground were minimal at best. With two of the heavy machine guns, she'd have a better chance, but she only had one of the teams despite their SOP of going out in pairs.

She could go aggressive and mount an assault, but with a huge kill zone, her Marines would be sitting ducks.

She raised her head over the small mound and increased her magnification to try and get a better feel for the legionnaires on the high ground. The problem was that they were in defilade, probably in fighting holes, able to rain down fire on the platoon while remaining almost impervious to the fire from below. Esther's AI pinpointed one of the chat-chats pouring a stream of fire onto Third Squad to the east. As she watched, one of Second Squad's grenadiers launched a Bushmaster, the short, stubby anti-armor rocket fired from the M333 "dunker" attachment to M99 assault rifle. The rocket rose to the Legion chat-chat, only to sail right past and over the high ground. It might have parted the machine gunner's hair as it sailed by, but the firing never let up.

"Grenades on blow-down," she passed to Sergeant Daniels-Graves.

The Bushmaster rocket was only semi-intelligent. It worked well against armor but was not as effective against soft point targets, especially those in defilade. The dunker could fire three different munitions, but its primary round was the 30mm grenade which could be programmed to detonate above a target, spewing its load of soft pellets downwards onto a waiting enemy.

Before the squad leader could acknowledge, Esther was reflexively moving as the first round impacted beside her, diving back. Mounds of dirt showered down around her as a dozen heavy rounds chewed up the ground where she'd just been. The Legion's battlefield optics were as good as the Marines', and they had easily spotted her. Luckily, at 600 meters from the high ground, she was out of range of personal energy weapons, and so far, there'd been no sign of crew-served plasma guns.

"You OK, Lieutenant?" one of the Second Squad Marines, Corporal Meyers, she thought was his name, yelled at her.

She gave him a thumbs up, her sides heaving in the adrenaline rush.

*If this was the company's PICs platoon, I could assault right up that hill,* she thought. *Hell, I might as well wish for a destroyer in orbit with her big guns at my beck and call. PICs probably wouldn't work, anyway. They'd be exposed climbing the hill, as big as they are.*

The Legion wasn't some piddly-ass, jumped-up local militia. Smaller than the Corps, it was still a professional, capable force. Esther's father had fought both with them and against them in his career, and he'd thought them the best fighters other than the Marines. And just as the Marines, the Legion infantrymen had weapons to knock out combat-suited opponents. The Marines' own Banshee anti-armor missile was basically a copy of the Legion's Gazelle.

Another Marine's avatar grayed out. Her command display identified him as Lance Corporal Kenneth Portis. She hadn't even met him yet, and now he was gone. She could only hope that Doc Quisenberry could zombie him for a possible resurrection. At least she'd put the corpsman with the First Squad. Bad for him, good for the squad.

She replayed the last 20 seconds, trying to spot where she'd taken fire from. Something caught her attention, but she wasn't quite sure what. She replayed the same clip.

*There!*

She scooted over five meters, then popped up, scanning and recording the high ground, then ducking back before she could draw any fire. She directed her AI to pull in whatever overhead images it could gather, and almost immediately, she had a 3D image of the jutting high ground. She rotated it back and forth through a range of angles.

"Esther, you've got the three Aardvarks inbound. Give them 20 minutes if the route is clear," the XO passed to her.

"Roger," she replied, as she continued to study her image.

The Aardvark armored personnel carriers were nice pieces of gear, and she could use them to medivac the wounded, but they were not suited for taking the high ground, and certainly not to enter the swamp. She was frankly amazed and impressed that the legionnaires were maneuvering through it. They'd made a tactical blunder by hiding too deep into the morass, she thought, but all that did was give the Marines more time before the inevitable fight.

Then as she rotated the image on its Z-axis, she saw it. The overhead image, or images, most likely, were very good. When combined with her lower-quality ground-level image, she hoped the topographical image on her display was accurate. Even being off by half a meter would screw her plans—and screw First Squad.

Using her eyes, she traced a route. A mortar round landed ten meters away, and she jerked, ruining the trace. She blinked it clear, then tried again.

"Sergeant Ngcobo," she passed on the platoon command circuit along with the 3D topo, which went to each of the squad leaders as well as her platoon sergeant. "On my command, I want you to hightail it forward along this route."

"Towards the legionnaires, ma'am?"

"Towards them."

Her third option, of going on the offensive, was the only reasonable course of action after all.

"Take a look. By my calculation, you've got 50 meters of open area where anyone on top can fire at you, mostly those legionnaires on the east side of their line. Once you're inside that, you've got a window of cover."

She didn't bother to point out that 50 meters under fire can be a huge, deadly expanse.

"We're going to give you covering fire, but once there, you've got to get your squad up the draw I've highlighted. You should be able to remain in defilade until the last 20 meters."

It was more of a crevice rather than a draw, but it should suit the purpose.

"Then we assault, right?"

She'd been worried about how the sergeant would take it. He might be a whiz in garrison, but he hardly had the air of a warrior about him. Sergeant Hammerschott, for all the gung-ho attitude he'd shown in transit, had turned into a wimp under fire. But Ngcobo sounded eager to give some back to the legionnaires who taken three of his Marines.

"That's right. You assault. Roll up their line as far as your momentum lets you, then break off and hightail it back down."

"Do I have two minutes? Doc is ziplocking Port-man."

Esther assumed "Port-man" was Portis, wishing she'd had time to get to know her platoon before being thrown into the breach. She checked her AI's latest projections.

"Roger. Give me a heads up, and I'll send you. Second, start suppression fire now. They'll react, thinking we're making a break for it, and I want to give them time to calm back down. Be ready to escalate the rate of fire on my command.

"Lance Corporal Wynn, keep them occupied, but save enough ammo for two intense engagements," she told the heavy machine gunner.

The M449 used implosive jacketing, where the casing became part of the propellant. This allowed the two team members to carry much more ammunition than with old-fashioned jacketed ammo, but still, the rounds were not small, and Wynn didn't have an infinite combat load.

"Hammerschott, so help me, you've got two minutes. If you're not in position, you're going to lay down fire wherever you are."

Almost as if on cue, one of the Third Squad Marine's avatars went light blue. Another WIA.

Fire started to increase from Second around her as Sergeant Daniels-Graves passed on the orders. Wynn fired a ten-round burst as well.

Esther opened up the circuit to the three Aardvarks. She was surprised to see that the armor detachment commander was personally with the three vehicles—normally, the lieutenants were with the tanks.

7

She passed an area target to the lieutenant, noting that she hadn't even designated registered targets. The mission had come up quickly, and it wasn't exactly on her planned patrol route, but that didn't negate standard operating procedures, she knew.

"I need you where you can take the target under fire with your chain guns on my command. You should be able to stand off a klick-and-a-half from here," she passed, highlighting a firing position.

The position would give them a clear shot to the swamp line, but it left them vulnerable to any infantry or recon skulking about the vegetation, and Esther couldn't spare them any bodies to clear the area.

"The target will be an infantry platoon emerging from the swamp. Chase them back."

There was a moment of silence, then "Roger that. We'll be there."

She focused back on her display, and to her surprise, Third was moving quickly. She instinctively popped up her head to see, and across the broad open area, she saw a few bodies rushing forward towards the raised roadbed. Another Marine's avatar went light blue, but the rest never faltered.

Her AI kept track of the platoon coming through the swamp. The AI was only as good as the input it was receiving, and the legionnaires would be spoofing the Federation surveillance, but it gave her a 72% probability that the lead element of the legionnaires would reach the open bottomlands in 21 minutes. She forwarded that to the armor lieutenant—she had attended several briefs with him both in transit and upon arrival, but she couldn't even remember his name.

"How're you doing, Sergeant Ngcobo?" she asked on the P2P.

"He's powering the ziplock up now. Thirty seconds."

"OK. We're almost there, then. Remember, you can't stop over those 50 meters. You've just got to haul ass."

"Don't worry about us none, Lieutenant. We'll be flying."

"Second and Third, get ready. . ." she passed, waiting for Ngcobo's OK, which she received 15 seconds later.

"Now!" she shouted, mindless that the AIs would normalize her volume over the net.

Immediately, there was an increase of fire. The standard arms sounded loudly, notably the M449, the reports echoing off the rock face above the home. Esther rolled over and added the fire from her M99, the muted zips of the hypervelocity darts barely noticeable. She hoped the legionnaires noticed the incoming, though.

The house blocked her view of First as they started, but after only a few moments, they angled from behind the house to dash towards the blind spot. Esther willed them forward as she kept firing, emptying a magazine. Once Marine faltered, went to his knees, and tried to get up before falling again to his face. Another Marine scooped him up to carry him to cover.

Esther was too busy to note the name, but her peripheral vision noted with relief that the avatar went light blue instead of gray, indicating a WIA instead of a KIA.

And then First Squad was clear. One Marine—PFC Yanghu, she saw now—was WIA, but the rest had somehow made it through unscathed. Nine Marines, three now wounded, were all she had to climb the hill. She contemplated sending Third forward. First had probably surprised the legionnaires, and they'd covered the 50 meters in about fifteen seconds. Third Squad was farther out, so they would have to cover 250-300 meters, crossing the creek, to get out of the line of fire, and the legionnaires were now forewarned. It was too much of a risk, and Esther wasn't sure of the potential gain.

One of the First Squad Marines turned and waved his arm back to her. A smile cracked her face—she knew it was Ngcobo. A moment later, the Marines filed into the tiny draw and were lost from her sight.

"Sustained fire, sustained fire," she passed.

While the M99-armed Marines had several thousand darts each, those with chemical arms were more limited. Esther wanted to make sure each Marine was still loaded for bear when the Ngcobo launched his assault.

She panned back her display to include the Aardvarks. The three vehicles were less than five kilometers from the turn-off.

9

They'd have to slow down along the winding dirt road up to them, but she figured they'd be in position a few minutes before the first of the legionnaires reached the open bottomlands.

*So, what now?* she wondered.

She was the platoon commander, so she felt she should be, well, "commanding." Her mind bounced back and forth like a canary in a cage as she considered her options. None of them provided any real advantage, and most put her Marines at greater risk. She squashed her desire to start giving needless orders.

Another mortar round arched over the high-ground, but this time towards Third. Esther's AI calculated the trajectory, indicating that it would hit pretty close to the squad. Esther held her breath, but the AI was maddeningly accurate, and the round landed between two Marines. If he was hit, Corporal Duerte's bones did their job, and his blue avatar remained steady. Lance Corporal Spandal-Myrk's avatar switched to light blue.

The Legion mortar had been a thorn in the platoon's side. It was well-situated over the high-ground above the house, and up close to the foothills to the east. Even with arty, Esther didn't think it could hit the tube with the foothills providing cover. If their roles were reversed, Esther would be raining shells on them. The fact that the mortar team was spacing out the shells either meant they were limited in their ammo load, or they were trying to tease the Marines into rushing across the bottomlands. At the cyclic rate, even one of the Legion's 90mm mortars could wreak havoc on Marines in the open.

Esther was a combat vet, and she knew she was smart. She'd been honor graduate at NOTC,[2] having excelled in the field exercises. But if she'd made a mistake back at school, she'd only suffer in grades. Here, if she made a mistake, Marines would die. Three of her Marines were already KIA, Marines she'd barely met yet.

"How's your progress," she asked the armor commander, despite being able to see it on her display.

"We'll be there," the calm voice replied.

---

[2] Naval Officer Training Course, where new lieutenants are prepared to be commissioned.

She remembered he was a first lieutenant. How much time he had in combat, specifically in tanks, she didn't know, and she didn't have access to his service record. But like all armor officers, he'd been infantry first, so he had to understand her situation. Esther knew she should just shut up and let him do his thing.

Esther's mental trigger finger was itchy. She had to do something. So she rolled over to her belly and inched back up her little slope, M99 at the ready. She'd let her physical trigger finger relieve some of her stress. Platoon commanders were not combatants in the same way as a lance corporal was. They weren't trigger pullers, something all of her instructors at NOTC had stressed. They couldn't get focused on specific targets. But for the moment, she had to let Sergeant Ngcobo get his squad up that hill, so she might as well contribute to the volume of fire.

She aimed where her AI indicated one of those damned chat-chats was and let loose 50 darts. She doubted she'd hit anything vital—the legionnaires had prepared their fighting positions well. Still, it felt good.

"We've got movement coming from the swamp," Corporal Westinghouse passed from her position as the far left fire team.

Esther immediately swung her head to the left, dialing up her magnification. Four legionnaires were crouched at the edge of the swamp, one of them glassing in the direction where First Squad had disappeared.

"Get fire on them, Westinghouse. Send them back."

Within a moment, a thump of a dunker sounded to her left, and she could see vegetation explode around the four legionnaires from the fire team's rifle fire. The legionnaires ducked back just at the 30mm grenade detonated, sending shards of wood and muddy water flying through the air.

Esther couldn't tell if any of the four had been taken out, but they had been pushed back, which was her main concern. If they had spotted First and relayed that to the legionnaires on top, then the element of surprise was gone. But she couldn't see the squad from her much better vantage point, so she hoped the swamp legionnaires hadn't seen them.

She turned back to the hill, and right then, saw movement, three-quarters of the way up. She zoomed in further. One after the other, the Marines climbed over something, exposing themselves before getting back into the crevice.

*Please believe First Squad is still huddled down at the bottom, waiting for reinforcement!*

The lead element of the swamp platoon was already in position. Her AI still gave her a 12-minute estimate for the main body of legionnaires. Four of them weren't a threat, but soon there would be more. For now, Esther did not want them to have eyes on any of her Marines.

She started to bring up Corporal Westinghouse again before realizing that she had bypassed the corporal's squad leader. It was her right as a commander, but that didn't make it a good idea.

"Sergeant Daniels-Graves," she passed on the P2P. "Have Westinghouse keep reminding those legionnaires that we're here. And let me know when any more of them arrive."

For the next four minutes, nothing much happened. Rounds were fired from both sides, but almost as placeholders. No Marines were hit. Esther, however, was getting more nervous in a way she'd never felt as an enlisted Marine. While her forces were maneuvering, the legionnaires were undoubtedly adjusting their own plans. Esther didn't know who else might be hiding, ready to spring yet another trap.

She started having second thoughts about sending First Squad up the hill. If the Legion swamp platoon managed to break through to the farmhouse, First would be cut-off. She keyed in Sergeant Ngcobo on the P2P to recall him, but held her tongue. She still needed to disrupt the platoon up there. She wanted to scream with frustration as the tension mounted, and all at once, everything broke loose.

"We're assaulting," Sergeant Ngcobo passed, not giving Esther any time to give orders to the other two platoons.

Second didn't need it. The Marines, along with Lance Corporal Wynn, opened up, peppering the line of fighting positions. Once again, Esther didn't think they'd be having much effect, but they should be keeping the legionnaire's heads down. Third Squad, though, was a little slower to add to the fire.

"Mind the beacon!" Esther passed.

On Esther's display, Lance Corporal Kunckle's avatar was flashing red. As the lead man in the assault, his beacon marked the forward progress, and the other two squads had to keep their fire to the west of him.

A tremendous cacophony of firing exploded to Esther's left. For a moment, Esther thought that Daniels-Graves had managed to increase her squad's output, but the sound was different. And then it hit Esther like a mule kick. She swung back around, fearing what she would see.

The legionnaires had either been adjusting on the fly—or, with a sinking feeling, this had been a trap within a trap from the very beginning.

The four legionnaires who had first been spotted had been close to the farmhouse. Now, erupting from the trees much closer to her, the rest of the swamp legionnaires were not engaging First Squad but rather Second. If First Squad was rolling up the legionnaire line on the hill, a platoon of legionnaires were in position to run up Second Squad's line in the same way.

"Second Squad, one fire team on the hill to support First, the rest shift fire to the left. Third, give me full support here," she passed, sweeping a sloppy overlay that covered from where they were taking fire."

It might seem counterintuitive to have a fire team from Second continue to pour fire up on the hill and to have Third fire across the bottomlands in support of Second, but Third Squad was not in great position to support First, and they had a much better angle to fire on the swamp legionnaires while Second had the better angle to fire on the high ground.

Esther had at first thought the legionnaires in the swamp had made a mistake and been positioned too far in, but now she was convinced it had been part of their plan. The most logical place to put a unit to support any Marines in the farmhouse would have been the treeline to the south—right where Esther had placed them.

"Ter, I need air now. Air, arty, anything. We're getting hit hard!"

"Still working. Eight minutes."

"That's too fucking long! I need it now!"

"Lieutenant Lysander, calm down," Captain Hoffman voice came over her speakers. "The XO is working on support, but you need to fight the fight until we get there."

Esther wanted to yell back, but she knew the captain was right. She took a deep, calming breath, then said, "Aye-aye, sir. Just get them here as soon as you can."

Two of Westinghouse's Marines' avatars grayed out, and an instant later, the concussion wave hit her. Whatever the legionnaires had thrown at her, it had been pretty big.

Something hit Esther in the back, her bones stiffening up for the instant it took to stop the enemy round, and she turned just as the Marines next to her opened up on three legionnaires who had managed to come up behind them. Esther fired as well, as the three jumped for cover. She dropped one of them before the legionnaire was dragged by one of his buddies into a depression.

*How the hell did they get behind us?*

Esther tried to re-scan for the enemy positions, but her display was flickering and re-booting. There was some heavy-duty jamming going on.

"Pull Westinghouse back and orient the squad to the west," she ordered her Second Squad leader.

One of the chat-chats started firing, the rounds reaching out to them—but not quite. They were impacting just beyond Westinghouse as he wheeled back.

"That you on the chat-chat?" Esther asked Ngcobo."

"Roger that, ma'am. Thought we'd get in the fun."

She highlighted the squad. Six of the avatars were a bright, welcomed blue, and the two walking wounded were still their light blue. They had moved down a third of the legionnaires' line and stopped.

"What's your status?"

"We've got three POWs, and two enemy KIA. The rest have retreated down their line."

"Can you advance?"

"Not too good of an idea now. They're keeping our heads down in the far position. But not the chat-chat's. We're clear."

That wasn't going to last long, Esther knew. The legionnaires weren't going to just sit there and do nothing. Her plan had been when Ngcobo had reached that situation, she'd break off and high-tail it back down, covered by the other two squads. But right now, she needed that chat-chat.

"Light them up, Charlie! Push them back into the swamp."

A mortar landed in the trees behind her, but she barely registered the zing of shrapnel hitting the tree trunk a good 50 centimeters above her head.

And then, the sweet, sweet sound of a chain-gun sounded in the distance. Moments later, two more opened up in unison. The Aardvarks had arrived! Esther turned back to her left to see trees disintegrate as the big rounds tore into them.

"Whiskey-two," she started, using the Aardvarks' call sign for the first time. "Give me two on the treeline," she passed, highlighting the area on the overlay. "And give me one on the hill, all west of the beacon Marine."

"Roger that. We've got you covered."

"I'm sending Third Squad to your pos now."

"We'd appreciate that. We're feeling a bit exposed to mudrats about now."

Esther didn't even blink at the armor slang for infantry. They could call her much worse now and she wouldn't care.

"Sergeant Hammerschott, pull two fire teams back to the Aardvarks. I want a security perimeter around them. Keep one team covering First and link up with them. As soon as they link, get back to the tracs."

"Charlie, you still OK?"

"Hell, yeah, ma'am. I'm just glad that chain gun isn't aimed at us. It's freaking awesome."

"OK, I want you to break contact. Spike that chat-chat first. Then get your ass back down the hill, link up with a fire team from Third, and move back to the tracs."

The tracs were pouring huge amounts of fire into the swamp. It didn't look like anyone could survive the devastation, but Esther knew that humans were tough sons-of-bitches. She couldn't assume anything.

"Sergeant Daniels-Graves, start moving back. Bounding overwatch. Keep on the alert, though."

The Marines might have the upper hand at the moment, but the Aardvarks couldn't fire forever, and the legionnaires could still have a surprise in store. Esther's goal now was to break contact. The farmhouse was empty, and this little plot of land was not worth any more Marines deaths.

"Staff Sergeant Fortuna, I want you to watch Hammerschott. Make sure he and First get back to the tracs."

"Roger that."

Her platoon sergeant had been mostly invisible since the battle started. She looked to the east and saw him stand and almost casually walk toward the sergeant's position. She pushed him out of her mind as Second Squad started to reach her. She had to retreat with them. Except for the mortars, incoming started to diminish, but Esther kept Second in the bounding overwatch.

"Golf-One, we're inbound in 30. Please don't shoot us," one of the Wasp pilots casually passed.

"We won't, but we'd appreciate the same," Esther passed. "Confirm."

"Beacons on!" she ordered. "Incoming air."

Command avatars worked by matched electrons, which theoretically could be hacked. But when dealing with air and ground fire, beacons were broadcast to limit friendly fire casualties. They could theoretically be hacked and copied, or they could be used by the enemy to target Marines, so they were used by the forward-most Marines. When air was inbound in a confused battle area, though, beacons for everyone made sense.

"Roger, I have yellow, I repeat yellow, at two-two."

"That's confirmed. Happy hunting."

The platoon beacon, set by Esther, was a yellow avatar, flashing brighter twice, then a pause, then twice. This pattern would continue until the beacons were turned off.

A moment later, two evil-looking birds swooped in from the south. Wasps were dual-purpose fighter/ground attack aircraft with limited space capabilities. They were not much when compared to a Navy Experions, but they packed a pretty good punch. As they passed and climbed, the entire swamp exploded, flames and black smoke rising as if hell had escaped the underworld.

As bad as it looked, the swamp was still a lot of water, and that could protect legionnaires. Esther doubted they'd all been killed.

The Wasps hit the high ground on the next pass, and upon Esther's request, hit the mortar position before heading back to the airfield.

Flames still crackled high in the trees, but the rest of the battlefield was oddly silent. Esther tried a scan, and to her surprise, it indicated a large number of legionnaires still alive and moving—but away from them. Whatever jamming the legionnaires had been employing had evidently been knocked out. She did a quick query—47 legionnaires were retreating. There were a few flickers from either dead or wounded legionnaires.

This could be another trap, but Esther didn't think so. With both the Aardvarks and Wasps, the advantage was now with the Marines.

Sergeant Ngcobo had left his three prisoners on the top of the hill when he'd left, unable to handle them, but Esther sent out a quick patrol to check the ghost flickers on her scans. Four wounded legionnaires were collected, and after being treated by Doc, were loaded into the Aardvarks, along with the platoon's five KIA and six wounded. Doc thought four of their KIAs were good candidates for resurrection. Even if he were right, that meant two of her Marines were permanently dead.

Esther had lost Marines before, on Requiem when she'd been thrust into command after Sergeant Kinder had been killed. This was the first time that she'd lost her Marines, Marines entrusted to her to keep them safe. She stood over the six Marines in their ziplocks, pulling up their personals on her display. Lance Corporal Portis, "Port-man," Charlie Ngcobo had called him, was one of the two who Doc thought could not be resurrected. Frandell Portis,

Junior. Twenty years old, from Dillon's World. Single, as most junior Marines were. Son of Helen and Frandell Portis, Senior. Esther had never even spoken with him.

She pulled up the second. Private First Class Vykky Tantamount Lorne. Esther had spoken with her two days before on the ship when she was doing her initial interviews. She was a bigger girl, with a page-boy haircut and purple eyes. She'd seemed very excited to have Esther as her platoon commander, and she wasn't sure whether that was because of her father or simply because of her gender. She was a Navy brat, enlisting on Station 1. When Esther had asked why she hadn't gone Navy, Vykky had simply said she wanted to be one of the best.

Now she was a mass of mauled body parts. Most of a human body can be regenerated, but not the brain. And they managed to scrape together only half of hers. The ziplock was wasted effort, but regs were regs, and it took a medical officer to declare someone officially KIA. Doc could only ziplock them and get them back to the aid station.

Esther had already made her preliminary report back to Captain Hoffman, who'd canceled the rest of the orientation patrol. They were to return to the base on the Aardvarks.

Esther helped her Marines load the KIA, taking one of the four handles on each bag. She kept her eyes straight ahead, not looking at faces. They'd won the battle; they'd driven the legionnaires from the field. But it didn't feel like a win. In her first day of command, real command, that is, where she was making decisions, she'd lost five of her Marines. Two more were due for long regens and had joined the KIA in ziplocks. That was 17% of her platoon, if she counted Wynn and his assistant. If that was a victory, she quailed to think of what a loss would be like.

"You all ready?" Callas Anderson, the armor commander, she'd found out, asked.

Esther gave one last look at the eight ziplocked bodies, seven of her Marines and one legionnaire, then nodded to the crew chief to close the hatch.

"Yes, we're ready. Let's get out of here."

# TARAWA

## Chapter 1

*Two months earlier . . .*

Twenty-one years after she'd first entered the hallowed ground, her five-year-old hand clasped in her father's as she peered into the gloom, lit by old-fashioned incandescent light bulbs, trying to understand what the tavern meant to the Marines, Esther Lysander returned to the Globe and Laurel. She'd been in the place several times since over the years, but this time, her nerves were fluttering, a sensation she wasn't used to. No one ever accused Esther of lacking confidence, but now she hesitated, just inside the doorway.

*Come on, Esther. Get it together!*

"You going in, or are you just acting as a door-block," a deep, gravelly voice asked from behind her.

Esther didn't need to turn around to know who it was. Midshipman Falcon Upshick had spent almost a year in regen after having most of his throat torn out, and as was occasionally the case, his regenerated body didn't quite match the original, giving him a distinctive voice that didn't match his somewhat diminutive size. As a sergeant, Falcon had stood off an assault from a rioting mob on Durbin II, earning himself a Silver Star in addition to his stint in regen. As a midshipman, Falcon had been Esther's closest competition—and one of the few classmates she considered as a friend.

"Nah, just trying to keep out the riffraff. This here's a solemn occasion, and we don't need Fifth Marines rejects lowering the standards, don't you know," she said, not turning around.

"Hah! We may be riffraff, but that's better than you 16th Marines. At least we're in civilization. I know which fork is the salad fork and which is for the main course."

Esther's thoughts flicked to her brother Noah for an instant. A dedicated foodie, Noah knew all about proper table etiquette, a topic that never even registered in her mind. She felt a twinge of emptiness, of missing her twin, but she shoved that deep within the recesses of her consciousness as Falcon put a hand on her shoulder. She turned to look at her friend, put an arm around his shoulder, and faced the main room again.

"Well, since we're both such hiso characters, let's get the party going."

Together, they crossed the main dining area, Esther's eyes straying to the walls. Photos and holos of various Marine commanders, commandants, sergeants major, and heroes covered them, some being signed command photos, some being taken with the pub staff. Memorabilia hung everywhere, but the entire back wall and part of one side wall had the class time boxes, the boxes that once had three bottles in them. The older ones were now empty, the newer ones with one, two, or all three bottles still. Esther had looked at each and every one of them before, the last time four months ago when she'd arrived on Tarawa for Phase 3 (Marines) of NOTC.[3] Now, her eyes avoided the box on the side wall, two from the top and three from the right side. That was Class 59-2's box, her father's box, whose name was now engraved on a small brass plate in the middle of it, engraved when he'd been the first in his class to receive a star. The box had one bottle left, a bottle her father would never open. Esther knew if she saw the box, the tears would well up again, and she didn't want anything to dampen the mood of her classmates.

They reached the back dining room, and Esther reached out with her free hand to the door. Mr. Geiland, the Globe and Laurel's owner, and part of history in his own right, swung it open first, though, and emerged, holding an empty box with the words "Krug Clos d'Ambonnay" printed on the side.

---

[3] NOTC: Naval Officer Training Course

"Welcome," Mr. Geiland said, stepping to the side. "Most of you are already here, but you're all set up. Give me a shout if you need anything."

Esther dropped her arm from Falcon's shoulders and pulled down on the bottom edge of her miner's blouse as if she were in her Bravos. She was dressed in civvies, not her uniform, but habits of the last five years were already ingrained in her.

The two midshipmen entered the room together. More than half of the class was already there, and a few looked to have been tapping the kegs that Mr. Geiland had put out for them while others were munching on the small snack line. The Globe and Laurel put on this little party for each class gratis. The three bottles in subdued wooden racks on the back table were paid for by the mids themselves.

"Glad to see you two lovebirds made it," Deri Tsu said, handing each of them a stein of beer.

*Lovebirds? Is that what they think?*

"You can't start without me," Esther said, attempting to change the subject.

The small cloud that seemed to cross over Deri's eyes made Esther regret the words. She knew she was confident—what some people might think of as arrogant, and this wasn't a time for that.

"It looks like we're still missing a dozen or so, and we need everyone before we start," she amended, trying to deflect her initial statement.

The thing was, she had meant it exactly how it sounded. Deri had read her right. Deri had been a run-of-the-mill midshipman, and Esther thought she'd be a run-of-the-mill officer. Unlike Falcon, who Esther was sure would excel, the fact was that most of the gathered midshipmen would be decidedly average officers.

*Average for Marine officers,* she corrected her thoughts. *Still better than any other service.*

Every one of the 72 midshipman in the room had proven him or herself as enlisted Marines. Eighteen of them had even received appointments to the Naval Academy back on Earth and completed four years there before joining the rest in Phase 2 (Marines). Each and every one of them had what it took to achieve. But even when grouped with other over-achievers, the cream within the cream still rose to the top. And Esther knew without a doubt that she would rise.

Esther spent the next hour drifting about, touching base with most of the others. More than a few toasts were called, and a few of her classmates were getting a little into the cups. Esther nursed the one beer Deri had given her, taking tiny sips for each toast. This was a solemn occasion, and she wanted a clear head.

It was good to relax, though. For once, he didn't have to worry about whether she would end up as the honor graduate or not. She didn't have to stress about her performance. All of that was over. She could listen to sea stories, and despite a desire to tell a few of her own, she held back. She would have to work with all of them in the future. These would be her compatriots going up the ladder. Some—most—would fall off that ladder at some time or another. But in the end, it would still be these classmates who shared a bond.

And then it was time. Esther walked to the table, picked up one of the wine glasses and clinked on it with an antique round casing Mr. Geiland had left there. It only took a moment for the gathered class to stop talking and turn to face her.

Esther ignored the piece of plastisheet in her pocket, the one Brigadier General Cousin Stapleton-Hargreaves had given her. She had memorized the words already, but still, it felt comforting to know that should she falter, she could pull it out.

Her father had never said the words. He hadn't been close to being the honor graduate. General Simone had filed that spot for her father's class, and while he'd done well in his service, it was more and more clear that he'd never pick up his third star. Being honor graduate at NOTC was not a guarantee of ultimate success, something of which Esther kept reminding herself. She could never rest on past laurels if she was going to make it to the top.

"Gentlemen, we are gathered here for comradeship, for one last gathering before we are sent out to serve our Corps. We have been forged from the same crucible, though, so we will always share that connection. We are brothers of the blood.

"To keep this connection, we now place three bottles of elixir in this sacred case, three bottles to be taken out when the time is right.

"If you can all create the chain, we will dedicate our box."

At that, each midshipman put his hand on the shoulder of the person next to him or her, until all were connected. Falcon, who was standing on one side of Esther and was closest to the class time box reached out to put his hand on it. Quince Smith, standing on the other side of her, reached out to touch her shoulder, keeping her in the chain.

"The port, the drink of remembrance, will be opened on the Marine Corps birthday following the first of us to fall. Any of the class present will open the bottle and toast our fallen brother."

Esther picked up the bottle of 304 Quinta do Vesúvio and almost reverently placed it in the first cradle in the box. She could almost feel the significance of what she was doing flow from the dark port into her arms, a wave of warmth rushing through her.

"In remembrance," the rest of the mids intoned.

"The champagne, the drink of celebration, will be opened when the first of us earns his or her brigadier's star. All who are present for the promotion will join in the toast as the stars are a reflection of not only an individual, but our entire class."

"In celebration," the class intoned as Esther placed the Krug Clos d'Ambonnay in the second cradle.

"The sherry, the drink of loyalty and service, will be opened by our last two surviving classmates on the Marine Corps birthday following the passing of our third longest surviving classmate," she said as she placed the bottle of 318 Massandra in the last cradle.

"In retrospect," the rest of the midshipmen finished.

The ceremony was over, but they stood there, unmoving. Esther knew that after tomorrow, they would never be together like this again. Some would spend a career in the fleet, leading Marines. Some of them would die. Others would leave the Corps and make their way in the civilian world. But right then, at that moment, they were all the same. They were a band of brothers. To her surprise, Esther felt a lump forming in her throat.

They kept their hands on each other's shoulders for longer than necessary, none of them seemingly wanting to be the first to break the connection.

## Chapter 2

The commandant's voice boomed out over the gathered midshipmen and guests, "I, state your name . . ."

Each Marine in the class repeated after the commandant, right hand raised.

*. . .do solemnly swear, to support and defend the Articles of Council of the Federation of United Nations, against all enemies, foreign and domestic; that I will bear true faith and allegiance to the same and above all others; and that I will obey the orders of the Chairman of the Federation of the United Nations and the orders of those appointed over me, according to the Uniform Code of Military Justice. So help me God.*

"Congratulations, lieutenants," the commandant said as he lowered his right arm. "Now get out there and lead. The Federation is counting on you. With that, I know you have family here, so celebrate today, for tomorrow duty calls. You are dismissed."

"Ooh-rah!" burst out of the throats of 72 very happy second lieutenants.

Esther smiled as she turned around, her class a mass of lieutenants milling about and hugging each other. The 18 Academy Marines among them had spent five years together—four at the Academy and one with the rest of the class—but even the direct commissioning lieutenants had been together for a year. That was more than enough time to forge life-long bonds.

A few were heading for the stands, family members rushing out to meet them. Esther watched them rush off, watched them hug each other. Bost Fraiser swept up a little girl who couldn't have been more than four years old and seat her on his shoulder as five adults gathered around him, all beaming with pride.

*No family for me*, she thought, trying to keep the smile plastered on her face.

"Hey, Congrats, devil dog," Falcon said, turning her around and pulling her into a hug. "Do you want to meet my great-granddad?"

Falcon had been raised by his great- grandfather, a former Marine who had fought in the War of the Far Reaches. Esther wasn't in the mood to stand among all the families posing for holos with their newly minted second lieutenants, but she couldn't turn Falcon down.

She followed Falcon to the stands were a wizened man stood, his back straight and tall. He had on a scarlet jacket with his Marine Corps service ribbons and insignia pinned to his left breast.

"Grandpop, this is Esther," Falcon said.

"Mr. Upshick, it's an honor to meet you," Esther said, holding out a hand. "Falcon's told me so much about you."

"So you are the General's daughter," he said. "He was a good man."

"You knew him?" Esther asked surprised, turning to look at Falcon, raising her eyes in a question.

"Not me. My grandson. Fal's father. Served with your father on Freemantle. He told me about the general, though. Of course, he was only a lieutenant colonel then, but my boy, he knew your father was going places.

"Told me that before they deployed, all excited. He never came back, though. I lost my boy there," the old man said, shaking his head slowly.

Esther was floored. Esther had known that Falcon's father had been killed in battle, and that he'd been mostly an absent father before that. But she had no idea that their fathers had served together.

And suddenly, she wanted to know more. The Corps was built by those who served before, and she felt a strong need to understand that better. She was raised a Marine brat. She'd served in combat as a Marine, but she realized there was a gap within her, a gap that was the very soul of what it meant to be a Marine.

"I'd like to . . . uh, if you don't mind, I'd like to talk to you, if that's OK. About your war. About your grandson."

"I'd be happy to, if you really want to hear the ramblings of an old man. But if you two have someone special for your first salute, I'd suggest you do it now. The sharks are circling."

Esther looked up, and she saw Falcon's great-grandfather was right. The commissioning had been on the lawn in front of Marine Headquarters. As the newly commissioned Marines started to break away from the pack, there was a slow maneuvering of the enlisted staff as they tracked down their prey. Esther had seen holos of sardines back on Earth, rotating in a ball of fish, with sharks and dolphins hovering just outside the mass, ready to pick off stragglers. Those predators had nothing on the enlisted Marines and sailors staking out the periphery.

It didn't make any difference to Esther. She'd never bonded with any particular instructor. But she did care where she received her first salute. Her father had told Noah and her about his first salute, under the statue of General Salizar. She even remembered the name of the Marine: Gunnery Sergeant Meader.

Esther didn't care who gave her the salute; she just wanted it to be under the statue. She'd even managed to find a 2123 O.R., Australian Kookaburra Dollar to present, the same coin her father had given to the gunny. It had been far more expensive than the typical Tarawa commemorative most new lieutenants gave, and whoever received it would never know of the significance, but it had just felt right.

"I'm going to head over to General Salizar. Look, let's get together tonight for dinner, unless you've got other plans. OK?"

"Sure," Falcon said. "We were just there last night, but the Globe and Laurel? Twenty- hundred?"

"Better call them for reservations," Esther said, taking in all the gathered people who might try and eat dinner at the tavern, too. "I'll see you there."

Esther cut through the bulk of her classmates, steering clear of the edges where she could be picked off. Half-a-dozen classmates stopped her to shake and offer congratulations, but as more and more classmates left and were pounced upon by Marines, her path to escape was getting narrower.

She finally broke away from Alvey Goins and focused straight ahead, refusing to meet the eyes of anyone as she tried to cover the last 25 meters to the statue. She could see two Marines in her peripheral vision break off to cut her off, but she picked up her pace, refusing to turn her head until she reached the base of the statue. She looked quickly at the face of the hero of old, then turned around to see who'd be saluting her.

With a look of victory in his eyes, a corpsman rushed up, his arm cocked to whip into a salute.

"As you were, Doc. She's mine," a voice called out with authority.

The corpsman stopped, and it looked like he was going to argue, but with a wry smile, nodded, and turned back to the remaining pack of new second lieutenants.

Esther slowly turned around. Shocked would be an understatement.

Emerging from the other side of the statue, Noah, in his dress blues, stood tall. He came to a position of attention, then slowly brought up his hand in a salute.

"Congratulations, ma'am!" he said, his face carved in stone.

Esther stood there, her mouth open, and when Noah didn't move, she remembered to return the salute. Noah brought his down smartly.

"How. . .what. . .how did you get here?"

"By spaceship. That's the usual way, ma'am, you know."

"But you're at Camp Ceasare!"

"And no ships ply the space lanes from there to here? And I'm not at Ceasare any longer. I've already been assigned. I sent you a whispergram to tell you that."

"You did? Well, I've been . . . I mean, with NOTC and everything, I don't check my personals often. I'm sorry. But why come all the way here? I mean, that had to cost a pretty credit."

"You have to ask? You're my sister, Esther. We only have each other. You needed family here for this."

Esther was confused. She and Noah had very little communication since she left Wayfarer Station. It simply boggled her mind that he'd come all this way just to see her get commissioned.

"How did you know I'd come to the statue for my first salute? That someone wouldn't grab me sooner?"

"As I said, Ess, you're my sister. You're my twin. I know you. Of course, you'd come to where Dad got his, and no one was going to get in your way for that. I saw you marching over, a woman on a mission. I'm surprised that corpsman even got as close to you as he did."

"Well, I guess you're right. And I guess I owe you this," she said, pulling the Kookaburra Dollar out of her pocket and handing it to him.

Noah gave it only a glance before a satisfied smile crept over his face. He slipped it into his pocket.

"I was hoping that's what it would be, but I looked online. A 2123 Kookaburra's pretty hard to find."

"I . . . well, you know."

"Yeah, Ess, I know."

The two stood looking at each other for a moment, the silence growing longer.

Finally, Noah broke it with, "There's one more thing. Miriam and I are getting married, and we'd love you to be there. It's up to you, though. I know you'll be busy snapping in with your platoon."

He said it matter-of-factly as if it was no big deal, his gaze shifting to the ground at her feet. But just as he'd said he'd known her because they were twins, so did she know him. He cared—deeply.

Esther didn't want to go. She had mixed feelings about Noah's marriage. She'd barely seen Miriam at the PX back on Wayfarer Station, and she thought Noah might be grasping at the first lifeline thrown at him. And he was right. She would be joining her first platoon, and she didn't want to take off on leave before she'd even settled in. It wasn't professional.

But when she looked at him, a piece of her wall that she'd erected after they'd both enlisted broke off. She still thought the Corps was not for him. She still sensed the wall keeping them from the relationship they'd once had. But he was right. They were family, the only family they had. Well, the only family she had. Noah was still in close contact with their mother's extended family, and he would soon have his own family, it seemed.

"When is it? And where?"

"May 4. On Prophesy. So, you know, Grandmama can help."

"Help, Noah? You mean take over," she said, a smile breaking through.

"OK, she'll take over the entire thing," he said with a small chuckle while looking up from the ground to her face.

"And May 4? Aren't we copying our parents a little much here? Me with General Salizar and the Kookaburra, you on Mom and Dad's anniversary?"

"Just like where you had to enlist Ess? In the same recruiting station where Father enlisted? We're just like each other, in so many ways."

*Only some. We are so different in others,* Esther thought but kept that unspoken.

May 4th was still a long ways off. She was surprised Noah was willing to wait that long, but if their grandmother were involved, she'd want a full ceremony. The more she thought about it, the more she was sure the wedding had been taken out of his hands.

*Oh, Noah, you can't even control your own destiny!*

"I tell you what, Noah. I don't' know my deployment schedule yet. I've been assigned to 2/14."

*Still in the Outer Forces. Can't sniff anything close to Tarawa,* she thought with resignation.

First Marine Division, headquartered in Tarawa, was the lifeblood of the Corps, and Esther wanted to be assigned to the division so badly she could taste it. But the powers-that-be seemed bound and determined to let her develop far from the attention given to Tarawa-based units.

"Ah, the Lagunari," Noah said. "Good unit."

It took a moment for Esther to switch gears before realizing he was mentioning her new battalion's patron, the Italian Marines.

"The what? 'La-goon-ary?'"

"The Lagunari Serenissima. One of old Italy's two Marine units. Two-fourteen chose the Lagunari as their name, but adopted the San Marco Brigade's motto, let me remember, something like 'Per Mare, Per Terram.' Do you know, the Lagunari were Army, not Marine or Naval Infantry? The San Marco Brigade was Navy, but not the Lagunari. It's one of only two Army patrons in the Corps today."

Esther looked at Noah in wonderment. Where had this thirst for history come from? Their father had been a history buff, but Esther hadn't known Noah might have developed the same fascination. Esther didn't care much for history. She studied battles of old, but the whole patron system within the Marine Corps infantry battalions, with each battalion adopting one of the 48 extant Marine Corps that had formed the Federation Marines, while it had political advantages, really had little impact on each battalion's ability to fight. Esther was going to 2/14, but Noah had just told her more than she'd known, or really cared to know, about her battalion's patron Marine Corps.

"OK, um, good to know," she told him. "But back to your question, I don't know my schedule, but if we're not deployed, and if I can get leave, I would be honored to attend your wedding."

"It's OK. I under . . . oh, you'll make it?"

"It's not a promise, Noah. But I'll try. You know the Corps, though. Remember how many times Dad missed birthdays and anniversaries?"

"Yeah, yeah, of course, I know," Noah said, excitement in his voice. "But thanks, Ess. It'll make Grandmama happy . . . no, strike that. It'll make me happy."

"You're my little brother, Noah," she said, using her being born nine minutes before him to claim the title of older sister. "Of course I'll be there."

A sergeant saw Esther standing by the base of the general's statue and started over, arm cocked to salute before he saw Noah and dejectedly turned to find a yet un-saluted lieutenant.

"It's a little late for that," Noah said as they both laughed and watched the sergeant's retreating back. "You've got to get an earlier jump on things."

Esther turned around to the grass where they'd been commissioned. A handful of her classmates were still there; many more were in the process of leaving.

"I think you're right. But, I need to get going. I've got a property pick-up in about an hour, and I'm not packed yet."

"You know, they only allow you two seabags," Noah said, his eyes glinting with mischief as he referred to her penchant for traveling with a wardrobe of clothes

And old penchant. The Corps had broken her of that habit.

"I don't carry that much!" Esther protested. "And now that I'm an officer, I get a load-out box, too."

"Lucky for you. I'm betting it's still not enough," he said, still teasing.

"You'd better watch it, Sergeant! I could always order you to pack my stuff for me and carry it to TMI."

The humor faded from Noah's eyes.

*Crap! I just blew it.*

Their lighthearted banter, something they hadn't shared for six years, was over. Esther had just reminded them of the gulf that now separated them. She was an officer, and he was a sergeant. It shouldn't matter, but it did—at least for now. The wall that Esther had erected between them now had another level added to it.

"Well, Ess. Lieutenant Ess," Noah said, forcing a smile on his face. "I need to get going. I'll let you get your things ready. Congratulations. Really. Mother and father would be proud."

He stepped forward, and the two awkwardly hugged. Their stiff dress blues were not the only reason for that.

"Thanks for coming, Noah. It was good to have family here. And I'm proud my first salute was from you."

"I couldn't miss this," he said, reaching into his pocket and pulling out the Kookaburra Dollar.

He came to attention again and gave his best drill field salute, which wasn't all that great, Esther had to admit. She pulled herself to attention and gave him her best salute in return.

"Well, OK. I guess I'll see you in May?" Noah said as he turned to walk away.

"Hey, Noah!" Esther said after he'd taken several steps. "When are you leaving to go back?"

"My shuttle's at 0530."

"Unless you've got something else to do, why don't you meet me for dinner? I'm going to eat at the Globe and Laurel with one of my classmates. His great-grandfather will be there. He was a Marine in the War of the Far Reaches, and his grandson—my friend's father—fought with Dad."

"I . . . I'd like that, Ess. But . . ." he said, trailing off as he pointed to the chevrons on his sleeve.

"Screw that. We're family. And Mr. Upshick was a corporal when he served. We're all Marines, right?"

"Well, right. But—"

"But nothing. Twenty-hundred, OK?"

Noah only hesitated a moment before he shrugged and said, "Twenty-hundred it is. See you then, Ess."

He turned around and walked off, but with more spring in his step.

The wall between them was still there, but Esther thought it now had a crack in it.

# REISSLER QUAY

## Chapter 3

"Hello?" Esther asked, sticking her head through the hatch. "Anyone here?"

She was met with a resounding silence. Shrugging, she stepped into the small office. "Small," was relative, though. With 2/16 on Wayfarer Station, the platoon offices were any clear spot between the platoon commanders' bunks. Here at Camp Salcedo, there was more than enough space to spread out, and each platoon had an actual office, complete with two desks and two small couches.

Esther had reported to Regiment two hours ago, meeting with the regimental XO, first, then over to the battalion headquarters to meet the CO. Each had given her the typical welcome-aboard-the-best-unit-in-the-Corps-work-hard-and-you-will-do-fine speech. Neither man mentioned her father, but she could tell the regimental XO was aching to do so. She'd bet the man had served under her father, and she was pretty sure she'd hear about it sometime. But she was also cynical enough by now to believe that all of the command had been directed to treat her like any other boot lieutenant. She'd been spared meeting the company commander, who was getting his annual physical, so she'd headed directly to the First Platoon office.

*Her platoon.*

She'd meet the skipper later that afternoon, but for now, she wanted to meet her Marines, starting with Staff Sergeant Conrad Fortuna, her platoon sergeant. But the staff sergeant was nowhere to be seen. She checked her PA. It was 1005, too early for noon chow. The battalion commander had told her Kilo Company was in garrison this week, so she knew he should be around.

She shrugged and took a look around the office. On one side, holes peppered the bulkheads, evidence of the plaques and pics that must have adorned it. Behind the desk, a pic of the chairman shared space with one of the commandant. Half a dozen frames hung from the third bulkhead. Esther put her AI on the empty desk, then took a few steps to look at her platoon sergeant's I Love Me wall. There was a copy of his warrant to staff sergeant taking center stage, right at eye-level. The rest were flat pics. One had a young sergeant posing with three civilians. She looked back towards the hatch to see if anyone was watching, then touched the bottom of the pic. Green identity squares immediately appeared around the four people's faces. The sergeant, not surprisingly, was Fortuna. Two of the people were flunkies—high-level flunkies, but flunkies none-the-less. The fourth person was Kenneth Détente, Federal Administrator. Esther had no idea who Détente was, but a federal administrator would be the senior federal official on a given planet.

The other pic that caught her eye was a group shot of eight young Marines: seven men and one woman. All were in t-shirts, all had their weapons displayed, most in the casual rifle butt to their hips that combat Marines seemed to gravitate to. Esther didn't already need to know that her platoon sergeant had been a sniper. The rifle cartridge hung around each of their necks was evidence enough. The fact that all eight in the pic had their "boar's tooth" was impressive. Esther knew only snipers who'd made their first kill rated them.

A younger Conrad Fortuna stared straight ahead into the lens, a tiny smile bending the corner of his mouth. He looked confident and ready for battle, which made sense. Esther had already pulled up his records. As a corporal, Fortuna had earned a Silver Star during the Evolution, compiling 14 kills.

Esther knew she was an outstanding Marine. She was combat-proven, as her own Navy Cross attested. But commanding a platoon wasn't something she'd done before, and she knew having a competent platoon sergeant would hasten her learning curve while simultaneously keeping her out of trouble. And from what she could glean from his records, she'd hit the jackpot with hers.

The front hatch opened with a crash, and Esther spun around. A sergeant stumbled in, holding a large supply pack in front of him. He started to put it down on one of the couches when he noticed Esther standing there.

"Oh, sorry, ma'am! I didn't see you!" He put the pack down, then stepped towards her, hand out. "I'm Sergeant Ngcobo. Charlie Ngcobo. I'm your First Squad leader. And I know who you are, ma'am, and we're happy to see you."

Sergeant Ngcobo was slightly shorter than Esther, but he probably had 30 kg on her—and not 30 kg of rippling muscles. He was slightly dumpy, reminding Esther of nothing more than a penguin. The hand that reached out was almost a tannish shade of gray, but his face was a mottled brown, with even darker freckles showing through on his complexion. His ice-blue eyes somehow seemed to be both piercing and vacant of thought at the same time— two attributes that were diametrically opposed. He was certainly one of the more unique-looking people she'd ever seen.

She took his hand and said, "Nice to meet you, Sergeant," while trying not glance from his hand to his face. She couldn't help but notice that his left hand was more in line with his facial complexion.

"I'm Lieutenant Lysander."

"Yes, ma'am, I know. We're all proud that you're with us."

*Proud of what? That I'm my father's daughter?*

Esther was proud of her father, and his memory was the force that drove her to excel. But she was also sensitive to others projecting her father's accomplishments onto her.

"Well, I'm proud to be here, too," she said, spouting the expected response. "Do you know where Staff Sergeant Fortuna is? I'd like to meet him before I meet the rest of the platoon."

Something passed over the sergeant' eyes for the briefest of instances before he said, "Ah, he's around, ma'am. Probably taking care of platoon business. We're in garrison now, after two weeks in the field."

"Yes, I know. The CO told me. But there are still schedules in garrison. Where's today's POD?"[4]

"Uh, I'm not sure ma'am. I've been on a mission, but I think this morning was for haircuts, PX runs, things like that."

The sergeant was smiling earnestly, but something didn't ring true, something Esther couldn't quite put her finger on. She decided to ignore whatever was scratching at her brain for attention.

"Mission? That supply pack?"

"Oh, yes, ma'am," he said, sounding relieved to move to another subject. "I had to pick up vix for the platoon."

"Vix? For everyone at once?"

The V106 was the battery pack for the M99 assault rifle. It powered both the sight display and the magnetic rings that pulled the darts down the barrel, accelerating them to hyper-velocity. They were rechargeable with a usage life of over a thousand cycles. It didn't seem likely that every vix in the platoon reached their end-life at the same time.

"Uh, we've had problems with the ones we had. They weren't holding their charges long enough. But the armory kept testing them and saying they were OK, so supply wouldn't replace them."

"So you did?"

"Yes, ma'am. Since we weren't doing anything else, I decided to see what I could do to fix that."

A couple of things became clear. First, there was no POD for today. He'd just let it slip that there was nothing else to do. Second, Sergeant Ngcobo was one of those NCOs who saw a problem, then fixed it. Which was normally good, but could turn around and bite her in the ass. A single V106 ran into the hundreds of credits. If the sergeant had done something illegal—or to be more accurate, something that was illegal and could be traced back to him—both he *and* she would be in trouble. She ached to ask him just how he'd managed to score a full pack of the batteries, but having been a sergeant herself, she knew that was something that as a lieutenant, she was supposed to ignore. She had to trust the sergeant to have acquired the vix in a way that wouldn't get anyone in trouble.

As a sergeant, she had been pretty much in direct control of both her squad and herself. As a lieutenant, she suddenly realized

---

[4] POD: Plan of the Day

that she had lost a bit of that direct control. She had to rely on others and focus on the bigger picture. She wasn't sure she liked that.

"I haven't downloaded the platoon contacts yet," she said.

*I can't believe the company clerk wouldn't do that until after I meet the skipper,* she thought, eyebrows furrowing. *Like the skipper's going to deny me that?*

". . . so can you call up the staff sergeant and tell him to meet me here?" she asked Sergeant Ngcobo.

"Uh, sure, ma'am. Only, sometimes he doesn't respond, like, uh, like if he's in the gym," he said.

*What the hell is going on here?*

"Lieutenant Lysander?" a voice called out from the hatch, forestalling Esther from ordering the sergeant to make the call.

Esther turned to see a Marine in PT gear poking half her body into the office, her hair cut in the high-and-tight.

"Yes, that's me," Esther said, frowning ever-so-slightly.

"I'm Ter Opal," the Marine said, entering the office, hand outstretched.

"Oh, the XO. Hi. I'm Esther," she said, taking the hand.

Esther had seen the XO's name on the roster, but "Ter" was normally a man's name, so she had expected a male Marine in the billet.

"Hey, Charlie. How're you holding out?" she said to the sergeant, hand still clasped in Esther's.

"Still kicking, ma'am. You know me."

"Yes, I know you, much to my chagrin. What's that? The vix you've been trying to get?"

"I wouldn't know what you're talking about, ma'am. Vix? Supply assures us we have what we need."

"Right," the XO said before turning back to Esther and finally dropping her hand.

"Charlie here, he's your go-to guy to get stuff done, even if you can't trust him farther than you can throw him," she told Esther

"Ma'am, you wound me!" the sergeant said, theatrically rolling his eyes. "I've only taken your guidance in all things."

"Yeah, right, Sergeant Never-Say-No. Why don't you bug out now and let me welcome in your new platoon commander. You know, secret officer stuff."

Sergeant Ngcobo came to attention and shouted out in his best boot camp voice, "Ma'am, yes ma'am," before performing an about face and double-timing out of the office.

Esther was floored. There was an obvious affection between the XO and her First Squad leader, but she'd never seen such, well, jovial familiarity between an officer and an enlisted Marine.

Her father's most trusted, well friend, had been Gunny, now Sergeant Major Hans Çağlar. But in all the time Esther had seen them together, there had been a degree of professional decorum. Esther knew that her father loved the sergeant major like a son, but she'd never seen joking between them like what she'd just witnessed.

The XO must have seen the astonished look on her face because she said, "Charlie's worth his weight in gold. He keeps the ship afloat."

"What about Staff Sergeant Fortuna?"

"Ah, yes. Fortuna. Well, I think you need to discover that for yourself, Esther."

*What the hell?*

"He's, well, let's say he's got a few issues going on. He still gets therapy twice a month."

"I didn't see that he's been wounded."

"Not that kind of therapy."

It took a moment to realize what the XO was saying.

"Oh."

If her platoon sergeant had some sort of psychological issue, she didn't know what he was doing in a line platoon. It couldn't be something too serious if he was still cleared for full duty, though.

"Anyway, Corporal Anthony told me you'd arrived, so I wanted to say hello. The platoon's been without a commander for three weeks, and that's three weeks too long."

*That's not a stunning endorsement of my platoon sergeant.*

"I wanted to go back to the platoon, but the skipper nixed that since we knew you were inbound. I miss it, though," she said.

"Spent two years with the platoon before Axes arrived and squeezed me up to XO."

"So what happened to the previous commander? The battalion CO said something about a shortened tour for him?"

"Well, yeah, if you consider four months as 'shortened.' He was pulled off-planet."

There was a note of finality in her voice that Esther didn't want to confront. She'd find out later what happened to her predecessor.

"Well, since you were here only five months ago, maybe you can give me a run-down on the platoon since I can't get a hold of my platoon sergeant?"

"Just call him," the XO said, her eyes drawn together in confusion.

"Can't. Your clerk wouldn't release the roster to me until after I met the skipper."

"Fucking Anthony. Sounds like that mealy pencil-pusher. I'll take care of that. But come to think of it, maybe it's better if we chat, first. I'm on the way back to the Q[5] to shower and change. Why don't you come with me? We'll talk, then go to chow. Captain Hoffman should be back by 1500, so we can meet up with him then."

The XO was a little different than most Marines, a little unorthodox, Esther got the feeling. And Esther didn't normally like unorthodox. She couldn't control unorthodox. She couldn't foresee unorthodox. But for reasons unknown, she kind of liked Ter Opal. And it made sense that she get the platoon gouge from her perspective.

"Sounds good to me, Ter," she said, subconsciously switching the woman from a simple billet to a fellow Marine. "Lead on."

---

[5] Q: Short for BOQ, or Bachelor Officers Quarters

# Chapter 4

A cold front had swept in from the high plains overnight, and Esther blew on her hands. She hadn't drawn her kit from supply yet, so she didn't have cold weather gear. The entire company was slated for their annual survivors benefit brief right after formation, so she wouldn't have a chance to draw her gear until COB unless she skipped noon chow.

*Oh, well, hopefully it'll warm up.*

Derrick Ganbataar, "Steel," was the only other lieutenant who wasn't wearing gloves. He stood easily, as if on a tropical beach somewhere. Esther thought it had to be mostly for show. She met Steel at the O-Club the night before, when the skipper organized an impromptu officer's call to welcome Esther aboard. Whip-cord rangy and with blonde hair, he didn't look like the Old Earth Mongolian he claimed to be. Esther suspected he was freezing, but was trying to uphold some sort of macho-Mongolian image, impervious to the cold.

With the first sergeant in front of the company passing the word, the five lieutenants were huddled in back of Second Platoon, waiting until the formation was dismissed so they could make their way into the classroom—and blessed warmth.

Nok Garrison looked rather worse for wear this morning. The Third Platoon commander had tied one on at the club and had either neglected to take a Soberup last night, or she was even too far gone for it to be effective.

*Heck, she only weighs about 40 kilos, so it didn't take too many brews, and then there were the shots*, Esther noted, feeling a touch of sympathy for the smaller woman.

Esther hadn't gotten too deep into her cups, so she hadn't taken a Soberup before hitting the rack, but the sour taste in her mouth was a reminder on why she didn't drink much. One beer or cider was fine, but the athlete in her didn't like not being in full control over her body.

"Heads up, the skipper's coming," Ter said, breaking into her thoughts.

Coming down the walk from battalion, Captain Hoffman was heading right for the first sergeant. The four platoon commanders scrambled to position themselves a step behind and to the right of their last squad or section leader. The first sergeant noticed the company commander and called the company to attention before performing an about face to wait. Captain Hoffman went right up to him, received the first sergeant's report, and took over the formation. Immediately, the four platoon commanders marched forward to take his or her place in front of his or her respective platoons, the platoon sergeants simultaneously marching to the back of each platoon.

"Kilo Company, good morning!" the captain shouted out.

He received a loud chorus of "ooh-rahs."

Esther hadn't quite pegged the skipper yet, but it was evident that he was pretty popular within the company. "Popular" didn't always equate to being a good commander, but it didn't preclude it, either, so Esther was going to withhold judgment.

"As I promised to you when I took command of the company, I will always keep you informed when I can. So now is one of those times. I just returned from a meeting with the CO. A situation has come up, and like always, when that happens, the Federation looks to us. So it looks like we could be deployed. We've received a warning order, and now we're just waiting to see if they're going to pull the trigger.

"Nothing has changed for the moment, though. We've still got our survivors benefit annual certification, and that's what we're going to do. However, commencing immediately, we are confined to base, and each Marine and sailor must sign out before leaving the battalion area.

"Staff and officers, I want you to get your certificates retinized first, then meet me in the conference room. For the rest of you, carry on the training schedule, but if you're missing anything for whatever reason, let your platoon sergeants know.

"That's all I know for now, but rest assured I'll keep you updated as soon as I get any more word.

"First Sergeant!" he shouted out.

The first sergeant marched to position himself in front of the skipper and received the company back. Esther, along with the other platoon commanders, left their post to be replaced with the platoon sergeants.

Esther's mind was awhirl. Upon reaching 2/16 as a PFC, Esther had rushed through her gear and weapons issue and was deployed on a mission within hours. Before even getting to know her fire team. Now, upon reporting to 3/14, she might be in the same boat. She hadn't even spoken with her platoon sergeant other than to shake his hand before formation, she had only met one of her sergeants, and she hadn't drawn her gear, yet here she was again, possibly going into the breach.

And her heart sang.

# FS Sergei Dillon

## Chapter 5

The company never finished its survivors benefit brief. The staff and officers had just gotten their forms retinized, looking into the retinal scanners that confirmed they were who they said they were and were leaving for their brief when a runner came from Battalion to fetch the skipper. The fact that it was a runner and not a simple call held significance. Esther joined the others and sat back down in the back of the auditorium while the admin chief continued his brief. All hands had seen the runner come get Captain Hoffman, and no one's mind was on who gets what in the case of their demise. Even the admin chief was wandering, losing his train of thought.

Twenty minutes later, the XO received a call. She nodded as she listened while 145 eyes were locked on her, all pretense of a brief forgotten.

"First Sergeant," she said when she was finished, "the brief is over. Get everyone back to the company area. We fall out in full Series 2 at 1400."

Series 2 meant full battle issue, with gear for 60 days. Only Series 1 was further along the scale.

A chorus of "ooh-rahs" echoed through the auditorium as Marines stood and platoon sergeants took over.

"We've got a brief in the conference room," Ter told the other lieutenants and the gunny. "I'll tell the first sergeant."

*Frigging great. We're deploying, and I've got jack.*

That wasn't exactly true. Esther had her uniforms and her bones, but not much else.

"Ter, I don't have my gear yet," Esther told her. "Am I going to have time for that?"

The XO hesitated only for a moment, then told her she'd cover for her at the brief. She had to draw her gear and weapons.

Eight hours later, the detachment, consisting of Echo and Golf companies and sections from Weapons Company, armor and arty battalions, and a modified squadron were on board the *Dillon*, heading off-planet. The battalion XO, Major Postern, was the task force commander.

The Marines received their first major brief as the ship maneuvered to enter bubble space. Brigadier General Costelano, the division assistant commander, gave the brief from back at his headquarters on Cornucopia.

The Evolution was a watershed in Federation history, where an oppressive regime more concerned with power than serving the people had been replaced. The turmoil, however, had resulted in 18 entire planets and 5 nations leaving the Federation (to include Ellison, which Esther's father had saved from annihilation, a lack of gratitude that still stuck in her craw). A few had become independent, others had joined existing governments such as the Confederation of Free States or the Brotherhood. At the time, the Federation wasn't in much of a position to do anything about it.

The process of leaving the Federation continued, though. Not all local governments moved quickly, and with the Federation back on its feet, it was taking action to influence local politics.

Nouvelle Bretagne was one of those planets where the wheels of politics moved slowly. Over half of the residents had emigrated from Indéfectibles with most of the rest being refugees of the Great Drought in Earth's Australia. Indéfectibles was one of the worlds that had pulled out of the Federation, re-aligning itself with Greater France. Now, the coming election would determine if Novelle Bretagne would follow suit.

The campaign had been nasty, with violence breaking out. Greater France, reacting to a riot that had broken out in Charlestown, had sent in two battalions of legionnaires to "keep the peace." There was already an FCDC battalion on the planet, and while the almost religiously loyal troopers were a good resource to counter the legionnaires, the fact was that they were a cross between a police force and an army and not organized to fight a professional military like the Legion.

As it had done five times over the last two years, the Federation responded in kind, sending in the Marines. Not a full battalion—for some reason beyond Esther's comprehension, a full battalion was considered too "militaristic," tantamount to declaring war. The theory was that the mere presence of Marines would be a deterrent to fighting. In three of the previous five times, this had not been the case. Three Marine task forces had fought pitched battles, one of them losing an entire platoon on Saint Grigori's Ascension. That seemed like war to Esther, and it certainly must have seemed like that to the families of dead Marines.

But humankind was in the midst of a war with the Klethos. Things had calmed down into the stylized combat for possession of challenged worlds, but the fear was that as the human gladiators became bigger and better, the Klethos could revert to open warfare, something the humans probably could not win. Couple that with the fact that the Federation was still consolidating again after the Evolution, and war was to be avoided at all costs.

So when Federation Marines and Confederation troops clashed on Eridani 2, that wasn't war, but merely an "incident." Like the Indians and Pakistanis back on Earth's 20th and 21st Centuries, like the Pathfinders and Franklites clashes on Royerson over the last 200 years, it wasn't "war." While Marines, soldiers, legionnaires, militia, and centurions fought and died, their politicians socialized over canapés at Brussels' finest restaurants.

The Federation and Greater France were not going to war, the general had assured them. But the Marines were going to ensure the elections on Novelle Bretagne were fair, and that the citizens (at least those loyal to the Federation) were protected.

The task force was landing at Corky's Waystop, which had once been a mere lodge in the Jordy Enclave but had grown to a city of over 4,000,000 after some mineral discoveries in the surrounding mountains. It leaned loyalist, but with such resources, the enclave was a prize. If the planet split up, the Federation wanted to make sure the entire province remained loyal.

"What do you think?" Esther asked Ter after the feed from the general ended.

"Five hundred Marines against 480 million people? Not bad odds."

No one expected the entire planet to turn on the Marines, but her point was valid. What could 500 Marines do if the entire planet blew up in open warfare? All the Marines, the FCDC, and the legionnaires, for that matter, would be swallowed up by the pure mass of humanity. Esther was cautiously eager to prove herself against the Legion. Her father had actually been awarded the *Croix de guerre des théâtres d'opérations extérieurs* by Greater France for saving some Legion butts on Tylaria, but he'd also earned his combat leadership chops against the Legion on Weyerhaeuser 23. He had always admired the Legion, but Esther didn't have the same admiration. Still, it felt fitting to her that she might face them in combat as a leader of Marines.

"The skipper's meeting with the major now, and we're to stand by. We've got a lot of shit to do and not much time," Ter told the other lieutenants.

"Well, we can stand by in the wardroom. Let's see if we can't get the chief to feed us," Steel suggested. "They've always got chow between meals there."

"Sure, why not?" Ter said.

"You go ahead," Esther told them. "I'm going to start on my platoon interviews, see if I can't get them out of the way when I can."

"Yeah, I guess it would help if you actually knew who was in your platoon," Nok said with a laugh.

Marines always took advantage of two things whenever they could: chow and sleep. They never knew when they'd get the opportunity to eat or catch some Z's in the future. Esther hadn't eaten since breakfast that morning, before formation, and she was starving. But Nok was right. She really needed to know her Marines, starting with Staff Sergeant Fortuna. And with the other lieutenant's gone to the wardroom, she had the stateroom to herself.

She buzzed her platoon sergeant to come over and popped up seats for both of them. She'd probably have time to do this after planetfall, but things in the Corps had a tendency to escalate quickly.

She just hoped that this time, she'd have the opportunity to snap in before being thrust into action.

# Camp Hope, Jordy Enclave, Nouvelle Bretagne

## Chapter 6

"Enter!"

Esther pushed open the hatch and entered with trepidation. His office was lined with built-in hardwood bookshelves. This was a far cry from most military camps, but it had been a two-year college in its first life. Now, it housed the task force as well as the local police force.

"Sit," the captain ordered, indicating a chair to the side of his large desk.

Esther sat into the over-stuffed chair, running her fingers over the padded armrest. The chair was soft, and she sunk low. She'd rather be on something a little firmer, a little more military. She scooted her butt up until she was sitting over the front edge of the chair, giving her more support.

"Thanks for coming in," the captain said as if Esther had a choice in the matter.

Esther was nervous. She'd taken her platoon out on a patrol for the first time and had lost five KIA and six WIA. Two of the KIA were declared dead, and the other three had long bouts of regen ahead of them, as did two of the WIA. Four other wounded were being treated at the local hospital and would return to full duty within a couple of weeks. In three years on Wayfarer Station, she'd hadn't seen that many casualties for the entire battalion.

For the last two hours since returning, she'd been going over in her mind what she could have done differently, but except for refusing the mission—which wasn't really an option—nothing she could think of would have made much difference.

Still, she had placed her squads in the most logical position, something the legionnaires had obviously foreseen. But switching things up should be to something that was an improvement, and she just couldn't see that. But Captain Hoffman probably could.

"I've had a chance to go over your report and recordings with the CO," he started.

*The CO?* Esther wondered for a second before realizing it had to have been a conference call.

"First, we jumped the gun. The administrator wanted a visible presence to announce our arrival, and that is why the six patrols were sent out even before arty was able to get online."

Ter had told Esther that the arty firing AI was down, whether from hacking or a simply failure wasn't known yet.

"Second, you were the wrong choice to send out."

Esther's heart fell. No one wanted to hear that.

"I looked at your logs, and you've only interviewed half of your platoon so far. We . . . I . . . should have realized that before assigning your patrol the mission. I thought an orientation patrol, which Intel thought had little chance of contact, would be a good way to snap you in. I was wrong."

*What? Is he taking responsibility?*

Esther hadn't been high enough on the food chain before to be part of the internecine warfare that sometimes took place over the blame game, but being the daughter of a general officer, she'd been exposed to it. She hadn't seen too many people willingly accept blame before.

"But I was the one who put my squads where they thought I would," she blurted out.

"True, but sometimes, that's the only logical choice. What you did do, however, was react to the situation."

Esther wasn't so sure as to that. In her mind, she'd been paralyzed for long stretches of time, wanting to do something, anything, but sitting back to let things develop.

"It worked out, but I've run over various situations in the battle gamer, and I'm not so sure sending Sergeant Ngcobo up the hill was the best move. It worked, but the risk, well . . .

"XO, bring in the others," he said into his PA, stopping that train of thought.

"We're going to dissect the fight. This is not a kangaroo court," he said as Esther looked up in surprise. "I want all of us to learn from it, myself included. You did well, Esther. You reacted, and you took it to the enemy. That's the bottom line. But we all can improve, and if we don't learn from history, we'll never get any better in our line of work."

Esther wasn't sure how to take his words. She was somewhat mollified that he'd said she'd done fine, but she wasn't looking forward to him and her peers tearing her decisions apart, seeking for better ways to have fought the battle. She began to feel exposed.

"It's your call, but if you think anyone is worthy of a commendation, I'd like that on my desk by COB tomorrow."

Esther had been thinking about that. In her mind, Charlie Ngcobo deserved something. He'd charged up the hill without hesitation, driven back a larger force, and used the enemy's own chat-chat to suppress the other Legion platoon. But now the skipper had said he wasn't sure that task had been the best option.

Still, if it wasn't, that was on her, not on the sergeant.

"Sergeant Ngcobo, sir. I'd like to write him up."

She thought she saw the slightest glint of approval in his eyes as he nodded and said, "Do it. I'll give my endorsement."

She was so worried about her own reception that she hadn't immediately pushed for Ngcobo. She'd already considered it, but had not given it much more thought at the moment. Captain Hoffman had, though, but he'd given her the chance to make the suggestion. She was sure that if she hadn't, he'd have done it on his own.

Her instructors at NOTC had stressed that a leader has to make the tough decisions in battle, even sending men to their certain death. They couldn't get emotionally involved. But they also were there to take care of their Marines. She shouldn't have had to wait for the captain to prompt her.

She'd been withholding judgment on the skipper until she got to know him better. Captain Michael Hoffman seemed to know his military science, from what she could pull up on the undernet, with more than a few well-written articles covering a range of military issues. Writing articles wasn't the same thing as being a good leader, though. However, his admitting he made a mistake and his concern that Charlie Ngcobo be recognize were pretty good signs that he was more than an academic. She still didn't know how good he was as a combat leader, but if he thought holding a dissection of the battle was a good idea, she'd give him the benefit of the doubt.

There was a knock on the hatch, and the other lieutenants filed in.

"Please, take your seats," he said as he turned on the flat screen.

An overhead image appeared with the platoon making its way up the dirt road. A green triangle overlay identified Esther, yellow triangles her squad leader, and a lilac Staff Sergeant Fortuna.

"We're starting here, at 1403. The lead element of the patrol is 700 meters from the objective. Lieutenant Lysander, as we go through, please interject your thought process as appropriate."

"Aye-aye, sir," Esther said, leaning forward as if she could get closer to the scene.

Despite her initial misgivings, she was getting into it, her interest piqued. If she could learn something from the dissection, that would make her a better Marine.

## Chapter 7

"Didn't see you at the Roost," Karl Hampshire, one of the Echo Company's lieutenants said as Esther slid her tray up next to his.

She turned so he could see the Officer of the Day brassard around her left upper arm.

"Oh, sucks to be you. It was a great fight. That's two for Iron Shot."

"Iron Shot" was Chief Warrant Officer 2 Tamara Veal, one of mankind's gladiators, and more pertinent to the task force, a Federation Marine, one of only five in the gladiator corps. Like most people, she tried to watch the duels against the Klethos, but she'd especially wanted to watch CWO2 Veal fight. She'd watched the gladiator's first fight on Halcon, but bad luck had it that for this fight, which took place at zero-dark-thirty local time, she'd been in the task force office, along with Staff Sergeant Fillipo and Corporal Gant-Jessup, manning the headquarters. It wasn't as if anyone expected any trouble. Gladiator fights were not holidays, but most of humanity tuned in to watch. Over at their camps, the legionnaires would be watching, as would be most of the civilian population.

Most of the Marines had watched in the old student center, now taken over as a general club. The "Roost" was the "Chicken's Roost," the name given to one of the small dining rooms that had been commandeered by the lieutenants and CWO Koricle. It wasn't much, but it had a top-of-the-line holo projector, and Echo's gunny had hooked them up with a chiller. The four captains and the major had taken over the old facility manager's office, and the other ranks had claimed the larger rooms.

"It was freaking frigid, Lysander. I mean, she'd just finished some twirling sword dance and the d'relle launched, no pause, and Iron Shot, she just skewers her, like a shish-kabob. Chicken-on-a-stick," Karl said, laughing at his own wit.

Esther rolled her eyes. She didn't need the reminder. She had contemplated pulling out her PA to watch the fight, Fillipo and

Gant-Jessup watching her eagerly. But regs were regs, and she had to follow them. She didn't know who'd been more disappointed with her decision: the other two or her.

One of the fabricators became free, so she left Karl and walked up to it, inputting Eggs Benedict. Twenty seconds later, the dish, hot and steamy, appeared in the chute. Noah had turned her on to the old dish, making it from scratch at home when they'd both been in secondary. Esther knew her twin would turn up his nose at the fab version, but she couldn't tell the difference. No one had ever accused her of having a refined palate.

She made her way to join the Ter, Steel, and Nok, who'd already staked out their table. The task force mess served all ranks in the school cafeteria, but the tables ended up segregated—whether by design or happenstance, Esther didn't know. What she did know was the far left table at the cafeteria's north side "belonged" to the Golf Company lieutenants. And now, all four of the other lieutenants looked a little worse for wear having been up most of the night for the fight.

"Hey, you should have seen—" Ter started.

"Yeah, yeah, yeah, I know." Esther said, cutting off the XO. "I've already heard all about it from Karl. I don't need you to rub it in."

"Sucks to be you. It was max copacetic," Steel said.

Esther rolled her eyes again and took a bite of her breakfast.

"You ready for tomorrow?" Ter asked, switching the subject.

First Platoon hadn't been outside the wire since the battle at Watson's Farm, as they were now referring to it. That was six days ago. Two of her WIA had returned to duty the day before, but she was still down seven Marines. Everyone else had gone out at least once since then, either on standard show-the-flag-patrols or to provide security for meetings between the major and civilian heads.

"Sure am. We're getting cabin fever here," she said, with a little more bravado than she'd intended.

Going out down seven did not thrill her, but when Captain Hoffman had broached the subject of some inter-company transfers to beef up her numbers, she had said the platoon was fine.

*It's not like its much of a mission, and next week, I get Das Salaam and Eire back.*

Major Postern was going to the city administration center to meet with the mayor, a representative of the *Frères Dans L'ègalitè*, a Greater France-leaning civil group, formed barely six months prior, and a Federation rep. The Francophiles were a decided minority in Corky's Waystop, but the Federation Administrator in Charleston, which was leaning much more toward Greater France, wanted to keep a lid on any violence leading up to the elections, and Esther's fight at Watson's Farm had not been received well. The administrator had demanded the withdrawal of legionnaires, but the governor had resisted, stating she had a contract with the Legion for the "training" of the local militia, and she couldn't break that.

The administrator had holed up in Charleston, the planet's main city, but he was sending his vice administrator, who would be protected by an FCDC security team. First Platoon would provide security for the major.

"Your mission brief's still at 1400," Ter told her. "Let me know if you need anything."

"Will do," she said as she took the last piece of English muffin and mopped up the gooey mixture of egg yolk and hollandaise.

She popped it into her mouth, licked her fingers clean, and stood up. Ter reached out and gave her forearm a squeeze before Esther left to return her tray.

She returned to the task force office, waiting for her relief. First Sergeant Caneletti, Echos's first sergeant and the task force's senior enlisted Marine came in to take care of some admin, soon followed by most of the headquarters staff. Major Postern arrived, and instead of waiting for the formal turnover, took Esther's report, which was basically a "nothing to report."

And she waited—and waited. The clock hit 0800 Greenwich, which for the moment was close to local time, and more importantly, was when she was supposed to get relieved. At 0815, she was still sitting there at the small OOD desk, waiting. Finally, at 0824, First Lieutenant Boron Wiesapp came into the office.

Esther stood there steaming as the pilot looked over the log, swiping through her routine entries.

He seemed satisfied, and said, "I'm assuming the duty as Task Force Mandrake Officer of the Day."

Esther stood there for a moment, expecting an apology, but none was forthcoming, she said, "I stand relieved."

She handed him her brassard, and started to leave, but she couldn't let it go.

"You know you were almost half an hour late."

"Couldn't be helped. Had things to do."

"So do I, but you kept me from that. Next time you have the duty, be on time," she said before turning and stalking out of the office.

Corporal Sandoval dropped her eyes and refused to look up as Esther stormed past. Esther knew she shouldn't have berated the pilot in front of the Marines in the office, but she couldn't help it. It didn't matter what he had to do. He was supposed to be there for the relief on time. Until evening, he didn't even have to stay in the CP. He could be out on the flight line or wherever the flyboys spent their days, so "things to do" was bullshit.

Esther held all Marines to a pretty high standard, but officers had to be held to even higher standards. Her father had always been clear on that. There were benefits to being an officer, but there was a price to pay for that.

Esther went to Danielson Dorm, which was serving as the officer and SNCO quarters. Esther thought it a little risky to have all the leadership in one building, but the overall alert status was only 2, and Intel was sure the Legion wouldn't launch an attack on their base. Evidently, there were "rules' to these quasi-wars.

Alert Status 2 or not, that didn't do Portis or Lorne much good. They were just as dead as had this been one of the big full-scale battles during the Evolution.

Esther entered her room. The walls had been painted a horrendous shade of magenta, but the color somehow struck a chord with her. It was so un-military, so unlike her. Normally, that would make her shy away, but she was getting rather fond of her little retreat.

She sat on her rack, and almost immediately, its siren song began to call to her. She knew if she lay back, she'd be asleep in seconds. Esther didn't like to take stim-tabs, much less a brain flush. She only had one body, and she didn't want to abuse it. She had to do something to stay awake until after the mission brief, however, and that left one thing in her bag of tricks.

Esther stripped off her clothes and neatly hung them up. She grabbed her PT gear from where it hung in the tiny shower and laid the shorts and shirt out on her rack. She caught her reflection in the vanity mirror over the small desk and stopped to look.

Esther wasn't vain—well, not too vain, she amended her thought. It was true she liked clothes, even if the Corps limited her in when she could engage in dressing up. But she wasn't that concerned with her face, and she had never gone for some of the more flamboyant make-up and nanoskins. She was, however, proud of her body. She worked hard to keep it in shape, and she turned back and forth slowly, looking at her reflection. Slim but not skinny, she had the taut muscles of an athlete. Satisfied that nothing on her had slumped, she put on her shorts, then the Boudica shirt, feeling the "hugging" as the upper support settled around her breasts, giving the support needed for athletic activity.

She snagged her bag and left, heading to the gym across the quad. The college actually had two gyms. One had courts and the pool, and both Marines and the local police made use of it regularly, with pick-up basketball, etherball, and volleyball, the regular bill of fare. Esther, though was heading for the smaller training gym.

She sniffed the air as she pushed through the front hatch. It was a habit she'd developed over the years after going into countless gyms for matches. While the muggy, overripe scent of bodies might give some people pause, to Esther, they touched synapses deep within her insula that resonated with memories—in her case, memories of a home, of belonging. No matter where they moved as children, following their father's orders, the gyms were always the same.

The gym was almost empty. Esther figured that Marines who might normally be working out were catching up on a few Z's they'd lost during the night watching the fight. She could hear someone going heavy on the free weights in the back as she settled on one of the padded mats to go through her Saturnalia Yoga. She'd been a proponent ever since she was introduced to it back at the University of Michigan on Earth. She'd planned a light workout on the weights, but even a light workout could result in injury, and she was convinced that the yoga helped stave that off.

She sat down, legs out in front of her, hands flat on the mat behind, ready to lift her butt. From this vantage, she could see under the squat rack to see who was on the weights. It took her a moment to recognize her platoon sergeant. He wasn't lifting heavy, but he was pumping out reps on the bench like a machine. The more he lifted, the more violent his lifts seemed, as if he was attacking the weights. He kept going, far beyond what Esther could do with the same 60 kg. She didn't know how many reps he'd done before she started watching him, but she'd seen him do at least 30 reps, his arms turning red with the effort, his grunt sounding muted in the gym, but still very evident. He started to slow down, arms trembling, then with a shout, he threw the bar up in the air, letting it fall down to catch the stops.

Esther's mouth dropped open. That was an extremely dangerous thing to do, especially when Fortuna thought he was alone. If the bar had missed the stops, it would have come down on his neck. Even 60kg could do him some serious damage.

The staff sergeant lay there for a moment, then suddenly sat up, bending over, elbows on his knees and putting his forehead into his hands.

Esther knew she wasn't the most empathetic person in the galaxy, but even she could tell that something was seriously wrong with the man. Yet he was cleared for duty. On the one hand, Navy Medicine was outstanding. It had saved her father a number of times. On the other hand, something obviously wasn't right.

Esther slowly edged back, pulling her bag with her, around the half-wall before standing up. Staff Sergeant Fortuna hadn't moved, so she didn't think he'd seen her.

*I'm not a doctor,* she thought before taking a deep breath. *What the hell do I know?*

She started whistling, then a few moments later, came around the half-wall as if she'd just arrived. She threw her bag to the mat, then looked up.

"Oh, Staff Sergeant, getting a good work-out in?"

He was sitting up straight, looking much different. Not happy, not excited, but almost normal.

"Yes, ma'am. Sergeant Ngcobo's doing a junk-on-the-bunk for tomorrow, so I came to work up a sweat."

Esther picked up her bag, then walked around the squat rack and up to the bench. The gym had six benches, but only Fortuna's had plates on the bar.

"Mind if I work in with you?"

"Sure thing, ma'am."

Esther hadn't warmed up, and while 60kg wasn't much, she still would have rather had done her Saturnalia first.

*Oh well, the enemy doesn't give you chance to stretch out first*, she thought as she lay down, taking a moment to push her shoulder blades flat on the bench.

Normally, she placed a towel on benches. Noah had given it to her, a goofy, purple Air Fairy towel he'd received in a goody bag at one of his gaming tournaments. She didn't particularly like lying in another person's sweat, and the towel was a good barrier. She left it in her bag, though, though, wanting to keep things as simple as possible.

She reached up, positioned her hands, then lifted the bar, bringing slowly down to her chest, before starting her reps. She did ten, then racked the bar in the stops.

Most men had a habit of moving to spot her when she was on free weights. Whether this was because they didn't give women the credit to be able to lift or they were in the low-key gym flirting mode, Esther hadn't been able to figure that out. But the fact was that most men either offered or moved into position without asking.

Staff Sergeant Fortuna just stood there, arms crossed over his chest as he watched. Esther didn't know what to make of that. Possibly it was their position as subordinate and senior that kept things at arm's distance.

She'd felt a twinge in her shoulder on the ninth rep, but nothing major.  Esther didn't lift free weights often in a well-equipped gym.  She liked the dynamic machines, which varied the weight throughout the range of motion.  But Marines had a traditional affinity for free weights (probably because they could make them out of almost anything no matter to where they were deployed), and if Fortuna was on the bench, she would be, too.

She stood up, then motioned to the staff sergeant.  His next set had none of the frenetic quality of his last.  Esther wanted to know what was going through his head, though.  Other than her initial interview with him, they hadn't spoken more than a few sentences at a time together, and he was still an enigma to her.

Esther tended to be direct, but she knew that was not the way to go here.  She had to break the ice.

"Did you see the fight?" she asked in a rush, trying to say something, anything.

"No, ma'am.  I don't like them much."

Which wasn't what she was expecting.  Almost all Marines watched the bouts, and this fight featured a Marine.

"You don't?" she said, her surprise leaking through into her tone.

"No, ma'am.  Don't like to see someone die.  It's your rep," he added without pause, pointing to the bench.

No one wanted to see anyone die, but that came with the territory, whether "regular" Marine or gladiator.  Whether a gladiator lost or won, maybe particularly if she lost, most Marines thought they had to watch to support her.

She didn't know how to respond, so she watched him complete another set before switching places with him and completing her next set.

"How's your family?" she asked.

*Shit, that sounds lame.*

"Fine, ma'am."

With that curt response, the talking ceased as they took turns on the bench.  Esther didn't know how many sets Fortuna had done, but after six, she was feeling it.  She needed to move to something different, but there was still unfinished business here.

She barely got up the last rep, her arms trembling, while Fortuna watched silently. Her arms were shot.

*I don't need to pussyfoot here. I'm the commander.*

"How's your therapy going?" she blurted out.

His eyes narrowed, but he said, "OK, ma'am."

"You think it's helping?"

"I just go where they tell me, do what they tell me."

"But is it helping?" she asked again.

He turned away, and Esther thought he was going to stride off, but after a moment, he turned back, pursed his lips, then said, "I don't know."

"Sit," she said, swinging her legs over to one side and giving him room.

He didn't argue and sat down heavily. He held out one hand, seemingly fascinated with his fingernails.

"Look, Conrad," she said, using his first name. "I don't know what's going on. I don't have access to your therapy, but I do see you here. I'll be blunt. Your performance has not been good. You almost disappeared at the farm, and I never know where to find you."

He started to stiffen up and pull away, and Esther hurriedly added, "But I know that's not you. I've gone over your record. You are a top-notch Marine. So something is getting in the way, and if there is anything I can do to help, well, that's what I'm here for."

She watched him for a moment, glad that he wasn't still pulling away, at least. He wasn't offering anything, though.

"Do you need some time off? I can make it happen. Nothing on your record."

He shook his head and muttered, "Just what I need, to be alone with my demons."

An almost electric wave ran through her.

*Demons?*

"What do you mean, Conrad?"

"Oh, nothing. And no, I don't want time off."

"Are you having problems at home?" she asked, her mind full of sickness, dying relatives, an unexpected pregnancy.

"No, ma'am."

*Then what?*

Esther knew she wasn't a professional, she knew she should leave it to them, but she had a duty not only to him, but to the platoon as a whole. She didn't want to, but she'd get rid of him if she had to for the good of the rest of the platoon.

"There has to be a reason for, well, for your performance. You're not 100% there. I know what you've done in combat. I've seen your awards. You've got 14 confirmed kills as a sniper, for goodness' sakes."

He leaned back and looked at the ceiling, his mouth in a smile, as he sardonically said, "Ah, yes, my kills. Fourteen of them."

Another electric wave ran through her.

*It's his kills! Something about them.*

"What, do you think you should be credited for more?"

"Oh, God, I hope not, Lieutenant, I hope not. Anything but that."

"Is there . . . I mean . . .did you do something wrong?" Esther asked, her heart dropping.

If he broke the rules of warfare, and he told her, she was duty-bound to report him. Suddenly, she felt out of her league. There was a doctor-patient confidentiality with the Navy psychiatrist, but that didn't exist between the two of them within their chain of command. She wanted to stop this conversation immediately.

But the dam suddenly broke, and the staff sergeant said, "No, nothing 'wrong,'" he said, and Esther could almost hear the quotations marks around the "wrong." "Nothing according to the Corps. I had fourteen kills, all righteous."

A wave of relief swept through her.

"But wrong? Yes. No. Does it matter?"

"What do you mean?"

"What I mean, ma'am, is that I killed fourteen people. I watched them die. But they weren't just people. They were Federation citizens," he said, turning his body to look Esther in the eyes.

"They were loyalists," Esther said, a hitch in her voice as she tried to process what he'd just said.

"From the Federation."

Esther sat back for a moment, letting that sink in.

"They were fighting us. No one wanted to go to war with them, but it was their choice."

"They were still Federation citizens. Half of my school beatball team joined the FCDC. Those were my friends, guys I grew up with. Were they my enemy?"

"Well, yeah, to be honest. Look, you know my father, right?"

The staff sergeant rolled his eyes.

*Of course he knows. Stop being stupid!*

"Well, during the Evolution, he gave the orders to take out a loyalist complex on Watershed, and 11,000 civilians died in the attack. That ate him up, but he had to do it for—"

". . .for the greater good. Believe me, I've heard it before. And no offense to your father, but he gave an order. He didn't pull the trigger. He didn't watch." He put a hand on her thigh and leaned closer. "On Kaptchaka, in Solsi Town, I was overwatching one of our security teams. I saw three troopers on the building above them. I took all three out."

"Saving the team on the ground."

"One of them was a little girl, I swear it. OK, she had to have been 18, but she looked 12. She'd been struggling to carry two Ogres. I took out the first two guys, and the girl, she just stood there, looking at them in shock. She was scared shitless. I told her to leave. I wanted her to leave. But she picks up one of the Ogres she dropped, and she carries it to the edge of the building. I wanted her to run. I wasn't going to kill her. But the stupid little bitch, I can see she arms the Ogre. Her eyes are so big, I don't need my scope to spot them. She drops the ogre again, and I hope she's going to run. But I know she's not. When she comes back up and starts to swing the Ogre around, I drop her. Bam! The top of her head is gone. A little girl, three years younger than me maybe. We could have been in school together. And now, she's dead meat rotting on the top of some abandoned roof."

He stopped his story, holding up his hand again, examining his fingernails.

Esther didn't know what to say. This was way beyond her pay grade. Hell, no matter how high she went, this was not what she was trained for.

"You had—" she started before he suddenly turned into her, head on her shoulder as he broke out crying.

Slowly, Esther put her arm around him. She was lost. She never should have opened him up. Part of her knew he wanted to vent, probably to a fellow Marine, not just a Navy psychiatrist. But she didn't need a pysch degree to know her platoon sergeant was in deep waters. And she didn't know what to do.

He cried almost silently for two minutes, and Esther could feel hot tears soaking into her shirt. Finally, he pulled back.

"Sorry about that, ma'am. That was unprofessional of me. It won't happen again."

He stood up, wiped his face with his forearm, and said, "I'll see you at the mission brief."

"It's OK, Staff Sergeant. I'm glad we talked."

But it wasn't OK, she knew as she watched him leave the gym. But she didn't know what to do.

# Chapter 8

"Yanghu, eyes forward, not back," Staff Sergeant Fortuna yelled out to the PFC.

"Sergeant Ngcobo, how about watching your Marines. Any threat is going to come from out there, not back at the municipal center," he passed on the command circuit.

Esther watched her platoon sergeant closely as she'd been doing since they left the camp. She hoped she wasn't being too obvious, but he had to feel her eyes on him. For his part, he studiously ignored her unless there was a specific reason to interact.

She had spent an hour with Ter the night before, asking for advice. Esther knew she shouldn't be sharing confidential information with the XO, but then again, she shouldn't have received that information in the first place. Part of her really wished Fortuna hadn't shared it.

The XO didn't have any easy answers, either. A Marine's medical situation was personal. If it were going to get in the way of his or her duties, a medical officer or independent duty corpsman would bring as much of the subject up as needed, but for the most part, officers did not have access to medical histories.

What it boiled down to was that for the moment, Staff Sergeant Fortuna was cleared for duty, and the day's operation was a low-risk mission. Between the two of them, they decided not to broach the subject with the skipper, but Esther was going to keep a close eye on her platoon sergeant. Depending on how he seemed, the two would decide on a course of action.

*So far, so good*, she thought, as she watched him walking up and down behind First Squad, alert and focused.

She checked the time. The meeting had already run an hour over with no signs of letting up soon. Esther could go inside and see for herself, but her platoon's job was exterior duty. She didn't want it to seem as if she was stepping on the toes of the FCDC security team that was providing security inside the building.

"Lieutenant, we've got some sort of commotion to our front," Sergeant Hammerschott passed on the P2P.

Esther immediately switch the personal comms to her command net, then replied with the more formal, "Golf-One-Three, what kind of commotion?"

"I don't know, Lieu. . .I mean, Golf-One-Six. We can just hear them coming."

"Six" would have been sufficient on the platoon command net, but overkill was better than under. Esther was just as guilty of being a little lax with comms procedures on the P2P, but on the command or open circuit, identifying who was sending and to whom was vital. In the heat of the battle, a simple thing such as looking for the avatar on a face shield display could be a distraction. She made a mental note to stress comms procedures after they returned to the base.

"Five, meet me at Third's position," she passed.

Esther was towards the north of the building, close to where Third Squad was placed. Keeping inside the line of permanent pylon barriers, she rounded the corner, and she could now hear the "commotion," as Hammerschott had called it. It was chanting, and it had the sound of a protest. She almost reported to Captain Hoffman, but she hesitated, wanting to get a little more information so she could give him some details.

She found Hammerschott and stood there, ordering her AI to filter out the rumble so she could make out the shouts.

"Froggies, out of Jordy! Froggies, out of Jordy!"

Within moments, the leading edge of the crowd appeared coming around a corner. They were two blocks away, but Esther didn't need magnification to read the signs they were holding. This mob was not in favor of the Francophones. One of the signs, a high-quality mono-pole screen was held high, the image a crude cartoon of a stylized figure in a beret bending over only to have a broad-shouldered image come up and kick it in the butt, sending the figure flying off the screen before reappearing to start the process over.

"They're not the enemy, Baxter," she passed on the P2P to Sergeant Hammerschott, forgetting her moment's ago promise to start stressing proper comms procedures. "Just take is easy."

She had placed Third over the north and north-east sector around the building because it was the least likely to see any confrontation. She was still concerned about the nervousness he'd displayed at the farm, and didn't want to put him in that kind of position again until she was more confident of his capabilities. Intel had briefed them that the part to the west of the building was where people gathered, and the west side had longer fields of fire for a sniper, so she'd put First Squad there. The gods of battle were perverse, however, so of course, it was to the north that anything was happening.

The protestors kept approaching, crossing Alder Ave and now only a block away. Esther looked back to the building. The conference room was on this side of it, on the second deck. She could see an FCDC trooper standing just inside the window.

*And that's why they're coming here. I should have thought of that.*

With the conference room on this side, and with the *Frères Dans L'ègalitè* rep and one of the governor's representatives, the protestors wanted to be where they could be heard. At the park, no one at the meeting would even know they had shown up.

The FCDC team had put up a simple tape barrier around the building, extending about 15 meters out to the other side of the street. It was a representative barrier, not a physical one. Anyone could just step over it. The protestors stopped at it, however, and continued their chanting.

Esther caught a glimpse of another sign, this one handwritten on a piece of fiberboard. It had a pretty strong suggestion for the Francophiles that was physically impossible—unless someone was extremely flexible—and she had to force back a chuckle. As a Marine and part of the Federation, she couldn't be seen as taking sides—despite that being the entire reason the Marines were on the planet.

"Steady," Staff Sergeant Fortuna passed over the platoon net. "We're just standing here watching the protestors. Nothing to be concerned about."

Esther reported to Captain Hoffman, who didn't seem too concerned, but the magenta icon that appeared at the corner of her display let her know that he was slaving into her feed.

"Keep your eyes open," Esther passed to Sergeants Ngcobo and Daniels-Graves.

While she didn't think the protest in front of her was anything serious, there was a possibility that it was a diversion. As always, Esther's mind was whirling with all sorts of possibilities, too many to address. The diversion possibility, though, was significant enough that she thought the reminder to her other two squad leaders was warranted.

In front of her were about 60-70 protestors. Most seemed willing to honor the barrier tape, simply shouting over it to the municipal building. A couple were more animated, striding back and forth. One young man had voice thrower, the tiny device amplifying his voice so much as he screeched and shouted that it drowned out most of the rest.

When he pulled down the tape with one hand, Staff Sergeant Fortuna ordered him with "Citizen in the blue shirt, do not cross the tape."

The shoulder speaker on a Marine's battle rattle was not as powerful as the voice thrower, which was designed for concerts, but Fortuna's voice had the element of command that could not be ignored, and the man stopped. He didn't let up on his shouts, but he stood on the other side of the tape.

"OK, good, good," Esther whispered to herself.

She started to feel better about her platoon sergeant. She didn't want to pat herself on the back (well, maybe a little), but maybe their talk in the gym had some effect on him.

She started to walk back toward First Squad's sector when Mr. Blue Shirt suddenly vaulted the tape and raised his sign, another mono-pole screen, as if it was a battle ax.

"Snatch!" Staff Sergeant Fortuna ordered Baston and Star of Justice.

The municipal building was surrounded by the squat shapes of pylon barriers, which protected against vehicle intrusion. These could be vaulted by individuals, but not easily. There were breaks in them at intervals, and the two Marines were at one such opening. And that was where Mr. Blue Shirt was heading, angling from where he'd stepped over the tape.

On Fortuna's order, the two Marines stepped back, leaving the gap open. Esther could see the look of satisfaction cross the man's face as he ran, his voice-thrower blasting an unintelligible screech. Staff Sergeant Fortuna moved to the opening, and the protestor, probably hyped in the adrenaline rush (if not something more chemically-induced) held his sign higher as he hit the opening and shifted his direction to the platoon sergeant.

*Oh, this isn't going to be pretty,* Esther thought as she took a step forward to watch better.

Esther was the platoon commander. She should be commanding. But she knew the man's fate was already sealed, so for the moment, she was simply an appreciative spectator.

Mr. Blue Shirt totally ignored Baston and Star of Justice, which was pretty difficult to do as they were both in full battle rattle, and Star of Justice was 2.2 meters and 110 kg of muscle. As the protestor reached them, his focus on Staff Sergeant Fortuna, the two Marines suddenly closed in on him like two halves of a clam. Baston hit him an instant before Star of Justice, knocking him back into the bigger Marine. His sign continued on toward Fortuna, but he didn't. He might as well have run into the stone wall of the municipal building. Actually, that might have been better. He'd have simply bounced off the wall without having 200 kg of that wall land on him right after.

"Oh, hell yeah," Captain Hoffman said over the P2P.

Esther winced as the man fell into a twisted heap, his head bouncing off the sidewalk. With Baston on his legs and Star of Justice on his torso, Mr. Blue Shirt was in a world of hurt. He was probably already knocked unconscious, but if not, Star of Justice's elbow to the side of the head as the Lance Corporal stood back up finished the job. Baston efficiently pulled the man's arms back and zip-tied his hands together.

The other protestors stood in silence, no one moving.

"Please stay on the far side of the tape," Staff Sergeant Fortuna passed over his suit speakers as if telling people which bus to board.

One of the protestors, an older man with razor tiger slashes shaved into his hair, shrugged and shouted out, "Froggies, out of Jordy! Froggies, out of Jordy!"

By fits and starts, the rest joined in, and in a few moments, were back to their full righteous fury. Like wildebeest in the eco-parks of Africa after a lion had made a kill, they had put the lion out of mind, their fellow wildebeest forgotten.

Staff Sergeant Fortuna picked up the man's sign, turned to read it, then slowly folded it in half before dropping it to the ground. With careful deliberation, he stomped on it, crushing it between his feet. A flash of first red, then blue, and the sign died.

That's got to be 300 credits down the drain, Esther thought, but without any compassion. What did the guy expect? How stupid could he be?

"Doc, can you come up here?" she passed. "One of the protestors ran into Baston and Star of Justice."

The magenta icon was still on her display, so she knew Captain Hoffman had watched the entire thing with her. She didn't need to report back immediately. But they had to take care of Mr. Blue—well now blue with spots of red—Shirt, and not just with the corpsman. Marines did not have authority to arrest a citizen. That had to be the FCDC. She asked Sergeant First Class Larrimore, the team leader, to send someone out to pick up the still unconscious man.

The magenta icon went out, and Esther let out a breath of relief. Having commanders observing her was part and parcel to the job, but she didn't know many Marines who actually enjoyed it.

The crowd seemed slightly quieter, but that might have been because of their prisoner's voice-thrower being out of the equation. What she did notice was that no one even touched the tape. They were more than happy to let only their voices cross it.

Fifteen minutes later, Captain Hoffman let her know the meeting was breaking up. She kept her Marines at their positions until after the governor's rep and his party lifted off, then collapsed them into the southern entry where the four vehicles were waiting to take them back.

"Good job out there," she told Staff Sergeant Fortuna.

He grunted what could have been a thanks as he motioned for Second Squad to mount up.

"Lieutenant Lysander, can I see you a moment?" a voice called out from behind her.

Esther looked back to see Major Postern by the Hyundai Rover motioning her over.

*What the hell? That was a righteous take-down. The idiot was warned, and he still came. What did he expect us to do?*

She straightened her shoulders and marched up to him, trying to look confident.

"You're going to come with me to the Landing Day Celebration in Charlestown on Monday. Make sure your Alphas are ready."

*What the . . .?*

She'd been ready to get her ass chewed, so this took her by surprise. Over the major's shoulder, she saw Captain Hoffman shrug his shoulders, hands palm up, telling her this had nothing to do with him.

"Uh, sir? Me?"

"Yes, you. I was just invited to the ceremony by the federal comptroller. The administrator thought it would be a good idea if we were there, showing the flag, so-to-speak. The election's only two weeks away, and he thinks we need to remind everyone what being in the Federation means, and that includes having the Marines to protect them."

*That is BS. There's more to it than that.*

"Is this because of who's my father?" she asked, heedless of how that might come across.

Esther was proud of her heritage, and she'd once been willing to use it to her advantage, but now, she'd evolved. She wanted to be Esther Lysander, not Ryck Lysander's daughter.

"No. Well, maybe. But your name was specifically added to the guest list. I got the feeling that it is more of a dig at the Legion. We've had only one confrontation, after all, and you lead it."

*And lost seven Marines,* she thought.

But that made more sense. Besides rubbing the Legion's nose in it, it was a reminder that the Marines were a potent force, and escalating the situation was not a good idea.

"I haven't cleared it with Battalion, but plan on it. And be looking good."

Her attendance was not really up to Battalion. As an official representative of the Federation, she'd have to be cleared by Division, as would the major and anyone else going. But that should be merely a formality. The warning about her Alphas was appreciated, though. This was a combat mission, not a normal deployment. Officers were required to bring one set of Alphas, but they were vac-packed into a tiny bundle, compressed as much as was possible. You couldn't just pop the seal and thrown them on, though. It took several steps just to get them to where they could be worn, and if this was an official function, she had to get them looking sharp.

"Aye-aye, sir."

She looked again at the skipper, hoping to get some guidance, but he silently mouthed "Later."

"Tell you what, why don't you ride in the Rover with me," he said, suddenly all smiles. "It's a little more comfortable than those Shannxis," he added, pointing to the trucks. "Captain Hoffman told me your Marines pulverized that negat who tried to rush you."

The Rover was a loaner, far nicer than anything the Corps had for company or field-grade officers, and the Shaanxis had a habit of forgetting that they were hover vehicles, supposedly able to smooth out the ride. But Esther only considered it for a moment.

"Thank you, sir, but I'd like to ride with my Marines."

"Well, OK, if you insist. I'll get the guest list confirmed, and I should know by tomorrow. Start on your Alphas today, though. Let them air out."

Esther came to semi-attention, and nodded, foregoing the salute as was normal for field operations. She didn't know what to make of what she'd been told. She hoped she really was being added to the list because of Watson's Farm, though.

As she climbed up into the truck's cab and sat on the thinly padded seat, she wondered if she should have taken the major up on his offer. The truck backed up and lurched into forward, the right skirt bottoming out for a second, sending a jolt that elicited a string of curses from the cargo bed.

*It's better than walking, I guess.*

The truck swung right, this time the left skirt hitting, as a louder chorus of curses sounded out.

*Maybe.*

## Chapter 9

Esther looked across the room, just taking in the entire surreal experience. She'd been to more than a few Founders or Landing Day celebrations in her life, but nothing was like this.

The elections to decide whether all, part, or none of the planet would withdraw from the Federation was in 18 days. Over 300 civilians had been killed during the campaign-related violence along with 17 legionnaires and five Marines. Those numbers might have been a drop in the bucket compared to other wars or skirmishes, but they weren't insignificant. Campaigns were supposed to be peaceful.

Yet here in the Charleston Mövenpick's ball room, all the movers and shakers on the planet were hobnobbing, kissing cheeks, and shaking hands as if nothing was wrong. Everyone was in the typical fervor of patriotism, and Nouvelle Bretagne's green and brown flag hung everywhere.

The Federation had sent the Honorable Franklin G. Rheinheim (who Esther didn't know from Adam, but she had gleaned the information from the engraved Schedule of Events she'd been handed at the door). Rheinheim was a career bureaucrat, the sector administrator and so responsible for Federation functions for over 25 planets and stations. He wasn't the center of attention, though. Nouvelle Bretagne's own favorite son, the football goalie Lamont Mulliare, had arrived with the sector administrator. Mulliare was a Francophile, but he'd been vocal about the planet remaining in the Federation. Now he was being trotted around by Rheinheim like a prized dog at Westminster.

Less than ten meters to Esther's left, two legionnaires in their *Tenue de parade*, their parade dress uniform, with the black kepis of officers, were helping themselves to glasses of Grackle. Three other legionnaires were mingling, to include their commander.

Representing the Marines, Esther had joined Major Postern, Captain Hoffman, Echo's Captain Tojinoru, and Captain Quince, the flight detachment commander. But while the legionnaires were in their full dress uniforms, the Marines where in the Alphas, their second-most formal uniform.

It still boggled her grasp of sensibility that both militaries were socializing together. The Federation and Greater France might not be officially at war, but Esther had been in combat with legionnaires less than two weeks ago, and for all she knew, there could be skirmishes happening at this very moment.

Esther took a small sip of her Grackle. The local bubbly wine was surprisingly tasty, with just the right fizz, but Esther was not going to drink more than one. Captain Quince had already had four glasses, and he looked to be enjoying himself. Esther kept expecting either the major or one of the other captains to step in and stop him, but it seemed that she was the only one concerned.

"Second Lieutenant Lysander, I don't believe we've had the pleasure," a voice from behind her said.

Esther turned to see a young legionnaire, smiling down at her. Esther wasn't a short woman, but the legionnaire towered over her by a good dozen centimeters. He was as thin as a rake, though, but with the wiry physique of an athlete instead of that of a scarecrow.

"Sous-Lieutenant Mark Donald," he said, his hand out.

Esther certainly had not expected to speak to any of the legionnaires, much less have one come up and introduce himself. She warily took his hand. His grip was firm, but not overbearing in an attempt to crush her hand.

"I believe you might know my sister. Ariel Donald?"

If she hadn't expected a legionnaire to introduce himself, she really, really hadn't expected to have a mutual acquaintance with one of them. Her mind raced as she tried to figure out who he meant before it hit her.

"From McGill? On the etherball team?"

"None other."

"And you just happened to know that we played in '13?"

"Oh, not really," he said with a laugh. "I looked you up, and when I saw you were at UM and on the team, I checked to see if you ever played each other."

"And why were you looking me up?" she asked, taking half a step back and narrowing her eyes.

"If you know the enemy and you know yourself, you need not fear the results of a hundred battles."

That was vaguely familiar to her, but she couldn't place it.

He must have seen the question in her eyes, because he said, "Sun Tzu," but without condescension in his tone.

"So, am I your enemy?"

"For now, possibly. Tomorrow, possibly not. The Federation and Greater France have been allies more often than opponents. And we are not at war now, true?"

"And what was Watson's Farm, then?"

"Yes, the Swamp. Grigori made a pretty big error, hiding too deep from the battle. It cost him."

*I knew it! I knew someone had blown it.*

"Now I have his platoon, so in a way, I owe my command to you."

"So are you thanking me?" Esther asked with the slightest curl of her upper lip.

She was extremely uncomfortable with the way the conversation was developing, so she was retreating back to the snide, aggressive persona she'd sometimes used back at UM when she was the subject of unwanted attention.

"No, I'm not thanking you. I merely have my command sooner than later. Rather I should thank Grigori for his lesson on what not to do."

"I'm sure he's pleased to have given you that lesson."

"I doubt it. Grigori didn't make it. There wasn't much of him left to mash back together," he said.

Esther stared into his eyes, trying to read into his mind. He stood there, drink in hand, and nonchalantly spoke of a fellow legionnaire, a fellow lieutenant, who'd been killed in battle as if it was just a passing event of no importance. And it was Esther who'd killed him. She didn't pull the trigger, and if this Grigori had been in the swamp, not to mention that his body had been too mangled for resurrection, then it had probably been one of the Aardvark crews that had killed the man. But Esther had been in command of the operation, and she'd been giving the orders.

"But enough of that. This is a celebration, and we should put our differences aside for the evening. Don't you agree?"

*What is your game? What are you trying to do?*

Esther was fairly lineal in her thinking. You went from point A to point B. Things tended to the black and white. She didn't enjoy, nor did she understand game playing, but she did recognize it when she saw it. Mark Donald, Legion sous-lieutenant, was playing a game. She just didn't know what game.

Noah, on the other hand, for all his "nice guy" attributes, could dance the dance of politics. He understood it. He probably wasn't cutthroat enough to succeed at it himself, but he could recognize and navigate past the traps and pitfalls. For a moment, Esther felt a longing for her twin. If he was there, he'd be a good sounding board to figure out what was happening.

She gave a non-committal sniff and took another sip of her Grackle. Unless the legionnaire was playing a very long game, whatever he said or did wouldn't have much effect one way or the other. Esther was still a second lieutenant, low man on the officer totem pole. Nothing she could do would have much of an impact on the Federation or even Nouvelle Bretagne. Major Postern had brought her as a not-so-subtle dig at the Legion, not because she really mattered to the bigger picture.

"Not much in the way of Landing Day celebrations," the legionnaire said, turning to scan the crowd.

She knew what he meant. Almost all planets celebrated either Landing Day, the anniversary of mankind's first landing on a planet, or Founder's Day, when a planet that was terraformed was declared habitable. Nouvelle Bretagne didn't need terraforming (other than the ongoing slow process of lengthening the planet's rotation until it matched that of Earth's), so it was Landing Day here. But there were no parades, no fireworks, no displays of military might. That last made her chuckle. There were two militaries here, so she guessed there was a display of military might. Neither was there in celebration, though.

"Could be because of the unrest you've created."

"Oh, please, *mon* Lieutenant," Donald said, "I'm surprised at you. Whatever unrest, as you say, that exists here was already brewing. Neither you Marines nor we in the Legion have anything to do with that. We're just marketing tools to help swing the vote."

"Or to fight each other."

"Or to fight, if necessary. It's all part of the entertainment. It's all part of the branding."

*I'm not an entertainer*, she thought. *I'm here to defend Federation citizens.*

"Once the vote is in, and Jordy Enclave stays with the Federation and rest of the planet splits to join Greater France, you and I will leave for new adventures. A year from now, we could be fighting a mutual enemy."

"We already are. The Klethos."

"Touché, Lieutenant. Yes, we are, but I was thinking more in terms of normal combat."

Esther hesitated a moment, then asked, "Do you think that is how the election will come out? With a split like that?"

"I would hazard a guess to say that's likely. But we'll see."

The Marines, at least at her level and below, had been given only the vaguest of briefs on the political situation. She hadn't given the election much thought other than it would be a yes or no to leave or stay. What he said made sense, though.

"Your Captain Quince seems to be enjoying himself," he said, raising his glass and lifting a forefinger off of it to point.

Esther rolled her eyes. If she had to say something, she would, but she hoped one of the others would intervene first. Even if she was right, it wasn't a good thing for a junior to correct a senior. Other officers agreeing with her actions would probably still label her as arrogant and as someone who felt privileged.

Then it struck her that he knew the captain's name as well.

"Do you keep track of all of us?"

A broad smile broke across his face, and he shrugged. "Only those on the guest list. Would you like to meet our representatives? That's Commandant Chelli over there, talking with Mr. Mulliare."

*Trying to convince him to change his views*, Esther thought.

"No, I'm fine without. Uh . . . it's been a pleasure, Sous-lieutenant . . ."

*A "pleasure?" Has it really? Geez, Esther. Get real.*

It might not have been a pleasure, but social niceties had a way of forcing themselves out, and she continued, ". . . but I'm afraid I need to see to our captain."

"Yes, it has been a pleasure, Lieutenant Lysander. I hope we meet again, perhaps when we're not on opposing sides."

For a horrifying moment, Esther thought he was going to take her hand and kiss it like some 18th Century court noble, but he merely gave a short nod and left.

That was one of the strangest conversations in her life. If they met tomorrow in a battle, she would have no hesitation to kill the man. But he'd been pleasant, and under other circumstances, she might have enjoyed speaking to him.

She looked up at Captain Quince again, who was now leaning way too close to a young woman who was giving every sign that she wanted to bolt. The captain was gesturing with his hands, Grackle sloshing out of the glass he held, as he was making a point that he probably thought was profound.

The easiest thing to do would be to ignore the captain. Eventually, one of the others would lasso him and get him out of there. She wouldn't be involved, and nothing would reflect onto her.

But she was an officer in the Marines, and she had a duty to the Federation. Maybe more importantly, she had a duty to the captain as well. Marines had each other's backs. That was the way it was.

She put her glass down on a side table, tugged at the bottom edge of her Alpha's jacket, then started marching across the ballroom floor to him. It was the right thing to do, but she hoped it wouldn't blow up in her face.

## Chapter 10

"How's he doing?" Ter asked as the two Marines looked out over the receiving station.

Esther didn't need her to elaborate. "He" could only be one person.

"I thought he'd pulled out of it at the municipal building, but he's back to where he was. He barely says a word, and he doesn't take any action on his own."

"Maybe it's when the shit hits the fan that he starts performing. Back at camp, he's got his thoughts to contend with."

"His demons, you mean. Maybe you're right, though. He was fine for that mission. When that idiot charged us, he was cool and professional. Uh, what did the first sergeant say? You never told me."

Esther had only confided with Ter so far on her concerns about Staff Sergeant Fortuna. Between the two of them, they wanted the company's senior enlisted Marine's input, but if Esther approached the first sergeant, it would be an "official" action. She was his commander, and technically, her concerns needed to go into the record. Ter was the XO, however, not in Fortuna's chain of command. She could do things without the formality that handcuffed Esther.

Ter pursed her lips and took a deep breath through her nose before answering.

"He thinks it's temporary. He's also worried about Fortuna's career. So his suggestion is just to stand by until the mission's over. The elections are in two days, and we're probably going to be terminated shortly after that. Fortuna's got another eight months until he's due orders, but the first sergeant is going to talk to the sergeant major after we get back, and between the two of them, they'll try to get him earlier orders to Tarawa or someplace where he can get therapy."

"He's getting therapy on Reissler Quay."

"Aye-yah, I know. But Tarawa's got the Naval Hospital, and he thinks that will make a difference. Bottom line is that he doesn't want you to initiate any action that'll screw up Fortuna's career. He wants the SNCO mafia to take care of it."

"He said that? 'SNCO mafia?'"

The term was quite common, especially among the officer ranks, but Esther didn't think SNCOs would use it, too.

"Yeah, he did. Why not? That's what they are."

Unlike Esther, Ter had been a staff sergeant when she was selected for a commission, and she wore the SNCO badge proudly. Esther hadn't meant anything derogatory—she just didn't know, and not knowing anything grated on her.

*OK, file that one away.*

"No reason. Just curious."

"I don't want to wreck his career," she added, changing back to the main subject. "He's served the Federation with distinction, and he deserves our support."

"Aye-yah, he does," she said with a note of finality. A moment later, she asked, "And what about Das Salaam and Eire? They doing OK?"

"Fine," she said of her two WIA who were now back with the platoon. "No problems at all."

"Well, I've got to get to Nok. She's got a bunch of protestors out in front of her," the XO said. "Gotta support the sisters, you know."

Esther dutifully gave her a fist bump. Female officers were still somewhat rare. Only 20%, or thereabouts, of the Corps were women. The officer corps was 7% female, although that was expected to rise as more women entered the enlisted pool from which officers were selected. There were only four female officers in the entire battalion, and three were in Golf. A cynic might believe that was gender segregation. Someone else might think it was just the luck of the draw. The three Golf lieutenants chose to declare they were assigned together to use "sister power" to make Golf the tip of the battalion spear. Patel never played along, but Steel jokingly declared himself an "honorary sister."

"Not going to see Steel?"

"The skipper's there with him. So that leaves me with you two."

As the elections got closer, Intel had picked up chatter from both sides of the political fence. As a result, all six of the task force's line platoons were out at perceived hotspots. Steel's Second Platoon was in town at the municipal building, which was the center of protests in Jordy Enclave. But where Esther's first platoon had faced only Federation-supporting protestors, both sides were there now. If Esther were a betting woman, she'd say that it would be either there or with Echo's First Platoon in Hummerstadt that any violence would break out. Captain Jonas evidently agreed with that assessment, and that's where he was as well.

"Well, tell Nok to keep her head down," Esther said as the XO motioned for her driver-slash-security.

Things could be too degraded if Ter and one lance corporal could travel around as they willed.

"Aye-yah, I will. You keep your head down, too."

"I don't think we've got much to worry about. No matter who wins, they need power," Esther replied.

"Complacency, my dear butter bar, complacency. You've got warm bodies out there to bring home when all this is over."

Ter was her friend, but she was also the company XO, and Esther bristled at the implied criticism. She was very aware of the people out there. She knew the platoon was under observation. But she agreed with Intel's assessment that they were there to watch over an even protect the receiving station as well. Like she said, however, the elections turned out, Nouvelle Bretagne needed power, and the receiving station supplied it for this entire region of Jordy Enclave as well as to more than 20,000 households in Green River, a Francophile-leaning county across the provincial border. But believing that the station would not be a target did not mean that Esther was complacent in her mission.

She knew Ter didn't mean any real criticism, but she frowned as her friend got in their candy-blue rental hover (yes, on a live mission, she was out in a rental as if on vacation somewhere). Still, the reminder made her double-check her positioning.

The receiving station, which accepted the transmission of energy from the orbital solar station and then distributed it out to the grid, was too large at six hectares for the platoon to set up around the perimeter. So Esther had broken up the three squads and placed them at three separate strong points within the station, creating a perimeter defense. Each squad could support the other two with fire, and each had scrounged enough material within the station to have fairly decent protection from small arms. They could function as interlocking pillboxes. With Esther, Doc, and Lance Corporal Mykystra at in the station control house—which she shared with four civilian employees of SDS Power—she could watch over each position.

Six dragonflies, guided by AI chaos programming to avoid patterns, covered the area surrounding them out to over a klick.

Nothing in warfare was a "for certain," but Esther was pretty confident that her platoon was in a good position. She didn't see anything that needed to change.

Her AI pulled some of the company data stream, deemed it important, and displayed it for her. The protests around the municipal building were getting more heated, but so far, nothing was directed at the Marines or the building itself. For a moment, Esther wished that it was her platoon that was there. But she knew Captain Hoffman had made the right assignment. First was still shorthanded, and that could make a difference should things get bad there. And as Steel has said to her after the mission brief, it was about time his Marines had their turn in the potential breach. It took combat to hone the steel of a platoon, after all.

Esther couldn't direct her feeds to any specific person in Second Platoon, but from the feed that was open to the rest of the company, she could see some scuffling between the protestors going on. A wedge of local police moved forward and professionally split the two groups without obvious injury to any of them. She had to give both the police and their FCDC trainers credit. That had been very well done. Proactive and aggressive action could be the key to keeping serious violence from breaking out.

She looked past her display to where her police were standing, chatting with the SDS jimmylegs at the station's main gate. She'd been surprised that the company had not beefed up their four-man security team, the same number they'd had every day since the facility first came online years ago. She was equally as surprised that the police had only sent three men. She agreed with the assessment that it would be self-defeating for anyone to attack the station, but it still was a strategic asset, and its loss could be devastating.

"Sergeant Hammerschott, you doing OK?" she asked, turning her mind from the local lack of concern to her own Marines.

"Yes, ma'am. We're ready for anything."

With her concerns over Staff Sergeant Fortuna, she'd given Hammerschott less attention that she needed to. In garrison, there wasn't another NCO as gung-ho and eager. In actual action, he was the polar opposite, hesitant and even frightened. That was not a good combination for any Marines, much less a squad leader. She had his bios miniaturized and running on the bottom of her display. With a simple blink, she could enlarge them. The bios wouldn't be an indication of anything specific. A rapid heartbeat could mean excitement to close in with the enemy just as much as it could mean fear, but she still wanted to monitor him.

She checked with Daniel-Graves, then Ngcobo. She had no concerns over Sergeant Ngcobo. She had come to trust the strange-looking—and sometimes strange-acting—Marine.

Satisfied, she pulled up the staff sergeant on her display. She'd placed him with Hammerschott's squad. Before using the P2P, she pulled up his bios. His pulse was a low 38 beats per minute. Esther frowned. It was all well and good to be calm, but they were in a potential combat situation, and she wanted her Marines to be on the alert, not drifting to the comatose.

She was just about to speak over the P2P when the raucous incoming alarm sounded over the platoon net. Her own heartbeat jumped as she switched her display to an aerial aspect, taking in the entire area. Three missiles of some kind were heading towards them from three different directions, each with impact in less than five seconds.

There was nothing Esther could do in that amount of time. It was up to her Marines and their training. Immediately, fire reached up from all three squads. Second and Third aimed at one of the incoming, which looked to be splitting their positions. That left First with two of them.

One of First Squads two Porcupines erupted in its angry chatter. The M-554 "Porcupine" was a small, man-packed projectile mine. It could throw up 50 small minelets out to 750 meters, each minelet capable of taking out smaller rockets, missiles, and possibly even mortar shells. The minelets were dumb munitions, unable to change their trajectory, but each had a proximity fuze that detonated the payload if something came near enough. And in this case, something did. Two of the minelets detonated close to one missile, close enough to send it crashing into the grassy field.

Something hit and knocked down the missile that was splitting Second and Third. It exploded in a five-meter ball of flame. The remaining missile kept coming, and for an instant, she thought First Squad was its target. But it passed right over the Marines to slam into one of the transmission tower pylons, sending flames and smoke into the air. Pieces of shrapnel and pylon peppered the area, hitting First's position, but their fighting position preparation kept anyone from being hit. The transmission tower lurched, and for a moment, Esther thought it was going to fall, but while knocked offline, it stayed upright, if canted.

Fire reached out from the surrounding area to hit inside the station, and her AI tracked mortar shells reaching up into the sky. On her display, the scattered figures that had been out there were coalescing into groups.

Beside her, Mykystra was reporting to the task force CP[6] back at camp. They would be following on the feeds, and she expected the captain or the major to demand her attention at any moment, but for now, she appreciated being able to focus on what was happening.

Her AI was having difficulty identifying the incoming. Neither the missiles nor the mortar fire matched Legion specs, so unless there was more subterfuge going on here than she thought, she was facing locals, not legionnaires. That was all well and good,

---

[6] CP: Command Post

but she knew the legionnaires and could guess what to expect from them.

She certainly didn't expect the technicals, at least not this kind of technical. From one of SDS' own construction sites 800 meters away, two heavy-duty dozers turned towards them, blades high, while a stream of heavy 13mm rounds poured from one of them.

"Banshees, Staff Sergeant!" Esther shouted into her mic, then to Mykystra, "Get us air."

"Esther, what's happening?" Ter asked over the P2P.

"Not now, Ter, we're under attack. You can work on our air request."

Once again, First Platoon was out of arty range. They didn't even have a section of mortars. Their mission had been considered low risk, so the heavier weapons had gone elsewhere.

There was a whoosh as a Banshee took off from Second Squad's position. Esther watched the missile zip downrange, impacting on the right dozer's blade in a bright flash of flame. The smoke obscured the dozer for a moment, but the blade pushed through the smoke as the dozer emerged. There was a gouge in the blade, surrounded by shiny, clean metal, but the machine hadn't slowed down—and it kept on firing. A series of sparks jumped off another tower's pylons as 13mm rounds struck it, but without effect.

"Mykystra, where's the air?"

"Working on it, ma'am!"

There was a pounding at the front hatch, and Esther wheeled around, her Ruger at the ready.

"Doc, let them in," she said when she recognized the police and jimmylegs. "You, get back and on the ground," she added to the control room's SDS staff.

She saw a shift in some of the avatars to the west. They could be bystanders trying to get out of the area, or they could be part of another assault force.

"Charlie—"

"I've got them. The minute they start towards us, we'll engage."

And so she immediately put them out of her mind, knowing the sergeant was on top of it.

The six dunkers in the two squads facing the dozers were firing, most with the Bushmaster rockets. Each of the stubby rockets hit the dozers, but if a Banshee hadn't knocked one out, the smaller Bushmasters hadn't a chance.

"Grenades, blow-down fuzes," Esther ordered.

The armed dozer shifted its fire from the tower to the control room. Esther hit the deck as the heavy rounds tore into the building, destroying equipment in ear-shattering blasts.

"Doc, Mykystra, with me," she ordered, crawling to the front hatch and outside.

Whoever was assaulting them obviously had a strategic mission to destroy the station, but ignoring the Marines was a tactical mistake. The dunker's "dunks" of outgoing grenades were music to Esther's ears, and she lifted herself up on her arms to see. The puffs of exploding shells above the dozers were clearly visible, and almost immediately, one of the dozers—the unarmed one, unfortunately—veered off. At least Esther had thought it was unarmed. After 20 meters, it exploded in a huge blast that shook the ground under her from 500 meters away.

The armed dozer kept coming, though, gun blazing. More grenades exploded above it, but with no obvious effect. Either the driver was under some heavy protection, or it was being remotely operated. She thought the latter was more likely, but that didn't explain why the second one had been knocked out.

More small arms fire reached into the station, and mortar rounds landed in the parking lot, another indication that it wasn't trained soldiers attacking. If it were the Legion, they'd be hitting Marines from only a klick away.

A volley of fire sounded from First Squad. Esther switched to a split screen. One half showed the approaching dozer, the other Ngcobo's feed. From well out in front of First Squad, several figures were in full retreat, leaving three motionless figures behind.

Sergeant Ngcobo would have seen her comms icon appear on his display, so he knew she was watching.

"They must have thought that with those dozers and the rest of the incoming, we'd miss them. We didn't," he said in his usual, almost flippant manner.

"No, I guess you didn't," she said, cutting his feed.

Most of the incoming fire was ineffective. The main threat was the technical.

"What's the air status?" she asked Mykystra.

"Four minutes."

Captain Hoffman's comms icon appeared on her display.

She blinked the connection open, then said, "We need that air now, sir."

"Four minutes, Lieutenant."

She ran a quick calculation. Four minutes would put that dozer into the station, right at Third Squad's position.

"Beacons on," she passed on the platoon net, then "Note the friendlies," to the CO.

"Staff Sergeant Fortuna, I'm going to pull you back. Sergeant Daniels-Graves, cover Third, but be ready to assume your alternate position,"

"Roger that," the Second Squad leader replied.

There was nothing from the platoon sergeant.

"Conrad, did you copy that?" she passed on the P2P.

A questing stream of the 13 mm hit the ground five meters from her, and she ducked down.

"Hammerschott, do you see the platoon sergeant?" she passed.

"Uh, wait one," he said, his voice tense but sounding like he was keeping it together.

She flipped to Staff Sergeant Fortuna's feed, but all she could see was a close-up of what looked like dirt.

*Has he been hit?*

His avatar had him right behind the squad's position.

"Lieutenant, are you getting this?" Hammerschott asked as he force-fed his feed.

Staff Sergeant Fortuna was standing above his utilities, which were crumbled in a pile at his feet. He slid off his smoothies, and stood there for a moment, stark naked.

"Staff Sergeant, what are you doing?" Esther could hear Hammerschott call out.

"Stop him, Sergeant," Esther shouted, overcome with dread.

Her platoon sergeant reached down and adjusted his helmet so it looked up. He smiled and gave the feed a casual salute. He disappeared from his feed, but from Hammerschott's, Esther saw him pick up something, and then disappear to the side of the position.

"Tackle his ass now," she ordered. "Bring him back in."

"Staff Sergeant, come back," the sergeant shouted as he scrambled to the side to bring Fortuna back into view. "Eire, Frogman, go get him."

Lance Corporal Carrigan, "Frogman," passed in front of Hammerschott to exit the position.

"What's going on?" Captain Hoffman asked. "What the hell's Fortuna doing?"

Past her display, Esther saw Eire and Carrigan emerge from the position just as Fortuna came into view in front of it. Both junior Marines bolted around the side of the position and ran forward just as the dozer's 13mm swung towards them, chewing up the ground and sending both of the junior Marines diving for cover. A few rounds hit near Fortuna, but he never faltered, just kept walking forward.

Another burst hit the position, sending pieces flying, and Eire wheeled around, bringing his left hand to his chest and clutching it with his right. His avatar changed to light blue.

Esther got up to her knees as the gun on the dozer fired off another burst. She didn't know how many rounds they'd stacked up on the vehicle. Unlike a military vehicle where the rounds would be stored inside, they'd be exposed in some sort of jury-rigged container. The rounds would be more vulnerable, but the dozer could carry a lot. And with a sinking heart, she knew what she had to do.

Carrigan, get Eire back inside."

Both Marines craned their heads to look back at her, Eire still clutching his hand. If the situation were different, she wouldn't have given that order. But Staff Sergeant Fortuna had made his decision, and it wasn't right that Esther risk the other two because of that.

"Sergeant Hammerschott, prepare to fall back to your alternate position."

"But the staff sergeant—"

"That's an order."

Fortuna kept marching forward, hands out at his sides, carrying what looked like toads in his hands. There was so much metal on the dozer that Esther didn't even know if one of the incendiary devices had enough fuel to melt through it to anything vital. Dozers were built to withstand a lot of abuse.

And still Fortuna walked forward. The dozer continued to fire, ignoring him.

And then it hit her. If the dozer was unmanned, as she was now sure it was, whatever weapons system had been hooked up probably had an AI directing its fire. Without a uniform, without gear, the enemy AI might be a low-enough-level AI not to recognize Fortuna as an enemy. For a moment, she felt her hope rise. Maybe there was method in his madness.

She barely saw Third Squad emerge from their position and sprint back. Two of the Marines were hit by small arms, but their bones stopped the rounds.

Esther told her AI to re-direct a dragonfly. Within moments, she had its view from behind the dozer, facing Fortuna, who was now 30 meters beyond the position, a beatific smile on his face as he walked forward. The dozer was 70 meters out and closing, heading at a slight angle away from the staff sergeant.

"Throw it!" she shouted, unable to stay quiet.

She knew he wasn't going to throw one of the toads. She knew he wanted release from his torment.

Suddenly, the dozer stopped, maybe 30 meters from Fortuna. The gun started traversing to him. Someone was observing them and had either taken over the controls or even directed the AI to recognize the staff sergeant as a threat. Even then, the gun didn't fire, as if the person on the other side couldn't believe what faced the dozer. And the staff sergeant kept walking forward, arms outstretched.

"Throw it," Esther whispered.

At 20 meters away, the 13 mm on the dozer opened up, and Staff Sergeant Conrad Fortuna was immediately blasted into pieces.

"Fuck!" Esther said, burying her face into the dirt.

She was vaguely aware of Mykystra talking in the Wasp.

*Get it together. He's gone!*

She flipped to the air tac net, and heard Captain Quince say he was two minutes out, then confirm beacon color.

The dozer continued forward, but it had swerved to kill Staff Sergeant Fortuna, and Second Squad's lone remaining Banshee took off from their position. Three seconds later, it slammed into the left rear corner of the dozer. The construction vehicle was massive, but tracks were tracks, and the Banshee knocked off a section of them. With the right tracks still working, the dozer started turning in a circle. After two revolutions, it stopped for a moment, then with several fits and starts, oriented itself back on the station. Its 13mm demolished Third Squad's now empty position, reducing it to splinters and rubble.

"Second Squad, displace!" she ordered.

A moment later, the dozer started turning again, this time towards Second Squad's position.

Sergeant Daniels-Graves stood just outside the entrance, urging everyone out.

"Move it," Esther passed needlessly.

The sergeant knew the situation, and she knew what was at stake.

With only one track, the dozer remote operator was having problems. It was just getting into where it could fire when Captain Quince started his run. With an angry-sounding snarl, the plane's 30mm cannon opened up. No matter how sturdy a dozer was made, it couldn't stand up to that. It looked like the hand of God smashed down on the bright yellow vehicle, driving it into the dirt. Black smoke started to rise into the air before a huge explosion enveloped it.

The first dozer had been 500 meters away, and that shock wave had been bad enough. This dozer was just outside the station, and Esther felt as if someone, someone big, had landed on her chest.

Even with her battle helmet suppressing the sound, her ears were ringing.

Something big, something that had been part of a dozer until a moment before, landed ten meters away with a thud.

The second Wasp pulled up, its run unnecessary.

On her display, Esther could see avatars heading away from the battle area. Combatants or spectators, they evidently thought discretion the better part of valor.

The battle was over.

# Chapter 11

Two days later, the elections were over. The vote was split along geographic lines. As per an agreement hammered out before, that meant Nouvelle Bretagne would divide, with the Francophile provinces retaining the name. Jordy Enclave and three other provinces would become a separate nation, still within the Federation. There were a few days of muted protests, then the decision became the new norm. There was a flurry of citizens exchanging homes with others who wanted to move to the other nation, and that somehow took up a couple of days of the news feed.

Esther thought that was crazy. Their planet was being divided, yet the newsies focused on home swaps. Ter thought that was on purpose, to bring a sense of normalcy to the populace.

A week after that, the task force received its orders to return to Reissler Quay and stand down.

It had been a rough deployment for Esther. The task force had suffered three permanent KIA during the mission, and each had been from her platoon. Five of the nine Marines now going through regen had been in her platoon. She'd been assured by the major on down that she'd performed admirably, that the KIA were just the luck of the draw. Esther knew better. She could accept Lorne and Portis as battle casualties, but not Fortuna. He'd been killed during the Evolution—it had just taken this long for death to actually arrive. But Esther could have stopped it. She'd known that something was wrong with him. She'd discussed it with Ter, and she'd had the issue brought up with the first sergeant. But Staff Sergeant Fortuna's career was deemed more important than his life.

And then there was the doctor who'd cleared him for duty. A quiet and subdued Ter had blamed him for Fortuna's suicide. Esther agreed that doctor was at fault, and the division commander had convened an investigation on him. But the medical officer was not Fortuna's commander. She was, and it was her duty to watch out for her Marines.

Her father had told her once that a Marine officer had two and only two duties: accomplish the mission, and watch over his Marines. Sometimes, those two missions clashed, and then an officer had to make a hard choice. But that wasn't the case here. Esther had failed to protect Fortuna from himself.

Esther had poured over the undernet to try and figure out what had happened. Staff Sergeant Fortuna had been killed by a condition known to soldiers ever since there were soldiers. Called "nostalgia," "soldiers' heart," "shell shock," "battle fatigue," "PTSD," "the empty," it was essentially a soldier's inability to come to grips with the experiences he or she suffered in combat. Treatment had improved over the centuries, and now, long-term effects were rare. A combination of drugs and therapy were usually enough to keep the demons at bay.

But not for everyone. Esther was surprised that there were certain individuals who did not respond to treatment. Staff Sergeant Fortuna's tissue samples had been sent for analysis, but the feeling now was that he was one of the few in that category. And that would be embraced as the cause of death.

Doc Quisenberry had looked over the staff sergeant's records, and while not a medical officer, he knew enough about military medicine to tell Esther that the investigation wouldn't result in any action. The doctor had followed established procedures. Esther didn't doubt that, but she felt it should have been obvious that Fortuna was not responding to treatment. He'd been on a long spiral into oblivion, and someone should have taken action.

Like her.

As she boarded the shuttle to lift off the planet, she vowed to herself that something like this would never happen again on her watch. Command came with responsibilities. Never again would she make a joint decision when she felt something was wrong. No more bringing in the XO or first sergeant. She could ask for input, of course, but she'd ceded this decision to others instead of making it herself, and that cost Staff Sergeant Fortuna his life.

*If I'm going to accept command, then I'm going to command!*

# PROPHESY

## Chapter 12

"She be beautiful, no?" Ruth asked Esther in a whisper.

"Yes, she is," Esther said, watching Miriam walking down the aisle.

And it was true. She was lovely. She'd confided with Esther the night before that she wasn't one much for the trappings of ceremonies, but Esther thought that at that moment, she was beaming.

Esther spared a quick look across the chancel to where Noah was standing, looking sharp in his dress blues. His eyes were locked on his bride-to-be, an expression on his face that Esther couldn't quite place.

*Pride? Longing? Fulfillment?*

Esther felt the slightest twinge of jealousy, which she quickly squashed. She was genuinely happy for her twin.

*So why am I jealous, even a little?*

She shifted her gaze back to Miriam, being escorted by Uncle Caleb. Miriam was estranged from her family, and despite Grandmama's best efforts, she would not relent and reveal who there were and how to contact them. Esther had to give Miriam credit for that. Not many people could withstand a full-court press from the family matron.

Esther still wasn't completely sold on her brother's fiancé. Her secretive nature, her lack of openness, these bothered her. She wasn't sure Miriam had even been open about her past with Noah. Knowing him, he probably happily accepted what little she'd told him without questioning. He was a trusting soul, too much so for his own good.

*But he seems happy. I guess that's what counts. But if she screws him over, so help me . . .*

She forced herself back to the ceremony. She was Miriam's maid of honor, and she wasn't supposed to be planning dastardly deeds upon the bride.

Not that she'd had much to do as the maid of honor. She'd only arrived on-planet two days before, and as she'd foretold to Noah back on Tarawa, Grandmama had pretty much taken over the entire evolution. Nothing had been done without her input or approval.

She hadn't done such a bad job, Esther had to admit to herself. The Roman Catholic chapel, which they'd rented for the occasion, looked amazing. Even the gowns for the bridesmaids were stylish, lilac and blue with clean, flattering lines. Popular culture was that bridesmaids' gowns were ugly things, planned that way to make the bride look better by comparison, but these were nice. Esther planned on keeping hers for future use or possibly repurposing.

She'd rather have been in her uniform, even being Noah's best man, but that position had been filled by Sergeant Skeets Harrak, one of his friends and fellow tanker. She couldn't blame him. She hadn't been the most supportive sister over the last six years.

When Esther had told Noah she'd come, she'd agreed only because they were twins. She had to support him, and she could put up with the extended family for a few days. But as she watched Miriam slowly march up the aisle, she was once again amazed at how many people had shown up for the wedding. That was why they'd rented the cathedral. Torritites normally met in small "brethren" halls for services, and there wasn't a hall on the planet that could hold so many spectators.

To Esther's surprise, she was actually enjoying reconnecting with family. There was a sense of community within the Torritites that mirrored the brotherhood of the Corps. Esther wasn't particularly religious, and she hadn't been raised in a Torritite household, but it was still part of who she was. Her mother had been born and raised within the community, and she'd held fast to her beliefs until the day she'd been killed. And despite Esther's lack of contact over the years, her family was welcoming her with open arms.

Miriam and Uncle Caleb reached the chancel, and with a huge smile that threatened to crack his face, Uncle Caleb handed over Miriam to Noah. Her brother hesitated for a moment, seemingly lost in Miriam's eyes, before he turned to Aunt Rebekah, who was officiating. While Uncle Caleb was her mother's brother, Esther wasn't even sure of her exact relationship with Aunt Rebekah—within the community, second, third, or further separated cousins usually resorted to age to determine how to address each other, and since Rebekah was a decade older, she was "aunt."

Noah and Miriam took two steps forward until they were a single pace away from Aunt Rebekah, who looked over the nave and spread her hands.

"Dearly beloved, we are gathered here today under the eyes of the Lord to join Noah Absalom Lysander to Miriam Seek Grace . . ."

*Holy hell! It's really happening. My brother's getting hitched!*

# REISSLER QUAY

## Chapter 13

"Look at all the lemmings," Ter said as at least two dozen Marines crowded around the airedale major.

"They're in for some disappointment," Nok added.

Which was true, Esther knew. The air community was one of the most difficult MOS[7] groups to get into, but that didn't stop starry-eyed Marines, visions of *Dax Puller, Fighter Pilot* and *The War Eagles* filling their heads.

All Marines, started out as infantry riflemen. And most support positions were filled by civilians. But combat specialties were pulled from the pool of infantrymen. To fill these positions, the Corps conducted quarterly "recruiting drives." Marines in various MOS's gave presentations touting the benefits of being an artilleryman, combat engineer, tanker, field logistician, pilot, or whatever.

The crowd around the major were chasing dreams. As the major had said during his brief, prospective pilots were drawn from either the officer ranks or from some highly qualified enlisted who were eligible for commissioning. There were limited slots for enlisted aircraft or ordnance techs, and they had to be eligible for warrant officer. Forsun Eisenstadt, one of Fox Company's platoon commanders, had just been approved for flight school, and a few of those surrounding the major might qualify to be a tech, but Esther thought that would be about it as far as airedales went.

Getting a secondary MOS was much easier. Except for recon, all of the infantry MOS's could be assigned by the battalion commander at any time during a Marine's career. A one-year

---

[7] MOS: Military Occupational Specialty

private first class could go to the mortar, rocketeer, or machine-gunner course. Primary MOSs such as armor, combat engineer, recon, arty, field communications, field logistics, the air billets, and the few support specialties open to Marines were board-approved, and were generally limited to NCOs and above.

"So, are you going to take off for the sky?" Nok asked. "You look like a beak-jockey."

"Yeah, you know me so well," Esther said. "I live to drive assholes like you around."

Esther was a diehard infantryman, and Nok simply liked to pull her chain. A "beak-jockey" was a less-than-complimentary term the grunt officers used for Stork pilots. Where the Navy had huge numbers of pilots covering many different platforms, the Marines only had two manned airframes: the cargo Stork and the fighter Wasp.

Esther didn't want to be a pilot, but what she hadn't told anyone yet was that she wanted Nok's job. Better yet, she wanted the PICS mission to simply transfer to First Platoon. She had served almost two operational tours so far, and the luck-of-the-draw had it that she had never been in a PICS platoon. The big combat suits were a vital component of the Corps infantry strength, and Esther knew she needed that experience if she was going to be a well-rounded senior officer someday. Getting it as a company commander would serve as a ticket punch, but it would not give her the same degree of knowledge and experience as being a PICS platoon commander.

She hoped with Nok already in receipt of orders, she could convince the skipper to give First the PICS mission. If not, she was willing to move to Third as the new platoon commander.

"Ladies, may I have a word with you three?"

Esther turned around to see Captain Vansant standing there. The captain had just given the recon recruiting brief. She was the only female recon officer in the Corps, so she had a degree of notoriety mixed with mad credibility. Another six or seven women had attempted the courses, but the rest had come out short.

This wasn't the first time Esther had met the captain. Rory Vansant had been an All-Federation etherball player, and at the

Federation championships when Esther was a sophomore, the captain's Fortress University had knocked Esther's UM team out of the tournament. Esther had shaken the then senior's hand during the team line-up after the match. Yet of all the billions of people in the galaxy, the two were crossing paths again.

She doubted that the captain remembered some sophomore, but due to Vansant's notoriety, Esther remembered it well.

"Yes, ma'am," all three chorused as they faced her.

"What did you think of my presentation?" the captain asked.

"Uh, fine, ma'am?" Nok said, a question in her tone as to why the captain asked.

Captain Vansant laughed, then said, "OK, I'm not really asking if I'm a great public speaker. But I'd like to know your opinion on what I said about women in recon."

*What had she said?* Esther wondered, trying to dig it out of her memory.

She hadn't been paying much attention to the captain's brief, or any brief, for that matter.

"Not many women in recon," Ter said, "so it's hard to say much about it. Not enough data."

"Which is why I'm here, Lieutenant, uh, Opal," she said after peering at Ter's name patch. "I'm on a tour of units now, and my goal is to get more women into the service."

"But why? Male or female, what does it matter, ma'am?" Nok asked.

"Twenty years ago, it probably wouldn't have mattered from an operational standpoint. But now, with the SpecOps initiative, well, it does matter."

Esther frowned as she tried to grasp what the captain was doing. Twenty years ago was before the Evolution, and women weren't even allowed in the military then, but that couldn't be what she meant. Shortly after the Evolution, the Marines had adopted a policy to keep the standard recon missions in support of infantry units but also adopt a SpecOps posture. Refered to as MARSOC, they were no longer going to leave those missions to the SEALS and the FCDC's Volaire teams. But why would that make a difference?

Then it hit her.

"Cover," she said.

"What?" Nok asked.

"Blending in," she said, looking at the captain for confirmation.

Much to the dismay of many of the Old Corps Marines, the MARSOC teams did not maintain Marine Corps grooming nor uniform regs. When they went out, they tried to blend in with the community. The problem was that military men tended to stand out, whether in uniform or not. Women had not been in the Federation military for long, and Esther was pretty sure that a female Marine, dressed as a civilian would attract less notice than a male counterpart.

Captain Vansant smiled and nodded before saying, "A good team has a variety of people who can contribute their skills. We need all types in the teams, and that includes women."

"But begging the captain's pardon, you're the only officer to have made it through those schools so far. Most wash out. You know, not lowering of the standards and all," Nok said.

"RTC, then MSOC," the captain said, for Reconnaissance Training Course and Marine Special Operations Course. "And your point is?"

"Well, ma'am, the course is hard enough for men, and, to be blunt, I think fewer women could make it through."

"Which is why we need more recruits. To make sure the Corps gets what it needs," the captain said, swiveling to look Esther dead in the eyes.

"I get that, ma'am. But it wouldn't be good on our records to try and wash out," Nok said, voicing her misgivings.

"Not many women earn the title of Federation Marine. Not too many men, either."

*Why is she looking at me?*

But Esther knew. The captain was recruiting her. Not Ter, not Nok, but her. She knew who Esther was, and she wanted Esther to volunteer. That wasn't ego speaking. It was just an acknowledgment of fact.

Nok was a good Marine, smart and personable. But while she was capable enough to manage boot camp, she wasn't a physical stud. Ter wasn't much better. If RTC was indeed as difficult as advertised—and it had been when her father had gone through— Esther might be one of a small number of women who could manage the physical aspect of it. Nine enlisted female Marines had managed it, but Esther didn't know how many had tried.

And she was just as sure that politics were involved. The recon community was somewhat of an outcast among the rest of the Corps as they received a significant share of the Marine Corps budget. The perception was that they took what they wanted while keeping separate from the normal command chain. More than a few general officers had advocated abandoning the MARSOC mission entirely. If Esther Lysander, daughter of Ryck Lysander was in recon, then that could mute some of the overt criticism.

*Or cause more if my presence brought in outside attention.*

The SEALs sure suffered from that. Being semi-mythological as the SEALs were had some advantages, but it sure made the "clandestine" parts of their mission all the more difficult.

"Things worthwhile usually require risk. To be the best, you have to try," the captain said, her eyes still locked onto Esther's, leaning forward like a lion stalking a cape buffalo.

An image flashed through her mind of the plaque that hung over her father's desk at home. It was a quote from an Old Earth 18th century naval commander, John Paul Jones: "He who will not risk, cannot win." That was true enough, and for a moment, the competitive aspect excited her.

But she knew that recon could be a dead end for an officer. Her father had gone into recon only because he felt that it was recon or resigning. The tour had reset his motivation (and earned him his first Federation Nova), but he was an outlier. Not as many officers within the recon community rose to senior ranks, and making senior ranks was Esther's goal.

On the other hand, a single tour as a lieutenant shouldn't hurt her. It might not help, but it wouldn't be the kiss of death.

*Not good enough. If it won't help, then it's not worth doing.*

She stared back at the captain, keeping her face emotionless.

"I just would like you three to consider it. The Corps needs women in recon, and they have to come from somewhere. Here, take my card," she said, swiping her PA near theirs. "If you have any questions, give me a shout."

Esther's PA buzzed, waiting for instructions on whether to accept or reject the captain's contact information.

The captain stood up straighter and said, "Thank you for your time, ladies. I've got another brief with First Battalion, so please excuse me. And I'm serious; call me at any time."

"Fat chance," Nok said as they watched the captain walked off. "No way I'm going to volunteer, only to wash out."

"Yeah, fat chance," Esther agreed.

The challenge was tempting, though.

# Chapter 14

"Fuck those assholes," Julio Santos, one of the Echo lieutenants said. "And of course, the Brotherhood ain't doing jack shit."

Esther looked up from her orange-honey cake to the feed. The twisted remains of a maglev lay smoldering on its side while numbers were flashed under the image. Thirty-two people had been killed with many more wounded, numbers that were expected to climb. Suddenly, the sweet dessert one of her favorites, lost its allure. She pushed it aside and watched intently. Throughout the messhall, talk dwindled as more Marines became aware of the newsbreak.

The Right Hand of God was taking responsibility for the action. The RHG was a fairly new group, either an offshoot or an allied group to the more established Seventh Revelationists. Esther wasn't sure why Julio was blaming the Brotherhood; just because both were religious organizations didn't mean they were aligned with each other.

They watched somberly as the story unfolded. Marines had fought the SevRevs often enough, and Esther knew they were all thinking the same thing. This could be the birth of a new enemy for them to face.

"Man's inhumanity to man," Steel muttered from across the table. "What the hell are we turning into?"

"That's San Isidro Labrador," Esther said as she saw the banner feed. "Is Nok coming to eat?"

"Oh, yeah, wasn't she born there?" Steel asked.

"Yeah, she's dual. Father from San Isirdor, mother from Heritage," she answered, still intent on the feed.

"Do you think she knows anyone there?"

With over three billion on the planet, Esther doubted it, but she'd certainly want to know.

"She and Bull went to Giorgio's," Julio told her.

Most of the lieutenants and a good number of the captains in the battalion were single, and with officers only being charged 2-

and-a-half credits for dinner in the messhall, most made use of Marine Corps chow to keep their cost-of-living down. Even a simple shwarma out in the ville would run four credits at a minimum, and most Marines couldn't imagine having only one schwarma for dinner.

Still, it wasn't very romantic, and as Nok's end-of-tour was getting closer, she and the Echo Company XO were heating up together.

Esther got out her PA, but Ter said, "Let them enjoy their dinner. It's not like she can do anything about it."

Esther hesitated, but then nodded. Ter was right. She could find out later. She looked back up at the feed, listening to the reporter describe in graphic detail what he was witnessing.

Talk gravitated to a possible Federation response. San Isidro Labrador was nominally an independent planet, but with ties to the Federation and Alliance of Free States. What the Federation could do and what they would do were not necessarily the same. Esther knew that throughout history, heavy-handed responses to terrorist often begat new terrorists, but a people couldn't stand by and ignore such acts. There had to be a response.

During her brief that afternoon, Captain Vansant had noted that one of recon's SpecOps prime missions was to combat terrorism. It seemed like a good idea to Esther.

*So why am I thinking about recon?*

She watched for another five minutes, but the reporter was repeating himself. She put her tray in the cart and walked out into the evening. The weather was a comfortable 19 degrees, and the last remnants of the sunset lit the clouds in reds, blues, and oranges. It was a beautiful, peaceful evening here, but light-years away, on San Isidro Labrador, 32 people had been killed, people whose only crime had been to take the maglev to work that morning.

She walked slowly through the Quad, past the company offices on her way to the Q. She didn't have plans for the evening (which gave rise to the briefest of jealousies of Nok). There were some interesting fellow lieutenants in the battalion, and more than a few had expressed interest in her, but Esther thought it better to keep her social life separate from her professional life. It took discipline, but she knew it was the right choice.

She'd had a few interludes over the last two years with Marines and one Navy ensign from other units, but not many, and none lasted past a couple of dates. She was too focused on her career to give much of herself, and she knew that was necessary for a serious relationship.

*Maybe later, after I'm more established.*

She suddenly didn't want to be alone, so she pulled out her PA to call Ter, but then she realized she didn't know what she wanted to do. She needed to think up something first or she'd sound like a morose baby who was lonely for company.

*Which I am, but I don't have to let her know.*

She glanced at the company offices, which took the back right side on the bottom deck of Building 188. The corner office light was on, which wasn't a surprise. Captain Hoffman might be married and with kids, all living out in base housing, but he often worked late.

Esther's feet changed direction before she knew it, and she headed to the building.

"Evening ma'am!" the duty Marine said, jumping to attention and saluting as she entered the front hatch.

"At ease, Lance Corporal. I'm just going back to Golf."

Esther didn't return the salute as she'd taken off her cover as she entered. She turned left down the main passage and made her way to the end office, rapping at the doorjamb.

"Sir, you got a minute?"

"Sure, Esther, come on in. Take a seat, and I'll be with you in a moment."

Esther sat on the couch while the captain's fingers flew over his keyboard while subvocalizing into his throat mic. Most people used voice-to-word while writing. Some used qwerty keyboards. But the captain used both subvocs and a syl-keyboard to record his writing.

Two minutes later, the captain turned off the keyboard projector and lowered his throat mic.

"What's up?"

Esther hadn't planned on bringing up switching the PICS to First Platoon yet. Nok still had more than three months left on station. But with the skipper working late, it seemed like a good time.

"Sir, you've told us that Marine officers are generalists, right?"

"Yes, I think I might have mentioned that once or twice . . . or 20 or 30 times," he said with a chuckle.

"I agree, but that means we have to have a broad array of experiences, right? I mean, we shouldn't stick with the same things we've already done."

"I was wondering if you were going to come to see me about that."

"You were?" Esther asked, confused.

"Yes, I saw you with Captain Vansant this afternoon. She's pretty impressive."

*Oh, crap! He thinks I want to go to recon!*

"And to answer your question, by all means, you should experience as much as you can. You've got two years with the platoon, and maybe it's time you experienced something else. I know you've told me you don't want armor or air, so recon would be a good choice while still keeping within the infantry."

*A good choice? Did he say a good choice?*

"But sir," she blurted out. "Recon's well, it's recon. It's a dead end for officers."

"Your father was in recon, and I think things turned out OK for him."

*But he got a Federation Nova out of it. That wouldn't hurt anyone's career.*

"He's one of the few, with all due respect, sir. I understand that recon is important to the Corps, and to the Federation, too. With MARSOC, well, we're doing more and more non-conventional warfare—"

"Which sounds pretty exciting to me. "

"Well, yes, sir," she admitted, realizing that she meant it.

"And with the Klethos war, with the rise of unconventional warfare, the MARSOC community should only increase in operational tempo.

"You've had two major battles during your two years. How many other platoons have had even one?"

"Fox's Second Platoon had one, and . . . uh . . . well, maybe that's it," she said.

"Esther, your career to date has been remarkable, and that's not even considering your Navy Cross. If you want to experience recon, I don't think it will hurt your career. In fact, I would say it would help you. As you become senior, it could give you a better perspective on how operators function.

"If you came here to ask me for a recommendation, of course, I'll approve it, although I don't think that would be necessary. I saw Captain Vansant lassoing you. They want you, I'm sure."

Esther hadn't come in to see the skipper to talk about recon, at least she didn't think she had. She wanted the PICS platoon, right? But the challenge of becoming a recon Marine was intriguing. Maybe her subconscious had wanted to discuss it with Captain Hoffman.

The challenge. That was the rub, though. Esther was athletic and capable. But so were many other women who hadn't been able to get through the course. Most men couldn't.

"Sir," she started quietly, "but what about the drop rate? I mean, if I can't make it?"

"If you can't, you can't. Neither can most Marines. Colonel Singh washed out of RTC as a captain, and he's done pretty well for himself."

*And rumor has it he won't pick up a star.*

"Uh, don't pass that around. I think I just let slip some confidential information."

"I won't, sir."

*But if it's OK to try and fail, then why not pass it around? You're telling me it doesn't matter.*

"You won't know what you can and can't do until you try, Esther. And I have confidence in you."

"Would you try?"

"I'd like to think I would. I've got orders to Tac 2, so those take priority, but after that? If they wanted an old fart like me? Who knows?"

She could understand that. Tactical Warfare II was a required course for post-command captains and majors that had to be taken for any chance at lieutenant colonel or colonel-level command.

Esther realized that she'd been mulling over Captain Vansant's words all afternoon and into the evening. That was probably why she'd been a little listless. Something was missing.

"Thank you, sir. You've been a big help. I appreciate your advice."

"Any time, Esther. Well, not now. I'm late, and Katie's going to kill me, so I've got to run."

Esther thought the skipper's wife had to have the patience of a saint. Captain Hoffman was almost always running late.

She stood by while the captain turned off his desk PA. Together they walked down the passage and to the entrance where the duty Marine jumped back up to attention.

"At ease, Lance Corporal Tennyson. You can log us out for the night."

The duty was from Echo Company, yet Captain Hoffman called him by name. It wouldn't have been hard to query his PA to get the lance corporal's name, but Esther hadn't bothered to consider it. Now she felt embarrassed that she hadn't.

"Have a good night, Esther," the skipper said as they reached the walkway. "Let me know what you want to do, and I'll support your decision."

"Thank you, sir. You have a good night, too."

She stood there, watching the captain stride away towards the parking lot.

*Recon? Would it be worth it?*

She realized that she'd never managed to bring up the PICS.

# Chapter 15

"Holy Apples, Nok. Let him up for air," Steel said in mock dismay.

Bull broke his kiss and looked to Steel with a self-satisfied grin plastered on his face. The Echo Company lieutenant had to mass 120kg. Nok was maybe 40kg soaking wet, and sitting on his lap, she still had to crane her head up to mack with him.

Esther rolled her eyes and pointed at the half-full pitcher.

"How about filling me up, boot," she said to brand new Second Lieutenant Gaylord Lincoln Masterson Nobo, IV.

Yes, there'd been three other Gaylord Lincoln Masterson Nobos. Esther was surprised there had even been one saddled with such a pretentious name. It was straight out of the Bollywood School of Bad Casting and Writing.

Nobo was technically Nok's replacement, but he wasn't getting the PICS platoon. Steel had moved up to Weapons when Patel had received orders, Second Lieutenant Jerome "Fish" Knightly had taken over Third, and now Captain Hoffman had shifted the PICS mission to the platoon.

Esther felt a twinge of regret, looking at Fish, who was deep into conversation with Monica Dupuis. He was a good lieutenant, and Esther was sure he'd do well. But she'd still have liked time in PICS as well.

The battalion officers had met at the O'Club for a hail and farewell earlier in the evening. Two lieutenants, to include Nobo IV, and a captain had come aboard that week. And the CO had introduced them before they each had the floor. Nobo IV had given his full name, to include the "IV," which had elicited a laugh from the other officers. Nobo IV had to be used to it. He'd made it to staff sergeant before getting his commission, so he wasn't some wet-behind-the-ears recruit, yet he still willingly entered the lions' den. Either he was oblivious to societal norms, or he just didn't care and was making a statement. Esther wasn't sure which, nor did she care much, if she was being honest.

Two officers were leaving. Nok had her orders, and she'd ship out on Saturday. She gave her speech, the CO gave her her plaque, and then the lieutenants gave her the traditional gag gift—in Nok's case, a basketball and step ladder. A sign on the ladder read "For Dunking." Nok had scrambled up the ladder and executed a wicked windmill dunk, slamming the ball to the deck—and which still wouldn't have reached a regulation rim.

"Hey, Lysander, good luck," Greg Yashua said, putting his hand on Esther's shoulder. "I'm taking off, so if I don't see you . . ."

"Hey, Greg. Thanks. Take it easy."

She reached behind her and pulled out her plaque, running her finger over the engraving. The battalion emblem of the burning lion, a book in its paws and crossed swords and an anchor behind took up most of the shield-shaped plaque. Above the emblem, the words "Second Battalion, Fourteenth Marines" were emblazoned in an arc with "Serenissima" in smaller letters underneath. Esther's attention was on the smaller brass inlay under the emblem on which was engraved,

*FIRST LIEUTENANT ESTHER LYSANDER, UFMC*
*7 March 412 to 9 July 414*
*"Per Mare, Per Terram"*

Esther had been the second officer leaving the battalion. She hadn't been as eloquent as Nok had been, and she just wanted to get it over with. But when the CO had handed her the plaque, she'd been struck with the heavy weight of tradition for maybe the first time in her life. Her father had understood it. Noah understood it. But tradition hadn't been important to her before. Looking at the emblem, which she now knew was taken from the both the old Lagunari Battalion and the San Marco Brigade, she felt the connection reaching back more than 700 years, and with her name on the plaque, that made her part of that tradition. She knew all of this on an intellectual level, but for the first time, she felt is on a visceral level.

The platoon had chipped in to get her plaque as well, which they'd presented to her that morning. She appreciated it, probably more than the battalion plaque. It had been given freely by her Marines, after all, and that made it personal. But the battalion plaque bespoke history, and that was daunting.

Esther had received her plaque from 3/16 on Wayfarer Station, but it had stayed in its box. She'd never started her "I Love Me" wall. She had a feeling that was going to change.

Her gag gift had been a sealed display case with an oversized set of stars inside and a "Break Glass When Needed" badge attached. Not as clever as Nok's, and possibly a little too close to home, but she had dutifully laughed.

"You gonna drink that?" Steel asked, pointing at her refilled stein.

"Oh, yeah, sorry. And thanks, boot," she said to Nobo IV.

"Lost in sweet memories?" Steel persisted.

"Yeah, lots of them. None of you, though!"

"Ah, you wound me, madame!" Steel said, bringing his hand to her heart, earning him a thrown napkin from Patel.

"You know, you never did tell me how you got your nickname," Esther said. "You keep putting it off, and now I'm leaving. Is there a dark past to you?"

"Oh, nothing so dramatic. It's just my last name. Ganbaatar. It means "Steel Hero.""

"You're shitting me, right?"

"I shit you not. That's what it means. Pull it up," he said.

"So why all the secrecy?"

"'Cause I like pulling your chain, Esther," he said with a huge grin on his face. "You should know that by now."

Esther reached over, took Steel's stein, and refilled it for him.

She lifted her own stein, clinked glasses, and said, "It's been real, Derrick Ganbaatar. Thanks."

"You're going to kick ass, Esther," he said with none of his normal bantering tone.

Esther felt a lump forming in her throat, so she nodded and broke eye-contact, looking instead at the four tables the lieutenants had commandeered. The official hail and farewell had been at the club on-base, but the junior officers had abandoned the club as soon as they could and taken over the rear of The Haunted Hound. The

"Hound" was not specifically a military bar, but it was off the beaten path, and it was generally left alone by senior officers as well as the shore patrol. When there was heavy drinking to be done, the Hound fit the bill.

Not that the drinking was excessive. Fox Company was scheduled for their BRQ, or Battle Readiness Qualification, recertification starting at the beginning of next week, and most of them had already slipped away for some last minute prep time. Nok and Bull could barely contain themselves and looked about ready to pull chocks.

Still, it was another two hours before the party started breaking up. Steel insisted on paying for the last two pitchers.

"You can't drink at RTC, you know," ha managed to get out, "so I've got to cover these."

Esther wasn't sure if drinking really was prohibited, but as hard as the course was supposed to be, she didn't think anything that could affect her performance negatively would be a good idea. Besides, she wasn't going to stand in his way if he wanted to pay.

"Got to pay the rent on the beer," he said too loudly, before heading off to the head.

"So, Esther. This is it, I guess," Ter said.

"I'm not leaving until Sunday, but yeah. We can still do something tomorrow."

The XO reached over and put her hand on top of Esther's.

"I'm going to miss you, you know."

"I'll miss you, too, Ter. Maybe after, you know?"

"You're gonna be a snake eater, a kick-ass recon Marine. I'm going to be babysitting recruits. It's a big Corps and an even bigger galaxy. We can say we're gonna get together, but you know . . ."

Ter was pretty deep into her cups, not plastered, but certainly happy. She reached up with her other hand, now with both hands cupping Esther's right hand.

"You know, I think we made a good team, me and you. We showed them."

Esther wasn't sure who "them" was, but Ter was right. They had been a good team. And good friends. That wasn't going to change just because they had orders to different duty stations. The

Corps might be big in most ways, but it was also small enough that they could run into each other again.

"Yes, we did, Ter. And I'm grateful to you, for your guidance. You're someone special to me."

Ter stood up, kicking her seat back, and leaned in to Esther, who looked up to hear what the XO wanted to say. But Ter didn't want to say anything. She dropped Esther's hand, grabbed her on either side of her head and pulled her forward—giving her a huge kiss right on her mouth.

Esther was shocked, and she froze, not knowing what to do. After an eternity, Ter broke off, and with her hands still framing Esther's face, backed away so she could stare into Esther's eyes.

*What the . . . ?*

A smile formed on Ter's face, but a wistful, sad-looking smile.

"Ter, I . . . I, uh, I'm not—"

Ter raised her eyebrows for a moment and said, "Aye-yah, I knew it, always did. But I just had to make sure, sweetie, you know, or I would have regretted not taking the chance." She sighed, then added, "It took more than a few glasses of liquid courage just to get up my nerve."

"I . . . I'm sorry," Esther said.

"No reason to be. I'm sorry. I knew what would happen, but I still did it."

"I like you, Ter. I really do. You're the sister I never—"

Ter put her forefinger on Esther's mouth, stopping her.

"No need to explain. I love you . . . like a sister, I mean," she added when she saw Esther's eyes widen. "And I love Steel, too, even if he is a gallump sometimes," she said as he returned from the head.

"What? What'd I miss here? We getting all maudlin with Esther abandoning us to go play recon?"

"Yeah, we're getting maudlin," Ter said, reaching out to take one of Steel's hands and holding out her other to Esther.

Esther could read the hope in her eyes, and without hesitation, she took the hand, and with her other, grabbed Steel's free hand. She pulled both of her friends into a deep hug.

"I'm going to miss you guys," she said. "Golf 2/14 forever, OK?"

"Forever," Ter mumbled into Esther's shoulder.

Steel broke the hug first, grabbed the empty pitcher and held it upside-down as a few drops fell to the tabletop.

"Looks like we're empty. One more?"

Esther pulled back from Ter, but gave her hand one more squeeze.

"No, I think I'm done. I've got some errands to get done in the morning if I'm going to be free later on. You still up for getting together, Ter?"

"I've got nothing better to do than kick it with my compadres on a Saturday night. Lonely Rose is playing at the Amphitheater. Sound copacetic?"

"Lonely Rose? They're all chick music," Steel said.

"That's cause they're chicks, dumbass. So you don't want to come?"

"Oh, no, I'll come. I kinda like them," he admitted.

"Well, then, it's a date," Esther said, standing up.

She gave each of her friends another brief hug, then made her way out of the bar. Ter had surprised her. Not her sexual orientation. She'd been vaguely aware of that, but it was something she never considered. A Marine was a Marine, no matter who they slept with.

But a Marine was also a person, just like anyone else in the galaxy. Ter was her friend, and that went beyond their interaction as XO and platoon commander. Esther knew that she was not the most empathetic person around. She wasn't sure she'd ever been that what with her drive to excel in everything she did. But after her parents were killed, she'd erected an additional wall between herself and others. And that wasn't good. It wasn't good as a Marine, and it wasn't good for her soul.

Esther hoped her reaction hadn't turned Ter away from her. She was serious when she said she loved her as a sister. Esther didn't have very many close friends, and she didn't want to lose one of those she had.

And in a way, it had been a compliment. It wasn't as if Esther was tearing up the intimacy playing field, so to have someone interested offered her a tiny ego boost. She didn't swing that way, but like any normal person, curiosity at the habits and proclivities of others had made her sometimes wonder about it.

She let thoughts on the subject fade as she entered the Q. She'd been serious. She had a lot to do to check out before she departed on Sunday. An entirely new chapter as a Marine was in front of her, and she was pretty excited about that.

# PART 2

Jonathan P. Brazee

# TARAWA

## Chapter 16

"Come on, Lysander, just quit. I know you want to," Gunnery Sergeant James McNeill said as he bent down to the prone Esther.

"I'm not quitting!" she shouted, pushing her body half-way back up from where she'd fallen and sprawled in the red dirt.

But he was right. She wanted to quit with every fiber in her body—what few fibers she could still feel.

*What the hell was I thinking?* she wondered for the thousandth time. *Me and my stupid ego. And now I'm royally screwed.*

Gunny McNeill put his foot on her back, keeping her from rising off her hands and knees.

"Look Lysander. You've done great," he said in a reasonable tone. "You've lasted beyond Holstein and Vioble," he told her, naming the two other female Marines who'd started out in the course. "Heck, you've lasted longer than half of the men. I think you've proven our point. Now it's time to move on. I'm sure with your, well, shall we say, 'connections,' you can get a nice plum billet. Maybe right here on the "T" at headquarters. Just think of it: a clean, air-conditioned office, steady working hours, a chance to hobnob with all those colonels and generals."

Esther didn't even feel guilty that she'd been thinking those very thoughts. It was true. She didn't belong at RTC. Life would be so much easier for her if she just rang out. It was right there. She could drop her 75kg pack in the dirt, catch a ride back to the school, and ring out. By evening, she'd be clean, comfortable, and with new orders to her next duty station.

She knew RTC would be difficult, but she'd never grasped just how difficult. Most of it seemed to be simple torture, to see how far the RTs[8] could push them.  This forced march was just one example.  In six years in the fleet, Esther didn't think she'd ever carried more than 35 kg into the field.  The Corps kept finding ways to lighten the load and still be able to take the fight to the enemy, and a Marine's gear was the best yet developed by man—expensive, but you get what you paid for.  So why was she kneeling in the dirt of Camp Prettyjohn with 75kg on her back?  Supposedly because a recon Marine could be assigned to train a foreign force that did not have access to modern, light-weight gear.  "Supposedly" was the key word here.  Esther thought the real reason was simply to try and break her and her fellow "polliwogs."

And it was working.  The class had started with 113 candidates.  After 13 days, 66 had been dropped with 63 of those DOR.[9]  Esther could make that 64 DORs right then and there, and her misery would be over.

*I can't! I won't.*

But she knew that was bravado.  She wanted to ring out, and she might as well do it instead of later and save herself days of misery.

*All I have to do is drop my pack.  That easy.*

Her right hand drifted to her pack's quick-release.

Maybe McNeill saw that, maybe he didn't, but he said, "Your father would be proud of you for even getting this far."

Esther's hand froze where it was.  No, her father wouldn't, she knew.  General Ryck Lysander was many things, and he was a good father, Esther thought.  But he was not "proud" of failure.  Results mattered, participation trophies did not.  If he was still alive today, Esther was sure he would still love her, but he would not be proud of the fact that she quit.

With a shout she pushed up, knocking the gunny's foot off her pack and him on his ass.

"I am not quitting!"

She fell into a crippled old man's shuffle, barely moving, but moving all the same.

---

[8] RT: Reconnaissance Trainers
[9] DOR: Dropped on Request

"Stupid fool!" the gunny yelled at her. "You've got 40 minutes to finish, and you're still five klicks away. Just give up."

Esther put her head down and willed her feet to move faster, not seeing the smile that crept over the gunny's face.

## Chapter 17

Esther had to bend forward at the waist, keeping her aching back straight, as she crept gratefully into her rack. The day and into the night had been a ball buster, and by the glory of the Divine Architect, there weren't any early-morning night evolutions on the schedule. The RTC staff had been known to add a few things to the syllabus, but after watching them leave together for the evening, for once, Esther thought they might be safe, and she should just lick her wounds and go to sleep.

After four weeks, the torture had almost become routine. The class was down to 38 polliwogs, but barring injury or academic failure, the general consensus was that those who remained would make it to the end.

That didn't mean Esther was home free. Physically, she was breaking down, but mentally, she'd reached her purgatory. The training was hell, but she knew she had the will power to just absorb it. All she had to do was avoid mistakes, and she'd reach her heaven, which was simply to leave Camp Prettyjohn, never to return.

"Come on, Lysander! Get your ass up," Delany shouted as he pounded on her hatch.

"Go away!"

Captain Delany Garrett didn't let up.

"You're coming with us."

"Eat me!"

Esther had spent most of her childhood with senior officers, and a general didn't faze her. But now, after seven years in uniform, the ranks structure had been welded into her mind, so it still felt odd calling the captain by his first name, much less yelling "Eat me" to him. But that was the recon culture. Members of a team tended to call each other by first names or nicknames. Outside the team, it was still rank and last name, so the class OIC was "Major Kierkirk," but among the polliwogs, everyone from the junior Sergeant Allison-Gibley to the senior Major Singh went by their given names.

Except for Esther. With only a few exceptions, she was "Lysander." She wasn't quite sure why that was, but there didn't seem to be any animosity to it.

Now that she was prone in her rack, all Esther wanted to do was to slip into Morpheus' warm embrace. Tonto, a decidedly weird staff sergeant, had pointed out that word "morphine" came from "Morpheus," and with sleep at such a premium at RTC, Esther now thought of sleep as an addiction, and she was always ready for her "Morpheus fix."

"The fight's about to start, and you said you were going to watch it with us," Delany said.

"Up and at them, Esther," Gator shouted through the door.

*The fight? Oh, hell! That's why the staff was leaving.*

Chief Warrant Officer 3 Tamara Veal was back up for a fight, her third. And just as in her last fight, it was taking place late at night local time for her. If this had been just any other fight, Esther would give it a pass and just sleep. But Iron Shot was a Marine, and Esther felt obligated to watch in support, especially as she'd missed the gladiator's last fight because she'd been on duty. What made this bout doubly interesting, however, was that this was the second time that it was the humans who had made the challenge, this time to recover New Budapest, which had fallen to the Klethos two years earlier.

"I'm coming, I'm coming. Give me a moment!" she shouted as she rolled out of the rack, her back screaming in protest.

Moving like an old lady, she slipped on a baggy pair of sweatpants and a micro-panel shirt and ran her fingers through her hair before opening the hatch.

"Where's Cowboy?" she asked, trying to blink the sleep out of her eyes.

"Already at the Club," Gator said. "He's been there since we got dismissed."

Esther followed the other two across the Quad to the all-ranks club. They could watch the fight on their PAs, but Marines tended to gather together to watch them, especially when a fellow Marine was fighting. They could go out into town, but Camp

Prettyjohn was out in the boonies, on the far side of Camp Charles, so the logical spot was the club.

Most of this class as well as the follow-on class were already in the small club, packing it tightly. As clubs went, this one wasn't much, but it had a top-of-the-line holo projector, and it had a 12-station Sanyo chiller, the same high-end device found in the top-of-the-line civilian clubs.

Esther's class had taken over the left side of the holo-room. Gator pointed at Cowboy, who'd staked out a couch in the front, and the three climbed over outstretched legs to get to him.

"About time you got here. I couldn't even get up to get a beer with these claim-jumpers ready to swoop in," he said.

Esther and the others flopped down beside him. The couch was lumpy, but it was right in front of the holo, which was still broadcasting the pre-fight commentaries.

"OK, what do you want?" she asked Cowboy.

"I want a Blue Peak," he said, referring to his favorite brew as he did whenever the occasion presented itself. "But since this is such a low-class operation, I'll take a Dilliards."

Esther got up, pulled a Dilliards out of the box, and popped the tab, letting it cool down. She picked a Nasty Red, thinking a cider might be a bit more refreshing and wake her up. The cider didn't have its own cooler, so she dialed in a 12 on the chiller and put in the cider. Ten second late, the door opened, and her cider came out on a tray.

"Make it last," she told Cowboy as she handed him his beer.

She was surprised to see Iron Shot already moving forward to her opponent, and she checked her PA. The fight wasn't supposed to start yet.

Then she realized that this was the gladiator's last fight. Esther had seen it several times on her PA since it happened, but never in this kind of setting. Watching it on the holo while surrounded by fellow Marines somehow made it seem more real.

The talking heads analyzed the short fight and gave their projections on the upcoming one. Not surprisingly, every talking head predicted an easy win for the chief warrant officer.

"Hey, enough of this analyzing shit. The fight's about to start," "Edgy" Hwei, a fellow lieutenant shouted out.

"Cassie, turn the volume," Cowboy said, speaking right at the projector's mic.

"Cassie" might be a fairly primitive AI, but she'd have learned by now the habits of the Marines. After measuring the ambient noise levels, she raised the volume so that everyone could hear.

Unlike the previous fight on New Budapest, where the human gladiator had been killed, there were few spectators on site for this one. There were more than a hundred of the Klethos surrounding one side of the ring, which had been constructed by the side of a river. A lone d'relle knelt at the side of the ring. It still seemed off to Esther. She'd watched 30 or 40 of the combats, and each time, the human gladiator was there at the fighting ring first and waited for the Klethos to arrive. This time, as the challenger, Iron Shot would come last.

As usual, Esther studied the Klethos, not just the d'relle in the ring, but the "regular" Klethos witnesses. Both species were sticking with the stylized combat for now, but that wasn't a guarantee that it would always be like that. Esther thought it probable that humans and Klethos would break out in total war at some time during her career.

Each Kethos was a nightmare, straight out of Lucas-Dreamworks. Three meters tall, with huge, taloned feet, the bird-like-looking creatures didn't need any of their four arms to take down a human. Esther knew that if it came to that, only human ingenuity and ability to improvise would carry the day.

"Here she comes!" one of the polliwogs from the follow-on class said.

CWO3 Veal came striding to the ring, her second in tow. Esther had seen pics of Veal before she'd become a gladiator. She'd been a big woman, a shot-putter on the Marine track and field team. But that was nothing compared to what she was now. Almost as tall at the d'relle she was going to face, she probably outweighed her opponent. Her muscles were huge, all genetically augmented, and she'd loss almost all female characteristics. The only feminine things about her was her glorious red and yellow hair, accented by the two braids for her two kills hanging across the left side of her face.

Esther felt a surge of pride, both as a Marine and as a human being. The genetic modification the gladiators underwent had a price. If a gladiator didn't get killed in the ring, she'd die of the Brick, Boosted Regeneration Cancer. Twenty percent of Marines who'd gone through regen came down with the Brick. Her father had. But it normally could be managed. With the crimes against nature that the gladiators had to go through to achieve their size, the Brick was deadly. They had at most five years before it claimed them.

"Iron Shot!" Delany said, the fanboy evident in his voice.

CWO3 Veal had reached the side of the ring where she stood for a moment before reaching behind her. Her second handed the gladiator her sword. Although it dwarfed Esther's dress sword, it was essentially the same weapon, a Marine Corps mameluke. There had been much discussion about that. Iron Shot was the only current gladiator with a mameluke, and she was one of five Marines in the corps of gladiators.

Esther felt her tension rise. CWO3 Veal had made somewhat of a name for herself for her hakas. Everyone leaned forward to see what she was going to do. She didn't unsheathe her sword, which was surprising, but stood there, staring at her opponent before breaking into motion.

The gladiator, with exaggerated, long-legged steps, moved to the center of the ring, drew her sword, then placed the scabbard on the sand, one end facing her opponent, the other back to the ten gladiator witnesses. She then placed her mameluke on the ground, making an X with the scabbard. She slowly backed up, and raising her arms gracefully over her head, started her haka. Stepping slowly, she touched each of the four quadrants made by the X, feet barely touching. Gradually, she built up the speed, her legs blurring into motion while her upper body remained still.

"A sword dance!" someone murmured.

Esther recognized it. She'd seen Scottish Sword dances on the holos, most done by lithe, petite dancers. Seeing the huge gladiator nimbly dance around the sword and scabbard was mesmerizing.

Esther kept expecting her to miss, to hit her sword. This was not a dancer's prop—this was a real sword with a real blade, one with which she would soon take into battle.

Iron Shot's feet flew through the steps, landing in each quadrant in turn, barely missing the sharp blade that lay there, waiting to cut an errant foot. Then she added bending to the side, one upraised arm reaching almost to the sand before coming upright to repeat the move on the other side, all the time her feet beating tattoos.

When she added spinning, the watching lieutenants burst into cheers. This was amazing, the best haka Esther had ever seen.

With a final flurry of spinning and steps, Iron Shot hooked the hilt of her sword with her foot and lifted it spinning in the air. As it came back down, she snatched it out of the air and converted the move into the challenge lunge with a loud shout.

Challenge issued.

Everyone one in the room watching jumped to their feet, screaming. Esther could hear the entire club erupt as a couple of hundred Marines screamed out their appreciation.

The d'relle waited almost ten seconds before she got up. She almost slid into her initial lunge, then started spinning around the ring, orbiting the gladiator. She did twelve huge spinning jumps in a row, her sword singing through the heavy air.

"Look at that. Iron Shot's enjoying the d'relle's dance!" Gator said.

Esther thought the XO was right. CWO3 Veal was watching the d'relle's every move with slight smile on her face.

It was a pretty good dance, Esther had to admit, powerful and graceful at the same time. She ended with a flourish, down on one knee, sword pointed at the gladiator.

Challenge accepted.

Then, the d'relle did something unusual, very unusual. Instead of retreating to the edge of the ring, instead of launching an immediate attack, she bowed low at the waist, pulling all four arms up at the elbows, exposing the back of her crest and neck.

"Do it!" someone shouted.

Esther knew what he meant. Esther could end the fight with one blow, killing the d'relle and reclaiming New Budapest.

Something told her that the gladiator wouldn't. Honor was the way of the Klelthos, as her father had discovered. She didn't know CWO3 Veal other than what was on the holos, but she didn't think dishonor was part of her makeup.

The d'relle slowly straightened up from her honor bow and stared at CWO3 Veal. Tamara stood still, then repeated the bow to her opponent—to the gasps of the everyone in the room. She stayed low for several heartbeats, her neck exposed, before straightening back up herself. The d'relle nodded once at Tamara before raising her sword.

"Freaking amazing," Delany said from beside Esther.

And then the fight was on. Both d'relle and human darted in and out, swords almost too fast to follow. Normally these fights were over within 30 seconds with either red human or blue Klethos blood staining the sand of the ring. This fight went past 30 seconds, past a minute. It was a beautiful, deadly dance. They were dance partners.

Esther knew what a parry and riposte were, if for no other reason than *Queen Killer*, the Hollybolly flick of Celeste, the first superstar among the new female gladiators. There had been resistance to the change in genders, which was predicated by the Klethos refusing to fight men, once they realized human physiology, thinking it dishonorable. Celeste changed all of that, and now it was simply accepted. Esther wasn't an expert in swordplay. Marines didn't use them in combat, after all. But still, she could appreciate expertise at work, and that was what she was seeing.

She gasped with the rest when the d'relle almost took off COW3 Veal's left hand, leaving it dangling by a thread of tissue. Still they fought on, scoring hits, mingling blood, red and blue, as they came together and broke apart. The d'relle darted in and the gladiator over-corrected. Esther didn't understand sword-play, but she realized the danger, and she cried out when the d'relle ran her sword deep into the gladiator's side.

She almost missed the gorgeous overhead swing by the gladiator, though, as it connected at the base of the d'relle's neck, mameluke biting deep.

The gathered polliwogs cheered, but the cheers faded as the two warriors stared at each other, dropping their weapons. To Esther's utter amazement, the two clasped arms, and supporting each other, sank to the ground.

On the holo, the UAM observers were shouting encouragement, but neither gladiator nor d'relle carried on the fight. They sat, facing each other, arms clasped as their blood mixed in the sand.

"What's going on?" Delany asked. "Why don't they do something?"

Esther didn't know how much time had passed while the two stared at each other. Five, ten minutes? Or an eternity?

The d'relle started leaning forward, ever so slowly, and finally, unable to stave off death, collapsed onto CWO3 Veals' lap.

Most of Marines in the room joined the humans in the broadcast as they erupted into cheers, and across the creek, the Klethos farthest away from the ring turned and started to leave. They had won. New Budapest was back in human hands.

The witnesses came into the ring, but the gladiator held up her one good hand, stopping them. Slowly, she reached over and smoothed out the crest of her opponent. With her hand still on the d'relle's crest, she started leaning forward as if to look into the d'relle's eyes, but she didn't stop the lean. She fell on top of the d'relle, covering her. Amid the cheers in the room, Esther knew Iron Shot was gone. She had regained the planet, but at the cost of her life.

Leaving her cider, she stood up. Someone pounded her back, but she ignored it and walked out of the club, out of the building into the night. She'd just witnessed something extraordinary, but she wasn't quite sure just what that was.

Esther hadn't known Tamera Veal. She'd never seen her, never talked to her. She wasn't given to displays of emotion, but as she walked back in the dark, a tear rolled down her face.

# PRIME DAVIS

## Chapter 18

"Hell, looking good, Lysander," Captain Sven Lugar said as he looked at Esther's naked body.

"Wish I could say the same about you. What'd they do? Drop you on an ant hill?"

The heavy-worlder did look a mess. His light skin was covered with red welts, and his thick neck was looking even more massive with an obvious swelling on the right side of it.

"Pretty close to it," he said with a chuckle.

Esther shook her head. Those bites had to itch like a bitch.

"Well, since you're here, do we stick together or go it alone?" she asked him.

"It might be a good idea . . . oh, hell. I'll just fess up. I knew you were dropped just before me, and I wanted to find you. I think we should team up. A couple might not draw as much attention as two singletons."

That was true, Esther knew, at least according to the classes they'd received. But it was more true that a single woman rarely attracted any kind of attention, at least the kind of attention they were trying to avoid.

"If I want to form a couple, then one of you trogs might not be the best choice. Not too many of you here on Prime Davis."

The captain ignored her baiting and asked, "Prime Davis? That's where we are? How do you know that?"

"I'm not positive, but it fits. I did some research on possible destinations, and with the double moon, I think this it."

"Lots of planets have double moons," the captain said.

"Yeah, but not many with such a small minor, with temperate deciduous forests, and what I'm guessing as 1.1 G. When you think of what was within the realm of travel possibilities and well, a population where we can operate, I'd be willing to bet that's where we are."

"I never took you for such a researcher. I have to say, I'm impressed. Very impressed."

Esther broke out into a smile before quickly suppressing it. Esther had always been known for her father first and for being an athlete second. But as General Simone had told her more than a few times, a Marine's most valuable weapon was his or her brain. And while RTC placed huge demands on the body, it was still the intellect that would pull a candidate through. Her hours spent researching potential worlds might have seemed like a wasted effort, but if she was right, then that little piece of intel could make the difference between success and failure. Sven's brief comment might have been the first time anyone ever complimented her intellect.

If she were being ruthlessly logical, then the captain would not be her choice for a partner. She'd called him a "trog" to see if it would get a rise from him, but the fact of the matter was that there wouldn't be many heavy-worlders here if they were in fact on Prime Davis. He'd stick out like an elephant at the ballet.

Still, he'd thought to track her down, which she admitted was self-serving, but was also smart. And he'd appreciated her analysis.

"OK, I'm up for it. First things first, though. Let's find some clothes. I don't want to be staring at your bug-bitten ass for longer than I have to."

## Chapter 19

Esther stood over the captain, almost against his back as he fiddled with the lock. They'd reached the small strip mall over two hours ago, but most of the stores had normal bio-locks on them. They had been trained on how to gyver them, but stark naked and with no equipment, that was out of the question.

*Please work*, Esther prayed as she watched him.

The larger of the two moons, which had given close to daylight illumination, had set, giving them darkness in which to skulk, but the red glow on the horizon was a pretty good sign that daylight was approaching.

It was Esther who had noticed the tall metal box to the side of the parking lot. Her heart skipped a beat when she was the familiar Goodwill logo on the side. Their luck held out when they saw the mechanical lock holding the door shut. Sven scrounged up a twisted piece of molding and was working the lock. He'd been on it for 20 minutes already, and Esther was tempted to take over. That was nerves, though. They'd been introduced to simple lock picking, but that hadn't been her strongest suit.

She almost jumped when she finally heard a click, then held her breath until Sven said, "That's it. Let's see what we can find."

He opened the door and reached inside, pulling out a handful of used clothing.

Esther gave them a quick scan and said, "Bring out some more."

She quickly pawed through them before holding up a dark Cossack blouse, checking it against the captain's stock y frame. Satisfied, she threw it at him. The Cossack blouses had been all the rage ten years ago, but there were still enough of them around that it shouldn't attract any attention. More than that, it was loose hanging off the shoulders, so it would serve to mask his wide body, at least to a degree.

"Find any pair of pants that'll fit, hopefully in a muted color, then try and find some shoes in there," she told him before searching for something she could wear.

She'd been ready to wear anything that she could find, but with so much to choose from, she wanted to pick whatever would help her blend in the best. Goodwill didn't accept underwear, so she'd be braless, so she tried to first find a tighter shirt to give her some support. She ended up with a man's Deep Six, the form-fitting collarless V that she thought did most men no favors. It worked for her, though. She found a pair of half-calves that fit, but she still wanted a looser shirt of some kind to put over the Deep Six.

"We're not at a fashion show," Sven said as he stood and watched. "Just pick something. We're going to attract some attention, if we haven't already."

Esther had noted the security cam, but she also noted that the power cord hung loose. Still, he was right in that people should start to arrive soon. One of the stores in the strip mall was a natural bakery, and bakers tended to come in early to start the day's bread.

"Hold on," she said, kicking some of the clothes aside and wishing she had more light.

She snagged light colored, probably yellow, shapeless blouse and threw it on. It wasn't muted, but maybe that was OK. While they didn't want to garishly stand out, they also didn't want to look like there were trying to avoid notice.

The captain handed her a pair of slippers.

"Is that it?"

"All I could find. I think it's those or nothing."

She slipped them on. The fit wasn't horrible, but she'd hate to have to try and run in them. Sven was already shoving the extra clothing back into the bin. Within moments, he was locking the door shut.

"Now that that's done, what's next? Yours or mine?"

Esther knew the captain was offering her a big advantage. If things went to shit after they recovered her objective but before they had his, he'd be out of luck. But she could analyze the situation as well as he could. With the time crunch, it made sense to get his first, then hers. That gave them the best chance for both of them to succeed. She could have gone it solo and not worried about order, but since she agreed to team up, she was going to honor that.

"Yours," she said without hesitation.

As if connected, both Marines turned in unison towards the planetary southeast. The Neulife bridge that let them know where their objectives were still freaked Esther out. She couldn't feel it, but suddenly, it was as if she had a nav AI inside her brain. She knew where she was and how to go somewhere else.

Recon Marines were often alone and often where any transmissions could be picked up. A simple uplink to a nav satellite could reveal their position. So the R&D wizards had come up with a way that while not as good as a simple nav app, allowed recon Marines and SEALs to navigate in stealth.

The first thing the docs did was stimulate the hippocampus to over-develop. This would allow recon Marines to have a much, much better sense of direction. But that alone was at most a marginal improvement. The brain had to be able to interpret what the hippocampus was sending. So second, two Neulife bridges, one for each hemisphere, would be inserted from the hippocampus to the rest of the brain, to enable the Marine to make use of that input in a more cognitive fashion.

The bridge was essentially a bundle of KD crystal connectors, bunched much like dried spaghetti in the hand before putting it into the boiling water. But KD crystals cannot connect into brain cells. So on each end of the KD bundle, Neulife "caps" were attached which could take the input from the hippocampus, transmit it to the crystals, then interface back into the entorhinal cortex, bypassing the fornix, in a usable format.

The same, if a little older version of the process had been done to her father when he'd joined recon, and he'd admitted to Noah and her that he'd almost refused the procedure. Neulife was an artificial organic tissue, and the thought of it inside his brain had terrified him.

Esther didn't have the same phobia. She understood the long-term risk, but knowing the bridge could be removed took care of that issue. It just blew her mind that given two coordinates, one at her origin and one at her destination, she always knew how to get there. It wasn't fireworks going off in her mind with a big reveal. It was just as she knew which way to look when she heard a noise. It was the "normalness" of how it felt that was so unreal to her.

"I'm thinking we head south on the road here. Somewhere up ahead, we'll need to take a left," Esther said.

"My thinking exactly," Captain Lugar said.

As the two stepped off, a hover pulled into the far entrance to the parking lot. People were awakening, and the city was coming to life. Things were about to get a lot tougher.

## Chapter 20

Three hours later, the two Marines were looking over where they both agreed Sven's objective was located. The Neulife improvements were significant, but they simply did not have the refinement to be any more accurate. The fact that both agreed was a good indication, but the objective could be within a 50 to 100-meter radius, and that covered a lot of area.

The fact that two militia guards were standing beside the small structure in the park was also a telltale, but people have been known to use guards as decoys, too.

"So now what?" Esther asked, trying to come up with a course of action.

"Should we just rush them? I mean, two Marines against two yokel militia. It shouldn't be too hard."

Esther frowned at that. There was a tendency among Marines to dismiss local militias as being inferior. It was true that there wasn't a militia or even and army that could match up, unit for unit, with the Marines. But it was stupid to underestimate anyone. For all they knew, either of the two guards could be MMA champions or wizards of hand-to-hand.

"ROE, Sven," she reminded him.

"I don't mean anything permanent," he said. "Just a little friendly contact, you know."

Heavy-worlders were stereotyped as brawlers, and it was true that a disproportionate percentage of them made up the premier rugby or NFL football leagues. Sven was doing nothing to combat that stereotype. But Esther knew that wasn't going to cut it. If nothing else, it would raise a hue and cry that neither of them wanted.

She ignored him just as she ignored his next two ideas which were even lamer than the first. He didn't argue for them, so she knew he was just thinking out loud. It took a few minutes as she thought and rejected a number of courses of actions. Then one hit her, which she promptly rejected, but a moment later, brought it back. It sounded just as lame as the captain's ideas, but as she re-examined it, she realized it might be feasible.

"Sven, how about this? Head on down that walkway, but before you reach the building, walk over to the water. Act like you've got something to feed the ducks with and get them to come up to you. Then wait for me. I've got an idea to distract those two. If it works, you might have a shot to sneak in."

"And if it doesn't work?"

"Then ignore what happens to me. You'll have to wait for another opportunity."

"Just what are you going to do?"

"I'm not 100% sure yet. I've got a few ideas, but really, I'm going to play it by ear."

"OK, Lysander, that's hardly a mission order."

"And this isn't a normal mission. You're not a company commander anymore. Things are different here."

He'd hit the nail on the head, though. Esther, just by being a Marine, was used to a normal Five Paragraph Order, a format that had been in use with various permutations for hundreds of years, or a Frag Order, which was a shorter version that adjusted the original order or was given when time was limited. This "I'll think of something" went against all her training. All her *previous* training. RTC stressed this kind of think-on-your-feet planning.

The captain stared at her long and hard before he shrugged his shoulders and said, "So you want me to just go down there and feed the ducks?"

"Yeah, that's about it."

"And where do we rendezvous after?"

Esther scanned the park, then said, "How about under those trees, the ones even with the Fidelity Life building?"

"OK, I wish I knew what you were going to do, but you've got it," he said.

He retreated 20 meters, and then got on one of the paths. He started walking as if just enjoying the pleasant weather, covering the 200 meters or so to an intersection. He took a right, and then Esther lost sight of him as he passed behind a row of bushes.

Esther held her breath until he reappeared, which she realized was kind of stupid. What was going to happen to the captain just because she lost sight of him?

As he approached the odd little building, one of the guards glanced at him, then turned back to talk to his buddy. Sven stopped as if noticing the ducks for the first time, then crossed the grass to the lake's shoreline. The guards didn't give him a second glance.

*OK, this is it.*

She backed away slowly, then moved to her right, in the opposite direction Sven had taken. When she reached another row of bushes, she stepped behind them and took off her yellow blouse. Look down at her Deep Six, she started having second thoughts. A Deep Six was a male fashion statement, not an exercise shirt. It was meant to show off a fit body. Her half-calves were not running shorts, but she thought they might pass. The slippers, though, which had been used when she got them and were now worse for wear after walking three hours, just wouldn't do. There was nothing else she could do about that but take them off. Some people ran barefoot—not Esther, but hopefully, she wouldn't look too out of place.

Knowing this was the best she could manage, she took off on a slow jog, first on the path, then quickly shifting to the grass as a softer, more giving surface. She slowly jogged about half a klick, always angling away from Sven's objective. Her legs warmed up as her gait smoothed out, and her feet felt fine on the grass. She might have been back at UM on a training run—except for her breasts. Esther wasn't huge in that area by any stretch of the imagination, but she was certainly a woman, and without an exercise bra, she was bouncing. She tried to smooth out her stride, keeping a more even keel, but with limited success.

When she thought she'd worked up a good enough sweat, Esther started back, making her way to the path that ran alongside the lake. The little building came into view when she was about 200 meters away. One of the guards noticed her approaching, and Esther saw the slight nudge he gave his buddy. They weren't being overt about it, but they were watching her while acting as they weren't.

*For all that is holy, I cannot believe I'm about to do this.* Esther didn't pay much attention to gender and gender politics, but she had an inherent dislike for women who played to their sex to get what they wanted. She was a competent woman who achieved success for her efforts, not simply because she was a somewhat attractive female. While at the university, she'd flirted on occasion, but she'd been determined to put that aside when she enlisted. As a Marine, she might have even gone overboard to avoid any "genderfication." She was a Marine, nothing more, nothing less. And she'd rather be back on that 75kg forced march at Prettyjohn than do what she was about to do.

While still more than 100 meters away, Esther straightened up her posture and stuck her chest out. She was very, very conscious of the bounce in her breasts, and she could feel her face turn red. She hoped the guards would attribute that to the exertion of running.

*This is so freaking lame,* she told herself. *This only works in the flicks, not real life.*

The two guards had quit pretending and were openly watching her as she ran up. Behind them, she could see Sven edging closer along the shoreline.

She started to speak, but her voice caught. She coughed, then said, "You boys, now don't look at my ass when I run by" in as flirty a voice as she could—which sounded anything but to her. She ran past them by about ten meters, then turned to look over her shoulder to see if they were watching her—and managed to get her feet tangled up, sending her flying to the ground.

Both guards were watching, and their looks changed to horror as Esther tumbled. She cried out and rolled to clutch her knee. The blood rolling down her lower leg was real. She'd wanted to make it look good, but maybe her fall had been *too* good. Her knee started throbbing.

Both guards bolted toward her, one shouting, "Are you OK, ma'am?"

Behind them, Sven was rushing up to the shack, which looked to be mere artistic cover for one of the pumps that fed the lake. One of the guards was kneeling beside her, asking if she was

OK. The second guard was standing five meters back, simply watching. If he turned around, he'd see Sven.

"You were looking. It was your fault," she yelled at the second guard while clutching the hand of the first.

The second guard scowled, not buying into her act, she knew.

"We weren't looking, ma'am, really. You just fell. We're so sorry!"

She saw the second guard, the suspicious one, start to shift his weight as if to turn back, so she blurted out, "What's your name! I'm going to report you!"

His eyes narrowed, but after a moment, he said, "Junior Sergeant Philip MacAdams. Thirty-Second Provisional Guards."

Behind him, ten meters away, Sven reappeared. He held up a brown envelope high, a huge smile on his face before he ducked behind the building. Esther knew he'd keep the building between them until he reached the shoreline and started casually making his way along it.

"Well, Junior Sergeant McAdams, you should have a little decorum when you're on the job. What are you here for anyway? Someone's going to invade the park?"

"Are you really going to report us?" the first guard asked her.

"I should, but at least you seem to care. Help me up, please."

Esther didn't have to fake the wince as she stood. She'd banged her knee up pretty good. She did make a show of flexing it, and she was relieved when it seemed to be working.

"Keep your mind on the job, soldier boys. I don't pay taxes so you can sit there and ogle anyone who jogs by."

She started limping away. She wished she could break into a jog, but she was afraid that if she tried, she might fall for real.

"Miss? Miss? You're bleeding," a young woman pushing a stroller said as she and Esther closed.

"Just a fall, but watch those two," she said, turning and pointing back at the guards.

They were back at the building, but both were still watching her. Beyond them, 100 meters farther away, Sven was still casually making his way around the lake.

Esther continued until she reached the trees she'd designated as their rally point. Luckily, it was well out of sight of the guards, and Esther was happy to see several benches. She sat down and examined her leg. Her knee was throbbing, and it was swelling up where she'd scraped it. The longer she sat, the stiffer it would get, but she needed to wait for Sven. It was at least half-an-hour before her partner in crime walked up.

"That was something," Sven said. "I guess they were right when they said they need more WAMs in recon. Those negats never would have come to help me like that."

Esther had called him a trog, so she ignored the "WAM," which she had only recently found out was supposedly a centuries-old term for 'wide-ass Marine." And she'd pretty much been sitting there thinking the same thing. As much as she detested what she'd just done, as much as it went against everything she stood for, in the end, she'd just used one more tool in her tool box. A 2.5-meter Marine might be chosen to emplace explosives high on a wall over his 1.5-meter buddy, but that shorter Marine might be chosen to worm down a tunnel to flush out whoever was in there. Neither the taller nor the shorter Marine was inherently better than the other—they just both fit different missions better.

Emotionally, Esther felt as if she'd done female Marines a disservice, but intellectually, she knew she'd simply done what was prudent for the mission. And the mission had been a success. That was the bottom line.

"Oh, crap, look at your knee. Did you do that when you fell?"

"No, Sven. One of the ducks attacked me after you left."

"Yeah, sorry, dumb question. Are you OK to keep going? Do we need to stop?"

"After I shook my ass to get you your objective? Fat chance. Now we're on to mine, and we've got nine hours until extract."

"OK, let's go, then."

Esther slowly got up, testing her knee. It hurt like a son-of-a-bitch, but she wasn't going to let that stop her. Barefoot now and without her yellow blouse, she took Sven's arm. If they were supposed to be a couple, she damned-well let him support her until her knee loosened back up.

"And if you have to shake your ass to get me mine, you'd better shake it right," she told him as they made their way out of the park.

## Chapter 21

Esther watched the entrance to the building for twenty minutes. At least a hundred people had gone in during that time. Both she and the captain had agreed that her objective was in the office building, and her mission order had included the entry "Room 1204." But where the captain's objective had been out in the open, hers was in a crowded office space.

She wished she was closer to the building, but she feared surveillance that would notice her sitting and watching, so she was 150 meters to the south, sitting outside a crowded café, sipping from someone else's abandoned cup of what she thought was a chicory blend. Esther was very conscious of her bare feet and her grubby appearance, and she kept expecting the lone harried waiter who was serving the outside tables to notice her and tell her to leave. She tried to exude that "I belong here" presence, but she didn't feel she was pulling it off.

*Confidence, Esther. You belong here. You're just a normal citizen taking a deserved break from her busy schedule.*

Sven slipped beside her and sat down, pushing something at her feet under the table. She didn't look but slowly felt the object with her feet. To her surprise, he'd brought shoes. She slipped them on while taking another sip of the coffee.

He placed a jacket of some sort between them on the table and asked, "Well?"

"Busy, how was your day?"

"Same. Too many customers."

She wished there was another cup on the table that he could hold. To her, the two of them screamed out that they didn't belong, and that they were up to no good. She'd initially objected to Sven going into their target building, but his logic was that if he went in and got caught, her mission wouldn't be compromised. And if she went in, looked around, then left only to come back again later, the security AIs might notice that and deem it suspicious.

"Are you going to get the registration done?" he asked.

*Registration? What did he find out? How do I ask?*

Esther didn't know if they were being overly cautious. The planetary security AIs would be analyzing conversations and transmissions for key words or patterns, but the sheer volume of communications was so great that they had to filter out the vast bulk of what was being said. With both her and Sven being off-worlders, their speech patterns would put them in a higher priority, but still, there had to be hundreds of millions of non-natives on the planet.

"Did you get the times?" she asked.

"Yeah, the Regional Tax Registry's in room 1204. They're open until 5:00."

*Regional Tax Registry. OK, thanks, Sven!*

"Well, then, I might as well get it done. You want to finish my coffee?"

She new Sven didn't drink coffee (or any drink with caffeine), but he said, "Sure, let me have it."

She pushed the cup to him, then stood up, grabbing the jacket and putting it on. The long coat was black with silver trim, and it almost reached the ground, covering her half-calves and the Deep Six. She straightened the front out and saw the shoes, which were surprisingly fashionable, and they even went with the coat. She had to resist turning her ankle to get a better look. Whether by accident or a taste for fashion, Sven had actually acquired a good combination. Where and how, she didn't know, but she was grateful she wouldn't be going in the building barefoot.

She wasn't going to dilly-dally. She was a woman with a purpose, so she strode along, ignoring her bad knee, straight to the Gartrelle Building. At the corner, she saw a street vendor with shoes on a blanket he'd spread out on the sidewalk. A dozen of the same shoes as she now had on were prominently displayed. Esther knew where Sven had snagged them, at least, and she stood at the crosswalk, avoiding the vendor's eyes and hoping he didn't notice her shoes. An eternity later, the light switched, and the mass of people surged across it.

She reached the front entrance and marched in like she belonged. On most planets, visitors had to sign in to gain access to the upper floors. The government floors in the Gartrelle Building, however, were open floors. Esther passed through the scanners without a problem and into the elevator. Moments later, she was entering Room 1204, the Prime Davis Regional Tax Registry.

"Payment or new registration," the concierge box asked.

"New."

A ticket spit out of the bottom of the box with the number "262" printed on it and "Estimated wait time: 84 minutes."

"Please wait in Room B. Thank you for making Prime Davis strong."

Esther followed the sign to a common-enough-looking room. A counter was in the front, divided into three sections. On her side of the counter were about 50 uncomfortable-looking plastic chairs. A guard was standing watch over the room, but with the intensity that bespoke military, or at least military experience. He didn't look like a normal jimmylegs.

As Esther turned to take a seat, she caught sight of a simple brown envelope in a wire rack in front of the far left station. She'd almost missed it because of the white envelopes in front of it. She tried not to stare as she took her seat, but she was sure that was her objective.

Most of the other people waiting were either chatting or on their PAs. Esther didn't have one, and that made her stand out. She leaned her head back and pretended to nap.

About twenty minutes after she got there, Sven came in. He was dressed better, but his face was still polka-dotted with bug bites, and his neck swollen. He didn't look at Esther but took a seat in the second row.

Esther watched the numbers count down, trying to see how long each session took. She had to get the left-hand clerk, she knew. As her number kept getting closer, she tried to calculate who would call her up. When she was one number away, she knew she'd get the center clerk.

Two people down was a woman who'd stopped talking and was watching the display intently. Esther leaned back and craned her head. The woman's ticket was number 263.

Without hesitation, Esther stood and stepped over to her, shifting her weight from foot to foot.

"Excuse me, but I think you came in just after me. Your number is 263, right?"

The middle-aged woman looked up at her, a confused look on her face.

"Yes. Why?"

"I've been trying to hold it in, but I can't. I've got to use the ladies' room. I'm number 262," she said, holding out the ticket so the woman can see. "I don't want to lose my place and have to wait again, so would you mind trading with me so I can go pee?"

Esther didn't know if she would really lose her place or not, but the lady gave her an understanding look and said, "Oh, of course, dear. Here, you take mine."

Esther changed tickets, then hurried out of the room and into the main office space. The restroom was out in the hallway, so she went inside. She didn't want to wait too long and miss her new number, so she counted out 45 seconds, then returned to the room. The lady was just approaching the middle station. Esther straightened out her coat and walked to a seat in the front row, a few places to the right of where Sven, in his second-row seat, was in deep conversation with a man in front of him. Esther could make out part of the conversation, which seemed to consist of the man telling Sven how successful he was and how he was going to make a killing in phosphates or something.

Esther gave up trying to listen just as her number was called. She stood up and went to the far left station. Her objective was twenty centimeters from her hand. She could just snatch it and run, but the guard at the door looked alert and ready. While she'd been sitting, her mind churning with ideas, the best she'd come up with was to "accidently" knock over the wire holder, then slipping the envelope into her jacket as she picked the rest up. Now that she was standing there, the guard seemed to be staring right at her.

"Application, please," the bored-looking clerk said.

"I don't have it now," Esther said. "I thought I could fill it out here."

The woman looked at Esther as if she was an idiot, and then with a voice that had probably said this a million times before, said,

"The forms are online. You are supposed to fill them out, get them notarized, and bring them here."

"I didn't know that. And I've waited for two hours. Isn't there something I can do?"

"Yes, you can go to the ground floor, go to FastPrint, and fill out the form. They have a notary there."

Esther was eyeing the rack of envelopes, ready to knock it off the counter as she left, when a loud voice interrupted the two of them.

"How come this lady went right to the front of the queue? I just saw her come in!"

Esther turned to see the man Sven had been speaking to. He pushed his way to the counter, shoving Esther to the side—and right in front of the envelopes.

"You are mistaken, sir. She has the next number. Please sit down and wait your turn."

Esther felt an almost malevolent force hit her. She turned to where the guard was on full alert, his body tense for action. He was staring right at them.

*Oh, hell!*

"Bullshit! I saw her just come in a minute ago. She can't slip someone 100 credits and get to the front of the line!" the man insisted, his voice getting high.

Esther didn't want any attention on her, and this fool was a magnet. She could see Sven standing and watching, as were most of the waiting people, but he wasn't moving to help.

"Sir—" the clerk started.

"I want to talk to your supervisor," the man said just as the guard launched himself.

Esther jumped back and turned to face him. She was not going down without a fight. But the guard tackled the man instead, bringing him to the ground as the clerk ducked back out of the way despite the counter between them. Esther turned away as if to protect her face, and leaning up against the rack of envelopes, she easily slipped the brown one out of the rack and under her coat.

She'd been right. This guard was either ex-military, a martial artist, or simply very well trained. With quick professionalism, he had the man face first on the ground and ziptied his hands behind him.

"I got one," he spoke into his shoulder mic as she stood up, hauling the sputtering man to his feet.

Esther looked at the clerk, opening her mouth as if shocked. She didn't think the clerk was faking her shock, though. The woman was gaping like a beached fish and trembling.

"I . . . I . . . I've never seen, I mean, what?" Esther said, sounding pretty genuine, she thought.

"Ma'am, I'm so sorry," the woman said, her professionalism taking hold of her. "We just got the new guards today, and well, I'm sorry. You can file a complaint, if you want."

"No, I'm just happy no one was hurt. My registration, I still have to get it done, though. You said FastPrint? On the first floor?"

"Uh, yeah. Yes. I'm sorry about this. Believe me, I'd do it here for you if I could, but I just don't have the capability. All I do is scan yours and then make my entries."

Esther was feeling sorry for the women, but the mission was the mission. Still, it didn't hurt to be polite.

"Don't worry about it. You didn't do anything wrong. It was that, well, can I say asshole?"

The woman smiled and said, "Yes, I think you can say that."

"It was his fault. Stupid of him, from what happened. Anyway, let me get going so I can be back before you close. Have a great rest of the day, at least, uh . . . Daylana," she said, catching the clerk's name on a small placard.

She shook Dylana's hand, then walked out of the room and into the hall. Two more guards had appeared to join the first to surround the man who was weakly protesting his innocence of whatever they were accusing him. Esther walked past them and to the elevator.

*Come on*, she pleaded to herself, watching the bank of numbers indicating where each elevator was at.

She kept expecting to feel a hand clamp on her shoulder, a firm voice telling her to "Come with me!"

Finally, the doors opened, and she stepped inside. Her anxiety kept rising while she tried to keep a calm, casual expression on her face. The elevator stopped at nine of the lower floors, and each time, Esther expected to be greeted by a guard.

When the elevator reached the ground floor, she wanted to run, but she kept an even pace, passing the FastPrint, until she exited the building. It wasn't until she was on the sidewalk and heading to the rally point that she allowed herself to pat the envelope under her coat.

*I did it! Mission completed!*

## Chapter 22

Two hours later, and with three to spare, Esther and Sven walked through the boutique, past the racks of clothes, and into the back room where Gunny McNeill and Major Kierkirk were waiting.

"Are we the first?" Sven asked.

"Yes, you are," the major said. "Congrats."

The gunny scanned their wrist implants and recorded them in.

"Ms. Alicia Lumsden wants her coat back," he said, hand out to Esther.

With a sigh, Esther took it off and gave it to the gunny. It was a very nice coat, and she'd been hoping to keep it. Sven had snagged it off a chair while the woman was leaning forward. This was after he'd grabbed the shoes from the street vendor she'd seen. He was a man of surprising talents, and if he left the Corps, Esther thought he could make it big as a shoplifter.

"Why didn't you just pay her?" Sven asked.

Every Marine during the operation had a micro-drone following him or her, tracking and recording their every move. If a Marine stole or damaged something during the course of the mission, a local government rep descended on the victim to pay for the damage.

"Because she refused payment. Says this was a 'special' coat."

"How's your knee?" the major asked Esther.

"It hurts, sir."

Within the teams, first or nicknames were generally used, which was why Captain Lugar was "Sven" to Esther. But the major was the school XO, so he was "sir" to the students.

"Have Doc check it as soon as we get back. You've still got Mount Motherfucker on Tuesday."

He didn't have to say more. The mission today was their last graded event. Technically, having completed it successfully, both she and Sven had passed the course. They were almost recon

Marines. However, tradition was that on the final day, there was a group run from the school to the top of Mount Snyder, better known as "Mount Motherfucker." It was not a timed event, but each Marine or corpsman had to reach the top. Esther only had a few days to get her knee ready.

"That was pretty copacetic, Captain, with that dickwad in the office," the gunny said as the two students started to change into their field uniforms.

"Am I in trouble for that?" Sven said, looking toward the major.

The exercise ROE was pretty stringent. There was to be no harm done to any citizen. Sven had staked out the waiting room, trying to pick a victim. The guy he'd chosen had been full of bluster, and when Esther had left and come back in, Sven had shifted his original plan and egged the guy on to complain. He hadn't realized that the guard's reaction would be so intense.

In retrospect, his plan was sound. If he'd done the diversion, he'd be in some holding cell now with a mission failure recorded.

"No. It was not your fault that the militia over-reacted. That's against their ROE, so they have to deal with it."

"Knew it," Esther said.

She'd been sure the guard at the tax office was military. The Marines and the local government had to jump through a million hoops for an operation like this. What sold it was usually that it was good training for a planet's security forces. But egos tended to flare, and a planet or country's local forces often tended to pit their best against the Marines. The forces who needed the training the most were pushed aside and the exercise, at least on the host side, became a thing of pride.

"Help yourself to pizza," the gunny said when the two were dressed.

Esther hadn't noticed the delivery boxes, but she hurried over to where the gunny pointed. Her stomach growled with anticipation. She'd been so hyped over the mission that she'd forgotten that she hadn't eaten since the night before. Popping open the top, the room was suddenly enveloped with the aroma of one of her favorite foods.

"Sven, what kind do you want?  We're first, so we get choosies."

"Bacon?  Is there bacon in there?"

Esther shifted the individual boxes, checking.

"Bacon and duck egg."

"That'll do."

"Major, Gunny, do you want some?" she asked.

"No, we've eaten.  You enjoy."

Esther had just taken the first wonderful bite when Doc Tee came in, wearing the robe of a Brother of the Light.  He looked disappointed that he wasn't the first one back, but he brightened up when Esther handed him a piece of pizza.  Doc was one of two corpsmen to make it through the course so far, and the common perception was that he was probably the most dangerous man in the class.

Esther didn't bother showing him her knee.  He couldn't do much more than say, "Your knee's fucked up" without any of his medical gear with him.

By one, twos, and even a group of three, the class arrived at the rally point.  Delaney was wearing a dress, but Tonto had him beat.  The staff sergeant arrived still naked but clutching his envelope.  Everyone laughed as he arrived, but he didn't say a word except to demand some food.  Esther looked forward to seeing the recording of his day.  How he'd completed the mission buck naked was beyond her imagination.

By Endex, 31 of the 35 students had arrived.  Three were in custody of the local police.  One was still out there, and gunny left to collect him.  The failures would be recycled to the next class to try again-except for one.  He'd already been recycled once before, and this had been his last chance.

As the class filed out to spend the night at the contracted hotel, Sven stepped up close to Esther and quietly said, "Thanks.  I'd never have made it without you."

"You got me through, too," she said.  "Pretty smart what you did with that poor guy."

"Yeah, I'm surprised I even though of it.  Not bad for a trog, I guess," he said, his ever-present smile even larger.

"And yeah, and I wasn't too bad for a WAM, I guess, either" she replied, giving Sven's extra-wide shoulders a squeeze.

Esther knew she was driven to succeed. She wanted to be better than anyone else, and she measured her success with every promotion, with every award. But as she looked around her joking classmates as they entered the hotel, she realized that reward was not just promotions. It was in belonging, to be part of something bigger than herself.

She'd been cast adrift ever since her parents were killed with only Noah left, and she'd done a pretty good job of shutting him out. It had left an empty hole in her soul, one she'd been trying to fill with hard work and dedication. But after boot camp first, after NOTC, and especially now with RTC, she was finally beginning to realize that there was more than one way to fill the void. It was also in the brotherhood, in the knowing that all of these Marines and corpsmen had her back and would die for her if need be. And she would do the same for them.

It was an awfully good feeling.

# OMAHA

## Chapter 23

Esther looked at her image in the mirror. She was reporting in, so she was in her Alphas, and from what Gunny McNeill had told her, it might be one of the few times for her to wear the uniform. Recon Marines were under "relaxed grooming regulations," but to wear anything other than utilities, they had to conform with the full regs.

Esther understood the need for the relaxed regs for MARSOC Marines, but she was going to battalion, and she didn't see why the normal regulations weren't followed. Maybe it was a gender thing, she wondered. She wasn't about to grow a beard, after all.

She thought she looked good in the Alphas. They fit her well and showed off a toned, athletic body. She only had four ribbons on her chest, which wasn't particularly impressive for someone seven years in the Corps. That was ignoring the fact that her senior ribbon was a Navy Cross, though. That one ribbon spoke loudly. It might not be a Federation Nova, but it was the next best thing, and Esther was proud to be wearing it. Now, with the simple crossed-paddles badge of a reconnaissance Marine just above it, she thought she looked damned sharp, and she regretted that she wouldn't be wearing Alphas or Charlies often over this next tour.

Esther thought she had a pretty good idea of who she was, and she was not ashamed to admit that she liked to show off. Some Marines made a show of not caring about medals or specialty badges. She was of a different mind, though. Marines who weren't proud of their accomplishments were somehow lacking, in her mind. Noah tended to be like that, she knew, and that was one reason why she thought he wouldn't reach the heights that she herself would reach.

Chasing medals was normally disastrous, however, and usually resulted in Marine casualties. But it was different to simply take pride after the fact. She was sure most Marines would agree with that, even if the culture of the Corps tended to demean that kind of attitude. Which was why Esther had never mentioned one of her goals as a Marine. There had never, in the history of the Federation, been a father-child tandem of Nova awardees. Esther wanted to be half of the first pair to earn Novas. She was not going to chase one by putting her Marines at risk, but she was sure, that if faced with a situation that demanded it, she would not hesitate over fear for her personal safety.

She tugged on her gig line and left her room the Temporary Officer's Quarters. Camp Iwasaki was a unique Marine base in that it was in the middle of a large, modern city. Sheelytown was not just the planetary capital, but the capital of one of the four or five richest planets in the Federation. Originally terraformed and developed by the Buffet Foundation almost 400 years ago, it had grown into an economic powerhouse. Some people from the core considered Omaha a hick-planet, bereft of culture, but from what Esther had seen since landing yesterday, it might give Earth a run for her money. On the short trip to the base, she'd been amazed at the art and architecture she'd seen.

Sixth Recon Battalion wasn't at Camp Iwasaki, of course. The camp housed only the division headquarters. But even away from Sheelytown, Esther thought she would enjoy exploring the planet during her down-time. She might still be relegated to the Outer Forces, (which she still thought was ridiculous. It wasn't as if the press was still interested in her. That ship had sailed long ago.), but at least she was back in civilization.

Esther's space-lag still had her screwed up. She wanted breakfast, but it was already approaching 1100 local. That left out the O Club, which had a reputation as being one of the nicest in the Corps. So she headed to the exchange food court where she dialed up an Eggs Benedict. She ate it carefully to keep from spilling any of the hollandaise on her blouse. As she ate, she kept looking around, trying to spot a familiar face. But it was a big Corps, and she didn't recognize anyone. Not one seemed to take any notice of her, either.

By the time she'd finished, it was 1145, and she knew the civilians in admin would be going to chow. So she decided to explore, starting with the Exchange. As expected, it was pretty good, far outclassing the ones on Wayfarer Station and Reissler Quay. The selection of civilian goods was impressive, and a good percentage of items were much cheaper than back on Tarawa. She checked out the commissary, then wandered over to the O Club, which was as impressive as advertised. Finally, at 1330, she wandered over to the HQ Annex to check in.

Esther had never reported in at a division level. But with the battalion on the same   planet as Division, the Joint Receiving Section handled all Marines and sailors arriving on Omaha. It was much smaller that she'd expected until she realized that with the regiments on other planets, most of the division's personnel went directly to check in with them.

Sven had told her that she wouldn't make a commander's call with the CG, but Esther had known Major General Molina since he was a major, so she thought he might make an exception for her—not that she'd admitted that to Sven. So she entered the JRS and scanned her wrist.

A middle-aged lady sitting at a desk behind the counter suddenly looked up and said, "First Lieutenant Lysander?"

*No, I just chopped off her hand and scanned it to throw you off.*

"Yes, that's me."

"Where have you been?  You were supposed to report in today."

"It is today," Esther said, confused.

"It's 1330, Lieutenant.  We've been trying to reach you all morning."

"Since I haven't checked in yet, my PA is only in civilian mode."

"Hester, I've got Lieutenant Lysander.  Call Bruce and get him working on her," she told the older man two desks over from hers.

She got up and came to the counter, holding her hand out for Esther's packet. A wrist chip should be more than enough to initiate a check-in, Esther had always thought, but the military liked to over-think things. So all Marines were given a data-cube and plastisheet printouts of their orders. The woman took the cube and placed it in the reader.

Esther stared at her, wondering just what the heck was going on, but with the officious manner of some mid-level civilian employees, the woman, who hadn't even told Esther her name, wouldn't bother explaining why all her consternation.

Esther was getting impatient while the woman made some entries, then stood at the counter, back to her, and facing Hester.

At last, Hester looked up and said, "1636 on Harmony."

The woman turned to Esther and said, "You've got a flight to Washoo Township at 1636. I hope you're still packed."

"But . . . but I haven't checked in yet?" Esther protested.

"What do you think I just did, Lieutenant? You're checked in; now we've got you on a commercial flight to your battalion."

"I'm confused. I already have a ticket for Thursday. So what's going on?"

The woman rolled her eyes as if Esther was an idiot, and Esther had to refrain from jumping over the counter and punching her in the face.

"That other ticket was canceled. Your battalion sent us a message that you need to get there immediately."

"Why?"

"I'm sure I don't know the specifics, but you're deploying at 0115 in the morning. I suggest you get going. You've got to be checked in and at the gate by 1606."

She turned around with an obvious dismissal. Esther stared daggers at her for a long few seconds before she wheeled about and rushed out of the office.

*Deployed? Like this again?*

One day, Esther was going to report into a unit and actually get to know her Marines before being thrown into the shit.

Jonathan P. Brazee

# LUCKY FORTUNE #9

## Chapter 24

"Anything?" Esther asked Grayback.

"Nada. Everything's routine," the sergeant said.

"OK, I've got it. Catch some Z's."

Esther settled in behind the P-2001. The passive surveillance console was a nice piece of gear: lightweight, a small footprint, and the ability to monitor 11 different spectrums. It was also very expensive. The Federation was paying 80,000 credits for it, part of an agreement the government had made with Novaset Industries to keep it exclusive to the Federation military and FCDC. The Two-Oh-Oh-One (an awkward nickname, Esther thought) didn't need a monitor. It could be placed and left alone, and it would function fine. However, even without the issue of security for the team, Esther wanted active eyes on the console to make sure it didn't walk off while no one was looking. Esther would take a long, long time earning enough to pay it off should someone take a hankering for it.

This was the third time Esther had joined a new unit in the Corps, and this was the third time that she'd deployed within 24 hours after arriving. That had to be some kind of record. She was either the luckiest or unluckiest Marine in the Corps.

On the one hand, Marines hated sitting on their asses. They lived for action, and Esther had experienced that with each live mission. On the other hand, she would have liked to have some time to get to know her unit before being thrust into the fire.

It hadn't been too bad, this time, though. Bravo Company had deployed as a unit to provide support to a task force consisting of the Sixth Raider Battalion and 1/15, a "normal" infantry battalion.

Both Sixth Recon and Sixth Raiders were division assets while 1/15 belonged to the 15th Marine Regiment.

Recon companies rarely deployed as a unit, but the huge expanses on Lucky Fortune #9 required orbital and extensive ground intel gathering. More than that, though, when Lucky Fortune demanded Federation assistance, they got it in spades. The corporation was one of the oldest in the Federation, going back 800 or more years to old China. Now, its reach was galaxy wide, and it was the 34th largest corporation in existence. So when the CEO called up the chairmen to complain about saboteurs on Lucky Fortune #9, the new chairman, just six months on the job, called up the Navy chief of staff and the commandant to take action.

Esther didn't pay too much attention as to why they were there. Sure, Lucky Fortune had a security force as large as a Marine division, and most of the Marines thought they should be able to handle their own brush fires, but the whys and wherefores of their deployment didn't matter as much to her as forging a tight platoon. Not being the primary recon unit in the task force had been fine with her. Major Carlstein, the company commander, had assigned Second Platoon to one of the more secure areas, which was fine with her. It was more time to get a feel for her platoon.

And after two weeks of sitting in the forested hills overlooking a refining complex, she'd at least gotten to know a third of them. A recon team was seven Marines and a Navy corpsman, unlike a 13-man rifle squad. Three days after landing on the planet, the platoon had gone out into the field, but as separate teams. Esther could have stayed back at the camp with the task force headquarters—in fact, that was the SOP—but with the company commander on the mission, that freed her up to attach herself to one of her teams. One of Esther's teams was 25 klicks away. The other was 60. She'd communicated with the other two teams, but that was about it. And if any of her three teams got into trouble, there wasn't a way for another team to get to them.

That wasn't a major problem, however. Between all three teams was a company of Raiders. One platoon was occupying a Forward Operating Position four klicks from Esther. The rest of the company was between her other two teams and sending out active patrols.

She pulled out her hadron phone, tempted to call Top Gann, her platoon sergeant, who had gone out with Third Team. The hadron phones were a tremendous resource, even if they were overkill on a single planet. The phones used matched technology to create instant communications no matter how far apart the phones were from each other. One "batch" was 16 phones. When one phone was activated, as in speaking into it, all of the other 15 phones reacted in the exact same way at the exact same time. Esther had listened to the explanation, which delved deep into quantum physics, but most of it had gone over her head. To her, what was important was that they worked. She had three of them in the platoon, and even if the skipper was back on Omaha, she could speak with him as if he was just down the hall.

Of course, the phones were ungodly expensive, so that was one more concern for her as the responsible officer for them. Recon got all the high-speed, low-drag gear, but someone had to sign for all of that expensive equipment, and that someone was in the platoon was her.

The expense and obvious size constraints also relegated the team phones to VBV, or voice-to-binary-to-voice. The big commercial and military hadron systems could broadcast, if that was even a word that applied, visuals and large data dumps, but the small team phones were far more limited.

She sighed and put the phone back in her holster. Top knew what he was doing, and she didn't need her to keep bugging him. She was just bored. While she had initially been glad to have the time to snap in with the platoon, they'd been sitting on the planet for going on three weeks, and there had been no sign of any violence. The Federation had two ships in orbit and more than 2,000 Marines on the surface, and so far, nothing of note had happened.

Esther knew that most of what a recon unit did was boring—that had been brought out ad infinitum by her instructors. They watched and reported. But there was a mystique about them that had perhaps clouded her visceral understanding. She'd let the crossed paddles on her patch become a symbol for derring-do. But the reality was that recon battalion was a support unit, providing the eyes and ears for the infantry. They were not MARSOC nor the SEALs. No Hollybolly moviemaker was going to be rushing to make a flick of six Marines and a corpsman who just sat around and watched.

It was true that battalion recon did do missions, such as taking out targets like bridges, calling for fire, even targeting enemy leadership. Esther had a school-trained sniper in the platoon as well as two school-trained engineers. During the Evolution, her company's Second Platoon had earned a Chairman's Unit Commendation for destroying a loyalist airfield, but the most common mission was just what they were doing now: sitting on their butts and watching.

And the boredom was driving her crazy. She had to do something, anything.

When her phone buzzed with the skipper's code, she almost fumbled taking it out.

*A mission! Finally!*

"Lieutenant Lysander, pull your teams now to their rally points," he said.

*Hell yeah! A platoon size mission!*

"Roger that. What're my orders?"

"You'll be picked up by commercial buses. I'll brief you when you get back."

*What? Commercial buses?*

"Sir? Buses?"

"Affirmative. I think you have Starlight Lines, complete with all the latest flicks," he said, the bitterness evident in his voice.

"Uh . . . Skipper? Can I ask what's going on?"

Another good thing about the hadron phones was that as they didn't transmit or broadcast in the normal sense, they were completely secure. Someone would have to physically take one of the 16 phones in order to listen in.

"Sure, why not? Lucky Fortune has negotiated a new deal with the local union, so now we're not needed anymore."

"The union?" she said with a sinking heart.

"Yeah, the union. Seems as if our mere presence convinced them that their factories are needed for the defense of the Federation. So in a fit of patriotism, they've agreed to the company's terms."

*Fucking hell!*

"Roger, understood. We'll start packing up now. Do you have a timeline for our pickup?"

Three of the Marines who were sleeping were up, listening in to her. They did not look happy.

"That's a negative at the moment. I'll get back to you on that. You are now in a Level Four status. However, if there ever were any belligerents in your area, and they have not received the word that we are all friends again, you may defend yourself."

"Roger that. Level Four."

Level Four meant that kinetic weapons were not to be loaded, and energy weapons were not to be powered up. Which would make it hard to defend themselves if they were hit. But she was pretty sure that not only would they not be hit now, they had never been in any danger of that in the first place.

"Stand down the Two-Oh-Oh-One," she told Grayback. "Everyone else, let's pack it up."

"Let me guess," Duke, the team leader, said. "We're all friends now that the Marines were called in as a show of strength."

"Got it in one, Duke. Now let me pass the joyful news to Top Gann and the rest of the platoon. Peace is at hand."

"Yeah, joyful. We're all so very fucking thrilled," Duke said as he kicked a clod of dirt across their hide.

Esther understood their anger at being used as pawns in a corporate negotiation. She was livid. Her father had fought against the pervasive integration of the big corporations and the old government. After the sacrifices of the Evolution, after her father and mother had been assassinated for the cause, it looked like it was business as usual.

# JOINT TRAINING AREA, GENERAL HABITATS #26

## Chapter 25

Esther twisted to look over her shoulder at the Top and gave him a thumbs up. He returned it with two thumbs up.

Master Sergeant Lee Gann had been in the community for almost 15 years and had come to the battalion after two tours with MARSOC—and he was going batshit crazy. In MARSOC, every Marine in a platoon was an operator, not matter how high the rank. In battalion, neither the platoon commander nor the platoon sergeant normally conducted operations. Their position was back at the supported unit's CP, both to control the teams and to give advice to the unit commander.

Esther and the Top had just spent an excruciating two weeks in 3/14's CP for the annual Valiant Force exercise. The fact that the purple forces, of which 3/14 was part, got their asses kicked by the green forces, had only added to their frustration.

Esther was too far down the food chain to be in the after action meetings, so she'd expected to cool her heels for three days while waiting for embark and the trip back to Omaha. And as the planet was still being terraformed by General Habitats, there wasn't even a city in the region where they could get some libo. So when the Space Guard liaison had asked for volunteers to get some of the Guard pilots their drop quals, she'd jumped at the chance.

Esther had never worked with the Space Guard. They were the "third" arm of the Federation military, with historical roots going back to the United Kingdom's 19th Century's Waterguard. Their original mission of combating smuggling had evolved to encompass anti-piracy and even local defense, although their cutters did not have the weaponry to take on most navy ships. Esther wasn't all that versed on the Guard. Like many Marines and sailors, she sort of considered them as younger siblings, well-meaning, but not that effective. She knew that Marines were occasionally attached to the Space Guard on anti-piracy missions. She also knew that the Space Guard had posse comitatus[10] and so the power to arrest, so a Guard officer had been attached to a few ships she'd been on, but that was about the breadth of her knowledge.

Except for two more things. Space Guard cutters were both space and atmosphere capable, and they were sometimes welcomed where Navy ships were not. In this case, it was the first that mattered. Because the ships could operate in deep space as well as planetary atmosphere, they could be used as platforms to insert small forces onto a planet. One of those ways was through jumping.

A space-only Navy ship could insert Marines with the "duck eggs," which were two-man capsules that were essentially shot out at a planet from up to a million klicks away. The duck eggs would hit a planet's atmosphere, then the outer skin would ablate away releasing the two Marines inside to parachute to the surface.

While this was still the primary method of clandestine insertion of recon Marines or SEALs, duck eggs were expensive, the process was wearing on the Marines, and it required a configured ship to conduct the operation.

A SG cutter had far less of a footprint, and it could enter the atmosphere. Within each cutter was a drop hatch where emergency supplies—or Marines—could parachute to the surface.

What Esther hadn't realized was that cutters needed to be certified for dropping personnel, and failure to earn the quals could affect a skipper's career. So if she could help an SG officer and crew like that, then of course, she'd do it, fellow serviceman to fellow serviceman.

At least that was what she told the SG liaison. Truth was, she'd have paid to do it. Aside from her boredom, she simply loved jumping.

---

[10] Posse Comitatus: the authority of a military force to enforce domestic polices, to include those normally granted to law enforcement such as the authority to arrest citizens.

Esther had 14 training jumps to her record. Thirteen were from aircraft, and one was from a duck egg. This would be something new. The cutter needed three successful drops to earn her quals, and with ten pax being the max load, that would allow each Marine in the platoon to get a jump. She pulled rank and made sure she and Top were on the first stick, and that she was the doorman.

The ship was an Ageon Class, the second smallest cutter and just slightly larger than a Marine Stork. There were only five crew with the skipper being a very young-looking lieutenant (jg).

The cargo compartment was extremely cramped with ten Marines; each Marine had to sit in a chain, the legs of one around the Marine in front of him. A Stork could carry 38 Marines (50 in a pinch), but the cutter needed much more room for its engine train.

The little cutter had shot into space, pulling a couple of G's that had not been compensated. Esther had been pressed into the Top behind her. She had expected it. G compensation was a drain of energy, and the cutter was a combat ship, so it was conducting emergency lift-off procedures. It was a long three or four minutes before the skipper cut in the compensators and Esther could breathe normally.

The ship entered the exosphere, which was the requirement for the quals. The control panel let her know the ship had turned and was reentering the planet's atmosphere. There was a slight vibration making itself felt through the dampeners as the ship reached the mesosphere, but nothing like she had experienced in her duck egg insertion.

Esther felt her heartbeat quicken. When the hatch over the compartment opened, she got even more excited. She edged forward and put her legs over the edge, dangling them 15,000 meters above the planet's surface. At the cutter's speed, they should be whipping about, but the ship was designed with a slipstream baffle that acted as a sort of shock absorber. Right at the skin of the ship, Esther barely felt a thing. When she jumped, she would gradually feel the bite of her forward speed as she progressed away from the ship. By 15 meters, she would have slowed enough so that she could survive the transition. She'd still feel a serious jolt, but a survivable one.

The cutter could slow down enough for a normal exit, but one of the three jumps had to be a high-speed drop, and Esther had eagerly asked that it be on her stick. If she was going to do this, she wanted to experience something new, and she already had 13 routine jumps.

The red light on the edge of the hatch switched to amber.

"One minute," Esther passed needlessly over the net; everyone could see the light change.

At thirty seconds to drop, the light shifted to a flashing amber. Esther put both hands alongside the edges of the hatch as she stared at the light. At ten seconds, the light started flashing faster, and the horizon shifted as the helmsman brought the cutter around and lifted the nose. When the light turned green, Esther let go, and with the helmsman applying a jolt of power, Esther slid out of the hatch, immediately tucking into a tight position.

The cutter was flying at 500 KPH, far too fast for a normal drop. However, the dampening system worked, slowing her down to a more manageable, if still fast, 220 KPH by the time she exited the ship's envelope. The slowdown occurred in a little more than a second, though, so it was still a jolt, even if not quite as severe as the exit from a duck egg.

The jolt knocked the breath from her and whipped her around, but she kept her position for a few seconds before opening up into the standard free fall arch which deployed her wings.

All ten jumpers had exited together, but the cutter's climb separated them by 10 to 15 meters, which was good. She would have hated slamming into Top Gann at those speeds. Esther watched as the other nine jumpers assumed free fall positions. Everyone was in control.

She turned back to the ground, ready to have some fun. Except for a few qualified "flyers" with MARSOC, Marines were issued standard freefall wingsuits. It took hundreds of qualification jumps to be certified on the advanced suits where a Marine could maneuver like a falcon, but the standard suits were no slouches. Esther brought her arms back slightly to increase speed when Top flew in front of her, completing a barrel roll and flashing her another thumbs up.

Challenge on.

Esther dipped under him, increasing her speed, then pulling up sharply on the other side of him. She was still falling, so "up" was relative. As she approached the vertical, she tucked her legs in and bent over backwards, completing the loop.

Esther hadn't ever completed the maneuver, which was pushing the capabilities of the wingsuit, and it was done much more easily at lower altitudes, so she was relieved when she transitioned smoothly back into controlled flight instead of flailing around like a neophyte.

"Not bad, Lieutenant," Top passed. "But how about this?"

He started spinning like a corkscrew. It made Esther dizzy just looking at him.

Doc B flashed by her and came up alongside the Top. He started corkscrewing, even if his were not as crisp at Top's. Top stopped after ten seconds, and Esther swopped in front of her. Within moments, the three of them were performing a "Thach Weave," an interlocking maneuver named for an old Earth Navy fighter pilot. They swept back and forth between each other like strands of hair being braided.

None of this was authorized on a training mission. But Esther didn't care. It was pure joy. And if they didn't want them to play like this, then why introduce them to the maneuvers?

She pulled out of the weave, then started experimenting with somersaults, trying to stop each rotation exactly at the horizontal.

Her AI flashed a warning on her visor. She was getting out of range if she was going to reach the DZ. Reluctantly, she checked to make sure no one was above her and released her chute. The shock as the almost invisible foil deployed was almost negligible when compared to the exit from the cutter. She oriented on the DZ in the distance and checked her altitude, quickly querying her AI on O2 levels. Satisfied that she could breathe, she retracted her visor, letting in a blast of frigid air. She didn't care. It felt great!

Far below her feet, 30,000 Marines, militia, and civilian contractors were grubbing around, trying to get ready to embark ships to return to their home bases. Up here, Esther didn't have a care in the world.

Too soon, she was coming into the DZ. She flared for a tip-toe landing, with less of a shock than stepping off a stair. As she gathered up her chute, Top came in, landing a little harder than her and taking an extra step.

"Hey, Top! There're four empty slots in the third stick. I bet if we get back to the paraloft right now, we can pack our chutes in time to grab two of those spots. What do you say?"

But Top wasn't saying anything. As soon as Esther suggested it, he took off at a run, making a beeline to the loft. He was still struggling to gather his chute as he ran, and that let Esther catch and pass him a few meters from the loft.

*And to think, they actually pay me to do this,* she thought as she slammed her chute on the table and started repacking it.

# SAINT TERESA

## Chapter 26

"I need that support now, Captain," Gunny Michael "Monty" Montgomery passed.

"I'm working on it," Esther replied, trying to keep calm while her emotions ran rampant.

"Top, what's the Navy saying?" she shouted across the CP to where he was standing over the Naval Weapons Controller.

"The 'Navy' is saying stand by, Captain," the Navy lieutenant shouted back at her. "Your yelling isn't going to speed things up."

"I've got Marines who are getting overrun, Lieutenant. I can't reach them. It has to be you."

"When can we get those fighters?" Lieutenant Colonel Bertolucci, the infantry battalion commander asked, putting himself between the livid Esther and the Navy lieutenant.

Esther knew that the delay wasn't the fault of the lieutenant. She was just the liaison between the Marines and the ship, and she'd put in the support request. But the Navy officer was a handy target for her anger, and she was letting her have it.

The request had been submitted, and now it was up to the operational commander to allocate his forces. He could send his two Experions to support four Marines on Saint Teresa's moon, or he could keep them around the *Fairfield Bay* as security against the six Uni Ramheads that hadn't been located yet. Esther was pretty sure what the commander would decide, but she had to keep trying.

"How about Osprey-Two," the colonel asked Major Baxter, his operations officer.

"Still 30 minutes until refueled, then 15 to the moon," Captain Francis, the FAC answered for the major, which was pretty much what Esther had expected.

Osprey-One had been shot down by a Uni missile two hours ago, and Osprey-Two had barely made it back from Bingo to refuel. The Marine Corps Wasp was a wickedly effective platform in an atmosphere, but not as good in space. It would be a sitting duck to a space fighter, but against a ground force as what was attacking Monty and his team, it should be effective if it could punch through into the tunnels.

"As soon as they have enough fuel to make it to the moon and back, have them take off," the colonel ordered.

"Aye-aye, sir," the major relied.

"Monty, hang on. We're trying to get a Wasp up to you," she passed.

"A Wasp? We're pretty deep for whatever one of them is packing."

"Can you get to the surface?"

"Yeah, we can, but we'd have to fight through 20 or 30 Unis to get there."

"That may end up being your only choice. Just hang tight."

"It's not like we're going anywhere soon."

Esther could hear the pounding of a jackhammer of some sort as it sought to break into the small compartment where Monty, Doc Juno, Hank, and Sputter were holed up. Monty was watching where the Uni troops were breaking down the metal bulkhead, so Esther switched her feed to Hank, who'd been hit and was sitting against the far wall. She could see the other three now. Monty looked calm, as if they weren't in deep shit. Sputter, a sergeant, just two months with the team, was trying hard to look collected, Esther knew, but his bioreadouts revealed a different story. Doc Juno looked back at Hank, and for a moment, Esther wondered if he was looking at the wounded staff sergeant or if he knew she was watching and he was looking at her.

This entire mission had been a clusterfuck. The platoon had been attached to the task force in direct support of the 3/14, her old battalion. The mission was to quell the fighting on Saint Teresa between the Progressive Coalition and the Unified Party. The Federation wasn't even taking a stand as to which side was right. Twenty-one percent of the planet's property was Federation-owned, and a nascent Federal bio-research complex had just begun operations there. The Federation's prime objective was that nothing threaten its holdings on the planet. All of the planet's FCDC troops had been consolidated on Federal property, and that led to the Navy and Marines providing a show of force to convince both sides to put down their arms.

Except that the Unified Force wasn't convinced. Three days after the task force arrived in New Goa, two Marines had been killed by a Uni suicide bomber, and the lines were drawn.

A single battalion was nowhere near big enough to pacify an entire planet if it erupted into full-scale war. There wasn't a single entity that could match up man-for-man to the Marines, but ten thousand army ants could bring down a lion. The Marines had to find the ant's burrows and stamp them down before the ants could emerge.

The Unis had seized the spaceport, where there had been six Ramhead fighters. The Ramheads were old tech even for frontier worlds, but even one could feasibly damage or take down a Navy ship-of-the-line in orbit. The Task Force commander was extremely concerned about that.

Esther had tried not to be cynical about that considering the commander was aboard the *Fairfield Bay*. She knew that the Federation valued a frigate and the sailors aboard as more vital than a single Marine battalion. That was simply a fact of life to those in the Corps.

With the Ramheads missing, Esther had been ordered to send a team to the area around the moon base, which was controlled by the Unis, to see if they Ramheads were stashed there somewhere. Esther had chosen Third Team, which Monty had split into two four-man teams. One was to the planetary north of the base, high on a peak, where it was monitoring emissions. Monty had breached the farm tunnels and had been physically searching likely spaces that could be serving as temporary hangars.

Esther didn't know whether the Unis had detected the initial breach or not, but when fighting broke out on the planet, a platoon-sized force had assaulted Monty's team at the same time. Esther had ordered Monty to surrender, but the Unis were having none of it, and Hank was hit. Monty had managed to retreat into an empty tunnel, hoping there was an exit somewhere. Dragging Hank, all four had made it to what they discovered was a dead end. As with most tunnels, an airlock was placed at the terminus as a safety measure. The four Marines were now barricaded in that airlock while the Unis were pounding away at it to break in.

"The Navy's not going to release the Experions," Top Gann said as he walked up to Esther. "The cowardly mother fuckers."

"Do you have any ideas?" Esther asked, not expecting much.

She'd been wracking her brain trying to come up with a strategy, but unlike in the flicks, there was no hidden trap door, no cavalry right over the horizon. She was sitting in the CP, safe and sound in New Goa, while four of her men were facing their deaths.

"That's it, then," Monty said as the hammer-head broke through the wall, splitting the metal fabric. "Top, it's been an honor. Captain, you, too."

"Let's kick some ass," he said, turning to the other three, Esther's view bouncing a bit as Hank struggled to his feet.

"We've got Osprey-Two lifting off. ETA in 15 mikes," the FAC shouted out.

"Too fucking late," Top said.

"Hank, you ready? You've got the coup de grace."

"Sure thing, Monty. I'm ready."

"Wait!" Esther passed. "You can try to surrender again."

"They shot Hank last time we tried that. No, Captain, this is for keeps."

All attention was on the four Marines as the breach in the wall grew. Monty fired a burst through the hole, but that only delayed things a moment.

"Maybe we can recover enough for regen," someone said from behind Esther.

That was about the best they could hope for, Esther knew. She kept watching the feed with growing foreboding. She felt helpless, watching events unfold when there was nothing she could do.

With a horrendous screeching, the bulkhead gave way, almost crushing Doc Juno. Blue-uniformed figures started to dart in only to be cut down by the four team members. Three, four dropped. An explosion rocked the room, and the feed jerked despite the compensators. All four were still standing, but Sputter's avatar now joined Hank's as light blue.

Two more Uni soldiers tried to enter and were cut down.

"Think they can hold out?" the major asked to no one in particular.

Esther hadn't thought so, but with what looked to be six Unis down, she had a glimmer of hope that they would retreat. It wasn't as if the team was going anywhere, and they were proving to be a tough nut to crack.

That was dashed when the compartment erupted into smoke and flames. Hank fell to the ground, and it took a moment for his cam to pick up Doc down, too. Monty was leaning up against the wall, and Sputter was not in the field of vision.

All four avatars were now light blue, and Esther quickly switched to Sputter's feed. He was sitting, looking at the stump where his hand had just been. Esther switched immediately back to Hank's feed.

A mass of blue bodies rushed into the compartment. Some of them fell, to be trampled by those rushing behind them. In a mass of confusion that was hard to make out through the feed, Sputter, Doc, and Monty were killed, their avatars turning gray. Hank was the last one. Up against the back bulkhead, he rolled four small grenades to the middle of the compartment. Esther didn't even think the Unis noticed them as they shot and killed the Marine. He fell to the ground, his cam still capturing the scene. Three seconds later, view erupted into an even greater display of explosive power. It took a good twenty seconds for the compartment to clear enough for an image to be seen.

From deck level, it was hard to grasp the full scene, but there were bodies—and body parts—everywhere. Some of those parts belonged to Doc and the Marines, but most were in tatters of what had been Uni blue uniforms. The death of the four Federation warriors had come at a very, very expensive cost.

Several more Uni soldiers could be seen poking their heads through the breach, weapons ready. They edged out, looking in horror at the carnage. Another Uni with the insignia of a senior sergeant on his collar, walked up to what was left of Monty. With sure movements, he drew his sidearm, a bulky Wallen Python.

"That mother fucker!" Top said just as Esther realized what the soldier was doing.

She stood up, helpless.

The soldier aimed the big energy weapon at Monty's head and pulled the trigger. There was very little to see, but Esther knew what he'd just done. Monty's body had been ravaged, but there was always hope of a resurrection and regen. With his brain fried, that hope had just disappeared.

The sergeant walked over to Doc as he stared at the Python's readout. When it had recharged, he fried Doc's brain as well.

"OK, back to your stations. We're still fighting a battle out there," the colonel said to the entire CP. "Focus on your mission."

Esther couldn't tear herself away, though. She tried to switch the feed to Sputter again, but his cam was out. Back on Hank's she watched the sergeant disappear to where Sputter was, then reappear a few moments later, heading right to Hank. He stopped, so close that only his legs were visible in the feed. Esther held her breath when the soldier bent down and aimed the Python right at Hank's head.

And the feed was cut.

Gut-punched, Esther didn't know what to do. She struggled to find a degree of normalcy.

Esther turned to Top. He was bent over, elbows on his spread knees, and staring at the deck. He'd been up for close to 30 hours now. She'd relieved him several hours ago, but he'd stayed in the CP.

"Why don't you get out of here for awhile. Maybe get some sleep."

"You think I can sleep now? After that?"

"I need you alert. We've still got teams out there."

He looked like he was going to argue, but he nodded his head and stood up.

"The Wasp is almost on station. What do you want me to tell him, sir?" the FAC asked the CO.

Taking out the compartment wouldn't affect the four team members. There was no hope now for resurrection for any of them, so whatever the Wasp did now would do them no more harm.

To go through with the attack would only be revenge at this point, however. There was no real tactical or strategic value in doing so, and it would be expenditure of ordnance that might be needed later. The logical thing to do would be to recall the Wasp and save its efforts for another day.

All the Marines in the CP looked toward the CO to hear his answer.

"Carry on the mission," Esther said in a loud and clear voice.

Lieutenant Colonel Bertolucci stared at his Reconnaissance Platoon commander for a long moment while she held her ground, staring back.

Finally, he nodded, and said, "You heard her."

Top sat back down, and together they sat in silence, following the Wasp as it acquired the target and made its run. They sat in silence as the Mole Missile did its thing, burrowing into rock until it either ran out of fuel and detonated or hit open space and detonated. They sat in silence until the Wasp made a second pass and forwarded a damage assessment. The Mole had reached the compartment and demolished it.

Top Gann slowly stood up once again and said, "I think I'll try to get some sleep now. Call me if you need me."

Esther sat there for a moment, then keyed in First Team on her hadron handset.

"First, give me an update."

There was a hollowness in her heart that she didn't know how long it would last, but there was a war going on and she had a job to do.

# OMAHA

## Chapter 27

"I just thought, you know, that it would be more hands on," Esther said.

"You're too senior. Hell, I'm too senior. All we're here to do is to provide training and support for the teams," Top Gann said.

"But my father, when he was in recon, he was in the middle of the action. That's where he got his first Nova."

"Yes, we all know that," Top said. "But that was a different era. Now, we've got MARSOC, and that has split recon into the two groups. Here in battalion, we support the infantry. And that means we deploy in the teams. In MARSOC, we support the Corps, if not the Federation," he said, not telling her anything she didn't already know.

"Recon, Force Recon, Raiders, Rangers, Deep Surveillance, Special Operations, MARSOC . . . it seems like we change the name every few years. What kind of consistency is that?"

"Commando, Dragoons, Scouts; don't forget those. But to be fair, the Raiders aren't part of recon," the Top said.

"Not to bring up my father again, but yeah, I know. He helped stand up the Raiders when he was a captain. But in other militaries, in other times, what we call recon had all the names we just mentioned and more. My point is what we call something has an impact. How can we function when our very organization changes every time we turn around?"

The two had been having much the same conversation since their return from Saint Teresa. Esther's attitude was in a downward spiral. She hated being in a support billet, and losing Monty's team had been the final nail in the coffin to her morale.

"I should have tried for the Raiders. I'd be a company commander now."

"What, and not earned the crossed paddles you wear on your chest?

The Raider comment had been Esther's newest refrain, and she'd probably said it once a day for the last month. The Top's reply was equally as worn.

He did have a point about the crossed paddles, though. She wore the badge with pride. Not many male Marines had earned it and only 14 females. Esther was the second female officer, and she knew that was an accomplishment. But she was chafing at the bit. Each of her teams had gotten into combat on Saint Teresa while she and the Top sat back at the CP. No other Marines had been KIA, but four had been WIA with Grayback undergoing long-term regen.

But she was handcuffed. Esther wasn't going to the Raiders or anywhere else. Her tour with Recon wasn't close to being completed, and while there was cross-pollination between Recon and Raider Marines, the organizational commands were separate. Even after this tour, the Raiders would be a long shot. As a new captain, she'd be going to Tac 1 and then staff billet somewhere.

And she knew she was just bitching. Top was her sounding board, the one person with whom she could get things off her chest. She wasn't going to rock the boat. There were plenty of other junior officers who would kill to be in her position, and if she was going to be in support, then she was going to be the best support Marine she could be.

What she did know, however, was that once this tour was over, and once her staff tour was over, it was back to the regular infantry. Maybe she could wangle a PICS company to get that under her belt before she got promoted.

"Of course," the Top said, "there is one more option for you, if you were interested in getting back in the thick of things."

The Top had changed the script. He listened while Esther bitched, told her to be proud of what she'd accomplished, and Esther agreed until the next day when it all would repeat. Nowhere was there another option in their set lines.

She looked up at him, waiting to hear what far-fetched idea he might have. She'd be able to shoot it down within moments. Still, her interest was piqued.

"And what might that be, oh Master Sergeant Extraordinaire?"

"There is another part of the community where officers are operators."

Esther's interest vanished like a puff of smoke.

"Yes, MARSOC. I know. I also know that you have to be invited in after your first tour with battalion. I've told you, Top, that even if I was somehow invited, after my next tour, I am back with the infantry."

If Recon was the premier branch of the Corps, then MARSOC was the premier of the premier. To be assigned to MARSOC, there wasn't some ass-kicking school like RTC that had to be conquered. If a Marine got orders, he or she went to MSOC for three months for advanced training, and then was in, just like that. But getting the orders was problematic. A battalion recon Marine had to be invited in, and any such invitation came after first proving himself or herself in the battalion. A mysterious MARSOC "mafia" did the selections, which were always approved by HQMC.

"Occasionally, I repeat, occasionally, Marines are invited before their first tour is completed," he said as if discussing the weather or what he was going to have for lunch.

Esther looked up in surprise, though.

"Uh . . . interesting. But that would mean someone would have to know said Marine, or said Marine might have done something remarkable," she said, trying to keep her voice collected.

*Could it be possible?*

"Normally, yes. But there can be many reasons for an invitation."

"So why are you telling me this?"

*Just say it, Top. Say it!*

"Well, it so happens that you do know someone from the community. Yours truly," he said, sweeping his arm over his head as if conducting a regency bow. "And you will be offered an invite."

*Holy Christmas! How? Why?*

She gathered herself, cleared her throat, and asked, "Why am I being offered this opportunity?"

Top Gann hesitated as if gathering his thoughts.

"The truth, ma'am? Or do you want me to blow smoke up your ass?"

*Hell. He never says "ma'am." What's going on?*

"The truth, Top."

"Well, first, the decision wasn't unanimous. As you said, you haven't completed a tour in battalion yet, and you haven't done anything remarkable in the billet."

*It's not like I've had an opportunity.*

"But, you proved yourself in RTC, and you're a good officer. No one doubts that you can be an effective operator."

"But . . ."

"Someone who's served with you thinks you're too self-centered, too much out for yourself."

"What?"

Esther wanted to argue, to take issue with that, but she realized this was not the time for that.

"Others disagree. I disagree, if it matters to you. So did Gunny McNeill back at Prettyjohn. But beyond that, there are three reasons."

She was only somewhat surprised that the gunny would be involved. It made sense that the mafia keep track of what was going on at RTC.

"And these three reasons are what?"

"First, you are a woman."

"What? Why does that matter?" she asked, getting a little angry.

"It does matter. There is only one woman in MARSOC now, and she's been a great asset to her team for more reasons than she's a kick-ass warrior. But right now, too few women enter the pipeline. To have another Marine, and an officer at that, in MARSOC, could convince other kick-ass warriors to go to RTC."

Esther wanted to argue with that, but as much as she tried to preach gender-blindness, there was some truth to what the Top was saying. The Marines had adopted the old MARSOC designation for

179

more reasons than having a clandestine capability. MARSOC was an answer to the longer and better-established SEALs, and the Corps took every opportunity to tout its achievements when it could without compromising security. If she was in MARSOC, other women in the Corps would know that, and it could convince some of them to apply to RTC. She still had problems with the concept, but now wasn't the time to get into another long conversation on gender.

"And the second reason?"

"You are General Lysander's daughter."

If Esther had been surprised at his first reason, she was floored by the second.

"What the hell does that have to do with anything?" she asked, her voice rising.

"Almost the same reasoning. People will take notice if your father's daughter is a MARSOC Marine. It could possibly open up the bankbook, but it will certainly raise our profile."

"I thought MARSOC was supposed to be swift, *silent*, and deadly."

"Operators, yes. As a branch, maybe not."

"So if I'm supposed to be some MARSOC figurehead, then how can I be an operator? It would be hard for my team to get anything done with legions of paparazzi following me around."

Top smiled as he said, "Discussed and dismissed. We have methods to ensure that does not happen. MARSOC might be using you in the big picture, but you would be a real operator. Anything else could actually backfire on us."

This wasn't going as Esther had hoped after Top said she was getting an invitation. Esther wanted to succeed on her own terms, not for being a woman or having the right father. She was about to tell the Top to shove it up where the sun doesn't shine.

"And, pray tell, what is this third wonderful reason?"

"Because you're a good officer. Couple that with your background and your drive to succeed, the general consensus is that you *will* succeed. You're on the fast track to stars, and if you don't screw up in the meantime, the entire recon community would like to have one of its own in positions of authority. We don't seem to do so well with officers, you know."

"Yes, I know," she said in an even voice while staring at the Top. "So you think I'll make flag because of my father?"

"Not in the least, Captain. If you were a shitbird, or hell, if you simply weren't an outstanding officer, your father could be God Almighty and you'd never make major. But facts are facts. You are who you are, and because of that, you will be noticed. If you continue to excel, more senior officer will hear of you, and that will help you during the boards."

"But in the universe according to Lee Gann, that means if I screw up, everyone will know and it can't be hidden."

"True, so I suggest you don't screw up."

Esther's mouth dropped open as she looked at him, shocked at his statement. Then she broke out into a laugh, unable to help herself.

"OK, Top, maybe I'd better not screw up."

She got control of herself and sat back, right hand on her chin as she looked at her platoon sergeant. She hated the first two reasons he'd given her and barely tolerated the third, even if they all had a degree of truth or logic to them. The question she had to answer was whether she should accept the invitation or not. If it was right for her, if it was right for the Corps, did the reasons matter?

"And what do you think, Top? I'm asking you as my senior SNCO, not as a MARSOC Marine."

"It's kind of hard to differentiate between the two, Captain. I am who I am. I'll say this. I recommended you. First and foremost because I think you will advance MARSOC's mission. Second is because I think you need it. You are unraveling here, and becoming an operator might just save your sanity. But that right there is where I have my reservations.

"Being blunt, ma'am, your attitude sucks right now. I know, I know," he said, holding up a hand, palm out to forestall what she was going to say, "that you're just bitching to me. You don't show any of that to the team members. I don't mind listening to you. But just by voicing your feelings, you can make them stronger, reinforcing them in your mind and making them more real. MARSOC is different that battalion, but it's got its own share of bullshit. There's an old saying that the Marines never promised anyone a rose garden, and ain't that the truth.

"I went out on a limb for you, Captain. I know you are dedicated, but I know losing Monty and the others was hard on you. But you've got to put that behind you now if you're going to succeed and serve the Federation.

"So before you say yes—if you are going to say yes—I've got to know if you can do that. You need to go into this without reservation."

"And if I say no, you'll put the kibosh on the invitation."

He didn't bother to insult her intelligence by denying it. He just sat there, watching her.

She stared back at him as her thoughts raced. Her attitude had sucked lately. And if it did when she was a platoon commander, crying because her Marines were getting all the action, how would she be in a staff billet at some headquarters? She couldn't expect to have all command billets during her career. If she'd wanted to stay a fighter, she should never have accepted her commission.

She hated the reasons she was being made the offer. The first two were things completely out of her control, and even the third was only partially her own doing. Sure, she'd made it through RTC on her own, but she didn't think she'd done anything so far to earn the invitation.

She knew she could do it, though. She could excel in MARSOC. So maybe the ends justified the means. Who cared what the reasons were if it was the right decision to make? And suddenly, it did feel right to her.

"OK, Top. I accept. When do I start?"

# *UFSGS MANTA*

## Chapter 28

"Have you ever been on a Space Guard cutter before, ma'am?" the senior chief asked.

"Yeah, just last year on the General Habitats JTA," she said, looking at the ship with reservation. "This is a cutter, though?"

The senior chief laughed, then said, "That's more of an honorific, ma'am, if you know what I mean. We kinda call all Space Guard ships 'cutters,' for tradition like. But the *Manta's* a good ship. We'll get you to Elysium nice and cozy."

The "cutter" was barely 20 meters long, which for a space-faring vessel was tiny. She didn't see how the ship had room for her crew, much less her eight-man team.

"It's going to be a tight trip, Ess," Gunnery Sergeant Tim Ziegler said beside her as they looked at the screen display of the ship. The station's docks in this terminal were designed for Class C ships, those up to 200 meters in length. Even in the "baby" docks, the *Manta* looked like a child's toy.

"I hope everyone's showered," she said to Tim. "It looks like we'll be living in each other's armpits."

She turned back to the chief and asked, "Where's your commanding officer? I'd like to go over a few things before we pull out."

"You're looking at him, ma'am. Senior Chief Arleigh J. Carpenter, at your service."

"You? You're the CO?"

"Yes, ma'am, in the flesh. I know, you were expecting some high and mighty officer, like an ensign or maybe even a JG, but I can assure you, I have enough experience to take you were you need to go."

*Oh, a little sarcasm now, huh Senior Chief?*

While almost all Marine officers were pulled from the enlisted ranks, most of the Navy officers were commissioned directly from civilians. Esther didn't know much about the Space Guard, but it probably followed in line with the Navy, so she got his point.

"I'm sure your capabilities are more than adequate, Senior Chief. I was just surprised. I wasn't aware that the Space Guard had enlisted commanding officers," she said, stressing the word "enlisted."

Esther had not doubt that someone who'd made it to senior chief would be far better qualified than a brand new ensign, but his sarcasm grated on her. She hadn't thought her question was out-of-line.

"Well, ma'am, we're just the Space Guard. We don't get the funding that you and the Navy get, and we're short of personnel. So all of the Class 5 ships are given to command-screened chiefs. That's what this star means," he said, pointing to the small badge on his chest.

*Oh, this relationship is starting out great. Just ignore him, Esther. Let him get us where we need to go, and then it'll be good riddance.*

"Thank you for explaining that, Senior Chief. Are we ready to board?"

"Once I have your orders, then yes, ma'am."

*You know we're who we say we are*, she thought, but she pulled out her PA to tap his.

The orders were coded, so they would only transfer to his.

He made a show of reading them, then said, "Welcome aboard the *Manta*, ma'am. If there's anything I can do for you, just let me know."

He nodded to the FCDC security who keyed open the gate. Juliette 6 was a civilian station, but as the ship and passengers were Federation military, the FCDC trooper was taking boarding gate duties.

"Let's get everyone embarked," she told Tim, who turned and motioned to the other six team members.

Esther had been with the team for more than a month now, and she still was amazed at the feral grace with which the men moved. They might look like average civilians. Heck, Merl looked like he never left his gaming chair except to get more snacks. But as soon as any of them moved, there was no hiding that they were bad hombres. She couldn't put her finger on just what it was, but it was patently obvious to her. These men were deadly.

At least for the first time in her career, she'd had time to meet her Marines and work with them before being given a mission. One month might not seem that long, but it was better than she'd had with her previous three units.

Esther followed her team down the docking tube to the ship. Each Marine and Doc saluted aft and requested permission to come aboard. It seemed a little ridiculous—they didn't do that when boarding shuttles, and most of them were larger than the *Manta*. But traditions were important in the naval service, and technically, the tiny cutter was a man-of-war.

Esther wanted to retract that admission as soon as she passed through the hatch directly into the bridge. Four "taxmen" were standing by the control stations, watching the team enter. Along with the senior chief, that mean the tiny ship had a crew of five, unless someone was hiding somewhere—but the ship seemed hardly big enough for that. Esther could see into a cramped berthing space to the rear of the bridge, and beyond that was a featureless bulkhead.

"Where do we store our gear?" Tim asked.

"We've cleared out Locker B for you," one of the Space Guardsmen answered, pointing to the locker.

Doc Buren opened it up, then turned to the rest and said, "Uh, I don't think this is going to work."

Esther stepped forward to look inside. The locker was about a meter-and-a-half square. The team had much more gear than that.

"That's it?" Tim asked.

"Whatever else you have, just stack it up over there. Try and keep it out of the way," the taxman replied.

Tim looked over to Esther, and she said, "Just make do. We're not going to be on here long."

"What about our weapons?" Bug asked.

"There's our weapons locker," the same man answered, indicating a four-place rifle rack on the rear bulkhead. "That's our total armament, in fact."

The spots were filled with two M99-A1s and two older plasma rifles that Esther didn't even recognize. The A1s were in use even before her father's time, so these were pretty old. The Marines sometimes complained about getting hand-me-down equipment, but if the weapons were any indication, the Space Guard might have it worse.

"Did he say those are your total armaments?" Esther asked the senior chief.

"That he did. The *Drum* Class used to be armed, but the guns were pulled out 20 years ago. Made us too 'militaristic,' doncha know."

"But, your mission is to stop smuggling, right? That and piracy. What do you do if someone refuses to heave to for an inspection."

"Why, we politely ask them to comply, that's what we do."

"That doesn't make sense. If you've got no bite, no one's going to obey, not if they've got a cargo hold of smuggled goods."

"You're pretty smart for a grunt, ma'am," the senior chief said.

"Tell her about the *Bonito*, skipper," a petty officer said.

She'd been wondering about how to refer to the senior chief. "Captain" seemed odd, so it was good to hear the petty officer call him "skipper."

"What about the *Bonito*?" Esther asked.

"Five months ago, in the Praceous System, the *Bonito* did ask a ship to heave to for inspection. She was blown into her component atoms. Evidently, the ship didn't want to comply."

"And they ain't never been caught yet," the petty officer said, her voice full of venom.

That floored Esther. The Space Guard might be a cross between the Federation Navy and the Ministry of Revenue, but they did sail into harm's way. She couldn't think of any valid reason for them to do that unarmed.

"And they took out your ships' armaments because they made you look too militaristic?"

"Well, to be honest, only partly. The old Pattersons were not very effective, so some brainiacs thought better nothing than something that wouldn't do the job. We were supposed to get upgrades, but that nasty funding issue keeps getting in the way."

*Damn! Sucks to be you, I guess,* she thought, but feeling more than a bit of empathy for the senior chief and his crew.

"Where're we supposed to rack out?" Chris asked.

"We've got six racks in berthing. That's where the fabricator is, too."

"The coffee program's corrupted," one of the crew shouted out. "Don't even try it."

"So, we hot-rack it. If the racks are full, stretch out on the deck," the senior chief continued. "Space is tight, so please clean up after yourselves and try to stay out of our way."

"You heard the skipper," Esther said. "Try to get settled the best you can."

She didn't even try to put her pack in the locker. She plopped it on the deck against the bulkhead, lay down using it for a pillow, pulled her cover over her eyes, and tried to get some sleep.

*No berthing, no space for our gear, an unarmed ship, and now, no coffee. This is going to be a frigging great transit!*

# ELYSIUM

## Chapter 29

The air tore at Esther's wingsuit as she descended into the planet's atmosphere. There were none of the acrobatics she'd enjoyed the first time she'd dropped from a Space Guard cutter. This was business, and it was a night jump.

She'd been grateful that she'd already had a cutter jump. This was the first time for three of her team, and considering how small the cargo compartment had been—barely able to hold all eight members of the team—and jumping at night, it had been beneficial to already know what to expect.

The transit on the *Manta* had been uncomfortable, but as she'd thought about it, she realized it had been a smart move. The old cutter was small and unarmed. She doubted that any watchers would think she had any combatants on board. If the team was supposed to be clandestine, then using the *Manta* for the insert gave them a pretty good start to the mission.

Now they were on their own. There was no one there for support if things went to shit. And she had to admit there was a very reasonable possibility that it could.

Esther watched her display. Jumping over water at night made determining altitude by visual means almost impossible. There were no references on the water for scale, so she didn't even try.

She couldn't see any of her team, but their avatars showed up on her display. Everyone was close enough to rendezvous after landing, but not so close as to constitute a danger of collision either while in flight or after their chutes deployed.

This jump was a HALO, or High Altitude, Low Opening. They'd jumped at 15,000 meters, and with the wingsuit's ability to cover ground, they'd have flown close to 50 klicks to just offshore. If anyone had been tracking the *Manta* as it entered the atmosphere to land at the spaceport Patra, there would little be reason to connect it to the island of Naxos, the team's destination.

At 1,500 meters, Esther deployed her chute. By instinct, she looked around to make sure her team's chutes deployed, but of course, she couldn't see a thing in the darkness, which was the whole idea of dropping at night. Below and in front of her, she could see the darker mass of the island in the distance as it rose from the sea. She was already about even with the top of Mount Zeus, the highest peak on the island.

At 100 meters above the surface, Esther unlocked her harness and dropped her pack, which was still attached to a 25-meter long equipment line. Ten seconds later, first the pack hit the water, then she hit. As soon as her feet touched the surface, she lifted her arms and slid forward, freeing herself from the chute which drifted down behind her to settle in a heap.

Esther was still in her drop helmet. She was not planning to submerge more than three meters, so it would do as diving gear. She needed mobility, though. With quick, sure movements, she stripped off the "wings" between her arms and her side and between her legs, then pulled the fins off her back and put them on her feet. She hauled her equipment strap, pulling in her pack, and deflated the small air bladders allowing her to submerge the pack and attach it under her chest. Finally, she removed the tiny impellor motor from its hook and oriented herself to the shore.

Esther couldn't see any of the rest of the team, but their avatars moving toward her was reassuring. The jump wasn't particularly dangerous, but any jump at altitude had risk. No one had broken radio silence, and that was a good sign.

It took almost 20 minutes, but finally, the team was in their diamond formation. Esther keyed her impellor, and it slowly started to pull her through the water. Within moments, all of the team was moving along at a steady 3 knots. The ocean had been seeded, so Esther's body was illuminated with bio-luminescence, but at three knots, it wasn't too severe, and at three meters down, she didn't think any of it could be picked up from the surface.

The trip to shore was frankly boring. It was hard to keep alert while simply staring into the void. The impellor kept pulling her along, and she only had to make occasional corrections with her fins to keep her position steady.

Fifty-two minutes after starting out, Chris, who was the point of the diamond, stopped. He'd touched bottom. Once everyone followed suit, Esther started forward again, this time at one knot. Together, the eight Marines crept towards the shoreline. One-hundred meters out, Esther gave her clicker two sharp squeezes. The simple piece of metal clicked, something that could be heard under water for up to 200 meters. The four in the rear of the diamond stopped while the front four Marines kept moving ahead. Esther followed their progress as they reached the shore and exited the water.

Security was paramount. They could not be seen emerging from the ocean. There was less than an hour before daybreak, though, so they couldn't dawdle. Esther watched the time tick by, anxious to get moving. She felt vulnerable. She had a meter or so of water over her head, but the waves were rocking her, and she was afraid of a larger one pushing her forward and breaking the surface.

It was a full twenty minutes before the welcome triple click that indicated a clear beach. With a sigh of relief, Esther swam, then crawled to the surf line. With Doc, Merl, and Bug, the four waited until they saw the tiniest of flashes, something less than a firefly. All four got up and hurried across the beach and into the brush.

Chris was already out-of-sight somewhere forward of them, but Tim and Lyle had already dug a hole in the sand. The chutes and wingsuit strips would disintegrate in the ocean within hours, but the fins and O2 cylinders were more permanent. Esther's orders were to remove all trace of just how they'd arrived on the planet. The fins and cylinders went into the hole, followed by the wingsuit skeletons. Within moments, the cache was covered, and the team looked as if they could have arrived by any means. Nothing connected them to the cutter or the ocean.

Chris was waiting for them on the narrow coastal road, another 100 meters inland.

"No traffic."

"That doesn't mean we're not under surveillance," Esther said. "Stay alert, but we need to move."

The faint lightening of the sky to the west gave urgency to the need to move. The team split on either side of the road and headed west, towards the coming dawn. Using the road was not secure, but time was of an essence. They only had 20 minutes to reach their objective.

Esther had thought that the planet, which was one of the rare ones that rotated clockwise, would be more disconcerting. But as she watched the sky turn from black to gray, while she knew she was facing planetary west, her brain simply interpreted it as east.

The speed at which dawn approached, though, was surprising. The western sky was already turning shades of dark red-yellow when they reached the small, dilapidated concrete building on the high ground alongside the road. Within moments, her team had it surrounded, four of them oriented in to it and three facing outwards.

*Time to get it over with. We'll just see how it plays out.*

Esther dropped her pack and slung her M114 over her shoulder before leaving the cover of the brush and casually walking up to the front door of the squat building. She could feel the crosshairs on her back, and her hands kept twitching as if they wanted to take the weapon off her back and hold it ready.

She stopped in front of the door, took a deep breath, and pushed it open.

"Captain Blue, I assume?" a voice called out from inside.

"That's me," Esther said. "And you are?"

A tall, lanky man stepped out from the shadows wearing one of the oddest uniforms Esther had ever seen. The tunic was somewhat ordinary for a planetary militia. Under that, the man wore tight white leggings of some sort with black bands just below the knees. On his head was a red, brimless and featureless cap. And older version of Esther's own M114 hung from his shoulder.

"I am Lochagos Constantine Stavropoulis, First Hellenic Brigade. Welcome to Elysium."

## Chapter 30

"OK, let's have it," Esther told Chris.

All members of MARSOC teams were operators, but for a team to have the capabilities to complete their missions, all team members had secondary or tertiary skills. Staff Sergeant Chris de Brittan was the team's armorer/weapons expert, and Esther had assigned him to inventory the weapons of the "First Hellenic Brigade." She had to know just what they had.

"'Brigade is rather a lofty title," he said.

"No shit," Merl said, which Esther ignored.

"We've got 87 soldiers. Fifteen are officers, and I think six are SNCOs and 13 are NCOs."

"No, I told you," Lyle interrupted. "That 'lochias' rank, what you've got as staff sergeant, well, there's two kinds of them. One had two upside-down chevrons, and the other's got two of those chevrons and two upside-down rockers. The first one is a non-rate, and the second is a SNCO."

"Wait, they've got two ranks with the same name?" Esther asked.

"Affirm on that. I even had them write it out. L-O-C-H-I-A-S."

*How did I miss that in my briefing file?* Esther wondered.

"Well, if that's the case, then I've got, uh, let me see, only four SNCOs. Heck, they've got almost as many officers as NCOs and SNCOs combined. As far as weapons, they have 38 Dierdres in good working order with about 50 rounds apiece."

"'About?'" Esther asked.

"They're thrown loose in five crates. I was just guesstimating."

"OK, go on."

"Let me see. Quite a few of them have brought hunting rifles. I counted 52 of them, and probably 52 different makes. They have two Gentry 12.4 heavy machine guns with 5000 rounds between them, ten 20mm grenade launchers, an old Gentry MRL firing 15mm anti-armor rockets, and get this, a 40mm field gun that they made themselves. I'm not sure I'd want to be standing next to it when it's fired, but it looks wicked cool.

"That's about it for major weapons. They've got grenades, side arms, and demo gear, that I've forwarded to you. And oh, yeah, the Locha . . .lacho . . ."

"Lochagos, but he said to call him "captain," Esther said.

"Yes, him. He's got a sword. He showed it to me, all proud and stuff."

"Hah! He'll chop up any Hands who show up," Lyle said.

"Chop the hands off of the Hands," Merl said with a laugh.

Staff Sergeant Merl Miller, their explosives expert, thought himself a comedian. Esther ignored his interruption, afraid to encourage him, even if he usually could draw a laugh from her.

"No energy weapons at all?" Esther asked.

"No, none."

"So we've got 87 poorly armed and untrained soldiers, and I use that term facetiously, to train to defend this crazy planet. Easy-peasy," Tim said.

Esther understood his point. This mission, which had seemed so clear when it was given, was rapidly falling down the rabbit hole.

The facts were straightforward. Elysium was a second-gen world, settled by Athína. It already had a barely breathable atmosphere and existing oceans, but Athína had got it on the cheap due to its lack of heavy metals and more importantly, to its extremely rapid rotation. Each planetary day lasted just over 13 hours, well beyond the range where terraformers could bring it's rotation in line with the Earth-standard 24-hour interval.

The terraformers arrived and sterilized large portions of the main continent so that the native toxins wouldn't kill the modified crops the first settlers brought, they tweaked the atmosphere to make it more palatable to humans, and stocked the oceans with fish and mollusks. On land, native vegetation was dominant where humans hadn't taken over, but in the oceans, nothing could compete with Terran sealife.

The first wave of pioneers was from Athína, but the 13-hour days proved to be too much for many, and the numbers of volunteers dwindled. Anxious to recover their costs, the Athína assembly opened up the planet to immigration, and a second wave arrived, only to peter out within a decade.

Two hundred years later, the population stood at barely 15,000,000 souls. The original ethnic Greeks from Athína occupied the top rung of society, almost as a noble class. The rest made do, mostly with agriculture and fishing. Athína still provided some material and financial support, but the planet relied primarily on self-sufficiency.

That support was why Esther had to bring in her team in secret. Athína was a fiercely independent world, often at odds with the Federation within the UAM.[11]

Normally, Elysium and the Federation wouldn't cross paths. But the Right Hand of God changed that. Elysium was a large, sparsely populated planet. As the RHG expanded, it needed places of refuge, places to call home. Elysium had seemed a likely target for some of them. But the planet fought against humanity and Earth plants. Outside of the sterilized regions, growing crops was a losing battle. So to survive, the "Hands" who'd arrived took to small-level raiding of Elysium farms and settlements.

The Elysium assembly requested assistance from Athína, but the patron world didn't think the problem was serious enough to send more resources to the planet. As the raids became bolder, the Elysium speaker prime travelled to Earth and petitioned the chairman of the government that was taking the strongest stand against the RHG: the Federation.

The Council was not about to send combat units to another government's world, but it was not above improving its influence, particularly when it might eventually stick a finger in the eye of an annoying little planet. So it agreed to send, in secret, a team of trainers to both survey the military needs of the planet and to train the trainers, creating a cadre that could upgrade the planet's existing military.

---

[11] UAM: United Assembly of Man

Elysium had six "brigades," and Constantine had assured her that the First Hellenic was the finest. Esther's team had been on the planet for about 15 hours, and night was already falling again. In that short period of time, she'd come to the conclusion that the planet needed far more than what she and her seven men could provide.

## Chapter 31

Two weeks later, Esther wasn't sure if they even made a dent in training the brigade. The individual soldiers seemed eager enough, but they'd been treating the brigade as a dress-up social club, not an actual military organization. There was nothing to build on—she had to start from ground zero.

One of the first major roadblocks had been the so-called uniform the soldiers wore. Most of the men wore a hodgepodge of military blouses of various kinds. On their legs almost everyone wore white leggings called *boudoiri* and white socks called *periskelides*. The socks were held up by *kaltsodetes*, a kind of traditional garter. A handful of men and all ten women wore white blouses and skirts called *foustanela*, which Esther had been told too many times to count had 400 pleats, one for each year of Greece's occupation by the Ottomans. If those weren't bad enough, everyone wore the red fez, called a *farion*.

Constantine had argued when she told him that needed to change. He stressed that this was part of history, part of what bound them together. Esther had to remind him that they weren't re-enactors. If they were going to fight the RHG, the Hands wouldn't give a flying fart about history. And he was making it easier on the Hands by giving them nice targets with red fezzes that provide no protection at all.

It had taken three days of constant pressure, but finally, Constantine had relented. It had taken him another day to convince his troops, though. Some of the most vocal soldiers arguing had names that didn't sound Greek, which Esther thought was odd.

The uniforms were a minor issue, however, when compared to their military skills. They essentially had none. Their idea of an assault was to charge the mighty Ottomans across an open field, shouting at the tops of their lungs, which they had shown the team on the third day.

Constantine had been rather embarrassed about their demonstration. From conversations with him, she knew he had a working knowledge of basic warcraft. But for a social club, actual tactics took a backseat to theatrics.

They weren't total incompetents. Bob had reported that most of the soldiers were adequate marksmen with their hunting rifles, with a few being excellent shots. Sergeant Bob Burnham was the team's designated sniper, a one-time bronze medal winner in the Federation Military Distance Shooting Tournament. If Bob was impressed, then so was Esther.

Their problem was a lack of training and proper equipment. Given a year, she could mold them into a proper fighting unit. The problem was, she didn't think they had a year.

She'd sent back two reports. One detailed the results of the equipment survey and a request for 100 U-22's, the gold standard of militia rifles. Made in the Confederation, the rifles were almost indestructible, and the barrel and housing could be switched between firing a standard 6.44 or 7.62 jacketless round or a 2mm hypervelocity dart. Nowhere near as accurate as the Marines' weapons, they were never-the-less durable, easy to use, and probably more than enough for the RHG fighters. The weapons, ammo, uniforms, and other supplies were in the pipeline with an expected arrival in three weeks.

The second report was a more candid assessment of the brigade, and it was not complimentary. Included was her unvarnished opinion that she would not have accomplished the mission in the three months allotted to her.

She was aware that her mission was more of a statement of support for Elysium than anything else, but she felt obligated to leave with a unit that could not only stand off the RHG but train others to do the same.

# Chapter 32

Esther lengthened her stride letting the slope of the mountain help her chew up the ground. Sergeant Lyle Jones was many things a recon Marine should be, but a cross-country runner was not one of them. Esther had paused at the top of the 800-meter Mount Zeus to encourage the soldiers as they clambered up the two-meter tall jut that created the peak and touched the cairn of stacked stones laid by years of tourists, but now on the way back down, she had her sights set firmly on the sergeant, who was Tail-End Charlie among the team.

Tim had instigated the every-other-day run to not only get the soldiers in shape but to instill a sense of unit. Esther needed it just as much. The crazy 13-hour "day" had her all kinds of messed up. With the diurnal cycle so out of whack with Earth's and eons of human evolution, the citizens just kept the entire planet on Greenwich Mean Time. That meant that one "day," Esther was going to sleep in the dark, and the next day, she'd be going to sleep as the sun came up.

The soldiers didn't seem to have a problem with it, but Esther was having a hard time adjusting. Running full-out seemed to help. She felt as if she was purging her body of Elysium craziness.

She closed the gap between Lyle and her, passing two soldiers until she was on his ass. The path at the upper reaches was narrow, and Esther waited for an opening to make her move. She juked to the right to pass him, but he juked as well. She darted to the left, and again he blocked her, his arms out at a 45-degree angle as he ran.

He was breathing heavily—and loudly—but he didn't slow down. Esther stepped off the trail and in her best parkour manner, started running on the slope. She thought she was going to pass him before he jumped up on the slope and shouldered her aside.

*Oh, it's on, Lyle-my-lad!*

She ran out of real estate and had to jump back to the trail. Coming around the switchback, she feinted to the inside, which she knew he was expecting. He moved to block her, but she let her centripetal force take her wide, and she scooted past him, almost going over the edge, but maintaining her footing.

"You're going to have to do better than that, Green!" she shouted, using his mission name. "Last one of the team owes 200, you know!"

"I know, I know," he said between wheezes.

He slowed down and was quickly out of sight.

Esther continued to run, passing several more soldiers who were more polite in getting out of her way. The view up here was pretty amazing, she had to admit. Naxos was one of ten islands stretching out 60 km from the mainland. It had been readied for agriculture, as had the other islands, but a lack of immigrants meant they had stayed uninhabited. Their remoteness made the islands a logical place for the training. Five kilometers to the east was Santorini. Thirty klicks to the south was Mykonos, the largest of the islands, but one where tourists sometimes put in. Between Mykonos and Naxos was the oddly named Jones Island, which, of course, Lyle claimed as his own. Esther had asked Constantine why there was a "Jones" amidst all the old Greek names, and he hadn't a clue.

She came around the last switchback, and Doc Buren was stopped along one of the soldiers who was sitting on the ground.

"Everything OK, Doc?" he asked, slowing down.

He waved her on, "Just a scrape. He'll be fine."

"You'd better hurry up. Lyle's just behind me."

Rules were rules, and last team member in was last team member in no matter the reason. Esther had been hit on the first run when she'd brought up the rear with the laggards, and the rest of the team had enjoyed counting out her 200 pushups.

Running downhill was exhilarating but hard on the legs. As the ground leveled out to the camp, Esther just stretched out into a loping run. It was 1920GMT, despite the sun having risen just prior to the start of the run, and Ester felt she could finally get a good sleep. She was beginning to suck a little wind when she spied a familiar figure ahead.

With only 500 meters more, she'd have a hard time catching up to him, but she had to try. She forced her legs to pump faster, and she closed the distance. Still, it took an all-out sprint to pass Constantine 20 meters from the finish. She put her hands on her head as she tried to walk it off.

"I didn't see you coming," Constantine said between breaths. "I would have run faster."

"Would of, could of. All I can say is Marine captain, one, Hellenic lochagos, zero. Ba-boom!"

"Next time, I'll crush you."

"Only in your dreams."

Both of them returned to the finish to cheer on the rest. By ones, twos, and threes, soldiers crossed the finish line, some collapsing in the dirt. One of the brigade's SNCOs, a man named Mamout, had dragged up a bucket of water and was offering ladles to the finishers. Mamout was one of the oldest, if not the oldest soldier on the island, yet he'd finished the run, had fetched the water, and looked none the worse for wear.

"Here comes your two," Constantine said.

Pounding down the straightaway, Doc was over-taking Lyle. Lyle was puffing like a steam engine, but he just couldn't get his tree-trunk legs moving fast enough. Doc passed him as if he were standing still. To Esther's surprise, though, Doc stopped just short of the finish and looked back to Lyle.

"Come on, Doc. No gimmies," Bug said.

Lyle started to speed up, but then he slowed, coming to a stop in front of Doc, who swept an arm urging Lyle forward.

"Nah, you beat me. Go ahead."

"Oh for St. Gladys' dirty drawers, just cross the line," Merl shouted out.

Doc nodded, and then walked over the finish. Lyle followed and immediately started his push-ups.

Lyle was a big boy—not tall and with short legs, but a big boy none-the-less. He started putting out push-ups like a machine. No one even counted. Lyle could do them in his sleep.

It took another twenty-minutes for the last person to cross, one of the junior officers on straggler duty pushing an exhausted soldier in front of him. The lieutenant gave Constantine a thumbs up.

*Epilochias,* or Master Sergeant Kang, started a head count while Esther helped herself to some of Mamout's water.

"Any word on the ammo?" Constantine asked.

"Nothing yet. I'll call again after chow."

The first supply run had arrived six hours ago under the cover of darkness. The uniforms were there, the rifles were there, but the ammo was missing. The lone fisherman who'd delivered the shipment knew nothing about anything else and had been anxious to get off the beach.

"I'm kind of anxious to try them out."

"That Koehler you have isn't a bad piece of gear," Esther said.

"So says the lady who has the latest model of it."

"Still, it's a good weapon for an officer. Bullpup design so its overall length is less. Great for self-defense, and it won't tempt you to get involved in the firefight."

"Captain Blue, we've got another problem," Tim said, walking up with Master Sergeant Kang.

"How many this time," Constantine asked, his voice heavy with defeat.

"Four, sir. We had the full head count when we started."

"And Michaelides' boat's gone," Kang added.

"Rebeth? She left? I've known her father my entire life. Hell, I've known Rebeth her entire life."

"I know, sir. And I'm sorry about that. But maybe we're better off with a solid core. We can build on that," Kang said.

"You're probably right. You're probably right.

"Well, I'm not too proud to admit that I'm beat. Mount Zeus will haunt me in my dreams. Captain Blue, Gunnery Sergeant Orange, shall we off to dinner?"

Tim caught Esther's eye, but neither said anything before turning to follow the brigade commander.

This was the third desertion in two days. After the first two had left, sailing to sea in broad daylight, Master Sergeant Kang had wanted to immobilize all the boats that had brought them to the island. Constantine had refused, saying that the brigade was volunteer, and no one would be kept on the island against his or her will.

Which was a noble sentiment, Esther thought. But also a foolish one. Their security relied on secrecy. Until they were combat ready, they were vulnerable, and they were far, far, from ready.

## Chapter 33

Esther slowly walked up the ravine, carefully choosing her foot placement, her senses on full alert. She was sure there were eyes on them, probably coming from the small copse of trees just ahead. She held up a hand, fist clenched, and the small patrol froze. The tiniest movement caught her eye, and a smile creased the corner of her mouth.

*Got you!*

She brought her hand down, and the patrol moved forward again, slowly making its way around dog-sized boulders that had rolled into the ravine over the years. Her eyes darted back and forth analyzing the terrain, working out her possible courses of action.

As she came abreast the leading edge of the trees, shouts of "Bang, bang!" filled the air.

"Buda-buda-buda!" Esther shouted, her M114 at waist level and sweeping the treeline

She spun on her heels and bolted in the opposite direction, climbing the small rise and over it to cover. Tim landed beside her, followed almost immediately by Constantine.

"I see what you mean, now. I was able to pick out the ambush before they sprang it," Constantine said, his voice full of excitement.

"Cease fire, cease fire," Bob shouted out from the ravine, where he'd remained while the rest of the patrol had rushed for cover.

Tim blew on the tip of his extended forefinger and made a show of holstering his hand.

"Don't forget 'Clear and lock your weapons,'" he added, which would normally be the next order made, but in this case, would be wasted breath.

Without rounds, even blanks, the soldiers had been relegated to shouting "bang, bang" over the last week, so there was nothing to "clear." Esther knew that simply carrying their new weapons was a benefit, so the soldiers were using them for training. At some point, however, they really needed to fire them.

Esther, Tim, Constantine, and three of the other brigade officers climbed back over the rise.

"OK, where to start. Who picked this ambush site?" Bob asked

"I did, Staff Sergeant Gray," Lieutenant Hansen said, stepping forward.

"Oh, sucks to be you," Tim said quietly, but not quietly enough as Constantine had to choke off a laugh.

Mild-mannered Bob Burnham, Staff Sergeant "Gray," could flay the skin off a student with wickedly aimed words. Esther walked closer to enjoy the show.

"And why did you choose this position?"

"Because, the ravine was a likely avenue of approach, and this was the only position that gave my squad cover."

"And if this patrol," he said, arm sweeping to encompass Esther and the others, "was only the lead element of a battalion?"

"He's setting him up," Tim whispered. "Watch the master at play."

Esther tried to shush Tim by waving her hand. She wanted to listen, and she didn't want to miss anything.

"Why, uh . . . I'd let them pass?"

"What's the frontage of a battalion?"

"Uh—"

"Where's your egress route. Are you a mountain goat? You can climb that sheer cliff behind you?"

"No. I mean, of course not. But—"

"But what? You think a battalion is going to meekly walk in file up the ravine and never be curious about these trees? You are trapped, that's what you are. I think . . . ."

"Sir, sir!" a runner came stumbling up the hill, eyes on Constantine.

Esther turned to see, forgetting Bob for a moment, who seemed to have things well in hand. She'd have Chris sit down with the lieutenant later and debrief him in a more academic setting."

"What is it, Kristos?"

"We've got boats coming, lots of them."

"Who are they?" Constantine asked. "I don't know anything about that."

Esther didn't like the note of concern in his voice.

"We don't know. Hassan flashed the interrogatory, but they didn't reply."

Esther looked around the ravine. Fifty meters ahead, the bulge of a finger jutted up a hundred meters or so before the spine rose to the peak.

"Follow me," she said as she broke into a run. Her thighs ached as she pushed her body up the steep slope, hands scrabbling to keep her upright. It took a long two minutes before she reached the top of the finger, and she scanned the deep blue waters in front of her. The sea was featureless. She turned towards the east, and her heart fell. At least 40 boats were between Santorini and Naxos, all heading right at them.

"They're not yours, are they?" she asked Constantine.

He slowly shook his head and said, "It seems as if the Right Hand of God doesn't want us combat capable."

"It looks like someone who deserted worked for the enemy," Tim said. "They knew we are here, and I'm betting they know how many of us there are and what we have to defend ourselves with."

Esther's mind was racing. Only a few of the soldiers and all of the team were armed. The rest of the soldiers were carrying empty weapons that were now little more than clumsy clubs. If those were RHG out there, and she had no reason to doubt Constantine, then clubs wouldn't do them much good. But they still had the old weapons at the camp. They were on the wrong side of the mountain, but if they ran, they might be able to reach the camp before the RHG landed. After that, she'd have to play it by ear.

"Recall everyone back to camp now and arm up with whatever we have there. And I mean now!

"It looks like were as ready as we're going to be. Ares is the Greek god of war, right? So let's get ready to render him honor!"

## Chapter 34

With a final swipe of her fingers, Esther sealed the armor pocket on her right shin. She stood and twisted her body in several directions, then jumped up and down. Her bones were in place, giving her a comforting feeling. The armor inserts, the "bones," were light and flexible while still giving kinetic protection. Esther liked their weight on her—in her mind, wearing her bones felt like getting hugged by a guardian angel.

She looked up to catch Constantine's eyes on her. She felt guilty having armor when he didn't, but it wasn't as if she could give him hers. Each section of bones was fitted to her as well as the armor sleeves in her utilities, her "skins."

Reaching down, she connected her hadron handset to the optithread fiber, making the handset hands free. With a simple blink, she could switch from the team comms to the handset.

On the run to the camp, she'd called up Major Filipovic, her company commander, back on Omaha and gave him a report. She couldn't slave him to her combat AI, but she could keep him on the line and up to date. Hopefully, he was trying to see if he could get any assets to them. Esther already knew that would be a dead end, though. There was nothing in the system, and nothing could get there until long after this battle was decided. If they were going to survive the coming day, it was up to them: her team of seven Marines and a corpsman and 81 barely-trained soldiers.

Constantine had reported to his command chain, but he didn't think anything could be mobilized to help them. There were on their own.

"Dragonflies and Gnats are away, Blue," Tim said. "Receiving now."

Esther blinked up the feed of the first Dragonfly. The team had three of the larger surveillance drones, each one about 10 centimeters long, and ten of the tiny Gnats, each half a centimeter in diameter. The Dragonflies were quick and maneuverable, and the Gnats were almost impossible to detect.

"You rea . . . dy?" Esther asked Constantine, faltering mid-word in surprised that he was strapping his sword around his waist. "What are you going to do with that?"

"This is for them," he said, patting his Koehler. "But I can't I just can't leave my *xiphos* for those bastards. This was my father's, which he passed to me."

A ceremonial sword was hardly something to carry into battle, but it wasn't worth arguing about. If he felt better with it, then that was his choice.

Dragonfly #1 was just zooming up to the beach. Several of the fishing boats had already stopped just offshore, and men and women had debarked and were making their way to the beach. Any hope that these were simple picnickers was washed away. All were armed, and all wore the payot in front of their right ears, the mark of the RHG. Ever the pragmatists, they could cut the sidecurls if needed, but when they could, they preferred to fight with payots displayed as an affirmation of their devotion to their god.

Their pragmatism made them a much more dangerous enemy than the SevRevs. Their fanaticism was no less than the group that spawned them, but while the SevRevs welcomed their own deaths and the End of Days, the RHG wanted to rid the world of all the "Fallen," or non-adherents to their beliefs. Once all the Fallen had been eliminated, the universe would transform into heaven.

As the RHG did not demand their members' deaths, it was not surprising that many SevRevs shifted to what had initially only been an offshoot, but was now the largest sect among the religious determinists roaming human space.

Esther tried to count the enemy, both coming ashore and still in boats. Without Federation satellites and their high-powered surveillance suites, both she and her little combat AI had to use the Dragonfly feed. She estimated that there were 450 of them, and her AI had 431. Elysium Intel had the total RHG on the planet at 300 men, women, and children, so their figures were obviously off by more than just a bit.

"Blue, we're ready. What're your orders?" Tim asked.

This was not going to be a MARSOC mission of subterfuge and stealth. The enemy was on the island, coming to kill them. This was going to be infantry battle, force against force. She had to think in those terms.

Esther knew it was too late to try and evacuate Naxos. It had been too late from the moment she'd see the oncoming flotilla. Still, she switched to Dragonfly #2, which she had climb to provide an overview of the entire island. To her surprise, there was already movement in the cove that sheltered the 13 remaining boats that had brought the brigade from the mainland. The RHG boats were another 800 meters farther along the beach.

She zoomed in, and the sour taste of bile filled her mouth as she recognized who they were.

"You've got six of your men boarding the go-fast," she told Constantine.

"What? Are you sure?"

"Sure as I'm standing here." She zoomed in closer, and said, "Lieutenant Lekas, and there's the guy who has the egg shop . . . uh, and that looks like Sergeant Roarke . . ."

"They must have run directly to the boat basin," Master Sergeant Kang said.

"That's Giscard, the one pushing the prow out," Tim said, slaving off her feed. "And Peony what's-her-name."

"Peony Truman," a dejected-sounding Kang said. "That's her boat."

"And, oh, Master Sergeant Hallas."

"Fuck Hallas. Fuck all of them," Master Sergeant Kang said.

Esther zoomed back out. What was done was done, and she needed a course of action to face the RHG fighters. The six might be leaving, but getting the rest of them off the island wasn't going to happen. They had to stop the Hands or make it so hot for them that they quit the attack.

She should have thought of this earlier and made contingency plans on what she'd do if they couldn't flee and they didn't have their ammo yet. With all of the brigade and all of their ammo, Esther's plan if they were attacked had centered around stopping a landing before an enemy came ashore, and if that failed, to consolidate around Mount Zeus.

Stopping them from landing was no longer an option, but Mount Zeus would still give them their most defensible position. It would be nice to be able to canalize them, though, and attrite their forces before they started climbing.

"Captain, I take it I have operational command?" she asked.

"Please, Captain Blue. My soldiers will do as you order."

"Very well. If the Hands follow form, they'll advance in a line, until they figure out our defenses and then maneuver to exploit what they perceive to be our weak points."

Assuming what an enemy would do could be shortsighted, and there was little enough data to see how the RHG had acted in past battles. They'd never attacked a Federation force larger than a platoon, preferring to move against planetary militias or police forces—or better yet, unarmed civilians. But from what Esther had studied, they hadn't yet shown much in the way of variation.

"Staff Sergeant Gray, take the two HMGs and a squad for security and set up on the overlook," she told Bob. "The guns can range across the breadth of the island from there, but I want you to focus to their right flank. Do what you can to augment the guns, but wait until they fire before you start picking off targets."

"So they commit to the north and the Vomit Gorge," Tim said, nodding.

The Vomit Gorge initially looked like a path up the mountain, but it narrowed down to a steep, space-constrained climb. The Marines had led the brigade up the gorge on runs twice, and each time, more than a few of the soldiers had lost their lunch in the process.

"They can still circle and come up from the southwest, so once they split to the north, displace the guns to that abutment there," she said, highlighting the position and sending it to Tim while pointing with her hand to where she meant for the soldiers. "If they pass the gorge to circle around, try and dissuade them.

"Pink and Green," she told Merl and Lyle, "take whoever you need and our demo. I want the upper end of the gorge mined. You've got probably less than an hour. Save, uh, save half of what you've got. When Orange and the HMG teams pull back, I want the trail up the mountain mined. You're running out of time, so go now."

Merl ran to the cache of demo while Lyle went to grab some soldiers.

"And if they don't go to the north?" Tim asked.

"You've got 5,000 rounds. Burn them to take out as many as you can and then displace back to the rest of us."

"Aye-aye."

"Chris, that MRL, it's got a remote firing capability?"

"Yes, I've already programmed it to our AIs."

*He did? I didn't notice, but good initiative.*

"Three salvos, right?"

"All at once or three?"

She pulled up the overlay, selected three spots, and pushed them to him.

"Target these three?"

He paused a second as he checked her orders, then asked, "The third one?"

"Just do it. And make it look abandoned."

"Roger that," Chris said before rushing off.

Esther knelt and wiped a clear spot in the dirt before making a quick sketch of Mount Zeus. It wasn't great, but without displays for everyone, it was the best she could do.

Mount Zeus was the major geographic feature of the Naxos, rising from the western half of the island. The north and east sides rose precipitously, while the south had a more gradual slope that ended on the southern shoreline. To the west, part of the face had fallen years ago, leaving a 180-meter cliff. The summit consisted of a relatively flat crown, a single small jut achieving the 814-meter elevation. There was a trail leading up to the summit, starting at the southeast, meandering back and forth, the last loop running from near the end of a gorge cut into the north face and running around the mountain's shoulder back to the southwest side where it bent around and onto the crown. Esther couldn't get all of those details into her dirt-scrapings, but they'd all run up the trail six times now, and they'd just been training on the eastern face, so this wasn't covering new ground.

There was an explosion in the distance, and Esther looked up. Out in the water, a small fire was burning. She pulled up the overhead feed and sent it back 30 seconds. On the display, the go-fast was escaping, its wake an arrow pointing to its position. There was a flash from one of the RHG boats, then several pops of light making their way to the go-fast. The speedboat was quick, but not as quick as a missile. It hit the boat and exploded, sending pieces of go-fast flying in all directions.

"Well, they have missiles," she said. "One less now, though."

RHG forces tended to be lightly armed, so if they had missiles, that was not good news. It didn't change her overall plan, though. With a larger island, more cover, and a better-trained force, she'd probably try and play hide-n-seek with the RHG, hoping to either wear them down or last long enough for major reinforcements. With the resources at hand, however, she felt that a strong defense, making the best use of the terrain, offered her the best chance to make it out of this alive. The situation still looked very bleak, but it was what it was, and it was up to her to give the best shot they had to survive the coming hours.

"OK, get close to where you can see. This is what we're going to do . . ."

## Chapter 35

The HMG's were singing their duet, the call of the first answered by the response of the second, together becoming more than the sums of their parts. The unbroken stream of fire tore into the Hands as they emerged from the coastal scrub, dropping a handful while the rest scrambled for cover. Slowly but surely, the HMGs were herding them to the north, all the while winnowing their numbers. Esther thought at least 20 of them had been killed or wounded, which was an impressive number for what she thought was about half of the two guns' 5,000 rounds.

Hands on the south side of their line crowded those to the north as they tried to get out of the line of fire. Esther wished she had some mortars to drop on their heads as they bunched up.

*Might as well wish for a battery of 155's or a flight of Wasps*, she thought.

Bob had probably picked off another 10 or 15 with his Windmoeller. The sniper rifle had a max effective range of 2800 meters, and the Hands on the south side of their line were only 800 to 900 meters away, so it was a turkey shoot for him. If someone started to move to the south to get out of the HMGs' line of fire, Bob dropped him with the .308, 172-grain, tef-sleeved round before others followed in herd mentality.

"It's working," she told Constantine who could see her Dragonfly feed. "They're shifting left. Your gunners are pretty good."

Due to the paucity of ammo, Esther hadn't seen the gun teams operate, but she had to give them props. Their fire discipline and targeting was excellent.

"They don't call us the Hellenic Weekend Gun Club for nothing," the captain said. "We do like to shoot, especially the HMGs."

"Merl, what's your status?" she passed, turning her attention away from Constantine.

"It's rough in here, Ess. We got four surprises emplaced, but it's tough going."

"I'd say you've got 30 minutes max. Whatever you have by then will have to do. Don't get yourself trapped there."

"Roger that."

Esther focused back on her display a moment before the Dragonfly feed cut out.

"Crap! That's the last Dragonfly," she said.

One by one, the three drones had been shot down, which meant that there were at least some energy weapons among the Hands—and not only that, but a way for the enemy to spot the drones. As far as she knew, this was an increase of capability never before seen from them.

"Switching to the Gnats," she passed on the team net as she flicked through the nine remaining working feeds. The Gnats were much harder to spot, but they were even more vulnerable to energy weapons, even from side lobes, and the resolution of their feeds was not as good as their larger cousins'. One of the Gnats was hovering over the wider path into the Vomit Gorge, so she panned it forward to watch for the Hands.

There was a break in the point/counterpoint of the HMGs, then a quickly aborted string of fire.

"The guns are out of ammo," Bob told her.

"Pull the firing assemblies and retreat back to our pos," she passed.

She doubted that the RHG soldiers had the HMGs' 12.4 ammunition, but better safe than sorry. Without the assemblies, the guns were useless.

"What about me? It's still a target-rich environment."

Esther hesitated a moment. Bob was a stereotypical sniper in that she knew he'd stay there if she let him, happily picking off Hands. But another five or ten kills wouldn't swing the battle, and it would leave him exposed. He didn't even have a spotter with him for security.

"I've lost the Dragonfly feed. What does it look like they're doing?"

"Most are moving up the north side. I've got a few stragglers on the south, but not many. I wouldn't say they're committed to the north, though. They could shift back, at least some of them."

It wasn't that imperative that all of the Hands assaulted the mountain from the north. A few coming up the gentler slope to the south wouldn't matter much. Still, it would take some of her soldiers to deal with that. She had a feeling that even if most of the RHG fighters initially climbed the mountain at the north side, they would scoot around once the hit the trail from the east as it looped around to the south and to the summit.

"Take out who you can and try to keep the rest pushing to the north, but you've got five minutes, no more. Keep the soldiers with you, and after five, I want all of you back here. We've got more than a few firing positions up here to keep you busy."

"Out of ammo on the HMGs. I'm pulling back the gun teams and the squad," she informed Constantine.

"How much damage did they inflict?"

"Between them and Gray? Maybe 30 or 40."

"So we only have 360 left? Child's play."

Esther heard the sarcasm in his voice, but if she had a platoon or two of Marines with their full combat load, while it wouldn't be child's play, she'd be cautiously optimistic about success. The RHG had wiped out a Marine platoon on Saint Grigori's Ascension, and probably with fewer fighters than what face them now, but that platoon had been trapped in an untenable position. Mount Zeus was a much better piece of terrain to defend. The west side was protected by the 180-meter sheer cliff, the south side was an open climb with little cover, and the north and east were steep and rough. The only quick way up the last 150 meters was using the trail. Anywhere else and the Hands would be fighting the mountain as well as the brigade.

Esther heard the crack of Bob's Windmoeller sniper rifle down the mountain.

*Keep smacking them down, Bob.*

If it were her firing, she'd take the Kyocera, the Marine Corps' sniper mag-rifle, she thought as Bob fired again. The hypervelocity darts were almost silent, and up to about 2000 meters, the rifle was more accurate than its slug-throwing counterpart. There were sniper rifles from all over human space that he could have used as well. There was always the Confederation's Pilum 42, she knew, and that was a good choice. But he liked the standard Windmoeller . . .

*Now's not the time to debate sniper rifles, Esther! Focus.*

The problem was that at the moment, she wasn't doing much of anything. Tim and Master Sergeant Kang were working on the choke points, Chris and Doc were supervising the construction of fighting positions, Merle and Lyle were still emplacing the booby-traps, Bob was sniping targets of opportunity, and Bug was preparing a little surprise should any Hands come up from the south. She, the team leader, was standing on the military crest with Constantine, simply observing.

If she had supporting arms, she could be registering targets and calling for fire. If she had air, she could be directing strikes. With a Navy ship in orbit, she'd have her hands full directing fire. But she had none of that, and her nervous energy was mounting.

She wheeled and strode to where three squads were digging in.

"Digging in" was being generous. Chris and one of the soldiers from the hastily organized First Platoon were shirtless as the two horsed around the commercial compacter, trying to dig fighting holes. The compacter was not intended as a military piece of gear, but it had been part of the construction equipment the brigade had brought. Its main purpose was to compact the ground as a foundation for tents or shelters. The compacter worked by decreasing the molecular space of anything in its beam. By changing the focus of the beam, it could switch from simple compaction to "digging" a hole as the molecules of the dirt or rock collapsed upon themselves. Esther did a quick count. Only five holes had been dug over the last 20 minutes.

"We need to step it up," she said.

"It's the ground here. All rock," Chris said.

"I know, but time's getting short. Just do the best you can."

A series of cracks sounded from the other side of the crest, followed by a cry of pain. Doc Buren looked up from where he was pointing out fields of fire to two of the soldiers.

"Keep up with what you're doing," she told him. "Let Doctor Willis handle it."

Doctor Willis was Sergeant Willis, whose day job was a physician. Doc Buren rightly took pride in his medical abilities, but Willis was a full MD, so he should be able to handle the situation. Doc Buren was frankly more valuable at the moment as a warrior, not a healer.

Another series of cracks sounded out as RHG rounds impacted on the rocks on the east side of the crest. Tim was already in motion with Master Sergeant Kang on his heels as they rushed to where panicked soldiers were trying to figure out what to do.

"Pull back," he shouted, grabbing one of the lieutenants by the collar and yanking him back to where he was out of the line of fire. Another one of the Second Platoon soldiers started downhill, which still kept him exposed, and Esther darted forward to grab him, spinning him around and sending him to the west side of the crest. Another scattering of rounds impacted around the summit, and one round made a nasty buzzing as it whizzed by her head.

All 15 or so soldiers were up and running for cover. Esther waved her arm, directing them behind the protecting bulk of Zeus' peak when one of the men dropped bonelessly to the ground. Keeping low, she rushed forward, grabbed the motionless soldier by his combat harness and started dragging him back. Within a couple of seconds, Constantine joined her, and together, they got him out of the line of fire.

*Hell!*

They'd lost their first man. Esther didn't need Doctor Willis to pronounce him dead. The big round had hit the soldier in the back and tore out half of his chest as it exited. He could probably be resurrected, she thought, but that was dependent them being able to withstand the coming assault.

Her anger began to bubble over as she looked at the soldier.

"Who had lookout duty?" she shouted.

"Soldier Tesler," one of the men said, using the Hellenic equivalent of "private."

"Tesler, step up, now!"

"That's him," Constantine said quietly, pointing at the dead man.

*Oh, shit. You killed yourself.*

She pushed Tesler out of her mind and focused on what had just happened. With the RFG soldiers getting closer, they couldn't directly fire up on the crown, which comprised the bulk of her battle position. The very bulk of the mountain blocked their fire. Esther had ordered that four lookouts be set up, each with a quadrant to watch for the enemy to crest terrain features and become a direct-fire threat. But the Hands weren't mindless automatons, simply marching forward into the face of fire. They knew about supporting fire, and they'd kept some fighters back far enough away to have an angle to take the east side of the summit under fire. Soldier Tesler was supposed to spot anyone to the east. He'd failed to spot them, and he'd paid the ultimate price for that failure.

Luckily, whoever was in that base of fire were not skilled marksmen. If they'd had their own Bob Burnham, Esther thought she would have lost six or seven of the soldiers. The RGH had wounded one man, who seemed to be more angry than incapacitated, and killed another, but they'd also played their hand. Esther could figure out where they were. She rewound her cam, then slowed it down. Rounds ricocheted off the rocks at various angles, but she didn't need her AI to get a back azimuth. With a quick set of orders, she sent two of the Gnats to track down the RHG positions.

"Bob, where're you at?"

"On my way. I'll be at your pos in 20."

"We've taken incoming fire. Track Gnat 4 and 9. When they've located the shooters, pick a spot within our perimeter where you can engage them when things get hot."

"Roger that."

Esther thought she was beginning to understand the RHG's plan. They were fine with coming up Vomit Gorge. Once they emerged and reached the mountain's shoulder, it would be difficult for the soldiers and Marines to engage them on the north and east sides without exposing themselves to the RHG base of fire. Climbing would be slow and difficult, and they could not bring their full strength en masse. But they wouldn't be under the same intense fire as if they were assaulting from the south.

*Should I have canalized them to the south instead?* Esther wondered, second guessing herself.

To the south, she had clearer fields of fire, and she'd have been able to keep assaulting forces engaged, but fields of fire went both ways. Her own soldiers would be just as vulnerable to RHG weapons, and the RHG had many more fighters than she had. If she got through this, the major and the rest could pick apart her decisions to their heart's desire. But for now, she had to play out her hand.

Now on the west side of the summit, the soldiers who'd just run for cover were milling about, most staring at Tesler. Esther realized this was probably the first time any of them had seen one of their number killed. She needed to get them active, but she couldn't very well send them to finish their positions.

"Tim, we're still going to need to cover the Second Platoon's AO. Work with Kang to get these guys organized to move forward when we can get fire on the Hands. I want them ready to move forward once Bob's in position and engaging."

It wasn't a very detailed order, she knew, but Tim didn't need to be micro-managed, and it was better than just to have the soldiers standing and waiting for events to reach them. Tim nodded and moved to the other side of them, away from where Doctor Willis was fruitlessly working on Tesler's body. The solders had to turn away and look at him as he started issuing orders.

A muffled explosion sounded from the northeast, down the slope.

Esther switched to Merl's feed, but it was jerky as he ran. She got a few glimpses of Lyle running in front of him. She switched to the nearest Gnat instead. A small column of smoke and dust was rising from Vomit Gorge, and she could see movement as Hands scrambled in reaction. She panned back until she could see Merl and Lyle running up the slope to where they could catch the trail. It took her a second or two before the scene registered.

"Merl, Lyle, stop! Do not climb higher!" Both slowed to a halt, and she continued, "We've got shooters somewhere along this axis." She highlighted it and pushed it to their displays. "Stay down low where you have cover and circumnavigate the base. I don't want you to climb until you reach here," she said, highlighting a position that should mask them from the shooters. "I'll send a runner to let the squad on that side know you're coming, but remember, they don't have telltale receivers. Make sure you let them know you're there."

"Thanks for the heads up. How much time do we have?"

She studied her map display for a moment, then said, "No more than 15 minutes. It's more than a klick, so get moving."

Esther had almost let her two Marines move into a position of vulnerability. She had their avatars on her display, but she'd neglected to overlay the incoming fire from the Hands. She still didn't exactly know where the RHG base of fire was located, but there weren't that many options for it.

Esther was feeling more than a bit overwhelmed. She just didn't have the resources she needed for a defense in depth, nor did she even have the normal command and control capabilities she expected within a Marine unit. Marines might be noted for succeeding despite the odds, but most of her command were inexperienced militia, and even with Marines, sometimes, the enemy was just too numerous. If the entire RGH force rushed them at once, she really didn't think they could hold them back. But Esther couldn't think of anything more she could do to break up their assault into more manageable waves.

"Ess, we've got the shooters' position," Bob said.

She quickly pulled up Gnat 4's feed. The RHG's base of fire consisted of about a platoon-sized unit on a finger some 1300 meters away. The soldiers were prone on the low grass. She had a sudden urge to creep back up and try to eyeball them, but that was a stupid risk. She could see them fine on the feed without exposing herself.

Thirteen-hundred meters was no easy shot for the average riflemen, and it was out of range of their ten grenade launchers. Bob had assured her that some of the brigade soldiers were pretty accurate out to 1500 or 1600 meters with their hunting rifles, but for most of the brigade, it would be more of a spraying the area and hoping to get lucky at that range. That was probably true for the RHG fighters as well. She was pretty sure that all they'd done was aim at the crest and fire, which meant they had to be lucky to get a hit. Or the brigade soldiers had to be unlucky, and unlucky was just as deadly as falling victim to skill, as Tesler had found out.

Thirteen hundred meters was well within Bob's range, however.

"Do you have a firing position?" she asked him.

"I've got two that I think will do. Give me five mikes and I'll confirm it."

"Roger, that, but I want you to pull three of the better brigade shooters. They may not be HOGs,[12] but if they can help."

"I've already got three in mind."

There was a distant thunk, and Esther wheeled around before the sound registered, shouting "Incoming! Thirty seconds!"

She swore under her breath and hit the deck behind a boulder. The RHG had never used mortars before, to the best of her knowledge. One of her base assumptions had just been shredded, and that could have deadly consequences.

Soldiers were diving to the deck, or in the case of one lance corporal, running across half of the battle position before sprawling to the ground as if the extra distance he covered would give him a better chance.

Doctor Willis, who'd been kneeling next to Tesler's body, stood up, looking confused.

"Get down!" Esther said.

"What?"

Esther jumped up, grabbed the sergeant by his uniform blouse, dragged him down, and then laid on top of the man. Her bones should be enough protection to withstand most mortars, but

---

[12] HOG: Hunter of Gunmen, a term used for a trained sniper who has registered a kill.

the doctor didn't have armor. She could feel Willis squirming under her as if he was trying to shrink himself.

Esther watched her display timer as it ticked down ever-so-slowly. The Gnats hadn't picked the round up, which wasn't surprising. They just didn't have the same capabilities as a Dragonfly.

At 40 seconds, Esther wondered if she'd made a mistake. It was possible that the "thunk" had not been made by an outgoing mortar.

It was almost a relief when an explosion sounded down the mountainside, at least 250 meters away. Her AI quickly analyzed the sound, but she was pretty sure she knew what it was.

"Did you get a Gentry 40mm?" she asked Tim after she read the display, who was down about five meters from her position.

"Sure did. Damned pea-shooter."

A 40mm mortar was not a "pea-shooter," but it wasn't much of a threat to Marines in bones. It could easily kill any of the un-armored soldiers with a close enough shot, however. On the positive side, if it was the Gentry "Knee-capper," it was just a basic tube and round with limited sighting abilities. It was super-cheap and very durable, but it took a lot of skill to use accurately—and it didn't look like the RHG mortarmen knew what they were doing.

On flat ground, the round might have missed them by 60-70 meters, which in and of itself was pretty poor shooting. But up on a steep slope, any lateral miss was compounded by the vertical drop. The round probably landed closer to the Hands coming up the slope than to them at the summit.

Esther rolled off Willis. She had been listening, but she hadn't heard another round go off.

"Think they're ranging us?" Constantine asked as he stood up.

"That, or they're limited in rounds."

A single rifle shot rang out from behind Esther, catching her undivided attention.

"I saw them!" The lookout towards the south, in Third Platoon's AO, shouted, his voice pitched high. "I shot at them."

Esther was beside him in a few strides.

"Where were they?" she asked.

"Right over there, by the tassle grass," he said, pointing.

"Right over there" covered a huge section of slope. She didn't know what "tassle grass" was, but she saw a line of what looked like three-meter tall sugar cane. She zoomed in, and sure enough, there were five bodies now prone at the edge of the grass. Another Hand was kneeling, glassing the mountain. Esther could almost feel the Hand's eyes on her.

She ranged the fighter. He was almost 1500 meters away.

"What's your name?" she asked the soldier.

"Pusser, ma'am. Erik Pusser."

"Well, that, Erik, is what a lookout is supposed to do," she said loudly for the others to hear. "Damned good eyesight."

"Did I get them?"

The Hands she'd seen didn't look overly concerned, so they might not have even known they'd been targeted, but she said, "If you didn't, you sure got their heads down," and clapped him on the shoulder.

The small RHG team was probably out too far to be much of a threat, but she knew that wasn't their job. They were there to have eyes on the mountain. And Esther wasn't about to let them have that. She glanced down at her M114. A bullpup configured rifle had a normal-sized barrel. The action was located behind the trigger, so the overall length of the weapon was shorter, which made it more maneuverable and a better self-defense weapon, but theoretically, it was just as accurate over long distances. Still the M114 was not designed as a sniper rifle, and its max effective range was only 750 meters.

"Doc!" she shouted, watching the watcher.

She put a big pink avatar on the kneeling man and pushed it to the corpsman.

"Can you take him out?" she asked.

Doc Buren was an excellent marksman and the team's alternate sniper. The Brotherhood SA-12-A2 he lugged around on his back had the range and accuracy to take out the Hand.

"I'll give it a shot," he said, chuckling at his own choice of words.

He put down his Grayson, brought his SA-12, and sank into an easy sitting position. He initiated his scope's interrogator to get the data he needed for the shot. Normally, a sniper would have an a-gunner who would run the environmentals and then spot the round, but Doc was the A-gunner, at least for Bob. Esther would try to spot the round for him, but the SA-12 was a hypervelocity mag rifle. She didn't think she'd be able to see the trace of the dart.

His thumb hovered over the selector. Esther knew he was trying to decide whether this would be a single shot or three-round burst. With a chemically-fired round, the recoil would throw off a second round, so snipers always fired single shots, re-acquiring the target before firing again. Mag rifles had negligible recoil, and the darts left the barrel so quickly that three rounds could be fired with a very tight pattern, even at 1500 meters. He pushed the selector down for three rounds.

Incoming fire hit the rock face on the east side of the peak. The base of fire was at it again, wasting more rounds. Esther ignored them, watching the Hand watch her. He had to see Doc getting ready for the shot, but he didn't seem fazed. Esther really had to wonder about their training. They'd shown a remarkable lack of understanding basic military tactics, and the fighter didn't seem to think he was in any danger.

Doc took a deep breath, let half of it out, and squeezed the trigger. There was quick, quiet buzz, and less than a second later, the Hand spun and fell back.

"Hit," Esther said.

A moment later, the man lurched up and almost dove for cover, his left arm dangling loose.

"Fuck. Shoulder or arm shot," Doc said.

"You sure got his attention, though" Esther said as bodies scurried back. "And his friends', too."

Another explosion reverberated through the air, this one sounding much nearer. More Hands had probably just been killed by whatever Merl and Lyle had left them, but they were getting closer. The battle was soon to be joined.

"Principles up!" she yelled.

Constantine and Doc were already standing beside her, but Tim, Master Sergeant Kang, Lieutenant Spiros, Captain Athanasciou , Bug, and Chris came jogging up. Each of the four platoons had a Hellenic officer commanding, but for Esther, the "principles" for the platoons were her team members. She had comms with them, not with the brigade soldiers.

Not having comms with everyone was a major headache—that, along with the shortage of ammo, was one of Esther's main concerns. She couldn't monitor each soldier, and she couldn't give orders other than by shouting them out. She didn't know how commanders of old fought battles without direct comms. She'd placed her team around the entire military crest to act as relays, but she was worried about the soldiers. They weren't a cohesive unit yet, and they hadn't been bloodied in combat. If they felt out of the loop, if they felt left alone to fend for themselves, they'd bolt, she was sure. She had to make sure they held together.

"We don't have much time, so I want to make sure we're on the same page. First, Lieutenant Spiros, get your best marksman left. I want him to plant his butt—"

"Her butt."

"What?"

"Her butt. Staff Sergeant Gray took the best three. That means Lachelle is the next best. Right Walt?" he asked Master Sergeant Kang who nodded his agreement.

"OK, have her sit her butt right here. Her job is to keep prying eyes back. Doc, make sure she knows where the targets are.

"Red, are you about done with the west wall? I'm pretty sure they're not going to ignore that."

"We're ready."

The sound of more firing reached them, but Esther couldn't see who was being targeted.

"I'm sorry we don't have comms. But we're not spread out that far, so listen up for orders. Don't get wrapped up in the fight yourself.

"We all know what we have to do. If we all do our part, if we support each other, we have a chance. If we don't, we'll lose, plain and simple.

"And our best chance is to break the assault. If they quit, we've won, our mission accomplished."

"And the boats?" Constantine asked.

"That's our back-up plan, as I've said. If it comes to that, the senior surviving Marine or soldier makes the call."

Constantine had become enamored with Esther's transition to retrograde. If it became apparent that they were going to get overrun, the surviving Marines and soldiers were going to try and punch through the assaulting fighters, focusing their strength at the weakest point in the assault. Once through, they were to conduct a fast retrograde to where the RHG flotilla was anchored, take over enough boats to carry everyone, and run. Esther knew that plan was more Hollybolly than real life, but she wanted the option if everything went completely to shit. That really was a last-ditch measure, though.

She checked Gnat 6's feed, from where it was hovering 400 meters above her head. A couple hundred Hands were visible as they converged on their position. Within ten, maybe 15 minutes, if they kept coming at the same pace, the first of them would be in sight—and in the line of fire.

"OK, it's almost time."

"Do you think we're going to win?" Lieutenant Spiros asked.

"No. I'd put our chances at 25% at best."

He pulled back in shock. Esther knew he'd wanted a "yes," but she wasn't going to blow fairy dust up his butt. This was the situation, and all 88 of them had to pull out all the stops.

"Captain Blue, no matter what happens, it's been an honor," Constantine said, his hand out.

Esther took it the hand and said, "Likewise. You've got a good crew." She only hesitated a moment before adding, "Captain Esther Lysander."

"Thank you," he said, nodding in a half-bow. He stopped, looked up, and asked, "Lysander? As in—"

"Yes, General Lysander was my father."

"I . . . I'm surprised. I'd heard that you and your brother had enlisted some years ago, but I didn't know you were still in, and I certainly didn't know you'd be here as the OIC of your contact team."

"Gunnery Sergeant Tim Ziegler," Tim said, holding his hand out.

Master Sergeant Kang simply smiled beside him. Esther was pretty sure Tim had already given Kang his real name.

"Sergeant Konor Suek, sir, but everyone calls me 'Bug.'"

"Pleased to meet you, Bug."

"I'm HM2 Buren Glover," Doc added. "Just Doc's fine."

"And I'm Staff Sergeant Chris de Brittain."

"'Pink' is Staff Sergeant Merl Miller, 'Green' is Sergeant Lyle Jones, and 'Gray' is Staff Sergeant Bob Burnham," Esther told the captain.

"I'm honored again, but why tell us, now?"

"Why not? Code names are a silly practice, anyway. And it just seems right. We're brothers-in-arms, and like I told the lieutenant here, we probably aren't going to make it through the next hour. If we're going to Valhalla, I think it'd be nice to go as comrades."

"Sir . . ." Master Sergeant Kang prompted the captain.

"Ah, well, yes. As long as we're in the sharing mood, my full name is Lochagos Constantine Stavropoulis Makos, at your service."

"'Makos,' as in the speaker prime?" Esther asked.

"My father."

"And now I'm surprised. I wouldn't have expected to see the speaker prime's son out with the soldiers."

"And the ex-chairman of the Federation's daughter is any different?"

"Chairman for three weeks, and he was a career Marine. But, uh, it's not common—"

". . . that out in the fringe worlds any of the elite serve in the military or constabulary."

Esther had been trying to think of a polite way to put it, but yes. In the newer worlds, the powerful didn't usually serve. Their interests tended to be a bit more self-serving, from what she'd gathered.

"My father is different. My sister and I were raised to serve, and we don't use our patronymic when fulfilling that duty. I'm a public works engineer when I'm not in uniform."

"Your father sounds like an interesting man," Esther said. "I'd like to know more about him."

Another explosion sounded to the southeast, possibly 200 meters down the slope, making them all instinctively duck.

"Merl just got another," Tim said. "Coming up the trail, though."

"I'd be most happy to tell you about my father sometime, hopefully, back at Patras a long time from now. But I think we've got a job to do at the moment."

"Right, and we need to get in position, " Esther said. "Any saved rounds?"

They shook their heads. This was a fluid situation, but the Marines had been trained well, and the soldiers didn't lack for heart.

"OK, let's kick some ass."

She grabbed Constantine by the arm as everyone spun to get into position.

"Keep your head down, OK?"

"Sure thing, Blue . . . uh, Esther, if that's OK."

"No, not Esther. Call me Ess."

## Chapter 36

Bob and his crew of four were plugging away with measured shots. Esther watched the feed from the Gnat above, and four of the Hands were sprawled motionless in the grass while the rest were scurrying back. Esther didn't know if any of the soldiers had made a kill or if it had been all Bob, but their combined fire was having an effect. One of the crawling Hands started to get rise up, and he immediately took a shot to the head. Even with the Gnat's relatively low resolution, the blowback of blood and brain matter was obvious.

"Now," she passed to Tim.

The first wave of RHG fighters were massing below the military crest to the east while another 30 or so were making their way up the trail which would loop them around to the south and then reach the summit from the southwest. If the ones below them charged up, they could be in among them in 30 seconds, and Esther wanted to hit them before that could happen. And now with Bob in position and keeping the base of fire's heads down, she could move her soldiers forward.

Twenty-three soldiers, "led" by Lieutenant Dillard, followed Tim and Master Sergeant Kang as he rushed forward to take a position close to the crown's brow that delineated the perimeter of their battle position. This wasn't like the cliff to the west. The crown itself was a shallowly-sloping platform that gave way over the brown to a much steeper slope. Each of the soldiers had been given two micro-grenades carried by the team. Ten soldiers rushed to the start of the drop-off and lofted a single grenade each before falling back to whatever cover they'd been able to prepare before the RHG base of fire had chased them away.

Esther couldn't see the tiny grenades as they fell, but she could see the results on her feed. One landed short, six went long and detonated below the Hands, but three landed on the trail amongst them. The fighters were packed tight, so their bodies acted as shields for each other, but at least ten of them were down.

"No more blind throws," Esther told Tim. "They need to see their targets. We just wasted seven micros."

There were three distinct thunks from off in the distance. It seemed as if the first mortar was merely ranging after all. They'd just fired three more rounds, and these would be much closer.

"Incoming!" she shouted. "Thirty seconds."

They couldn't just hug the ground and wait for the rounds to impact. In thirty seconds, a lot could happen, to include Hands breaching their perimeter.

"Stay here," she told Constantine as she rushed forward.

"You and me," she told Tim, taking out two micros out of their pouch.

The little 40mm mortars wouldn't do much to either of the two Marines, and a few more grenades should blunt an over-eager rush up the steep slope.

With Tim a few meters to her right, she edged forward, forgetting the Gnat feed for a moment. She couldn't deal with two spatial references at the same time, and she wanted to simply rely on her eyes.

One more step forward, and she saw the heads and shoulders of half-a-dozen soldiers rushing up. She could see them, so they could see her, and one fighter raised a rifle to fire at her, but missing by a wide margin—firing up hill was something that had to be practiced to get it right. Esther thumbed the micro-grenades live, then with simple underhand tosses, lofted the small, but power-packed spheres out about 20 meters. Four seconds later, she was rewarded with two blasts, followed almost immediately by two more. She pulled up the Gnat feed.

Both Tim and her grenades had gone a little long, taking out a handful of the fighters, but leaving the leading ten or twelve still climbing.

"Get ready," she told Tim, raising her M114.

And the hill was rocked with two huge explosions, one knocking Esther to her knees.

*That's no freaking 40mm!*

There were shouts from behind her.

"You OK?" she asked Tim, her heart falling as his avatar switched to light blue.

"Fuck that hurts," he said, shaking his left hand, drops of blood flying with each shake. "Yeah, I'm fine. Fucking shrapnel got me in the glove line," he said as he pulled at the glove's edge with his right hand and looked inside.

Shouts for Doctor Willis and Doc Buren were called out. Behind her, soldiers were down, a couple horribly mangled.

"Doc, get up here now," she passed.

"Can you shoot?" she asked Tim.

"Just give me a target," he said.

She spun back around to engage the oncoming Hands and saw a cloud of dust rising from below. Finally focusing on her feed, she couldn't see anyone rushing up the slope. More Hands were arriving on the trail below, but the slope to the crest only had mangled bodies, and four men dragging themselves back down the hill.

Knowing what she'd see, she backtracked 20 seconds and re-ran the feed. She saw their four grenade blasts, she saw the damage, and then both Tim and her getting ready. Then came three blasts, not two, all within a second. Two were on the crown among her men, and one hit the slope below them, right in the middle of the group of Hands rushing up. Bodies and body parts were lifted into the air.

The initial wave had been stopped by their own side.

"They suckered us," Tim said after the feed jumped to real-time.

The first mortar shot probably had been a ranging round, but that wasn't its only purpose. It also lulled Esther and her men into thinking all they faced was the 40mm. Her decision to have Tim and her lob the grenades was predicated on that. The Marines' bones were adequate protection against a knee-capper, but what was fired looked to be 90mms. And a direct hit with one of those would have killed either one of them.

"What do we have, Doc?" she asked on the net, turning her attention away from the four wounded Hands.

"Looks like six or seven KIA. Another six WIA."

Esther looked at the mess. As Tim had said, they'd been played, and soldiers had been killed.

Three more thunks sounded in the distance.

"More incoming! Thirty seconds!"

There was an immediate sense of urgency on the peak. One of the soldiers who'd just survived the blast took off at a dead run away from the area.

"Bug, you've got someone running. Tackle his ass when he gets to you."

"Roger that."

"Everybody down!" Tim shouted, running among the survivors.

Esther got down, too, still on the Gnat feed, watching for another attempt, but the mass of fighters was a confused mess. It would take time for them to reorganize, even longer with them on the constrained mountain trail.

To the south, out of her sight, firing opened up. The second mass of RHG fighters were within range of Third Platoon.

The next three rounds landed just to the north of the summit. The closest showered the nearest soldiers with small rocks, but it had landed below the military crest, and Mount Zeus had absorbed the bulk of the blast.

Even without further casualties, what had been 23 soldiers facing east was now down to half that. She needed to shore them up.

"Constantine, shift ten men to fill in the gaps," she shouted.

He raised a thumbs up and darted off.

On her feed, one of the Hands got back to his feet and swung what looked to be a massive, but century-old plasma rifle of some type. He pointed it up and started waving it around as he fired, the air shimmering as it ionized. Esther wasn't familiar with the specific weapon, but by holding the trigger like that, it had to run out of power in pretty quickly.

She started to tell Tim to keep everyone back until the rifle ran out of juice when her Gnat stopped transmitting, and she immediately knew what had happened.

On a childhood vacation with Ben, Noah, and her mother while her father was deployed, they'd gone to Tarawa's Big Mushy, the wetlands that had been an engine for terraforming and were now a tourist destination. The wild wetlands were packed with Earth wildlife, to include mosquitoes (although Esther had always wondered as to why anyone would introduce mosquitoes onto a new world). Each room at the resort was equipped with what Ben had simply called a zapper; a brightly colored tennis-racquet-looking tool that they swung in the air to clear it of the buzzing blood-suckers. They couldn't really see the tiny bugs well, but a loud zap and a blue flashing light of victory let them know when they'd fried one. Noah had demurred, but Esther and Ben had enjoyed being mosquito hunters, swinging the zapper wildly in hopes of connecting with one.

The RHG fighters knew that their opponents surely had surveillance drones. And while they might have detected the Dragonflies, they didn't have anything sophisticated enough to locate a Gnat. So they were resorting to the mosquito-zapper method. And unbelievably, by simply firing a plasma rifle into the air and waving it around, they destroyed another of her drones.

"We're blind until I get another Gnat here," she told Tim. "Do not let the Hands gain the crest."

Constantine returned with ten soldiers, all of them with eyes wide when the saw the carnage. Tim grabbed them and physically put them into position, sometimes in the middle of a gory mess.

Esther kept listening for more thunks, but through the now scattered firing, the distance was thankfully quiet. It was possible that the RHG had shot their load, but she wasn't about to assume anything else.

"We've got movement to the west," Bug passed to her.

"Can you see what they're doing?"

"Not yet. It looks like . . . shit, they've got dunkers."

Esther couldn't hear the grenade launchers fire, but she said, "Keep their heads down" as she ran forward, Constantine on her ass.

Part of her knew she should keep the brigade commander away from her. If she went down, he needed to take control of his troops. But she ignored that as she rushed to Bug's position.

Several small explosions sounded, but only one within their lines. Lofting a grenade up a 180-meter cliff was no easy feat even for a skilled grenadier. The rounds had to travel well above the top of the mountain, then fall back to the target. The grenades were landing everywhere, including two that came back down almost among the Hands that fired them.

Given time, though, anyone could learn to walk the grenades in to hit on top. Esther had figured the RHG would try to hit them with grenades from the west, and this time, she'd foreseen correctly. And she wasn't going to give them a free pass to do so.

Below the cliff was a steep slope interspaced with trees that had managed to poke through the centuries' accumulation of fallen rocks. The talus provided excellent cover, which, when combined with the steep angle, made hitting them with rifles or their own grenade launchers problematic. But there was more than one way to shuck a goober, as her mother used to say, and the mountain top provided two weapons: rocks and gravity.

Esther had Bug and his team arrange as heavy rocks as they could handle along the edge of the cliff. While sitting there, the rocks provided cover from any long-range firing to the west. If pushed, the rocks became missiles: big, heavy missiles.

"Go ahead," she told Bug.

"Gardner, Deng, Morales, on me," Bug said.

Each soldier and Bug had evidently been already assigned a rock. They quickly got behind, and while one of them had a pry-bar, the rest simply put their shoulders to the rocks and pushed. Within moments, all four rocks were falling, and Esther stupidly leaned forward to watch. One rock shattered upon impact, sending out shrapnel 20 or 30 meters. The other three landed and bounded forwarded, snapping trees and glancing off boulders. Several bodies dove out of the way, fleeing for their lives.

Esther didn't know if they'd actually hit anyone, but she knew they'd gotten their full and undivided attention.

"Good job. Don't shoot your wad, but keep reminding them what's up here. Don't forget your hunters or your own dunker, though," she added, pointing at three soldiers who were standing there, two with their hunting rifles at the ready, the other with a dunker attached to his Diedre.

More firing sounded from down the trail, towards the southeast. Esther could hear the steady pops of Bob's Windy, but the rest was a cacophony of various weapons. She couldn't tell who was doing the bulk of the firing. She switched feeds to Merl, and she could see he was firing at someone, but she couldn't see a target.

Flipping to the Gnat feeds, she was surprised to see she only had five left. Gnat 2 was heading toward the trail where it looped around the east side of the mountain. She gave the AI instructions to bring three of the other four closer as well, leaving only one to cover the route to the east side of the island and the RHG anchorage.

"Lyle, what's going on?" she asked.

"The lead element is coming around the corner. We're keeping them occupied until more show up. We've got the slope mined, ready to bring down on them, but it's one shot, so we want as many as possible."

After Merl and Lyle had reached their lines, she had left them with the soldiers manning the southern approach. Bob was also to the southeast, but higher within their lines. That left Doc and Chris to the north with First Platoon, Bug to the west with the small Fourth Platoon, and Tim to the east with Second. The brigade had seven men and women making up Fourth with Bug to the west, and the rest were somewhat evenly split along the defensive lines, but a little heavier to the south. That was the easiest route up for the Hands, so she had more firepower facing that direction, to include five of her dunkers. She would have liked to have spread-loaded them more, but to the east and north, the distances were just too short to make much use of them.

If she'd left a small hunter-killer team out on the southeaster slope, they could be using the dunkers to hit the Hands on the mountainside. She'd even considered it, but while she could justify it from a tactical standpoint, it would have been a suicide mission. If she'd thought it would have a significant effect on the battle, she would have been ready to order it done, but while it would have killed Hands, she didn't think it would have turned the tide of the battle. A suicide mission was sometimes necessary, but only if it would do the larger unit some good.

She headed for the top of the military crest to where it looked over to the south, where Erik Pusser was still on lookout duty and where Lachelle was prone, rifle in hand.

"Are our friends still there?" Esther asked the designated sniper as she crouched low.

"Yes, ma'am," the lance corporal said. "I've fired each time they've poked their noses out, and I got one of the bastards."

"Good job. If you get a glimpse of anyone else, shift to them."

The little knoll on which they were perched did not offer much in the way of visibility of the trail until it bent back towards the west, so Esther doubted that the lance corporal would get a shot off at someone else—at least until the Hands overran the peak.

And, as usual, the Gods of Battle punished her complacency as a shot hit Esther high on her right shoulder. The round bounced off her as her bones hardened, ricocheting to spin around like a top on the ground a few meters in front of her. She ducked down to a knee.

"Did that hit you?" Constantine asked, his voice incredulous as he dropped beside her.

"Sure as hell did."

"Sorry, ma'am! But I'm sure none of my targets just shot you!" Lachelle said, her voice rising in panic.

"Not your fault. My fault for just standing up here. But that means someone else has eyes on us."

*Get your head in the game, Esther*, she admonished herself.

Getting hit was a wake-up call for her. Despite the fighting going on, despite the incoming, she was wandering around like a referee in a war game. She was getting so wrapped up in her plans that she somehow forget that she was just as vulnerable, just as at risk, as anyone else. Luckily, she had better equipment, and she wasn't hurt. If the unseen shooter had targeted Constantine instead, he'd be down for the count now.

"Erik, keep scanning for anyone else. But both of you, keep your heads down."

She motioned to Constantine to follow her, and keeping low, backed off the rock until she could stand.

"Your armor really did work," Constantine said, looking in awe at the torn fabric of her skins.

She reached up to finger the tear. The shot might not have been fatal even without her bones, but she'd be in a world of hurt.

"When all of this is over, we need to see about getting a milspec fabricator and the license for you to make your own STF armor," she said.

A huge explosion reverberated through the air, the shock wave reaching from below and somehow bending around to take the breath away from her. She immediately bolted back to the trail M114 at the ready.

"Oo-fucking-rah!" Lyle said over the net.

Esther came to an abrupt halt, Constantine, who'd taken off after her, running into her back before he could stop. She switched to Lyle's feed, back-tracked 15 seconds, and watched as 40 or 50 Hands were doing a credible job of bounding up the trail's long straightaway. They were taking some light harassing fire, and Esther saw one of them drop to slide off the trail, when the entire side of the slope above them erupted in a flash of flames and smoke. Tons of rock descended, sweeping Hands over the side.

"Oo-fucking-rah is right!" Esther passed as Tim chimed in with, "Get some, Merl!"

"What's the tally?" Esther asked.

The feed was all well and good, but it was still a feed. Both Lyle and Merl could see with their naked eyes.

"I'm saying 40 down."

Esther did some quick math. With what she'd seen, the RHG was probably down to close to 350 fighters. She was down to 67 effectives.

"And that's it with our mines," Merl passed.

"You've still got the field gun. I want you two to stay there with the gun team," she ordered.

The 40mm field gun had been hauled up the mountain, and it had been sitting out of sight just behind the sharp bend in the trail at the end of the straightway. Whereas a 40mm mortar was a relatively underwhelming weapon, a 40mm field gun could take out a tank. The problem was that its potential was not maximized at close ranges. Esther could have used it to take out or drive off the Hands' base of fire, but Bob could do that, too, without revealing the gun's presence. So her best option was to put it on the trail where it could be pulled out and fired down the 150-meter long and slightly concave straightaway. With no more mines and boobytraps, now was the time to commit it.

"Roger that. We're on it."

Shouts of "incoming" echoed over the top of the mountain. Esther and Constantine both hit the deck a few moments before something large whooshed overhead, passing right over Bug and his team of soldiers.

"What was that?" Esther asked over the net.

"Another missile, fired from one of their boats," Chris answered.

Whatever its fuzing system was, it hadn't worked, and the missile was probably half-way to the west coast of the island by now. But the fact that they had a missile launcher on one of their fishing boats was a huge concern. The field gun could range the boats, but unless anyone of the brigade had happened to see the launch, she didn't know which boat it was. Even if she knew, she was not confident in the accuracy of the home-made artillery piece over that distance. No, the field gun was better left where it was.

"Now we've got naval gunfire," Esther told Constantine.

"What are you going to do about it?"

"Not much we can do. Just bear with it."

The RHG force had already shown a fair number of weapons at its disposal, but combined arms had to be just that, "combined." Their fires had to be coordinated. If they had simply kept their base of fire quiescent until the first rush up the north slope and used that, the mortars, and the missiles in support of that rush, Esther was sure they'd have gained a foothold within her defensive area, and that would have been the beginning of the end. Poor planning and execution by the RHG commander had kept Esther and her force in the game. But very soon, things were going to devolve in a melee.

"Here comes another one," Tim passed as calls of "Incoming" were shouted.

Esther got back down, hoping for another flyover.

No such luck.

The missile hit on the east side of their position, sending rocks and rubble up over to shower the two on the reverse slope.

"Medic, up!" a voice cried out.

Esther switched to Gnat 2's feed. A few figures were rushing to two motionless soldiers. Esther didn't know the payload of the RHG missiles nor how they were configured, but two soldiers down was better than she could have expected. She breathed out a sigh of relief before she saw the massed RHG fighters.

"Tim—"

"I see them, Ess. I think this is it."

If there were 350 Hands left, probably 230 of them were massed within 200 meters of her defensive position along the shoulder from the north to the south. The closest were above the trail on the east, barely 30 lateral meters away and down the slope. And they were disbursed. Someone had taken charge, and a handful of micro-grenades thrown would not be as effective as Esther needed them to be.

Something in their posture, something is the tiny movements in their leading edge, triggered a certainty that the mass assault was only moments away.

"Get ready!" Esther passed as she jumped up and ran up the slope to the peak where she could see most of her entire AO.

Esther was ready to call for the FPF the moment the Hands moved into the assault. It should break up some of it, but they were spread out too much to stop the attack. And if things got too hot, she needed that massive Final Protective Fire to allow her to punch out and make the run for the coast and the RHG boats, so she held her hand, not willing to commit just yet.

She'd told Lieutenant Spiros that she thought their chances of survival were 25%. In her heart, she knew they were much less. If they didn't smash the assault, the RHG boats were six klicks away, and even if some of them could break through the assault and survive a running retrograde, the Hands undoubtedly had fighters there who weren't going to simply sit by and allow them to commandeer the vessels. Constantine still wanted the break for the boats to be their main effort, but Esther knew their best chance, as poor as that was, was to beat back the assault.

Three thunks sounded off in the distance, followed by three more. It was on.

Esther saw the first rank of Hands start to move just as her Gnat feed failed. Gnat 3 and 7 went down almost immediately after. The Hands must have been simply spraying the sky with their energy weapons, and on full dispersion. That wouldn't be effective against any sort of protected troops, but against the tiny Gnats, it was evidently enough.

Orders were being shouted, and around her, Esther could feel a collective sense of determination.

In the southern AO, the 40mm field gun fired, and a moment later, mortar rounds started landing. At least four hit within the perimeter, and soldiers fell. Two were short, and they had to have landed among their own fighters again. Her battle position wasn't large, but Marine mortarmen would not have missed with six rounds. Four landing within here battle position where the soldiers were either dug in or hugging the ground were bad enough, but upright and in the open, the assaulting Hands would have been much more vulnerable.

The short rounds had been on the eastern slope, and Hands appeared over the edge of the northern AO's perimeter. They were immediately cut down by First Platoon, but more kept appearing. Micro-grenades started detonating, and the wave faltered.

The short rounds hadn't stopped all of the assault from the east. Second Platoon began to fire, first a few shots, then more and more as Hands scrambled up. Esther brought up her M114, sighted in, and dropped first one, then a second.

The field gun opened up again, but Esther didn't have time to pull Merl or Lyle's feed. As long as she could hear it, then she hoped that meant the southern approach was still held.

Soldiers from First were dropping under the onslaught, but more of the Hands were falling, creating a barrier for those below to surmount. Chris was throwing grenade after grenade in machine-like frequency, while Doc was popping Hand after Hand with his big Grayson, the combat shotgun tearing off limbs and creating gaping holes in bodies that were charging moments before.

"Bug, pull your men and reinforce Chris," she passed.

Beside her, Constantine was sitting, cooling firing round after round. Several rounds pinged on the rocks between him, but he never faltered.

Somehow in the heat of the battle, Esther saw an RHG grenadier as he leveled his launcher at her and fired. She instinctively started to duck away, but the grenade whizzed past her head to disappear somewhere to the west of the mountain.

From below the perimeter, a siren sounded, followed by three or four more. There were 20 or so Hands within the perimeter, and all of them wheeled back and bolted. Most were cut down, but a few jumped over their dead companions and disappeared back down the hill.

Shots followed them until Tim yelled, "Cease fire, cease fire!"

Someone shouted out, then another, and within a few moments, cheering filled the battle position.

"Did we win?" Constantine asked, looking up at Esther with a confused look on his face.

"Back to your positions!" Esther screamed, jumping down from the peak. "Give me a head count!"

They hadn't won, she knew. As massive as the assault had been, it was only a probe, done to determine their posture and weapons. The assault could have succeeded if it had been pressed, she thought, but she was grateful they'd pulled back. And she was grateful she hadn't fired the FPF. That was still in her pocket.

"Head and ammo count, now!" Tim shouted.

Esther looked around her. There were at least 40 bodies of the dead and seriously wounded just in the north and east AO. A good many of them were Hellenic soldiers. All of her team's avatars were a healthy blue, but the brigade had taken a hit.

"What's your status?" she asked Merl.

"We took a missile hit. The gun's still operable, but the team is KIA. Me and Lyle had to man it."

Esther hadn't noted the incoming missile in the heat of the fight, and that was part of her mission as a commander. If she had a company of Marines, she could have sat back and monitored the battle, giving orders as needed, but things were desperate, and every trigger mattered.

The count came in. First Platoon had nine KIA and nine WIA, three of them being out of the fight. Second had six KIA and four WIA, two being combat ineffective. Third had four KIA while Fourth was at full strength. The force was down to 51 effectives, and ammunition was running low. The RHG had taken heavy losses, but they probably still had well over 250 combat effective fighters to throw into the next assault.

And there would be another assault, Esther was sure.

## Chapter 37

"What do you think?" Esther asked Tim.

"It's your call, Ess. As for me, I just don't know. Our chances aren't good either way. Maybe a few of us could break free and hide out, but that's about it."

Constantine, Captain Athanasciou, and Master Sergeant Kang had asked Esther again about attempting to break out. She'd stressed that option was a last-ditch effort if they were totally overrun, but she had to acknowledge that if they were going to attempt it, they should do it with as much strength as possible. Still, she felt their best chance was to retain the high ground and limit the frontage that the RHG could attack. She knew that Constantine disagreed with her decision, but he wasn't pushing the issue.

That attack was coming soon, she knew. The first assault had broken off almost an hour ago, and except for the occasional shot by Bob, the top of the mountain had been relatively quiet. Twenty-one of the Hellenic soldiers were ziplocked, both KIA and WIA, waiting in stasis for an attempted resurrection or regen. Ten of the KIA were so dismembered that resurrection was not an option.

The dead Hands were pushed to the edge of the defensive perimeter and down the slope. That had been a necessity as well as an opportunity. Private Jillian de Marco had suggested that they could make use of the bodies, and Chris had brought the idea to Esther. She listened and immediately agreed, wondering why it took one of the least-experienced soldiers to come up with the idea.

The RHG fighters all wore their normal gray and tan cammie-patterned uniform blouses and gray skulltops. The rest of their gear could be haphazard. Private de Marco had suggested that a few of them don the blouses of the dead Hands and get pushed over the side as just so much carnage. They could then listen and watch for signs of the next assault. With all of her Gnats now off-line, Esther had embraced the idea. Four soldiers had volunteered, and they were now scattered among the dead on the slope below the perimeter.

Technically, donning an enemy's uniforms was against the Harbin Accords, but *technically*, Esther didn't give a rat's ass about that at the moment.

Esther looked up at the sun. The day cycle was five hours gone. Nightfall would be in another hour-and-a-half. If the assault didn't materialize by then, she might reconsider the break-out, but she didn't think it would get to that.

She was right.

One of the volunteers scrambled back over the perimeter, almost getting shot in the process by another soldier.

"They're moving again," he said, breathing hard. "Most going to the south, but some look like they'll hit the slopes again."

"Good job, Mason," Constantine said.

"How many to the south?" Esther asked.

"More than a hundred."

Esther closed her eyes, trying to put herself in the enemy commander's shoes. The push to the south could be a feint to pull soldiers away from First and Second Platoon's AOs. The trail had been costly to the RHG, but still, it was the quickest way to reach the summit. The Hands could move that way, but then quickly backtrack along the trail.

If this were a nice, geometric summit, she'd just ring her troops around the crown, right along the collar where the slopes became steeper. But while the east and north formed half of a rough circle, the west was a sheer cliff, and the slope dropped to the south, creating a summit of two levels. She could pull back the perimeter to the south, but that would leave the trail open and uncovered. The three chokepoints along the trail were natural places to defend, and even if the RHG was aware of that, there wasn't a lot they could do about it.

If all her platoons were still at full strength, she'd feel more comfortable shifting forces, but First and Second had been hit hard, so she left Bug and his tiny Fourth Platoon augmenting First.

There was firing from below, and a moment later, Private de Marco came tumbling over the wall of dead bodies.

"All of them are moving. The attack's coming."

"That's it, then. Let's do this," she passed on the team net.

She waited for the thunk of outgoing mortars as she climbed the up the jutting rock that formed the peak again. This had become her personal battle position. The rock's two extra meters didn't seem like much, but it gave her a good view over First and Second Platoon's AO as well as Third's down to the closest choke point. Her hand rested on the bottom stone of the cairn left by tourists who'd climbed the mountain over the years—none probably realizing that the same summit would someday be a bloody battlefield. Amazingly, despite the incoming, the 30 or 40 rocks still lay on top of each other. The concussions hadn't knocked them down.

*Hell, if I run out of ammo*, I can chuck these at them, she thought.

Esther could hear movement, and Tim inched forward, looking over the edge. He ducked back as a volley of fire tore through the air.

"Now!" he shouted to five soldiers who each threw their grenades. Four seconds later, explosions boomed, followed by battle cries from the throats of 250 Hands.

No mortars landed, but another missile hit just on the other side of Esther's perch. The soldiers of First and Second opened fire as the first of the Hands tried to clear the dead bodies at the perimeter.

To the south, the field gun fired. Unlike before, the gun fired again five seconds later, followed by yet a third shot five seconds after that. And Esther knew this was the final push. The Hands weren't going to let themselves be rebuffed.

Beside her and one step down, Constantine was back to his mechanical firing mode. He had more ammunition than most of his troops, and he seemed bound and determined to expend it all.

A wave of eight or nine Hands poured over the perimeter, firing wildly while the soldiers picked them off. Rounds hit on either side of Esther, and she joined the firing, dropping at least one of the RHG fighters. As soon as the last one of the initial wave fell, another ten were coming over the edge. A soldier threw a grenade at them, but it bounded up against a dead Hand, and the corpse absorbed most of the blast.

The field gun fired again, then Lyle passed, "Merl's down, and we're out of ammo. We're pulling back to Pine."

Esther pulled up Merl's bios. He was in shock, but it didn't look too deep. He should be functional.

Pine was the second coordinating point along the trail. Esther couldn't see it—she wouldn't be able to see anyone until they reached Maple, which was the bend in the trail 40 meters away.

"Merl, you OK?"

There wasn't an answer.

"Lyle, how is he? His bios aren't that bad."

"Not good. I'm sending him back now."

Two Hands emerged through a crease in the perimeter. One of them saw Esther and charged. He was armed, but he wasn't firing. Esther wondered if intended to try and snatch her or Constantine, but that was a casual thought as she shot him in the chest, then as the second came to a halt and stood there looking stupid, she shot her as well.

With more of her soldiers falling, there were more gaps in the perimeter, and RHG fighters were making it through into the battle position. Fighting had devolved into hand-to-hand combat in places, and the soldiers weren't always coming out on top. She caught a glimpse of Doc blasting a Hand almost in half with his Grayson, then swinging the big weapon in an overhand arc to crash onto the head of another Hand who was grappling with a soldier.

"I'm out of ammo!" a voice cut through the cacophony of battle.

Esther knew she'd be hearing more of that. They hadn't started out with a normal combat load, and the fighting was rapidly using up what little they had.

Esther still had ammo, so she started picking off Hand after Hand, debating if she should switch and order a breakout. That would leave Lyle and those soldiers with him exposed, though.

Three more Hands rushed her position. Constantine whirled around and took out two, but the third one juked to the left, firing a small hornet.

A hornet was the generic term of any number of hand-held anti-armor personal rockets. They might be a little light for a main battle tank, but they'd do a number on even a Marine in a PICS.

If he hadn't been diving to the ground as he fired, Esther was sure she'd be toast, but the little rocket shot through the space between Constantine and her. Esther shot the man before he could try again.

The unmistakable whine of an aircraft enveloped the peak, and Esther's heart fell. It was too late for a breakout if the RHG controlled the air. They'd saved their final surprise for the last.

Expecting a strafing run, Esther brought her M114 to bear, a fly against a lion—and her mouth dropped open. Obviously coming in for a landing, the *UFSGS Manta* was an amazing sight.

Esther wasn't the only one who'd expected to be strafed. Hands and more than a few soldiers were diving out of the battle position and down the slope.

The main hatch opened, and Petty Officer Krüger looked out, holding one of the ship's rifles. She spotted Esther and shouted out, "HF-I 9200."

It took a moment for her to realize what she was saying, but then she immediately instructed her AI to switch to the band and frequency.

"That you, Senior Chief?"

"Sure is. You need a ride out of here?"

"Damned straight. How many can you take?"

"Probably twenty. Sorry, it won't be more, but I'll be weighted out as it is. But get aboard now. There's a shitload of bad guys all around you."

"Who is—" Constantine started to ask.

"No time. You've got to get out of here," she told him.

"All of the WIA, on the ship! Now! Move it!

"Tim, give me security. Kang, get 20 to go. You've got 30 seconds!"

They probably had less than that. It wouldn't take long for the Hands to figure out this wasn't a Wasp or Experion.

"Krüger, we need your ships' rifles, all four," she shouted, forgetting for a moment that she was now on the Space Guard ships' net and could have just passed it.

The petty officer nodded and ducked back inside

Shocked or not, Master Sergeant Kang got his people moving. Within ten seconds, he was directing people to pick up the ziplocked WIA and haul them to the *Manta*. Hope gave people wings, and they rushed. Most of the other soldiers were looking back at the ship, probably calculating whether they'd be able to fit onboard.

There was a single shot, and one of the soldiers fell. Tim shouted and bounded forward, firing on full auto.

"Eyes front! That's where the enemy is!"

"I told you to get onboard," Esther told Constantine.

"Not unless all my men get onboard first."

"You don't have a choice. You're too important to your people."

"No one is more important than another."

"Bullshit. You can make a difference. You can let your father know just what your planet is facing. You accepted my command, so I'm ordering you to get onboard," she said.

He looked at her for only a moment, let out a deep breath, and made his way to where the *Manta*, as small as it was in comparison to other ships, dwarfed the small battle position.

"What's going on?" Lyle passed. "Some of the Hands have pulled back."

*Not all*, Esther realized as more fire erupted from the southern AO.

"We've got the *Manta* here, ready to take us off," Chris answered.

"No shit? All of us?"

Chris looked over at Esther, who shook her head.

"No, Lyle. Sorry about that. Not for us."

There was a pause, then "Understood."

The loading was taking too long, Esther knew. Krüger had reappeared with the four ships' rifles and passed out three to eager hands, keeping one for herself. Two more of the *Manta's* crew were on the mountain, trying to hurry the process.

Esther hadn't even got close to the point where she would have been teaching the brigade how to withdraw while under pressure, and if the Hands recovered from their surprise quickly enough, it would all be over. A withdrawal under pressure had to leave soldiers in contact while others withdrew. The perimeter couldn't be abandoned at once, which despite Tim's best efforts, was pretty much what was happening. Focus was on the *Manta*, not on the mass of RHG fighters still just meters away.

"Shit . . . Merl," Bug said.

Esther turned, and being helped by a soldier, Merl staggered around the corner of Maple and started up the crown. His left arm was gone a few centimeters below the shoulder.

"Bug, get him on the ship!" Esther shouted.

Bug took off to help as Master Sergeant Kang selected the lucky few to join the wounded. Evacuating them would cut Esther's remaining firepower, but better that some survive.

Bug was short, but he was immensely strong. He'd grabbed a barely coherent Merl, slung him over his shoulders, and sprinted to the *Manta*. Esther had been counting, but as Bug reached the ship, the 20th soldier was loaded aboard.

"Stop, bug, there's too many. The ship can't fly."

"Two more!" Petty Officer Krüger said, contradicting her.

*Did I miscount?*

The petty officer was looking at the bottom of the ship, which was still aloft, half a meter off the deck.

*Oh, she's going by weight,* she realized. *If the ship bottoms out, she's overloaded.*

Bug looked back at Esther, so she motioned him to load Merl.

There was a thunk in the distance. The Hands had at least one more mortar round they'd been saving.

"That's it. We've got incoming!" Esther shouted, running down to the *Manta*. "Get back onboard," she told Krüger.

The petty officer said something into her headset, then slapped the side of the ship. She stepped back as the *Manta* slowly-lifted off and edged backwards, barely clearing the Esther's perch. It spun around, then plunged over the cliff to the west. Esther rushed forward, but a moment later, the *Manta* flew into view, low along the treeline.

The *Manta* could carry tons in space, but she was not the most airworthy plane in an atmosphere. Her lift surfaces were minimal, and her ion-drive, even with the ram assist, relied on power rather than aerodynamics to fly. Minimal didn't mean no lift surfaces, though. Weighted down, Senior Chief Carpenter had used the cliff to gather just enough lift from those surfaces to get the ship flying once it had had lost the ground effect.

Esther watched the ship reach the shoreline and start to climb over the water.

"Everyone down!" Tim shouted out. "And get ready for another assault."

Esther had almost forgotten about the incoming, and she hit the deck less than five seconds before the round hit, right on the edge of the perimeter in the north AO.

*They'll be coming now*, she thought, resigned to her fate.

She felt a moment of joy when the *Manta* appeared, thinking she'd get out of this mess. But when she found out the ship could only take 20 people, there really had been no choice. It had to be the Hellenic soldiers.

*Except for Merl*, she amended. *Do us proud.*

Now it was time to take as many of the bastards with them as possible. They weren't defeated yet, and it was theoretically possible that they could still prevail, but their numbers were now down to 35 effectives.

Her eyes lingered on the KIA. She could have sent them out. But there was no guarantee that those in the ziplocks could be resurrected, and while the Marine Corps told the universe that they never left anyone behind, given the choice between a dead soldier and a soldier who could survive, she'd chosen the living.

"Where do you want us, Ma'am?"

Esther turned around and asked, "Petty Officer Krüger, what the hell are you doing? Why didn't you board?"

"Me and Randy, we thought you might need some help, Captain. I'm not a bad shot with this," she said.

She was about to respond when Constantine stepped up beside her.

"I told you to get on the *Manta*," Esther said, shocked.

"You seem to forget that you are not my commanding officer. In fact, I outrank you on Elysium. I gave you operational command, nothing more. So I guess you're stuck with me."

Part of her was angry that he'd disobeyed her. Part of her was sad with the knowledge that he'd soon be dead. Inexplicably, though, she was glad that he was still there.

"So where do you want us?" Krüger repeated.

"We've got a lot of holes in our perimeter. One of you go to First Platoon; that's right over there," she said pointing. "The other can go to Second."

As they started to get into position, Esther said, "And thanks."

"Ain't no thing, ma'am. We was getting bored jus' hanging about."

Esther took a moment to look around. It was eerily quiet for the moment. Two minutes ago, the *Manta* was on the summit; three minutes ago, the brigade and the Hands were locked into combat. Now, while the stench of war filled the air, the sound of battle was missing.

*Or that could just be my ears ringing after the Manta took off*, she acknowledged with a smile.

"Bob, do you still have targets?"

"There're a few left, but they're keeping low."

"I need your firepower back here."

"That's a negative, Ess. We're sort of cut off."

Esther pulled up his avatar, and he'd moved a good 50 meters from his last firing position.

"What the hell, Bob?"

"It's a better firing position," he said matter-of-factly as if he wasn't now cut off from everyone else.

"Shit, Bob. You should have asked."

"And you'd have said no. And I hate to disobey officers, so I don't ask."

"You . . . we're going to talk about this later, you and me," Esther said.

"I sure hope so."

"OK, support as you can, but after it's over, you and your team, you get off this frigging mountain and hide out. Do not engage, just make yourself invisible until someone can come get you."

"Understood, Ess. Go with God."

Fire erupted again in Third Platoon's AO, and a blast of a grenade hit the crown 15 meters to Esther's right. The lull was over.

"Well, Constantine, you ready for this?" she asked, cutting the comms with Bob.

"As ready as I'll ever be, Ess. And I'm sorry."

"Sorry? For what?"

"Sorry for this," he said, sweeping his right arm to take in the battle position. "All of this. None of this is your fight. We're not even in the Federation, but you're here anyway. And you could have taken your ship out of here. No one would've complained, you know."

One of the soldiers in First was up at the brow, firing down the slope. Esther watched him blow through a magazine before he hopped back.

"Chris, watch the ammo discipline. We don't have enough to waste," she passed before looking back at the Hellenic commander. "That's not the way the Marines do things, Constantine."

Firing intensified to the south, and Esther asked Lyle, "What's your status?" cutting off anything else Constantine was going to say.

"We've got a shitload of Hands pushing at us. We're holding our own, but I don't know for how much longer."

"Get ready to pull back to Maple," she passed. "We can't fire the FPF with you still out there."

"Roger that."

Esther wasn't too confident that the FPF would be that effective. Normally, the Final Protective Fire was an intense, sustained, fire of all available weapons systems, from rifles to crew-serves to mines to artillery to air to naval gunfire. It was unleashing the full might of the defending force and was intended to break the back of the assault. But Esther didn't have all those assets, and the enemy was still spread out too far. She hadn't told anyone, even if some of her Marines had most likely figured it out, but her intent now was to bring in all the Hands she could before bringing the fire right on top of their own heads. If they were going to leave the mortal plain, then they might as well drag as many of the RHG scum with them as they could.

A roar sounded from below them, rising up the slope and enveloping the battle position. It was the same roar that had been sounded from millions of throats over the eons as man clashed with man, intent on dealing death.

"Here it comes, Constantine."

The time for planning, the time for observing was over. Esther unlatched the top of her holster and checked her Ruger, making sure she could draw it quickly. She flipped over her M114 to see the readout; she had 18 rounds left in this magazine and two more full mags in their pouch.

*Time to die*, she told the unseen Hands—or maybe she was telling herself that.

It didn't matter.

The first Hand appeared 20 meters in front of her, rifle held high as he screamed out in wordless rage. Esther raised her rifle, but someone else beat her to it, and the man fell back and disappeared from sight. And then there were more targets for her—many more.

The summit turned into a free-for-all. Esther fired, then fired again. Hand's fell—but so did soldiers. She emptied one mag, dropped it, and slapped in a new one. A haze of propellant settled over the summit like a fog, the setting sun lighting the haze in reds and oranges.

"I'm pulling back to Maple," Lyle passed a few minutes into the assault. "I've got six effectives."

Esther fired again, dropping a fighter who'd just shot one of Second's Platoon's soldiers. Another Hand poked his head over the brow, searching for a target. She didn't give him a chance but put a round through his jaw and out the back of his neck.

The dead Hands were becoming more and more of an obstacle to those still climbing. The living clawed at the dead for purchase, but that broke the bodies free, sending both back down the slope.

"I'm out of ammo," Constantine said.

"Grab yourself another weapon," Esther said as she dropped her empty mag.

Two Hands chose that moment to rush her, one firing twice and hitting her low in the belly. Esther pulled her Ruger as the man closed in on her, firing up and under his chin. His momentum kept him falling forward and crashing into her, knocking her to the ground and off her perch. Her hand was trapped, holding it up just long enough for the second Hand to loom over her, the butt of his rifle ready to smash into her face. She twisted her head and took the blow to the helmet. It rang her bell, and the helmet flew off.

With a look of triumph, the man reared back for another blow, one that was going to smash her face. She tried to roll out of the way when there was a flash of silver, and the man doubled over to fall at her feet.

Esther twisted to see Constantine bent over, arms to the side—and holding his sword. She didn't know who looked more surprised: him, her, or for a spit second before he died, the Hand Constantine had just killed.

*With a freaking sword!*

"Holy shit, man!"

"Yeah, I know!"

She pushed the dead Hand off her and stood up. She seated her mag and handed him her Ruger.

"That was awesome, but maybe you'd better take this."

Another five Hands reached the battle position. Esther snapped off a quick shot at one just as he stumbled over a body, and she missed. With the thickening haze, she lost sight of him, but she put another round where she thought he'd be.

Bug's avatar switched to gray, and she spun around to where he should be, but she couldn't see him. She jumped off the rock and ran to his position, taking down one more Hand as he appeared in the haze in front of her.

"Bug!" she shouted.

"He's gone," Doc said as she ran up. "No hope."

Esther wanted to see him, she needed to see him, but she still had a job to do. She was going to kill as many of the Hands as possible. They had to be given the object lesson that taking on Marines was never a good idea. That was now her final mission.

Firing reached a crescendo, and Esther spun around, but the firing was below them. She was confused. The RHG still on the slopes couldn't engage them unless they reached the brow of the crown.

Something tickled her ears for a moment, then the high-pitched whine of an aircraft reached her through the firing. The haze parted as the *Manta* came in for another landing.

Esther dove for her helmet and slammed in on.

" . . . ASAP. We've taken some hits."

"Roger that," Tim answered. "Glad to see you."

"I'm back," Esther passed.

"Couldn't leave you all alone, but if you can hurry, we'd really like to haul ass out of here," Senior Chief Carpenter said.

"Lyle, fall back now," she passed.

"I've got bad guys ten meters away. You load, and when you're done, give us a shout, then cover ourt asses."

"Roger that."

With the haze blown off the summit by the *Manta*, most of the battle position was visible. Bodies littered the crown, and those still alive were fighting. There had to be a dozen Hands locked in combat, with more arriving. Some were using bodies as shields, firing away at someone else five meters away. Several soldiers were already bolting for the *Manta*.

Esther had to break contact and get everyone on board the ship with Hands still within the battle position. She raised her bullpup and shot two Hands as they reached the top of the slope. That only highlighted the problem. No matter what, more of them were pushing forward.

Something exploded behind her, probably a grenade, and she felt her armor harden as she was hit by shrapnel. Constantine didn't have armor, though, and he went down to one knee. He grabbed his side, and put a hand out to keep from falling, dropping her Ruger.

"You," she shouted, grabbing one of the soldiers by the arm. "Get the captain on that ship!"

It had been 40 seconds since the *Manta* landed, and Tim and Master Sergeant Kang had already managed to load ten or twelve wounded aboard. That left another 15 or so to load, and the ship couldn't lift with that weight.

"Chris, Doc, start collapsing the perimeter, but keep firing! Lyle, get ready to pull back," she said, picking up her handgun form the ground.

She hesitated a moment, then selected the second FPF option, telling her AI to put it on a dead man's broadcast. If she were killed, the order would go out with a 30-second delay.

With surprising discipline, the remaining soldiers began to move back, closing in on the ship. To her utter amazement, instead of breaking and running to the ship, one soldier was actually saying, "Bang, bang!" as he backed up alongside Doc, jerking his rifle as if firing, refusing to leave his comrades.

Despite the situation, or maybe because of it, Esther laughed out loud.

*Oh, to be one with such marvelous men, such brave, brave men!* she thought, pulling the quote out of who knows where.

And suddenly she was at peace with herself. She was proud of being a Marine, but these Hellenic soldiers, without the training, without proper weapons and armor, were fighting just as hard with just as much discipline as any Marine.

She rushed forward between Doc and the soldier, firing from her last magazine.

"Get to the ship," she told him, and when he hesitated, added, "That's an order."

She dropped two more, as she backed up before stumbling over something. She caught her balance and looked down. Randy, the Space Guardsman, was at her feet, his body torn apart.

*Can he be resurrected?* she wondered for a moment, hesitating.

But as she glanced back, she knew she could not tell one of the living to give up his place for him.

The *Manta* had to be close to full, the bottom sinking closer to the mountain's surface. Krüger was shoving one of the soldiers up into the side hatch, taking an inadvertent boot to the face as the man scrambled to get inside.

"Lyle, now!"

Only a few meters now from the ship, she swung around her right to spend her last rounds covering what was left of Third Platoon. Within a few seconds, two soldiers appeared running hell bent for leather, their faces grimacing with effort. One's leg was stained red, but he ran without a limp, probably overcome by adrenaline. Another soldier appeared in view, turned to look back, then fell as if poleaxed.

*Come on, Lyle! Don't be a hero!*

And there he was, his standard-issue M99 firing bursts down the trail. Only he didn't keep coming. He stood there, sending dart after dart into the advancing Hands.

"Lyle!" she shouted.

He looked up at his name, caught Esther's eye, and smiled before turning back. Something hit him in the chest, and he staggered. Then more rounds impacted, and Esther could see the fabric of his skins part. The STF bones inside the skins were proof against most small arms, but single shots. They could be defeated by multiple rounds impacting, setting the fluid into an oscillating state. Esther was moving forward when his armor was defeated, and he fell onto his back, motionless as the Hands kept riddling his body.

Esther looked over her shoulder. Most of the soldiers had been loaded, but it would probably be another 30 seconds before it could take off, and the first Hand appeared coming around Maple. This wasn't the steep slope that slowed down the Hands to the north and east. They would be able to pour out into the battle position and take the *Manta* under direct fire. The ship had already been hit multiple times, but Esther didn't think it could survive an onslaught.

*I've got to stop them,* she knew as she turned back and started firing.

The red light flashed on her receiver group—she was out of ammo. She dropped her M114 and drew her Ruger, and just as she started forward again, she was hit from behind and knocked to the ground.

She bounced hard and looked up as Tim and Master Sergeant Kang ran to the chokepoint, weapons blazing.

"Finish the loading, Ess," Tim passed on the P2P.

She hesitated. Her mind had been ready to charge, and Tim and Kang had stolen that from her. But looking back to the ship, there were still a few more to load. Scrambling back to her feet, she ran back, firing her Ruger at a Hand andmissing, but making him duck back.

"How many do you have on?" she asked Krüger.

"Maybe enough for you three, that's all. We'll see when you get aboard what the weight is."

"What about you?"

"I guess I'll just stay here with Randy, but if you're going, you've got to go now!"

Two rounds hit the fuselage over their heads, piercing the skin. The ship had some shielding for energy weapons, and she was built to take entry into a planetary atmosphere from space, but she couldn't take too much of this. Already, Esther was pretty sure she wasn't spaceworthy.

Esther took a quick glance to Maple. Master Sergeant Kang was down, but Tim was in full berserker mode. Rounds were pinging off of him as he fired back. A grenade blast took him to one knee, but he kept his assault.

*I guess it's you and me, Tim.*

"Doc, Chris, onboard, now! No arguing."

Doc fired off one last burst, temporarily clearing the space in front of them and then dove into the ship, hands pulling him up and in.

"Chris, help me," Esther said.

"I've got you," Petty Officer Krüger said, reaching her hands down, cupped for a boost.

Chris bent over and took one of the petty officer's arms while Esther took the other, and between the two of them, they picked her up and threw her into the ship. She landed hard, then turned around, her face screwed up in anger.

Esther ignored her as Chris stood and then vaulted himself up. The edge of the ship's bottom sank to hit the deck, and then slowly came back up five or six centimeters

"Die well, ma'am," Chris said, hand raised to his brow in a salute.

"Get the ship out of there," she passed over its net.

"About time," the senior chief said. "We're taking too much damage. Hang on back there."

Esther didn't bother to tell him that for her, "back there" was "out there." For a moment, she was tempted to jump on board herself. She was bigger than the small petty officer, so if the weight was that tight, then she was the logical choice to stay behind. But if she jumped on, too, then that would probably be too much for the now-damaged *Manta* to get airborne.

She turned away, refusing to watch as the ship lifted another few centimeters off the deck, relying on the ground effect to keep it moving.

She didn't turn when Tim's avatar grayed out.

Shouts of "Now, now!" and "Get up there!" reached her, and alone in the battle position, she turned to face the Hands. She ignored the pile of weapons discarded to keep the weight on the ship down, but faced them with her Ruger. For a moment, the sun, just beginning to dip below the horizon, shone a deep orange.

*That's beautiful,* she thought.

As they started coming over in mass, she turned back from the sunset and fired. Maybe she hit some, maybe she didn't, but their eyes were on the *Manta* as it turned and floated toward the cliff edge. They didn't just watch—they were firing everything they had, and it sounded like a botchee beat band as the rounds pinged against the ship's skin.

"Fire the FPF, 30 seconds," she instructed her AI.

"And Bob, get off the mountain now."

To her left, several Hands were motioning to one of their fellow fighters. To her horror, that Hand knelt, a long tube on his shoulder which he pointed at the *Manta*. Esther didn't need to know what model or make it was; she knew it was an anti-air missile.

She fired her Ruger, hitting another Hand as just as the man fired. With a clap and a whoosh, the missile took off, covering the 40 or 50 meters and hitting the side of the *Manta*. Instead of detonating in a fireball, it punched right through it and exiting out the still open hatch—and taking two bodies with it.

Lieutenant Spiros, or what looked like half of him, and Petty Officer Krüger came tumbling out of the ship as it continued to rotate. Esther took a few steps forward, hoping to help her up and somehow back on the ship, but the Petty Officer was badly mangled and obviously dead.

Esther knew what had happened. Most missiles had a minimum arming distance, especially man-packed missiles. Soldiers had a habit of hitting the ground or trees right in front of them, and this kept those idiots alive. Forty meters was too close for the missile to arm, but it's engine packed a powerful thrust, and the missile had simply punched through the Manta's skin—and taking Spiros and Krüger with it. It had probably killed more or hurt more inside, as indicated by Chris' avatar which had just switched to light blue, but only two bodies had been ejected.

*Two bodies! It can take more weight now!*

Suddenly, Esther didn't want to die. She'd been resigned to it, but now, she felt a surge as her survival instinct kicked in, flooding her body with adrenaline. But the ship was just about to reach the cliff. She couldn't call it back; she wouldn't call it back.

Without even thinking about it, she spun and bolted into a sprint. Shouts sounded behind her, and firing reached out to her as the Hands seemed to finally notice her. She barely felt the two rounds slam into her back as she ran up the rock pinnacle, launching herself into the air, knocking over the cairn, just as the ship's nose began to fall over the edge of the cliff, its stern raising. RHG rounds sent flashed of sparks as they hit the underside, but Esther was focused on the stern, looking for anything to grab.

Pure space-going ships were usually round spheres, but for dual space-atmosphere vessels, that was not a viable structure. The *Manta* was not a mass of struts and planes, but she had a few. Esther was not going to reach them, though, she realized as she fell, the ship just out of reach. She almost screamed out her anguish as she hit the deck, rolling. She got to her feet as the ship started to slide over, but it was too late.

And with a screech of metal and ceramics, the bottom of the ship scraped the edge of the cliff, hanging it up for only a second, but just enough that when the senior chief goosed the engines to get it over, Esther was able to leap of the cliff and smash into the *Manta*'s underside.

The collision almost knocked her senseless, and it took a moment to realize that she was clinging to what looked to be a strut of some kind.

And she almost lost her grip as the *Manta* pulled out of her shallow dive, meters above the trees. She pulled up her legs and wrapped them around the strut, taking the strain off of her arms.

The wind began to whip at her as the ship started to gain altitude. She lost her helmet in the jump, but she looked back at Mount Zeus just as 100 25mm anti-personnel rockets, each with a 15-meter ECR, impacted the crown and north, east, and south faces. The old Gentry MRL she'd had Chris target in had been the entire FPF. She'd called it on herself, but all things considered, she'd much rather be hanging under a Space Guard ship than actually being on Mount Zeus then the rockets hit.

"Holy Hell!" she shouted, unsure if that was because she'd made the leap and survive or because of the rockets demolishing the Hands. Either or both, it didn't matter.

She craned her head back to watch the huge combined column of smoke and flames reach up to the sky, the last of the sun's rays giving the smoke an orange tint, imitating the active volcano that it once was.

The strut was round and a little hard to hold on. Esther forgot the mountain behind and settled for a long ride to somewhere, the wind buffeting her body.

*That's going to suck if I fall off over the ocean and no one knows what happened.*

She shouted out a few times, but the ship kept going, 50 or 60 meters over the water. She started calculating how far they had to go, how fast the ship was flying, and how long that would take. For a moment, she worried that the ship would go into orbit, and she considered dropping off into the water before the *Manta* climbed too high, but then she remembered the damage. The senior chief was probably keeping the speed down as it was to keep the ship from being torn apart, and there was no way he was going to take it into orbit.

After less than a minute, much earlier than expected, the ship started a low turn, the same that a Stork might make coming in for a landing. Esther craned her head back, and in the gathering darkness, she saw a white beach. The ship's landing lights turned on, and individual lights appeared as the ship came in low and slow. Esther didn't know if the ship would land on the sand, and as she really didn't want to get crushed, she dropped off, hitting the sand hard as the *Manta* settled down ten meters away. More lights from the sides of the ship came on, illuminating the beach. Soldiers rushed the ship and started to help others off.

Esther walked through the sand to get around to the passenger hatch, and as she looked up, she could still see the smoke from Mount Zeus, and she knew what the senior chief had done. She'd assumed that he would have taken the first load back to the mainland. Instead, he'd flown them to the nearby Santorini, offloaded them on the beach, and returned for the rest.

She rounded the ship's bow and jumped up on the bow lip to pound on the cockpit's windows to thank him. Inside, Senior Chief Carpenter was slumped over face-down on the controls. It was only then that Esther noticed the ragged gashes puncturing the ship's skin right at his level.

She jumped off the bow lip and ran around to the side hatch where soldiers were reaching out to assist the debark. Two soldiers were lowering Chris out of the hatch, and another couple were there to catch him.

Esther brushed by Chris to look into the ship, shouting, "Doc Buren, Doctor Willis!"

"Ess?" Chris asked.

"Where's Doc?"

"Up there, but how in the . . . I . . . how the hell are you even here?"

"No time, Chris. Doc Burren!"

"Yeah, who wants me?" Doc said, pushing forward. When he saw Esther, his mouth dropped open.

"No time for that, Doc. Where's Doctor Willis?"

"Back on Naxos. He didn't make it."

"Shit! The senior chief's hurt bad. You need to get to him," she said.

Airman Pokstra looked up from where he was helping to get the soldiers unloaded.

He looked and simply asked, "Senior Chief? I've got to go," before rushing after Doc towards the cockpit.

Constantine pushed his way to the hatch and said, "Ess! You made it!"

"I still don't fucking believe it," Chris said. "How did you, uh, you know?"

"I've got to get my head wrapped around it myself, and I'll tell you, but not now. Let's get everyone off and find out what's next. Some of the Hands had to have survived, and they've still got their boats. We're not that far from them, so we've got to figure out what happens next. I'll tell you what happened when we get everyone together."

"My command knows what's happened, and they're scrambling to find some transport," Constantine said.

*Shit, command! I don't have my handset, and the major's going to be shitting bricks!*

"Can you ask them to contact our command and let them know what happened?" she asked.

"Make a hole, make a hole," was shouted from inside the ship, then "Get out now! We need the room!"

There was a tumble of the whole and walking wounded as bodies almost fell out of the ship to the sand, forcing Esther away from the hatch. It took a minute for her to be able to get back.

Senior Chief was limp, his flight suit dark with blood. Doc and Pokstra were sliding him into a zip-lock. Doc sealed and activated it, watching as it deployed. Finally, the red indicator turned green, and Doc seemed to relax.

"How is he? Is he going to make it?" Esther asked.

"He's dead. Died just after I got there. Can he be resurrected? I hope so, but that's out of my hands."

"I'm going to sit here with him," Pokstra said, his eyes glistening with tears.

Doc turned to look at her, then said, "Ess, I saw you on the rock when we took off. How did you get here? How the hell are you alive?"

"That's what I want to know," Chris said.

Constantine looked at her, not saying anything, but obviously waiting for her answer.

Esther was on the verge of collapse. Her arms and legs were rubbery and without power, and her mind was fuzzy. When she spoke, it sounded to her like she was trapped inside a huge ball of cotton that ate up her words. As she thought about what happened, about jumping off the cliff, about hanging on the bottom of the ship for dear life, the only thought she could conjure was *Did that just really happen?*

She'd like nothing better than just to collapse onto the sand. But what she'd said about the Hands was true. If they were still in the fighting mood, angry about their fellow fighters, they could probably hit Santorini in an hour, maybe two. And most of their weapons had been left on Naxos to cut weight for the *Manta*.

With a weary sigh, Esther said, "I'll tell you later, I promise." She took a deep breath, and as if full of energy that she just didn't possess, she shouted out, "This isn't over yet. Captain Stavropoulis! I need a working party to get our ziplocked WIA off the beach and into cover. Everyone else, I want into squads. Chris, get a weapons and ammo count. I want that back to me in five minutes. Let's go! Let's go!"

263

No matter how tired she felt, she had a job to do, and she was going to do it.

## Chapter 38

"Damn! You look, well, you look martial, I guess," Esther said, trying not to laugh as Constantine entered the room.

"I can't expect a Marine to understand what a true warrior looks like," he sniffed, resplendent in his full Greek Guard dress uniform.

If Esther had thought their white leggings, the *boudoiri*, had been a little much, the captain was now decked out in the complete kit and caboodle, from a kind of sandal to the red *farion* on his head. In between, well, Esther didn't know what to call it.

"Warrior? I didn't know warriors wore dresses," Master Chief Carpenter said from his seat on the couch.

"Dresses? Did you say dresses? This, my friend, is a *foustanela*, which has—"

"Oh my gosh, Master Chief, did you have to get him started? Now we're going to get a lecture on the 400 pleats and 400 years of Ottoman rule," Esther said, interrupting the lecture. "You look cute, so come here and give me a hug."

She stepped up and into a strong embrace. She hadn't seen much of her friend over the last six months. Both of them had been pretty much occupied.

"You know, you can't wear that on Tarawa," Esther said.

Constantine had been accepted to the Marine Corps Affiliated Officer Course. It wasn't boot camp nor NTC but rather a six-month course designed for planetary and national military officers to bring them up to professional standards.

"Why not?"

"Why not? Because you need a sense of personal pride to attend AOC, of course."

The master chief broke out into laughter while Constantine struggled for a snappy comeback.

"Senior . . . excuse me . . . *Master* Chief, how are you feeling?" Constantine asked, changing the subject.

"'Bout as good as can be expected. I've still got another five or six months until I return to full duty."

"I appreciate, we all appreciate, you returning for this."

"It's my pleasure, not that I had much choice. When the commandant tells you your presence would be appreciated, that's pretty much an order.

"And I have to say, it felt damned good seeing the *Manta* again. You boys did a good job with her. It . . . it touched this salty heart."

Esther understood the political importance of the master chief being present at today's ceremony, but she'd still been surprised when he made the trip. He'd died on Santorini, too badly hurt to survive. His resurrection and initial regen had not been without problems, and he'd only recently started exo-tank regen. Frankly, he didn't look good, which was why he was still sitting on the couch, marshalling his strength.

"I met that actor who's playing me, too. Not good enough looking, I'm saying," the master chief said.

Hollybolly hadn't come knocking on doors, but a local production company was already recording the flick. Esther had met the actor playing her as well, and it had been a weird, yet rewarding sensation. Esther had been portrayed by Hollybolly before, but only as a minor character in the four flicks about her father. This time, even if it was a fringe-system production, she was one of the major characters.

Constantine, fully recovered from his wounds, was playing himself, though. Esther knew that the long-game was in play, with her friend being groomed for bigger and better things. And if he took a more central role in the flick's version of the *Battle of Naxos*, then she was fine with it.

"Besides your new rank, I heard about the Nova," Constantine said.

The master chief let out a puff of air, as if blowing away an annoying fly.

Master Chief Carpenter and BM2 Krüger had been recommended—and approved for the Federation Nova, the first two Space Guardsmen ever to be so honored. The ceremony was scheduled to take place in four months during the Space Guard's birthday.

Esther was fully aware that politics were once again involved in the decision. She didn't resent the honor for the master chief and Krüger. Both earned it, and without them, not only would all of her team been killed, but Elysium's entire future would be different. What she didn't like was that her putting up Tim Ziegler and Lyle Jones for the Nova had been short-stopped. The division commanding general had given her the word himself when he'd come to Elysium as part of the negotiating team. This was being presented as a Space Guard play for reasons she didn't quite understand.

Both of the Marines were going to receive the Navy Cross—as was Esther. This was her second award of the medal. If a tiny part of her wondered if this had been her last and best chance to earn the Nova, the same medal her father had been awarded twice, she was able to push that thought down deep within the recesses of her mind and gladly accept the Navy Cross. She would personally receive the award, after all. Tim's wife and Lyle's parents would be the people receiving their medals.

"Did you hear that the new station is being named for Krüger?" Esther asked the master chief.

"No, when did that word come out?"

"Yesterday," Constantine said.

The master chief nodded, then said quietly, seemingly more to himself that to the other two, "Good for her. She was a great shipmate."

The Space Guard station had been a priority, more as a statement than for tactical reasons. It was there to show the galaxy that Elysium was now part of the Federation, but that this wasn't a Federation land-grab. A Coast Guard station didn't have the same militaristic connotation as a Navy or Marine base.

Esther was still surprised that everything had happened so quickly. The Battle of Naxos had galvanized the population, a population that resented the fact that their patron planet of Athína had ignored their plight, and it took the unaffiliated Federation to step in and "rescue" the planet from the Right Hand of God. The general consensus was that if the Federation cared more about the Elysium's security than their own patron, then maybe they should formalize ties with them. A special vote was taken, and 74% of the people voted to secede from Athína and request membership in the Federation. For the first time since the turbulent redrawing of the maps after the Evolution, a planet or government entity had joined the Federation. The Federation Council had acted almost immediately, approving the request. The Memorandum of Intent was filed with the UAM,[13] and in three weeks, on July 1, the formal transfer would be made.

It had been a whirlwind six months for Esther and her surviving teammates. Instead of being recalled to Omaha, they were kept on planet until Major Filipovic and another team arrived to prepare for the influx of FCDC and Marine trainers. FCDC engineers had already started the expansion on the Elysium recruit training base, and the first of the 10,000 new recruits, the best of those who'd tried to enlist after the battle, were already in-processing.

*Two days and a wake-up,* she thought. *And then I'm out of here.*

Esther had been more of a staff officer since the battle, and she was anxious to get on with her career. She'd been told by her monitor that she had orders to Tac 1, to start in the 9 September class. The course was 11 months long, and then it would probably be to a staff billet for a year before returning to the fleet, but this time as a company commander. She was glad she had come to recon, and she would treasure her time there, but she wanted that company command. As it was, she'd probably make major before the end of that tour and get promoted out of the billet.

"They're ready for you," a baby-faced Hellenic lieutenant said, coming in the hatch.

A lance corporal followed, pushing a hover chair up to the master chief, who gave it one look and said to the lieutenant, "If you think I'm going to be pushed in this thing like a damned invalid, you've got another thing coming . . . sir."

---

[13] UAM: United Assembly of Man, the over-arching organization of humankind.

Esther fought hard—and lost—to keep the smile off her face as the lieutenant fumbled around, saying nothing that made sense except for a few "sorries" that he managed to get out. The lieutenant waved off the lance corporal who quickly made herself scarce.

"Let's get this over with," Constantine said, as the three of them walked out of the brigade headquarters together.

"She's a beauty," the master chief said as they emerged from the building.

In the oval in front of the headquarters, the *UFSPS Manta* was displayed on a gleaming silver pylon. She'd been beaten up so bad that when coupled with her age, the Space Guard had decided repairs didn't make much sense. So when the speaker prime requested her, the Federation transition team immediately agreed.

None of the damage on the outside had been repaired. The Elysiumites wanted her in all her battle glory. On her underside, the strut that Esther had hung onto was already beginning to gather a sheen where soldiers rubbed it for good luck.

At least she thought it was the strut. She hadn't noticed at the time that there were several there, so she wasn't 100% sure that it was *her* strut, but that is the one she'd identified as it.

There were hundreds of spectators between the *Manta* and the stage, and a separate stage for the press was set up to the side. The VIPs were already in their seats, but they stood up when the three of them approached. The conditional planetary administrator, the quadrant administrator, the Sixth Division commanding general, the Fourth Fleet commander, and the regional FCDC commander, and the Third Minister himself represented the Federation. There were dozens of Elysium notables, but Esther only recognized the speaker prime and the Hellenic Army commanding general. And all were gently applauding as the Space Guardsmen, the Marine, and the Army captain approached their seats on the stage. On an elevated purple cushion behind the podium, lay three of the gaudiest medals Esther had ever seen.

The Star of Nikólaos was a large, multi-pointed gold and platinum star hanging from a huge blue ribbon festooned with gold circles. The circles made it look like a child's costume, to Esther, but she'd been told that pattern came from the flag of Saint Nicholas, the same saint who gave the universe Santa Claus. That didn't make sense to her—wasn't Santa dressed in red and white? Be that as it may, the Star hadn't been awarded for more than 45 years, and that was a Vance Hold star. The new status of Elysium resulted in adding a few points and the platinum highlights to the star, differentiating it from any other of the Greek Diaspora governments.

In the stands, Daren Poulsen, and Elysium native and holder of the Athína version of the Star, awarded 68 years ago, sat as a guest of honor. The three of them, though, were to be the first living recipients of the new Elysium Star of Nikólaos.

"Classily subdued," the master chief whispered to Esther as they paused at their seats behind the three medals, acknowledging the polite clapping.

Esther had to stifle a laugh, and she made sure to elbow the master chief in the ribs as they sat.

The ribbon would probably cover her entire chest once it was put over her neck, a far cry from the much more subdued Federation Nova. Luckily, she wouldn't have to wear it again unless she was on Elysium. There was also a more normal-sized ribbon and clasp to hang the medal from her chest during formal dress functions off the planet and then a simple ribbon for her existing ribbon bar. Still, the medal for the Star was at least twice the size of either her Navy Cross or BC2.

The Hellenic Army chaplain took the podium to issue the evocation, and all the sitting guests and awardees stood. Esther looked out over the crowd, barely listening to the chaplain as she tried to put the last six months into perspective, something that had been eluding her.

She'd lost three teammates: Tim, Lyle, and Bug. While two trawlers had been diverted to pick up the survivors on Naxos several hours after the battle, it had taken a full standard day for the Army to recall and send the Second Brigade to Naxos where they'd picked up Bob and his three soldiers, collected their dead, and taken sixteen wounded prisoners. Many of their dead would have had reasonable chances at getting resurrected if they'd been placed in stasis immediately. Bug's body was too ravaged, either from the fight or from the rocket FPF, but both Lyle and Tim would have stood a good chance. Twenty-six hours after getting killed, though, their bodies had deteriorated too far to be resurrected.

She'd also lost 44 brigade soldiers and two Space Guardsmen, and she sometimes had to remind herself that their losses meant just as much to their families and friends as Tim's lost meant to Adrianne and his little Barry and Neosha, as Lyle's loss meant to Horty, as Bug's loss meant to his parents and siblings.

She glanced at Constantine, his head bowed as he listened to the evocation. He'd been in command, and he'd lost more than half of his men and women. Yes, he hadn't the weapons needed to fight a battle; yes, he didn't have the support even a half-assed military would have. But he was still the commander, and she knew the losses were eating at him.

She reached over and gave his hand a squeeze.

"What's that for?" he whispered.

"For them," she said. "For who we lost. But also for who survived."

He nodded and squeezed her hand back.

The chaplain ended, and those with seats sat down, settling in for maybe an hour of speeches. The battle would be extolled, the sacrificed of so many lives lost mourned, and the righteous fortitude of Elysium going forward proclaimed. And, Esther, knew, the three of them would be held up as examples of the warrior incarnate.

Sometimes, maybe many times, soldiers were awarded for actions that did exemplify what it meant to be a selfless warrior. Her father's own actions as a lieutenant for which he was awarded his first Nova, for example. He'd simply kicked ass. More often, though, it was not really an individual who earned the award, it was the unit. The medal may hang on an individual's chest, usually a commander of some sort, but it was earned by everyone there.

Esther, Constantine, and the master chief were about to receive Elysium's highest award, but without Tim and Lyle, without Petty Officer Krüger, without Bug, Lieutenant Spiros, without de Marco, Pusser, and Master Sergeant Kang, without all of the brigade, the *Manta*, and her recon team, whether they survived or died—the battle would have been lost.

As was usually the case, the awards sitting on the purple cushion were being awarded to individuals to wear, but they were an acclamation of the unit.

Esther looked at the gaudy, almost cartoonish medal, one that had given her pause at first, wondering what other Marines would think of it as she continued her career. But it wasn't her medal. It was *their* medal, all of those who'd fought.

And she would wear it with pride.

# OMAHA

## Epilogue

"I've got your link now, ma'am. Booth B," the civilian tech said, nodding at the small, soundproof room.

Esther thanked the tech, entered what was little more than a closet, and sat down. The terminal was blinking green, ready for her connection.

"May I have your desired waypoint connection?" the AI asked.

"Tarawa, United Federation Marine Corps Headquarters."

"May I have your desired terminating connection?"

Esther rattled off the number. Within a split second, her call was already on Tarawa. It would take longer for her call to be patched through a few klicks from the headquarters than to have it sent halfway across the galaxy.

Esther had gotten used to her hadron handset. Now, back on Omaha, she had to jump through the administrative BS to use the division facilities to make her call. Technically, the call was supposed to be for official business. Non-official calls were only authorized at the Marine Corps Personnel Welfare Center, but Esther didn't want to have to wait in line for an hour or more for her turn, and it did involve the Corps.

She sat there waiting while the call went through. It took a few moments, then the screen flashed on and a familiar face appeared.

"Esther, this is a surprise. How are you doing?"

"I'm fine, General. I hope I didn't wake you up."

"No worry about that. Too many years on the Corps' schedule have got early rising imprinted into my DNA. I've been up for an hour."

"Are you . . . I mean, how are things going?"

"You mean to ask, what's an old fart like me doing now that I've retired? Well, I'm bored as hell, Esther."

Major General Jorge Simone had retired six months ago after failing to be selected yet again for his third star. Personally, Esther thought that was a travesty. General Simone was both one of the most capable human beings she'd ever met and someone who'd probably done more for the Corps and Federation than anyone else alive. As far as she was concerned, he deserved his third star for his past service alone. But with Chairman MacCailín out of office, Esther thought the general had finally seen the writing on the wall and tendered his resignation.

The general had been her father's right-hand man throughout the Evolution. But too much blood had been shed during the fighting, and sadly, probably more pertinent, too many political careers had been ruined or destroyed. General Simone's elevation would have been a reminder to many of the sacrifices made on both sides, and that might have been enough to curtail his advancement in and of itself. Throw in political infighting, with many of the players holding a grudge, then it was a foregone conclusion that the general's career was done. The politicians couldn't tarnish the memory of her dead father, but they could reach out to his lieutenant in revenge.

He might be out of uniform now, but he was still about the smartest man she knew, and he understood the workings of the Corps. More than that, he had her back and would always be honest with her.

"I thought you were going to take up golf or something," Esther said.

"Tried it when I was still on active duty. Didn't understand the appeal then, and retiring didn't bring me enlightenment."

Esther felt a wave of worry sweep over her. She hadn't called to discuss the general's retirement, but it was obvious he wasn't adjusting well. He'd never married, so he was alone in the condo he'd bought in Valiant Overlook, the civilian housing project that had become de-facto officer housing for most of the O4's and above assigned to Headquarters and retired officers who couldn't break themselves away from at least being close to the flagpole.

"You need to do something, sir, you know—"

"Please don't tell me 'get a hobby,' Esther. That's what everyone says. And don't worry. I've got the VIW, I volunteer for the USO and the library, and I get the faded stars brief every two weeks."

The "faded stars brief" was a presentation made to all retired flag officers twice a month, bringing them up-to-date on the state of the Corps.

"And you didn't call me all the way from Omaha just to listen to an old man complain. What's up?"

"You're not old, sir," she said, unwilling to let that pass. "But yes, I need some advice."

She'd almost said "fatherly advice," and that would have been an accurate statement, but the loss of her father was too close of a wound for both of them.

"Eh, maybe I can help you there, Ess. What's up?"

"Well, I've got my orders, only they're TBA."

"To Be Accepted orders? But I thought you were going to school next. They think you'll turn them down?"

"I thought I was going to school now, too, sir. I need it. What with three years in recon, I'm a little behind the curve if I'm going to get a rifle company."

"You're not behind any curve. Your running mates have all been in staff or support billets."

"For two years, not three. And I had six months in RTC, too."

General Simone flipped up one hand as if brushing off her complaint.

"You worry too much. You're doing fine. But I assume you're going to tell me just what was in these orders?"

"Yes, sir. See, they're APOC."

"Hmm," the general said, sitting farther back in his chair. "Commandant or Chairman?"

"They didn't say."

"Curioser and curioser. They didn't specify?"

"No, sir."

"At the Pleasure of" orders mean a Marine, sailor, or FCDC trooper would be reporting directly to the designated letter. For Marines, a "C" meant either the Commandant or the Chairman himself.

"That sounds serious, Ess. What have you heard?"

"The CG personally handed me my orders. He said that because of my training, and because what happened on Elysium, I've been proven to have an 'aptitude' to complete unique missions of a more strategic reach."

"Which can mean you would be the designated butt-boy for whatever might have to be done."

"I'm not sure why Elysium has anything to do with that, though."

"Really, Ess? You're a bright young woman, so you can't have missed that the Federation gained an entire planet."

"But that wasn't me. I just happened to be there."

"It happened on your watch. And if it had all gone to hell after, you'd be paying the price for that."

"Maybe . . . OK, you might be right, sir. But the fact is that I don't have any 'special skills' like the CG said. I know I'm a good officer, but I lead Marines. I'm not a schmoozer. My social graces are lacking. So if I'm supposed to go out and be a junior attaché somewhere and be a super-spy, I don't think I'm cut out for that."

The general laughed, and then said, "I think you watch too many Hollybolly flicks. The Federation has spies. What they probably need, however, are trained operators to do what has to be done without landing a full Marine battalion somewhere."

"Like what?"

"I don't know. I never had ATOC orders. But it could be anything."

Esther put both elbows on the desk and lowered her head to her hands, rubbing her temples for a few moments.

"I don't know, sir. It's just that if I get further behind the curve, I won't have time for Tac 1, and I might not get my rifle company."

"And then you'll never make major, and that means no colonel's eagles, no stars, and no commandant."

Esther lowered her hands and stared at the general's image, her mouth dropping open.

*Am I that transparent?*

"There's nothing wrong with ambition, Ess. If you didn't have it, you'd be a pretty lousy officer."

"So, what do you think, sir?" she asked after digesting what he'd just said.

"What do I think about what? Whether you should accept the orders?"

"Well, yes, but do you think I could be committing career suicide?"

Tac 1 was more than training for the next level of billets. It was more than a ticket punch. It was also where bonds were formed between a year-group of officers, bonds that could be extremely beneficial as they advanced through the ranks.

"You could be," the general said.

*That's not what I wanted to hear!*

She'd called him for advice, yes, but also to assure her that if she took the orders, she wouldn't jeopardize her career plans. Frankly, the orders intrigued her, and just as with her decision to go to RTC, Esther had a hard time turning down a challenge. The idea that she was specially chosen played to her ego as well, something she acknowledged.

But more than any single billet, Esther was firmly focused on the end goal: Commandant of the Marine Corps. Everything she did was intended to be a stepping stone to that goal. If she failed along the way, it wouldn't be for lack of trying, and handicapping herself in her pursuit of that goal didn't make much sense.

"Did you ever meet Major Potsdam?"

"No, sir."

"OK, he served with your dad and me on Quail Hunt, so I thought you might have met him. He's the only Marine I know personally that had ATOC orders, his to the Chairman. He was out of the loop for five years, ostensibly a Marine, but not really acting as one. He was promoted to major while on the orders. Potsdam had a good rep before his orders, and he did well for us. But he never made lieutenant colonel. He retired and ended up working for a security lobbyist, last I heard."

"Did he go to Tac?"

"No. And before you ask, he never had a rifle company, either. I didn't sit on either of his promotions boards, so I don't know why he wasn't selected, but there were murmurings that maybe his loyalties were no longer with the Corps. We weren't on great terms with the chairman then, if you remember."

Esther lost her focus on the general's image as she thought about that. It made sense.

"What if the 'C' in this case is the commandant?"

"That might make a difference. But you won't know until you accept them, correct?"

"That's what the CG said. He told me he didn't even know the scope of the orders."

*That's the problem with secret-type orders. You have to accept them before knowing what they are.*

"So, as you can guess, I'm asking you for your opinion. Should I accept the orders?"

The general made a slight, almost sad smile, and said, "Ess, you know better than that. I'm not the one to tell you whether you should or not. That is a personal decision that only you can make. No one else."

Disappointment came over her. She asked him because she didn't know what to do, and with her father gone, the general was her only father-figure. She half-way wished he'd just tell her what to do, taking the decision out of her hands.

"But I will say this, Ess. I told you that having ambition is fine. It's laudatory, in fact. And I've known since you were a little girl that you were brimming over with it. But, in my opinion, it shouldn't rule your life.

"The fact of the matter is that you are on track for colonel, maybe even general. If everything fell into place, and you showed as much skill as a senior officer as you've done as an NCO and a junior officer, then maybe your ultimate goal could be in reach. But is it a certainty? Not even close. How many Marine officers are there who would be considered for commandant along with you? They will be just as ambitious, just as disciplined, in pursuing the position as you are.

"So as I see it, you can keep marching in step with your peers. It'll be difficult to stand out marching along with them, but you also won't stand out for the wrong reasons. And if you keep marching in step and more and more of your peers fall out, then at some point, you might be among the 30, 40, heck, a hundred potential candidates. If you grasp the brass ring, you will be able to put your signature on the Corps, just like your father did.

"Or, you can take a chance now on having an impact on the Corps, or even the Federation. ATOC orders are not given out freely, and you can assume that whatever your missions are, they will be important."

"So you think the orders are for something important?"

"I don't know for sure, but yes, I think so. By their very nature."

*It shouldn't be this hard.*

"But just as marching along, getting every box checked won't guarantee the ultimate billet, neither will accepting these orders preclude it. All it would be is an obstacle that you'd have to clear."

"So you won't give me your opinion as to if I should accept or not, but basically, you're boiling it down to handicapping my career in order to possibly have an impact on the Corps or keeping with the expected progression and go to school, get a company, and so on."

"That's not quite how I'd put it, but essentially, yes."

"But father said having a rifle company was his best billet ever."

"And so he was right. It is the finest billet in the Marine Corps."

"Better than becoming a general?"

"It's not even close, Ess. Not even close. General officers get the accolades, but the work isn't fun, not even close. A rifle company commander, now that's fun!"

"So I should be a company commander?"

"Absolutely!"

"What? You're telling me to turn down the orders?"

"Absolutely not. You should be a company commander. You should be in a logistics billet. You should train recruits. You should do ever billet. The problem is time, of course. So you have to pick and choose what the Corps offers you.

"There's one last thing that should go without mentioning, but you know me. I'm going to go ahead and mention it."

"What's that, sir?"

"Why are you in the Corps, Ess?"

*What?*

"I . . . I'm not sure what you mean."

"It's an easy question. Why are you a Marine?"

"To serve the Federation, of course."

"To serve the Federation, or to serve yourself?"

"I . . . I . . . " she started, getting a little upset with the question.

General Simone held up a hand to stop her.

"They are not mutually exclusive, Ess. And from a philosophical standpoint, possibly irrelevant. But it is a valid question. Do you want to serve where you can best contribute to the Marine Corps' mission, or do you want the Marine Corps to assign you to the billet that best serves your interests? I think if you answer that, then the decision will be easier to make."

"Are you saying I only care about myself?"

"Far from it, Ess. I'm not judging. Maybe both are one and the same.

"But I'm rambling, aren't I? You don't need me pontificating to you. It's easy for me—I won't suffer the consequences. Just think about it, Ess, and you'll make the right decision for yourself."

"You've given me food for thought, sir. And you're not pontificating. You've been a great help."

"When do you have to tell them?"

"COB tomorrow."

"Well, think about it. Go with your heart, whatever that is."

"I will."

The two fell into a silence that stretched out, before the general broke it with, "So, what do you think of Esther? She's a cutie, huh?"

It took Esther a moment to switch gears and realizing that he was talking about her niece. Noah and Miriam just had their second child, and they'd named the little girl Esther. She'd been happy when they'd named their first daughter Hannah, after Noah's and her mother, but "Esther" was a little disconcerting to her for reasons she wasn't quite sure. She was honored, but she wondered if that incurred a commitment of some sort on her.

Still, the little girl was adorable.

"Yes, she's a cutie."

"Did Noah tell you they want me to be the godfather?"

"No, he didn't. Are you going to do it?"

She was ashamed to admit that she hadn't spoken with Noah for awhile.

"It's not like my time here is too crowded. Yes, I'm heading out there in two weeks for the ceremony. Are you coming?"

"I'm not sure. It depends on my schedule. You know how it is."

"Yes, I know," the general said, his eyes boring into hers from light-years away.

She broke contact and took a sincere interest in her fingers.

"Remember, Ess, they're family."

"Yes, sir," she said, accepting the implied criticism.

*He's right, as usual. Whatever I decide, I need to visit them. Isn't an aunt supposed to show up and spoil her nieces or something like that?*

There was a knock on the hatch, and the tech asked, "Ma'am, I've got a Cat 2 call that needs to go out, and you've been on the longest."

Esther's call was a Cat 4, the lowest priority.

"I've got to go, sir. Thank you for your time and advice."

"Any time, Ess. I'm here for you. And I hope I see you at the christening."

Esther cut the connection and stepped out of the tiny room. A lieutenant was waiting, holding a sealed folder. She nodded at him, thanked the tech, and left the comms shack, stepping out into the muggy, late-afternoon air. Marines were getting off work and going home to loved ones, an empty quarters, or out into the ville to eat and relax. She knew that whatever choice she made, they'd be doing the same thing a year from now, a decade from now, a century from now. The Marine Corps was timeless. The name might change in the future, but the spirit would remain the same forever.

*Don't get maudlin, Esther!*

General Simone had made some good points, which she knew he would. But she was focusing on his last statement. Was she in this for herself or for the Corps? She really didn't know.

Esther didn't give as much credence to his comments on her chances to make commandant. She was confident that it would be within her reach. No one had ever accused her of having a lack of self-confidence. But just because she had that, well, many people would say hubris, that didn't mean she was wrong. She knew commandant was a possibility, and she also knew she could serve the Corps admirably in the position. And the fact of the matter was that as commandant someday, she'd have more of a positive impact on the Corps than she could as a captain, no matter the billet.

On the other hand, the Corps wanted her for the ATOC billet. For whatever reason, the powers that be thought she was the best fit for it. And as a captain, that billet undoubtedly gave her more of a chance to do something significant, something that could affect the Corps or even the Federation.

Part of her wanted just to let go and accept, to experience whatever it was that faced her. The challenge was undeniably pulling at her. But she'd sort of done that with recon, so the other part of her wanted to get back into the pipeline and start checking off the required boxes. Going to recon had been a slight risk to the normal career progression, but one she thought she could overcome. Accepting these orders would double-down on the deviation, and pretty soon, she'd run out of time to get back on track.

The more she thought about it, the more she wanted just to go to school and get her rifle company. Being a company commander had been her near-term goal since she was commissioned.

She'd been walking aimlessly, lost in her thoughts, when her decision crystallized. She stopped dead in her tracks, and a major on a bike almost ran her over. He shouted out, but she ignored him and turned, walking over the grass straight to the headquarters. She didn't need to wait until COB tomorrow. And she didn't need a sleepless night as she second and third-guessed herself.

Marines and civilians were pouring out of the headquarters as Esther walked up the steps, like a salmon fighting the current. She had to push to the side to get by them. She walked up to the second deck and down the passage to the modest office at the end.

"Captain Lysander," Ms. Porter-Effrieti said as she walked in. "Is the general expecting you?"

"No ma'am. But I've made up my mind on my orders."

"OK, if you're sure. He's in a meeting now. Would you like to wait?"

"I don't need to bother him with this. If you could, just tell him I accept."

Esther turned around and left the office, a huge weight taken from her shoulders. There really hadn't been a choice, and she wasn't sure why she'd even had to think about it. She was a Marine, first and foremost. She took the orders assigned to her because that was what Marines did. If she never made it to school, if she never got her rifle company, that was just the way things went, and if she couldn't rise above that and still make commandant, then maybe she didn't deserve it in the first place.

She still had no idea what the billet entailed or what she'd have to do, but she was pretty sure she was in for some interesting times.

Thank you for reading *Esther's Story*. I hope you enjoyed it, and I welcome a review on Amazon, Goodreads, or any other outlet. The series will continue with *Noah's Story*.

If you would like updates on new books releases, news, or special offers, please consider signing up for my mailing list. Your email will not be sold, rented, or in any other way disseminated. If you are interested, please sign up at the link below:

## http://eepurl.com/bnFSHH

## Other Books by Jonathan Brazee

## The United Federation Marine Corps' Lysander Twins
Legacy Marines
Esther's Story
Noah's Story (Coming)

## The United Federation Marine Corps
Recruit
Sergeant
Lieutenant
Captain
Major
Lieutenant Colonel
Colonel
Commandant

Rebel  (Set in the UFMC universe.

## Women of the United Federation Marines
Gladiator
Sniper
Corpsman

High Value Target (A Gracie Medicine Crow Short Story)
BOLO Mission (A Gracie Medicine Crow Short Story

# The Return of the Marines Trilogy
The Few
The Proud
The Marines

# The Al Anbar Chronicles: First Marine Expeditionary Force--Iraq
Prisoner of Fallujah
Combat Corpsman
Sniper

# Werewolf of Marines
Werewolf of Marines: Semper Lycanus
Werewolf of Marines: Patria Lycanus
Werewolf of Marines: Pax Lycanus

To the Shores of Tripoli

Wererat

Darwin's Quest: The Search for the Ultimate Survivor

Venus: A Paleolithic Short Story

Secession

# Non-Fiction
Exercise for a Longer Life

# Author Website
http://www.jonathanbrazee.com

Made in the USA
San Bernardino,
CA